THIS BROKEN WOLF
SOUL BITTEN SHIFTER 2

EVERLY FROST

Copyright © 2021 by Everly Frost
All rights reserved.

No part of this book may be reproduced or used in any manner whatsoever without the express written permission of the author, except for the use of brief quotations in a book review.

This book is a work of fiction. Names, characters, places, and incidents either are the product of the author's imagination or are used fictitiously. Any resemblance to actual persons, living or dead, is purely coincidental.

Frost, Everly
This Broken Wolf

Cover design by Luminescence Covers
For information on reproducing sections of this book or sales of this book, go to
www.everlyfrost.com
everlyfrost@gmail.com

Shout. Roar.
Howl like a wolf.

CHAPTER ONE

I refuse to scream. Ford Vanguard's eyes fade rapidly from crimson to hazel as he leans close—far too close—and rests his cheek against mine in a move that claims me for all to see.

His whisper only moments ago has left me cold.

You're mine now, little one.

He is the white wolf. A creature who has been pursuing me ever since he became aware of my existence.

A creature like me.

I can't deny his claim over me. I willingly gave myself over to this monster and now I will play a game of survival for as long as it takes to make sure Tristan and his pack are safe. Even if it goes against every instinct in my body that tells me to fight back.

Tristan stands only a few paces behind me. I don't need to see his face to feel the full force of his wrath. It's like a storm that threatens to tear strips off my heart, piece by painful piece. The melding bond I formed with him allows me to sense his inner emotions, to experience the true nature of the darkness that grows within the shadows of his mind.

Tristan's darkness is a thief that has stolen his future. And mine.

Now, his instincts are flooded with only one intent: to fight his way to me no matter the cost.

He wants to die tonight.

But... *damn him...* I won't let that happen. No matter what price I pay.

My own rage rises to meet his and I allow him to feel it—to feel my emotions like a violent shove that pushes him away from me as hard as I can. If I could reverse the true mate bond he formed with me, I would. If I could take away his pain, I would. But my choices were narrow and dangerous from the moment we entered Baxter Griffin's home tonight. Now, I have one path to walk. Only one chance to subvert Tristan's fate.

As Ford presses his cheek against mine, the tension in the room around me becomes a wildfire waiting to ignite. Baxter stands at the corner of my vision, having just shoved me into Ford's arms. A victorious gleam grows in Baxter's eyes with every second that Ford holds on to me. Baxter blames Tristan for the death of his daughter, Ella. He doesn't know that she's alive, but still healing within the safety of Hidden House.

By tearing me away from Tristan, it's Baxter's intention to cause Tristan the same pain he felt at losing Ella. Baxter won't let anything get in the way of his revenge tonight. His guards line the walls and even though I can't see them all with my back turned, I know they have one target: Tristan.

Every sound and move I make is being watched. Any small indication of rebellion on my part will be the spark that compels Tristan to act and explodes this glittering room into a bloodbath.

Already, tables have been overturned and the blood-splattered floor is littered with broken wine glasses, while the golden pendant lights hanging from the ceiling continue to shine a pretty glow that defies the horror awaiting me.

I have promised to allow myself to be taken away from Tristan, and I have no choice but to follow through.

Ford's fingernails dig into my biceps, a painful grip on both of my arms that commands me not to fight him. My hair is tangled around his right hand, allowing him to tug on my scalp and force my face closer to his.

Swallowing my revulsion, I turn my lips to Ford's ear and whisper, "I will come with you willingly. I won't fight you. I will walk the path you want me to walk. But only if Tristan leaves this place alive. He and his pack must remain safe."

Ford draws back a little—enough for his eyes to meet mine. He's a tall man, dressed in a dark blue suit. His jaw is shadowed with light stubble and his cheekbones are high, but his other features are oddly difficult to determine. His hair is a shade of light brown that seems to darken as I stare back at him, while his eyes shift from hazel green to brown.

His whisper makes my stomach fall. "You continue to deceive me, little one."

The last time we met, he accused me of eluding him. He can only sense me when I release my wolf's energy, and then I'm like a flaming beacon to him. Unfortunately, he knows what my human form looks like now. I won't be able to hide from him again.

I grit my teeth. "I don't intend to fight you."

Ford's threatening smirk remains. With his face only inches from mine, he continues to wind his fingers through my long ruby red hair. Finally drawing several toward his face, he inhales the scent of my tresses. "Your power ripples through every part of your body, and yet you don't know your own nature. You will never come with me *willingly*. It's not in your blood to submit." His smile turns into a snarl. "Ever."

The cold menace in his gaze makes me shudder. The absence of an aura around him kept his true identity from me until it was too late. He smells human, with only a faint waft of spiced cologne. Far too human—an absence of animal scent that deceived me into believing he was no more than a shrewd businessman who chose to make deals with dangerous wolf shifters.

Just like me, he is able to hide within his human form, completely undetectable by other supernaturals. The angle of his head and his proximity to my body will have concealed the shifting color of his eyes from everyone around us. I suspect, but don't know for certain, that nobody else in this room is aware of Ford's real power or identity. Except, perhaps, his mercenaries.

The ice jotunn and the warlock are threatening sentinels standing on either side of Ford and me, their shoulders tense, both taking fighting stances, ready if anyone interferes with us. When I first encountered them tonight, the warlock used his magic to protect their supernatural status from me, but now they're displaying their power openly.

Electricity crackles around the warlock's fingertips, a reminder of the lightning with which he can strike down his enemies. He's a tall man with long, dark hair slicked back and an eyepatch covering his left eye. The first time I saw him, he carried a wand shaped like a crooked shotgun that he used to draw lightning to kill his prey. He shot a bullet infused with lightning at me, but my ability to resist magic saved me. Until that moment, I was only certain that I am resistant to light and dark magic, but my survival of that attack made me suspect that I'm resistant to elemental magic as well.

Despite that, I don't seem to be immune from the ice jotunn's power. The air temperature around him has fallen rapidly, a creeping freeze that makes my breath frost and goosebumps rise across my arms. I brushed up against his arm earlier tonight and the icy temperature of his skin startled me. Now, his power is thrumming through him forcefully enough that the air burns inside my chest with every breath I take.

I lean toward Ford, my survival instincts urging me to take advantage of his body heat. "You're right," I whisper to him, allowing a growl to enter my voice. "It's not in my nature to obey. I won't follow commands. But I will come with you without a fight. Just this once."

There was a time when I had to hide my power and strength, to remain submissive and take the knocks that others inflicted on me. But now I'm an alpha in my own right. Even with all the firepower surrounding me—even with all these enemies ready to attack—I am ready to fight all of them.

I *choose* not to.

What's unsettling to me right now is that despite my promise not to fight, Ford still hasn't whisked me away. When I met him in his white wolf form, he seemed determined to bring me under his control. Now that he has me, he's delaying, and I don't know why.

Ford's thumb brushes across my other cheek. "Perhaps I underestimated how well you know your own nature."

He leans close to me again. His voice whispers across my cheek, lowering to a hum that vibrates beneath his speech like an echo of his wolf's growl. "I should take you away right now, little one. But you've given me a rare opportunity that I can't let slip through my fingers. To provoke a beast to his end."

Ford licks his lips as he pulls back and allows my hair to slide through his fingers. "It's time to find out whether or not you know who our true enemy is."

My forehead creases. *Our enemy?*

Without warning, Ford spins me around in his arms so that I'm facing Tristan. My instincts scream at me to fight back—to take my chance to elbow Ford's stomach, kick his shins, and free myself from this nightmare—but Ford's right arm circles my waist, hauling me hard up against his chest and thighs. His left arm closes around my neck, yanking upward beneath my chin, forcing my head back at an awkward angle against his left shoulder.

I choke, fight my instinct to struggle, and force myself to stop.

A single cry of pain from me will trigger a violent response from Tristan and then the guards will kill him.

I won't be the spark that lights this room on fire.

Tristan paces the floor close enough to cross the distance in three steps and drive his claws through Ford's throat. Tristan is the most beautiful, wild, ferocious man I've ever seen. Naked from the waist up, his chest is bleeding, his face bloodied, and strands of his raven-black hair fall across his crisp, green eyes. He is partially shifted, his incisors descended and claws dangerously extended. His chiseled chest rises and falls with every growl he makes. Each muscle in his body is ready, coiled like a wire waiting to attack.

He pulls to a stop directly opposite me. His claws press into his palms, but he seems unaware of the blood dripping to the floor.

"Ford Vanguard," Tristan says. "I will fucking kill you and send you back to your master in pieces."

Ford has a master? My thoughts spin because I'm not sure who Tristan could be referring to. Who does he think Ford answers to? Nobody could possibly command the white wolf... could they?

Even so, the pure vehemence in Tristan's promise sends a shiver down my spine.

Ford responds with a harsh laugh. His left arm clamps hard beneath my jaw, pulling me up so far that I struggle to keep my balance, my bare toes pointed to the floor. "If you don't want to lose another person you love, then you should take your chance to kill me right now, Tristan. Attack while you can." His voice rises. "Do it!"

Tristan's rage rolls across me in waves that scorch my heart, but his sudden smile throws me like whiplash. "You don't know who you're holding on to," he says. "Your master will end you if you harm her."

My thoughts swirl with deeper confusion. Nobody could possibly control the white wolf. Unless... Tristan has met Ford in his white wolf form and believes they are two separate beings. A master and a servant.

"Oh, you'd be surprised," Ford says, and I hear the delight and derision in his voice. "My *master* has special plans for this one."

Tristan's furious glare passes across every part of my body that I could use to free myself—from my loose arms and my still legs to my head, tipped back, my chin caught in Ford's hard grip. He knows I'm strong enough to fight my way free.

"Fight back, Tessa." Tristan growls into the tense silence. "Your deal is with Baxter Griffin, not with this butcher."

Tristan isn't the first to call Ford a butcher.

Baxter's eldest son, Cody, paces back and forth behind Tristan, following the arc of the upturned tables behind them. Cody's prowling is quiet, but his focus is wide, appearing aware of everything from the guards to his far left all the way to the door on his far right. He is Baxter's alpha-in-training, but his father gave him an ultimatum—Baxter will only step aside peacefully if Cody kills Tristan. Otherwise, Cody must challenge and kill his father for the right to rule the Eastern Lowland pack.

Cody's focus stops on me. He pauses in his pacing and draws himself to his full height to return my sharp gaze, his own eyes narrowing. His sandy blond hair is cut short, his brown eyes are the color of hickory and flecked with gold while he maintains a partial shift. His eyebrows are drawn down, his shoulders tense. The glittering gold tattoo of a snarling wolf's head inked into his chest and left shoulder is backlit with the shadow of a cobalt blue wolf—*my* wolf. He once tried to mark me and now he has chosen to have me permanently marked into *his* skin.

Once again, I'm reminded that he is my enemy. He is not my friend. And yet... I need his help to keep Tristan alive tonight.

Cody lost his sister, Ella, three years ago. He blames Tristan for her death. He has every reason to hate Tristan and wish the same pain on Tristan that his family suffered when Ella disappeared. He doesn't know that she's alive and I can't tell him that she is.

Now, Tristan wants me to fight.

I will.

But only once Ford takes me out of here and I know that Tristan is safe. Then I'll fight tooth and claw for my freedom.

But until then... All I can hope is that Cody will recognize the plea in my eyes—that he will honor the deal I made with his father to allow Tristan to walk out of here alive.

Tristan's fists clench and unclench, an increasingly agitated movement when I remain where I am, silent and still.

"Fight back, Tessa!" He poises on the spot, fixated on me as if he believes I'll obey him. For once.

But I never have, not from the moment we first met.

My focus flicks from Tristan back to Cody, willing Cody to understand my unspoken request: *Don't let Tristan fight for me.*

Cody is frozen, his eyes narrowed, his lips drawn into a fierce line. He has no reason to help me, and I don't know if he will.

To Tristan, I attempt to shake my head, forcing a quick back-and-forth movement despite Ford's arm clamped around my neck.

Ford presses in behind me, his cheek brushing against mine again. I sense his lips stretching into a sneer. "I think that was a *no*, Tristan. If you want to free her, you're going to have to do it yourself."

With a snarl, Tristan begins to prowl back and forth, reckless steps left and right that dare Baxter's guards to riddle his body with bullets.

"Tessa!" Tristan roars, fists clenching so suddenly that blood splashes across the floor. Teeth bared, he roars a command at me that I would never disobey if I were an ordinary wolf shifter. "*You will fucking fight back!*"

Two silenced bullets bite the marble at Tristan's feet in quick succession. They're warning shots, but I have no doubt the next bullets will be aimed at Tristan's heart.

Panic builds inside me.

I understand Ford's game now. He's deliberately trying to goad Tristan into retaliating. He called Tristan our enemy and now Ford is willing to risk losing his control over me to orchestrate Tristan's death.

I need Ford to take me away. The longer we remain here, the more likely Tristan will try to fight for me. He came here to die tonight. Death is his answer to avoiding his father's fate and keeping his pack safe—from *him*. His wolf is in control of his actions now. He won't care that another step toward me is an invitation for his body to be riddled with bullets.

It's what he wants.

"No!" I scream at Tristan, my voice raspy, my vocal chords compressed by Ford's grip around my throat.

I've forced myself to keep my arms at my sides, to be submissive to Ford, but now I make a swift move. Drawing on my wolf's energy to increase my strength, I grab the arm Ford squeezes around my throat, drop my weight, and drive my elbow into his stomach at the same time. The air whooshes from his chest for a beat before his arms open reflexively. I spin, the flat of my right hand colliding with the center of his chest and knocking him backward.

I read the surprise in his eyes, his raised eyebrows and parted lips as my wolf's strength gives me the power to maneuver against his wishes. I know in my heart that he's as strong as me, but he's in his human form right now and I had the element of surprise.

He won't be so easily evaded again.

Lightning crackles across me when the warlock jumps forward to defend Ford. His magic bites at my already wounded chest but rolls off me without leaving a mark.

I snarl at him. "Back off!"

Ford reaches out to stop the warlock in his tracks, but I'm already spinning out of the warlock's reach, headed for my real destination: *Tristan*.

Crossing the three paces it takes me to stand immediately in front of him, I plant both of my hands on Tristan's muscled chest, inhale his power and meet his stormy eyes.

Oh, give me strength.

I shove him as hard as I can, putting all of my physical strength into my planted feet and my extended arms in a powerful hit. At the same time, I push against him with my emotions, a raging, fucking-angry mind-shove that will rip through his consciousness.

He jolts, snarls, prepares to retaliate, but I grab his head before he can move, forcing him to feel the impact of my rejection.

"No!" I scream at him again. "You don't tell me what to do. Not now. Not ever!"

Recklessly—possibly the most reckless thing I've ever done—I allow my power to surface, my scent to build, and dare him to inhale.

"Tessa, don't do this." His eyes widen, but his chest stills. He's holding his breath, refusing to inhale.

If I were like other wolves—if I could have bonded with Tristan like he bonded with me—I would never be able to make myself hurt him like this. But I was never like other wolves.

"Breathe me in for the last time," I whisper, gripping his head so hard that I'm sure I'm clawing his scalp. I stand in a tattered evening dress that hangs by threads across my shoulders. My chest and stomach are clawed and dripping with blood. I'm barefoot and my tulle skirt is in ruins. Sharp pain strikes me with every breath I take.

My *heart* hurts.

I remind myself that I have only one goal: Keep Tristan alive for long enough to find a way to destroy the three minds of Cerberus before they destroy Tristan. I will find a way to subvert the Deceiver, the Coward, and the Killer.

"I'm walking away from you now, Tristan Masters. I will keep you alive no matter what it takes," I say, willing him to obey my next commands, even though I won't obey *him*. "You will *not* fight your way to me. You won't follow me or die trying to free me. You will not allow *anyone* in our pack to come after me."

Our pack. He will know I'm talking about Iyana and Danika—the fierce vampire and hawk shifter who are like family to me. They are like sisters. They are my pack.

Tristan once slipped up and called his territory '*our* territory.' He revealed to me tonight that he had a plan that I would take over his pack when he died, but I don't think he realizes how much his pack loves him. If he were to die tonight, they would be devastated. They wouldn't follow me, no matter how much strength I show them. He needs to hear my deliberate choice of words and remember what he's responsible for protecting: his pack and my friends.

Not me.

"Tessa." He growls my name, shaking his head at me, making me a promise. "There will never be a last time for us."

My hand slides away from his head and his response is to try to grab my shoulder, then my waist, but I fight my way free, punching his arms, deflecting every attempt he makes.

Tristan and I have never fought each other, not intentionally.

We've collided, disagreed, raged against each other, but we've carefully avoided a confrontation that would test our strength against each other. A true confrontation between us must never happen, least of all tonight.

My focus flickers to Cody, the briefest, sharpest glance asking for his help.

Painful gratitude floods through me when he responds by leaping at Tristan's back. Cody's powerful legs give him height as he crashes into Tristan, knees Tristan in the spine, and knocks him to the ground.

Tristan immediately releases me to defend himself.

I jump away from their fight. As they fall to their knees, Cody wraps his arm around Tristan's neck from behind, squeezing tightly and refusing to let go—even when Tristan elbows him and threatens to tip Cody onto his head. In a rapid movement, Cody retaliates by wrapping his free arm around Tristan's chest and presses his clawed fingers over Tristan's heart.

"I'll cut your heart out if you move again," Cody snarls. His voice lowers. "She's trying to save your life, Tristan. Don't fucking forget what you've got."

The way Cody's fist is positioned, his claws would spear through Tristan's skin and muscle fast enough to do what he threatens. Cody doesn't match Tristan's true animal strength —*hell, who could match a descendant of Cerberus himself?*—but he's strong enough to impale Tristan before Tristan can stop him.

And Tristan knows it.

He freezes, watching me walk away from him, his green eyes filled with tormented rage before he hides his emotions and becomes blank.

"What heart?" he asks. "Without Tessa, I have nothing more than a beating muscle inside my chest."

I falter. Nearly crumble.

Tristan has rarely made himself vulnerable to me, rarely voiced his feelings for me. The closest he came is when he told me tonight never to beg. Maybe when he said that I was meant to be his pack's future, not his. Maybe when he asked if he could mark me and told me that it felt right.

I hate him for choosing to speak now when I don't have any options left. I allow my anger to build, knowing it's the only emotion that can sustain me through the next moments. Cody won't be able to hold Tristan for long and I need to force Ford to take me out of here. *Now.*

I walk swiftly back to Ford, who considers me with a cold smile. Off to the side, Baxter's gloating face crosses my vision, along with the ice jotunn and the warlock, whose scrutiny of me is intense, boring deep.

"If you plan to take me away, then do it now," I say to Ford. "Otherwise, the deal is off and I'll kill every last shifter in this room before I leave."

Determined to force his hand, I raise my fist and prepare to smack his face, a deliberately provocative gesture.

Ford reacts swiftly, seizing my arm with one hand, my face with the other, squeezing his fingers around my chin. "You have deliberately squandered an opportunity to watch our enemy die by his own choice, and instead, you choose to bring pain upon yourself. You disappoint me, little one."

I glare up at Ford, my eyes watering as his fingers claw against my jaw, scraping me. "Tristan is not my enemy," I whisper.

The corners of Ford's mouth turn down. "You have much to learn."

His fingernails scrape down my chin. He wrenches me to

the left before he shoves me backward, both hands planted on my wounded chest.

I stumble away from Ford but right myself a split second before I register the sudden change in the temperature around me.

It's like I stepped onto an icy mountain and sank neck-deep into snow.

My heart in my throat, I spin to find myself standing a mere inch away from the ice jotunn's chest. He's an enormous man, descended from ice giants, seven feet tall with a strong jaw. His head is shaven and his eyes match his power—a frosty blue. The rolled-up sleeves of his white collared shirt strain around his massive biceps as he reaches out to take hold of me.

He casts his icy gaze across my face and the awful wounds across my chest. "It is my honor to carry you," he says, his speech overly formal.

I curl my lip at him. *A weird honor.*

"Bring her," Ford commands him, spinning on his heel and striding in the direction of the door. "Let her ruin begin."

The power pouring off the ice jotunn envelops me, growing in strength. Even without touching him, I know I'm in trouble. A single punch from this man knocked Iyana flat. His powerful grip nearly killed a member of Tristan's pack within seconds.

My eyes widen as the jotunn's power bites me, sharp and frightening—even without touching me. It's a thousand times stronger than when I brushed up against his arm earlier tonight. My breath frosts and the blood oozing down my chest and stomach freezes over, paling to a sickly brown color as icicles spread across every visible part of my skin.

The last time I encountered this man, I defeated him by releasing my wolf's energy and striking her through him, which tore at his insides and subdued him. I can't do that now. I can't release my wolf in front of these shifters. She is my last secret and I won't expose my abilities until I have no other choice. But more importantly than that, the moment that I release her from my body, Ford will be able to take control of her. The only way to protect her—to protect *myself*—is to remain in my human form.

That doesn't mean I can't use my wolf's energy to make myself stronger. I gather my strength to leap away from the jotunn, one hand raised to ward him off. "I can walk on my own. Do *not* touch me."

He ignores my command, smoothly tackling me before I can turn and hurry after Ford. The jotunn's thick arms close around my waist and in the time it takes me to gasp a breath, he hoists me upward and throws me across his left shoulder.

The moment he touches me, ice particles rush across my chest, shoulders, and stomach, forming down my arms and legs all the way to my fingertips and my toes, leaving my skin blue and glittering. It is the most visually beautiful but physically painful contact I've ever experienced.

I inhale. A moment of silent agony.

Pain shrieks through my body and screams wrench out of me against my will. My mind explodes with the onslaught of a freeze that rips through me like a thousand icy knives. A glacial darkness follows the pain, flashing up through my neck and into my head, halting rational thought and reducing me to my most basic instincts.

I have to get away from him.

I have to make the pain stop.

Now, now, now!

My reflexes kick into a frenzy. I thrash in the jotunn's arms, thumping his back with my fists, kicking his chest with my feet, smashing my knee into his face, trying to force him to let me go. Struggling only brings more of my body into contact with his, increasing my pain, and does nothing to make him release me. He's as physically strong as his giant stature indicates, the strength of his hold seeming only to increase the harder I struggle to free myself. He barely jolts, let alone falters.

"Tessa!" Tristan's roar breaks through my agony, cutting through my screams. "*Tessa!*"

Beyond my pain, I'm aware that Tristan is hitting back at Cody, savage, desperate blows, but Cody refuses to let him go.

Retaliating, Cody thumps his fist repeatedly against the location of Tristan's heart, rapid hits before he lays into the side of his face, punching Tristan so hard that he hits the floor.

Grabbing Tristan's head on the way down, Cody uses their falling momentum to smack Tristan's face against the marble. Dropping his knee onto the side of Tristan's neck, Cody pins him with a vicious roar. "Stay the fuck down!"

The echo of Cody's command repeats on me, a painful reminder of the first order Tristan ever attempted to give me.

Both men's eyes are turned toward me now. Tristan's head is tipped far enough back that he can see me. His focus is glazed and both his nose and forehead are bleeding. If he shifted into his wolf form, he could beat Cody in an instant, but he doesn't shift.

Cody's expression is drawn and pale. His focus on me is intense, his head lowered and lips pressed together in a tense line. His muscles bunch as if he's about to release Tristan and leap after me himself.

His focus suddenly shifts from me to Tristan when Tristan reaches up to grab Cody's shoulder.

Tristan's lips move. He's saying something, maybe in a whisper, but I'm in too much pain to gather my wits fast enough to try to overhear what they're saying. Even if I could, my own screams are too loud in my ears—so loud that I'm sure I'm preventing their murmured conversation from being overheard by the watching guards and especially by Baxter.

Cody's father has stepped into the shadows at the corner of the room, finding a spot behind the guards. The blood has drained from his face as my screams hurtle around the room. I wonder if he knows how numbered his days are now. I came here intending to end him. I only stopped because of Ella, because of my shock when I discovered that she was his daughter. I need to find out what really happened to her and then I'll be back. He murdered my father and I can never forget that.

I register the look that Cody suddenly gives his father—a hard stare that carries hatred more pure than I was expecting. Cody's incisors descend before he makes the slightest motion of his head. I can't tell if he nodded or shook his head at Tristan.

Cody shouts another order that seems completely unnecessary. "Stay down!" he roars, even though Tristan isn't fighting back now.

Cody follows up his order with a final fist to Tristan's face, a punch hard enough to smack Tristan's head to the side and knock him out.

Tristan's head rocks a little while his body sags against the floor.

Cody's focus flashes to me again, every muscle in his body tense.

He roars into the space between us, a sustained wordless howl that follows me all the way to the door. My heart wrenches around in my chest at the possibility that he's trying to drown out the sound of my screams so he can't hear them.

I pray that I'll pass out as the ice jotunn passes through the doorway into the front foyer. I'm struggling to understand how he's affecting me at all. His magic appears to be elemental, so it should roll off me like the warlock's did. At Hidden House, Helen determined that I'm resistant to light magic and dark magic. I was sure I'm resistant to elemental magic too.

All I know for certain is that I'm hurting—body and heart—and no matter how hard I wish to be unconscious, blissful darkness eludes me. Maybe that's part of the jotunn's power—to keep his victims awake and conscious while he hurts them.

He stays on Ford's heels, unmoved by my screams.

"Don't fight your power," the ice man says as he walks. His voice is low and calm. Terrifyingly quiet. It somehow breaks through my screams, a projection of power directly into my mind. "Let the pain dull your human mind. Feel the wolf within."

The warlock paces close behind us. Lightning pools in his palms, ready in case anyone tries to follow us. The eyepatch he wears across his left eye partially obscures his expression, but the rest of his face is blank, dispassionate, unaffected by my cries.

I swallow my sobs as the jotunn carries me into the beautiful foyer at the front of the house. Instead of turning toward the front door, he follows Ford toward the main staircase, veering to the right of it. Because I'm facing backward, I'm not sure where we're going. I can only see what we pass.

A row of guards lines the foyer, protecting the 'fun' side of the house where the younger shifters were celebrating Cody's brother's birthday. The thumping music on this side of the house that I heard when I first arrived has stopped.

Pain is dulling my mind now, tearing at my consciousness, even though I can't seem to escape it. I'm aware of a sudden movement in the doorway behind us that leads into the other room. A lithe figure swathed in a silver gown suddenly darts between the guards.

I recognize Charlotte, Cody's mother, her long, blonde hair streaming across her shoulders.

One of the guards tries to grab her, but she carries out a preemptive strike, stomping her heel onto his boot, making him yelp. I'm sure he's more surprised than injured since nobody in their right mind would want to come near me right now. Her silver stiletto sticks in his boot, but she seemed prepared for that, shedding the shoe with ease and darting out of his reach.

Another guard shouts as he makes a futile lunge for her. "No! Lady Griffin!"

She races away from the line of guards and runs toward me while the guard who shouted raises his hand to stop any trigger-happy comrades. "Hold your fire!"

The ice jotunn suddenly pulls to a stop, easing to the side so that Ford can step between me and Charlotte. The jotunn has stopped in a position that allows me to see both Ford and the blonde-haired woman.

I'm not sure why she approached us. When I first met her tonight, she looked at me as if I were the weapon that will tear her family apart. Her response to me told me that she is afraid of me. Maybe she just wants a better vantage point to witness my pain.

My entire body is trembling now, convulsing, and I can't control it. I've screamed so much that my voice is turning hoarse and my cries are nearly soundless.

Charlotte's face is flushed and her eyes are wide as she faces up to Ford. She's petite, forced to tip her head back to see him. "What is your man doing to Tessa Dean?"

Ford's voice is like honey, reminding me of how he sounded when I first met him. Soothing. Convincing. "My dear Charlotte, you know very well that the jotunn's magic is lethal to all but a rare few. My warlock has cast a spell to protect anyone who accidentally comes into contact with his body, so you have nothing to fear."

"I know that!" she snaps. "So why is *she* in pain?"

Ford shrugs, an overly indifferent gesture. "Sadly, Tessa's power is strong enough to cut through the protective shield around the jotunn's body. She feels his power in its most primal and painful form."

Charlotte's gaze flickers to me. "Then make the warlock carry her."

Ford shakes his head, leaning close to Charlotte. "Lady Griffin, please don't presume to tell me what to do with my possessions."

The corners of her mouth turn down sharply while a fierce crease appears in her forehead. "Possession," she whispers.

"Don't worry so much," he says, cooing at her. "Tessa is one of the rare few who is strong enough to survive the jotunn's magic. She won't die."

"But—"

"You do realize—don't you?—that the longer you delay us, the more she suffers?" Ford's smirk increases as he stares at Charlotte, waiting for his message to sink in.

She takes a quick step back, her lips pressed together, her head thrown back and a snarl on her lips. "Then be gone, butcher."

A shout from the far end of the foyer precedes Baxter Griffin, who hurries from the room I left behind. He's as tall as Cody, but his hair is a darker blond and streaked with silver. Charlotte is his true mate. According to Cody, Baxter doesn't love anyone, but he would die for Charlotte. He must have sensed her distress through their bond.

He storms to Charlotte's side, casting angry glances at the guards who let her past them. Drawing Charlotte behind himself, he inclines his head at Ford sharply toward the back of the foyer. "You know the way out."

Ford pauses, still smiling. "You have given me a valuable prize, Baxter. I'm rarely in anyone's debt, but I'm now in yours."

Despite his apparent concern for Charlotte, Baxter's eyes light up. The power to claim a favor from Ford must be worth gold. "Then we'll discuss terms when you're ready."

"Indeed." Ford swings toward the back of the foyer and the ice jotunn follows him.

I'm barely lucid now.

My screams have become whimpers. My struggles to free myself are jerky, my muscles twitching beyond my control. I have enough rational thought and control left to strain to the side to pick out the shape of the shadowed door we're heading toward—only ten or so paces away.

I can't survive the agony. I need the blessed relief of unconsciousness—even if it will only last a few minutes—and right now the wooden doorframe is my best option.

Using every remaining shred of strength in my body, I engage all of my stomach muscles as the ice jotunn carries me through the doorway. Timing my maneuver, forcing myself to wait another split second, I lift my head and chest as we pass through.

As hard as I can, I bang my head against the wood.

My skull cracks into it, a perfect hit designed to knock myself out.

The jotunn jolts at my sudden movement, adjusting his grip, but continues on his path. I sense him shake his head in disapproval. "You are too powerful for that to work," he murmurs.

My head and arms flop against his back, my bloodied hair cascading down my arms, but…

The jotunn was right. The darkness should have been instant, but I remain conscious.

I register Charlotte's gasp, her pale hand flying across her mouth at what I tried to do to myself. My focus swings across her, past Baxter and the guards, seeking the room where I left Tristan behind.

Whimpering, I reach out instinctively for him with my heart, seeking his emotions through the melding bond, needing the force of his fury to sustain me—even if his fury is aimed at me.

He must be conscious again because his rage hits me hard, a volcano I would gladly die in.

CHAPTER TWO

While the warlock leads the way, Ford takes up the rear, walking behind me where I can see his shiny shoes—or his face if I crane my neck.

We pass through another corridor in Baxter Griffin's vast home. The shapes around me are overly sharp and bright, as if my pain is highlighting them. Expensive plush and wooden furniture gleams in the rooms we pass, along with abstract paintings with swirls of vibrant color like the one in Ella's room. The colors are sickening.

Ford reaches out to brush his hand against the new wound on the back of my head where I tried to knock myself out.

He sighs and shakes his head at me. "You can try to hurt yourself, but you can't escape your power, little one. Your wolf's strength will keep you awake and alert no matter what you do."

"I don't have a wolf," I snarl, barely able to lift my head to see him. "I only have me."

Ford reaches out to run his hand down my hair, pulling the long strands away from my arms. Again, he sifts through them, choosing a clump of strands. He folds the ends in his outstretched fist, tugging on my scalp when he doesn't stay in sync with the jotunn's steps.

My hair extends between us like a rope.

He sighs again. "You know so little."

Pain makes me reckless, goading him into retaliating. "I suppose you're the fucking clever man who intends to teach poor little female me what I don't know."

A flash of crimson washes across Ford's eyes. "I intend to teach your *wolf*—once I can reach her," he snaps. "She is locked away so tightly that you only feel her energy, not her true desires. Once she's free, she will thank me for what I've done to you, even if you don't."

Another snarl builds inside me. "If she's locked so deeply inside me, how do you know she's there?" I raise my head again. "When you finally succeed in breaking open this cage you believe exists, what if there's nothing inside it but me?"

His fist clenches around my hair. White light glimmers at the edges of his fingers. I recognize the energy that he uses to form his white wolf. The sparks travel along my hair like shots of electricity. They bite my scalp, bringing fresh tears to my eyes.

"I will soon find out," Ford says.

Without warning, the jotunn's steps become heavier and my body begins to tip alarmingly in his arms. I grab his sides, not sure what's happening until I realize that we're ascending a set of stairs. His arms clamp more tightly around me, his fingers clenching around my hips to keep me from sliding headfirst down the steps behind him.

My scalp aches where Ford continues to grip my hair, the irregular and unpredictable sharp tugs eclipsing the constant pain of the jotunn's icy power.

We ascend two flights of stairs and my head spins by the time we reach the top. We must be at the eastern end of the house now and it's confusing that we're traveling upward instead of out to a parking garage. Facing backward makes it impossible to see where we're going and what awaits me.

We pass through a doorway that the warlock holds open for us, his single pale blue eye following me. The jotunn carries me through a small entryway before he pauses for the warlock to unlatch another door for us.

A strong breeze hits me as we exit onto some sort of platform. It's possibly one hundred feet wide with steel mesh about six feet deep rising up from the edges that I can see, the mesh angling gently upward instead of sitting straight up like a fence. A motion-sensor light flickers on as soon as the jotunn steps onto the platform, but it's not so bright that it's blinding.

The smell of rain fills the moist air. It must be past midnight now. The sky beyond the platform contains a dull sheen, a promise of sunrise a few hours away. The ice particles on my arms and hands glitter in the light, revealing a swirling pattern that pulses slowly up and down my limbs, a cruel beauty. I can't see my legs or my face, but I have no doubt that my whole body is glowing where I'm covered in ice.

"Get the chopper started, Silas," Ford says to the warlock, who removes his jacket with a "Yes, boss" before he strides out of view.

While I'm facing the door, I can't see the helicopter that Ford spoke about, but I feel the full impact of its rotor blades when it whirs into life.

The wind it creates buffets me and flips up my skirt. I'm in too much pain to care about my dignity—*damn G-string underwear*—although the location of the ice jotunn's arms clamped around my hips stops my skirt from flying up completely.

The strong wind finally tugs my hair free from Ford's grip. Despite releasing my billowing tresses, he grips the back of my head for a moment, an overly-familiar gesture that increases the pain from the wound I inflicted on myself.

"Let's get her strapped in," he says to the ice jotunn.

The jotunn has only carried me a few steps toward the source of the billowing wind when the back of my neck prickles and my instincts kick in.

My senses hone in on the entry room we left behind.

Without making any sudden movements, I lift my head toward the doorway we stepped through.

The far door into the entry room slips open and Cody

races through it. Surprise makes me jolt, a dangerous move since the jotunn will be able to feel it.

Cody's brown eyes gleam as his strong legs speed him through the entryway toward us. He's still dressed in his suit pants, naked from the waist up, but now he carries a weapon belt around his hips sporting two handguns and two daggers. A second harness is strapped around his chest that appears to hold a rifle at his back.

His surveillance is quick—he takes in the ice jotunn's location, along with Ford's position slightly ahead of us, and then his focus flicks beyond me to what I can only assume is Silas—the warlock—where he must be sitting inside the helicopter.

In a fluid movement, Cody drops to one knee just inside the second doorway, flips the rifle out of the harness at his back, and takes aim at the jotunn. My eyes widen at the weapon. I've never seen a rifle like the one he's holding—the magazine is much larger than normal and reminds me more of a grenade launcher.

I follow the barrel of the rifle in the split second that Cody takes aim, anticipating the weapon's blast.

The barrel shifts to my left.

I brace as Cody pulls the trigger multiple times.

Three large darts thud into the jotunn's back in rapid succession, making the ice giant miss a step and stumble with me in his arms. I've never seen darts like these, but I'm close enough to the point of impact to witness fluid inject from the thick barrels into the jotunn's body. It has to be tranquilizer fluid or poison, I'm not sure which.

The jotunn roars a warning. Beside us, Ford reacts at lightning speed, his focus flashing across me, skipping across the darts protruding from the jotunn's back to their source: Cody.

Ford's suddenly crimson eyes narrow to threatening slits. He whirls, muscles bunching as he runs at Cody.

I count his movements in heartbeats, everything happening so fast that I can hardly follow it.

Cody shifts his aim and fires at Ford. Cody's finger moves another three times on the trigger.

Two of the darts thud into Ford's chest as he runs, the impact point of each dart higher than the one before. Ford flails and, with a shout, he drops to his knees only two paces from Cody's location. In the act of falling, Ford snatches at the air in front of his face. He opens his fist as his knees hit the tarmac, revealing the third dart caught deftly in his palm before it would have hit him.

He squeezes his fist so hard around the projectile that it cracks and shatters in his hand, dripping silver liquid to the platform. "You're a fool, Cody Griffin," Ford says. "Nothing can... stop... me..."

Cody lowers his weapon and growls back at Ford. "These tranquilizers can stop anything."

Ford opens his fist. He landed on his knees at such an angle that I can see the side of his face and the disbelief in his widening eyes as he stares at the liquid spilling across his palm. "How... the hell... did you get these...?"

Ford sways, tilts to the left, and crumples all the way to the ground.

I'm in shock. The tranquilizers actually worked. Against Ford fucking Vanguard, the white wolf.

The ice giant takes a beat longer to fall. Shaking his head like an angry bull, he roars into the wind before he drops heavily to his knees. His arms clamp more tightly around me, refusing to let me go until he tips to the left. Forced to drop his left hand to plant it on the ground, he attempts to support himself at a sharp lean. His torso is so big that my toes barely scrape the ground even now that he's kneeling.

Even though the jotunn's right arm continues to clamp around me like a metal vise, without his left arm curled up around me, I have a much better chance of fighting my way free.

I grit my teeth and allow my fighting instincts to take over. My stomach muscles scream at me as I engage them to rise up and bash my elbow into the back of the jotunn's head, knocking him farther forward so that his right arm twitches.

Damn. He still doesn't let me go.

I don't know how I can make myself move again. My stomach has had the closest contact with his body and the pain is beyond endurance. I force myself to rise up and hit him again, screaming with effort as my elbow connects with the back of his head once more.

Then—*finally*—he tilts forward. His right arm loosens around me as he prepares to plant his hand on the tarmac and stop himself from falling face first onto the ground.

The easing of his hold on me and the touchdown of my toes on the ground is all I need to gain traction to twist and shove myself out of his arms, punching at the side of his head to give myself momentum.

Dropping to the ground, I lean back as fast as I can and kick hard into his side, angling my foot to make sure he continues falling forward. The sole of my foot was one of the few places that didn't come into direct contact with his power until now. Fresh ice tears across my skin during the brief moment that I kick him. The initial contact is like acid, making me realize the extent to which the rest of my body had adjusted to the pain. Just how cold I've become.

I'm freezing.

Colder than the moist wind that buffets me.

The water droplets in the air turn to ice as soon as they hit me, adding to the intricate pattern of snowflakes that decorate my chest, arms, and legs.

My body adjusted to the jotunn's power in a way that feels like I've formed a second skin of freezing glass, and now I'm terrified about what will happen when it shatters.

Gasping air and trying to control my fear, I backflip away from the jotunn as fast as I can. I land at a crouch nearby. His icy-blue eyes follow me as he punches both hands down onto the tarmac in front of his chest. He leans forward but refuses to kiss the ground.

I have his unwavering and unnerving attention. His voice is calm, deep, striking through me. "You can't escape… your transformation… It has… already begun…"

My chest rises and falls, my breathing increasing as I

quickly ascertain what threats await me, my hair billowing around me as I remain in a crouch.

I can finally see the sleek, black helicopter resting on the helipad to my left and the warlock in the pilot's seat. He's bent over, his back to the cockpit window, but I don't think it's because Cody has hit him with a tranquilizer. The cockpit door is closed and there aren't any breakages in the glass. He must be reaching for something. He won't be able to use his magic to hurt me, but I estimate Cody has only a few seconds before he becomes the warlock's target.

Already, I sense the warlock's magic building around the helipad, a shimmering shield that is rapidly closing around its outer edges and will trap Cody inside it.

Cody's energy hits me like a whip's lash as he runs toward me, still brandishing his rifle. "Tessa! Come with me!" His shout catches in the wind as he crouches and reaches for me.

I prepare to run with him when his fingers close around my bicep.

Cody's touch is like fire after the jotunn's ice—too earthy, too heady. Too animal. *Too hot!*

I fight the pain as I jump to my feet. I need to know whether I can trust him—I have to believe that Cody wouldn't jeopardise Tristan's pack right now—but there's no time to ask questions.

He's partially shifted, his brown eyes glowing with golden flecks. "My wolf let you go once, Tessa." Cody's deep growl thrums through me. "He won't let you go again."

I can't take his hand—his touch is too painful—but I launch into a run with him, trying to push away the aching memories that strike through me of the night my father died, of Cody standing on the road behind us as Tristan drove away with me.

I'm sprinting with him toward the exit when the warlock's power crackles in the air around us. We're too far away from the stairs. We won't make it.

I act on instinct.

Grabbing Cody's arms, I throw myself in front of him like a shield. "Get down!"

Wrapping my arms around him, I count a single heartbeat before the lightning hits us from above. The bullet is a fraction of a second away. Cody's furious eyes meet mine, but I pull him closer, covering his face and torso.

I scream as the bullet hits my back. The projectile draws a greater surge of electricity from the sky and directs it through my body. I sense my skin split, another wound to crisscross the claw marks I already have on my back. The explosion is blinding, the magic biting. It's impossible not to arch as a mess of pain and heat blows through me.

But I succeeded in my intention. My body formed a shield between Cody and the blast. He's safe and alive. Even if he can't get off the roof now because I sense the warlock's magic has closed across the stairs. The only way we're leaving is if I force Silas to retract his magic.

Cody is frozen in my arms while the light glows white around us, his arms clamped awkwardly between our chests, his knees pressed to the side. His body is a source of intense warmth that sears my skin as I freeze and burn in turns.

I try to breathe. Focus on basic survival.

Breathe in. *Violet sunrise.* Breathe out. *Silver forest.*

"Fuck," Cody says. "You can repel magic."

"Not without pain." I grit my teeth.

The bullet was the last straw.

I've passed my point of endurance and now my instincts have become basic. *Fight. Survive.*

Rising beneath those instincts is a new impulse whose full force I haven't felt before.

Kill.

As lightning continues to flicker around us—the next bullet only moments away—something cracks inside me.

A storm rises inside my mind, carrying my wolf's howl, drawing my power upward.

The ice jotunn promised that his magic was dulling my human soul, that my transformation has already begun.

Whatever that means, I will use it to fight the warlock. Kill him if I have to.

My hand closes around one of Cody's daggers. Before he can stop me, I slide the blade free from the harness at his waist, leap to my feet, and spin to face the helicopter where it rests twenty paces away.

The cockpit door is flung open. Silas leans through it, his arm outstretched, holding his crooked wooden shotgun with the warped barrel pointed in our direction.

He slides forward and leaps from the cockpit, hitting the tarmac with his knees bent, the wind billowing around him as he takes up position beside the chopper. I'm sure it's incredibly unsafe to leave a helicopter running without a pilot inside it, but I sense the power building around him. My ears pop when the air pressure changes. I have no doubt the warlock has full control of the chopper with his magic, keeping it ready for a quick takeoff.

He raises his weapon and takes aim—this time, a little to my right, where Cody remains.

I don't hesitate.

Flipping the dagger into my left hand, I position myself between them and run straight for the warlock.

Light flashes around the chamber of his gun a heartbeat before another lightning bullet fires.

I step right into its path, but this time, I don't intend to take the hit.

My arms pump, rising and falling at speed, my reflexes firing as fast as Ford's must have been when he caught Cody's dart at close range.

If he and I are the same, then I can do what he can do.

If he can catch a dart, then I can catch a fucking bullet.

The projectile speeds toward me, magic bursting around its surface my only focus. With split-second timing, I judge the distance it still has to travel, the miniscule moments as I raise my right hand, palm out.

The bullet hits my hand dead center. My fingers close around it. Lightning cascades from the sky as I pull it with me,

29

spinning in a full arc to reduce the burning impact of its momentum against my skin.

I land in a crouch, cradling the bullet inside my clenched fist. Lightning strikes the tarmac in a circle around me, burning in a downward spiral, following the arc that I spun with the bullet.

My head snaps up, my focus zeroing in on the warlock while the glittering sparks float around me.

Fuck. That actually worked.

The warlock's lips part. His weapon drops a little as he stares at me. I guess he's as surprised as I am, but his shock won't last forever.

I don't have time to waste.

Dropping the bullet and leaping back to my feet, I continue on my path toward him.

Behind me, at the edge of my vision, Cody rises to one knee, positions his rifle, takes aim, and fires two darts at the warlock.

Silas retaliates quickly. Sharp crackles of energy burst into life around him, forming an enormous shield that encompasses the helicopter and stretches several paces in front of the warlock's position.

He isn't quite fast enough. The first dart gets through before the shield is up. Light bursts across the warlock's hands and the dart flies off course, dropping to the ground and rolling to a stop a few paces from where the warlock stands. The second dart burns up in the shield.

Cody flings his rifle to the side, draws both of his handguns, and fires repeatedly. Every bullet he shoots burns up in the warlock's magic—but the distraction he creates splits the warlock's attention between Cody and me. It gives me the seconds I need to plow toward the warlock without being fired upon.

A deep energy continues to rise inside me. Parts of my body burn icy, snowflakes clinging to my stomach, outer arms, and calves. Other parts of me—my chest and thighs—

burn with heat that rages through me from my contact with Cody.

Both sensations tug at me as I tear through the shimmering orb of energy that the warlock created to protect himself. As soon as I pass through the shield, energy from his magic bites my skin, sharp and prickling.

It's the final layer of pain I can bear.

Claws, ice, heat, lightning. A broken heart. Shock. *Tristan.* I've experienced as much as I can stand tonight.

The distant howl inside my mind becomes a scream and my wolf's energy bursts to the surface, a savage ripple of power, stronger than I've felt before. I've learned to control it, to calm my power, but I don't subdue it this time. *Can't* subdue it.

I sense the warlock's shield repairing itself behind me, sealing us both in. I continue to sense his power around the helipad all the way back to the stairs. The complete shield across the stairway will stop anyone getting through. It must be the only reason why Baxter and his men haven't rained hell on us already since we've made enough noise to draw an army.

Silas's focus remains on me as I run the final paces to him, preparing to leap and strike him with the blade I'm carrying, to force him to let us go.

With a swipe of his hand through the air, the dagger leaves my fingers, joining the dart on the ground.

My claws extend from my fingers instead.

Just before I would reach him, the warlock's uncovered eye gleams. He drops his wand, plummets to his knees, and extends both of his hands in my direction.

A different kind of light bursts from his fingertips.

It's not lightning. Not elemental. I've only felt power like this once before and then it was a tiny flame, quickly extinguished.

Dark light envelops me, inky like the darkest night, filling my field of view. It pushes at me, slowing me down, and then...

A savage blast shoves me backward so fast that I spin midair and hit the side of the helicopter.

Struggling to breathe, I slide to the ground, landing on my knees, the darkness pressing down on me like a dead weight. The hairs at the back of my neck stand on end, my head bows, and a scream builds inside my chest.

This is dark magic.

I taste blood on my tongue. It fills my mouth, choking me. Dropping to my hands and knees as the magic pounds down on my spine, I spit crimson fluid onto the tarmac. Not only my sight, but my head fills with darkness like sinking into a vat of oil and trying to see through it, trying to breathe in it.

Helen proved to me that dark magic can't hurt me, but this... *this* darkness... is as immense as the depths of malice at the heart of Tristan's fate, the darkness that he hid from me.

Worse, Helen's warning about dark magic is like a scream in my memory.

Dark magic comes from draining life.

Struggling to swing my head, I seek Cody's position halfway across the helipad.

He is doubled up, gripping his chest. His other hand claws the tarmac, his back arching and rippling as his wolf appears and disappears. His wolf must be trying to fight back against the force that is sucking away his life. The warlock is killing him in an effort to fight me and now Cody's life is in my hands.

I raise my head. Grit my teeth. Gather my strength.

With a roar, I burst through the dark light, splitting the stream of power in two. Knocking the warlock's right arm to the side, I create an opening for my right hand.

My claws rip across the warlock's chin hard enough to tear off his jaw. A wave of magic ripples across his cheek—healing him as quickly as I injure him. The only impact is the momentum of the hit. He knocks against the helicopter, loses his balance, and falls to the ground.

I land on him in a straddling position. Desperate to stop him, my fists crash into his face, left, right, one after the other, over and over. My arms thrash through the dark light, making it swirl.

With every blow, he heals himself. The splits across his cheeks seal up. The cuts through his neck mend. His blood never flows.

And still Cody writhes on the tarmac.

"Stop killing him!" I scream. "Stop, stop—"

I knock the warlock's eyepatch aside. Beneath the covering, his eye socket holds a glass orb that swirls with light like wisps of smoke—silver, charcoal, and electric blue. A haze of dark light fills the space between the glass orb and his eyepatch, released now that the patch has shifted out of place.

The power inside the orb is like a shimmering storm, but I can see my reflection in its surface. My hair is bloodied and flying in the wind, my bodice ripped and clinging by threads that just barely cover my breasts, my fist hovering above the warlock's face.

The orb must be some sort of receptacle of power held within his face. As long as he has it, I can't kill him.

Just as I prepare to drive my claw through the orb, he slaps his hands against my temples. Darkness pours across my face. I inhale it, choke on it, fight it as it tugs at my heart.

His voice sounds directly inside my mind, as if he's using the stream of magic he's pouring across my temples to communicate with me.

"*I see you, War Wolf.*" His voice snarls into my mind. "*The ice giant's power has dulled the cage of your human soul and now you are ready to be freed.*"

"Stop!" I scream, grabbing his hands, trying to pry them from my head.

"*Come out,*" he whispers into my mind, his fingers like claws against my cheeks. "*If you want the pain to stop—if you want to save the shifter—you must come out.*"

I gasp for breath. My chest is heaving. My body is in agony. Every movement I make hurts. Cody is dying only paces away from me and the warlock wants to control me. Ford wants to control me.

Everyone wants to fucking control me, but I won't be controlled.

Not by anyone.

Crimson light bursts across my vision, flooding the space around me. The warlock's face and chest blush the color of wine, the magic streaming around the helicopter burns like flames, and the sky above me glimmers brilliant scarlet. Cody's struggling silhouette turns blood-red at the edge of my view, his power shocking me with its strength, but it's fading as his life drains from his body.

At the corner of my vision, the dart and the dagger are both within reach, but the dagger is closer. I snatch up the blade, gripping it in my fist.

My voice changes, a guttural growl ripping through me as I drive the dagger toward the warlock's good eye. *"You will stop!"*

A sneer breaks across the warlock's face that shocks me to my core. His voice sounds again in my mind. *"For you, War Wolf, I would die."*

I halt, the tip of the dagger a mere hairsbreadth away from impaling his eye.

My reflection glints in the glass orb in his eye socket, demanding my attention.

Even through the crimson wash that burns across my vision, I can discern the colors of my reflection. My ruby-red hair billows around my face. My skin glitters icy blue where the ice jotunn's magic remains, while a dark, oily substance coats my skin where the warlock has poured dark magic across me.

But it's the color of my eyes that stops me dead.

My eyes are as ruby red as my hair.

I have the white wolf's eyes.

CHAPTER THREE

The warlock grabs my hand, but instead of pushing me away, he tries to pull the dagger toward his eye.

"Do it!" he roars, not inside my mind this time. "Hurt me. Use the blade. Let your anger out. Let *her* out!"

I stare at him in shock, knowing I have to fight against him, fight against what my reflection could mean.

No...

Please...

The warlock grabs my hand with both of his, dark light spilling around us as he compels me to hurt him. "Do it!"

My inhalations and exhalations rage in and out of my mouth, my blood pounds, and my heart is a hammering muscle inside my chest as I struggle against what I want.

I want to hate him.

I *want* to hurt him.

My crimson eyes grow brighter in my reflection, a vivid flame as I moan against the impulse that tells me that ripping out the warlock's eye won't be enough.

I want to cut my enemy to shreds—

"Tessa! No!"

The violent roar of my name cuts through the darkness growing inside my mind. *That voice.* It's like a hook that takes hold and rips my heart right out of my chest.

"Tristan?"

He sprints toward me, arms and legs pumping, chest gleaming with sweat. Like Cody, he's naked from the waist up, blood splattered across his body, the top button of his pants undone. Barefoot. His power blazes in my heightened vision, blinding flashes. But he isn't carrying any weapons.

Dragging his scent into my chest like a greedy thief, I inhale all of the layers of bitter orange, nutmeg, cedar... each note somehow making it through the warlock's shield and cutting through the mire inside my mind, giving me clarity.

Tristan shouldn't be here.

I used every power at my disposal to push him away, to tell him to let me go, and still he came after me.

Oh, but he and Cody... Tristan said something to Cody before Cody knocked Tristan out. They must have come to an agreement. Their own deal.

Tristan runs straight for me while the warlock's hand tightens around my fist, clawing at me, trying to draw the blade closer. His other hand remains on my temple, dark light continuing to stream from his fingertips no matter what I do to make him stop.

With a scream of effort, I knock his arm away from my face with my left forearm, slide forward into a sideways kneeling position so that my left calf presses down on his throat, and wrench my dagger hand free from his grip.

"You must strike me!" he shouts, his voice carrying the first hint of desperation. "You must do it now!"

I ram the dagger into the surface of the tarmac right beside his face. "You can keep your fucking eye."

This close, my crimson eyes glow bright in his glassy orb, making my heart squeeze inside my chest.

Reaching for the tranquilizer dart while the warlock struggles beneath me, I snatch it off the ground, managing to maintain my balance despite the warlock's fists pounding against my torso and my left thigh.

His good eye widens a moment before I thrust the dart into the side of his neck.

His voice is a fading whisper. "You can't cage her… forever…"

"I don't have a wolf!"

His fingers claw at my forearm and thigh before his natural eye closes and his head lolls. His dark magic fades, the inky light finally dissolving in the air.

Despite his state of unconsciousness, the glass orb in the warlock's other eye socket continues to swirl, bright and clear. His shield remains around us and the helicopter stays in place. The glass orb flickers continuously, and I can only assume it must be maintaining the basic safety protections around the warlock's body. I should rip it out now and kill him, but that's what he wants.

Silence falls around me, broken only by Tristan's pounding footfalls. It's a deep, disturbing silence after the sharp crackles of lightning, the rush of the warlock's dark magic, and Cody's roars of pain. The wind continues to blow, an unnervingly soft whistle in comparison to the chaos moments ago.

My reflection also remains, showing me a face I don't want to see. Magic drips off me, a slew of melting snowflakes from the ice jotunn's power mixing with the oily black remains of the warlock's dark magic. When the warlock shot me with a lightning bullet that one time, the bullet's magic exploded against my chest, splitting my skin, but the bullet itself melted off me into a silver puddle.

Sliding off the warlock onto the tarmac, I remain at a crouch, trying to breathe. Trying to get my legs to work. I wobble, make it up an inch before I crash down again. I scream at myself to move but I can't do more than wait for Tristan to reach me.

My vision is still crimson, a haze I can't seem to shake.

Outside the shield, Cody pushes at the tarmac, attempting to get his arms and legs beneath himself. His eyes are glazed, disoriented, his face deathly pale.

Tristan veers in his direction with a shout. "Get the fuck up! Ford won't sleep forever."

My eyes widen and my heart pumps harder.

There are only two ways off this roof: the stairs or the helicopter. Or maybe three if I count jumping to my death. I still have no idea how I'll get Cody through the warlock's magic. Silas's shields haven't broken even now that he's unconscious.

Tristan remains focused on me, his partially shifted eyes flecked with amber that burns in my vision. Without stopping, he runs at me like a wrecking ball.

He hits the warlock's magic and rips right through the shield, the same way I did.

My breath stops, and... *hell, I can't be shocked by anything anymore.*

Tristan once broke through the lock that Helen placed on Hidden House. She tried to warn me that Tristan is stronger than I could imagine. Even the old magic at the foundation of the house can't control him. He's a descendant of Cerberus, for fuck's sake. A creature of the old gods.

The full force of his power wraps around me moments before his arms close around my torso, the strength in his biceps and shoulders lifting me back to my feet. I take a breath at the same time that he does. As he pulls me close, my head bent to his chest, I sense our heartbeats syncing, a slow, deep beat.

I can finally breathe.

Finally think.

But then he runs his hands all the way up my shoulders to my face, tipping my head back.

He looks right into my crimson eyes.

"Fuck," he whispers. "Am I too late?"

"Too late for what?" I ask.

A muscle ticks in his jaw and I sense a shift in him, nearly imperceptible. I wouldn't see it or sense it with my human eyes—possibly not even with my wolf's energy before today—but I see everything with my crimson vision. So much is visible to me now that wasn't before, not even with the melding bond.

I thought he'd shown me his worst when he revealed that he is destined to become a mindless killer like his father was.

Now I see what Tristan doesn't want me to see—all the shades of his power and all its tiny variances. I can sense his impulses, perceive his thoughts faster than my own—even faster now that my vision has changed. I can see every facet of the three minds that he's destined to succumb to.

He wants to lie to me.

He wants to run from me.

He wants to…

I gasp. Recoil. Struggle in his arms.

Fear rises inside me, a panic worse than what I felt when the ice jotunn grabbed me.

Tristan wants to *kill me*.

The depth and constancy of his impulse tells me that he has always wanted to kill me. Possibly since the moment we met.

Despite my struggle, he only grips me harder. "Fight it, Tessa." His voice is like daggers, hurting my ears. "You have to fight this power. Don't give in to it."

I have to fight *him*.

How could I have ever trusted him? How could I have fallen asleep with him, been vulnerable with him, when his rage, his anger, his unbending hatred for me was hidden beneath his deepest thoughts?

I don't understand why. Why does he hate me so completely when I don't know what I've done to deserve it?

Why, why, why?

"Get away from me!" I push against him, my claws appearing, scratching his chest.

He grabs my wrists, holding tight. "I was wrong, Tessa," he says, his voice low and urgent. "I thought you could be my end. I only saw your power. I only heard the cries of my pack. I only saw an end to generations of devastation. A final end to my bloodline. I didn't see your mind. I didn't see your heart—"

"My heart!" I snarl. "My heart is not yours to rip apart."

Instead of trying to pull away, I punch forward. He sidesteps before my hits land, catching my waist and turning me. I attempt to spin to face him again, but he grabs me, holding me from behind, his arms clamped around my chest.

"You should have let me die tonight, Tessa." His voice breaks, tearing at my confused feelings.

I moan, a deep, wrenching pain shuddering through me. Now that my back is pressed to his chest, I can feel his heartbeat again.

That beat.

I *need* it.

I *hate* it. More than anything.

"How could you plan to give your pack to me when you hate me this much?" I ask.

"Because you're strong enough to fight who you are," he says, his voice sounding like it's ripping from his body. "Because if anyone is going to fight their path, it's you."

My body heat has increased a thousand percent. I've gone from panicked to burning in the space of seconds and all of the magic I've been exposed to is finally taking its toll—icy snowflakes and oily darkness.

What's more, my head aches, a sudden pounding throb like a hammer swinging from side to side, trying to crack my skull from the inside.

It's a million times worse than the pain of hitting my head against the doorframe. I gasp when the crimson light in my vision increases, brighter still, nearly taking over all of my mind.

"I know you want to find a way to change my fate, but you won't," Tristan says. "I am what I am."

I grind my teeth, an aching resignation growing inside me. I need to know why he wants to kill me. He won't reveal his reasons to me unless I make him. Only my uncontrolled power—my scent—can force him to answer me.

Relaxing into him, I close my eyes and loosen my grip on my power, imagining that I never learned to control it, taking myself back to when my power was wild.

He flinches so violently that his body rocks against mine.

THIS BROKEN WOLF

He inhales sharply at my ear. His hands claw against my stomach. "Tessa. Stop."

"No," I whisper. "Not this time."

Using all of my strength, I turn in Tristan's arms, but I don't try to free myself. "You've been keeping the truth from me since the night we met. You said you knew at that moment what I am."

I press closer to Tristan, sliding my arms around his waist, up his back, into his hair, until I'm gripping him as firmly as he's holding me. My voice becomes raw, guttural, like a wild animal emerging and snarling into the wind. "You played a dangerous game with me, Tristan Masters. A game you thought you could win."

His response is a deep growl. His pupils dilate and his biceps flex where he holds me, a shiver running through his body.

I lean into him, my lips whispering across his jawline, returning the seductive pull that I feel when his power is overwhelming to me.

"Deceiver," I whisper, trying to cut through the facet of Tristan's mind that stops him from telling me the truth. "Stop lying to me. Fight your nature and tell me what you know about me."

"No." His incisors appear so fast that they cut his lower lip. The blossom of blood on his skin is bright in my crimson vision.

I rear up toward it, my mouth brushing the corner of his lips and lingering, tasting his blood on my tongue. "Tell me why you want to kill me, Tristan."

He jolts away from me with such force that I teeter on the spot, reeling from the violence of his movement. He leaves claw marks on my upper arms. More claw marks. There's very little of me that hasn't been clawed, scratched, or bruised tonight.

His chest heaves and his fists clench.

"Your scent brings back memories I need to forget," he

41

says, his voice rough, and this time, I'm sure he's telling me the truth. "Memories of a death I can't avenge."

Ford challenged Tristan tonight—telling Tristan to attack if he didn't want to lose another person he loved. "Whose death?" I ask, pushing for more truth.

"My mother's." Tristan's pupils remain dilated, his focus on me intense.

Confusion cuts through my anger. I know so little about Tristan's family history. Tristan himself told me nothing. I heard more from Cody, who told me that Tristan's father killed Tristan's mother. It was the same night that Tristan had promised to challenge his father for control of his pack—the night Tristan said he was prevented from fighting his father. But Tristan did eventually end his father, so surely he already took revenge for his mother's death?

Tristan gives himself a savage shake. I'm sure he's trying to fight my power. He returns to me as fast as he left me, a blur of movement. Partially shifting, he grabs me so fast around my waist that he wrenches me off my feet and hard up against him. His right hand whips around my head. His other hand grips my hip.

I sense the darkness inside him rising, the killer instinct not held so tightly within his mind now. My power over him is slipping, but I can't relent in my pursuit of answers.

"Why can't you avenge her?" I ask, letting him hold me, making myself fluid in his arms, malleable to his wishes as long as it gets me closer to knowing the truth.

"Because my father didn't kill her. The wolf who murdered her is unstoppable," he snarls.

"Who was it?" My demand is sharp as I sense that my control over him has nearly slipped completely. Deep down, I'm afraid of the answer.

Tristan gives a quick shake of his head, finally dismissive, before his gaze rakes across my face. "I need to end this nightmare." He says, not answering my question.

Damn him. He's too strong to succumb to my power for more than a few moments.

His mouth is so close to mine now that his incisors brush against my lips. Heat flushes from my head to my toes, an unexpected pleasure. I should be terrified right now. I've exposed his deepest need to end me, but instead of causing fear within me, his uncontrolled rage triggers my own darkness.

Drawing his head down to mine, I brush my lips against his, tantalizingly soft, the tip of my tongue tasting his scent.

Tristan breaks the contact, a slow movement that brushes his cheek against mine. "The truth of our fate belongs to our fathers."

I stiffen as the echo of his voice tonight repeats on me. He told me that he wanted me to live without the sins of my father weighing on my shoulders.

His grip tightens around me as he takes a deep shaky breath. "You don't have to walk your father's path," he says, leaning closer, pressing his forehead against mine. The nuances of his darkness change within my vision, surprising me when they calm and soften.

"Tessa," he says. "Impulses are nothing without actions. My deepest instinct is to end your power. But I turned away from that. My decisions determine my actions. I choose not to act on these impulses. I won't hurt you."

Pain jabs at my heart. "You're destined to lie to me," I say. "You're destined to make choices you don't want to make. You're so sure that you will succumb to the three-headed wolf that you were prepared to die tonight." For a moment, my rage dims, giving way to despair. "How can I trust any promise you make me?"

His hands soften against my cheeks. "I have no choice about my future, but you do. You can fight your power, Tessa. Hold on to your mind and your heart. Go with Cody. He can take you to a safe place—"

Tristan jolts. His focus shifts to a spot behind me and he snarls, his green eyes suddenly so flecked with amber and so darkly rimmed that they are pure animal as he zeros in on a new presence.

I spin to face the growing power on the tarmac—a power that rivals Tristan's.

The white wolf has always appeared to me in a burst of light, but this time, his presence is like a quiet scream at the back of my mind. I sense him in the same way that I could sense malice in my half-brother's sneer right before he hurt me. The same way a cold breeze makes me shiver. The white wolf is a creeping sensation that makes the hairs on the back of my neck stand on end.

Streams of energy ripple across the air as his shape builds —head and forelegs first, then his body, and finally his hind legs and tail. His eyes are as crimson as mine, glowing like hot coals, while his fur is as crisply white as snow. His head is lowered and his teeth are bared.

Tristan wrenches away from me. He doesn't scoop up the dagger I pitched into the ground next to the unconscious warlock. Instead, Tristan's claws descend as he steps back through the warlock's shield.

"Finally, the master reappears," Tristan says, taking careful steps toward the white wolf. "I've been waiting to fight you for three years."

The white wolf's crimson eyes glint at me before he speaks to Tristan. He talks in growls and snarls, and I'm surprised that I can understand them even in my human form. "You will never have revenge, Tristan Masters."

"My mother's blood is on your hands," Tristan says, the muscles across his shoulders and thighs tensing as he moves into position opposite the white wolf. "So is Ella Griffin's lost life, along with the lives of countless others."

"You're outnumbered now, Tristan," the white wolf says. "Tessa will join me and everyone you're trying to protect will die."

Tristan's snarl is instant. "Tessa's strong enough to resist you. She won't give in."

The white wolf smiles. "She didn't resist you: her real enemy. I think I have a chance of convincing her to join my side."

My thoughts whirl. Fighting the white wolf will get me nowhere. He's insubstantial. The real target should be his human form—Ford.

Ford has remained lying still on the tarmac nearly twenty paces away. He's turned in the other direction so I can't see his face, but he must be awake now to control his wolf's energy.

Bending to scoop up the dagger, I edge through the warlock's shield, keeping the white wolf within my sights as I head for Ford.

Only a few steps past the shield, my attention is suddenly drawn to Cody, who lies on the tarmac only five paces away. Cody's eyes are open. His arms shake and sweat pours down his face as he pushes himself upright. Grimacing with pain, he reaches for the rifle at his back, aiming it at the white wolf, even though his arms shake.

I guess he doesn't know that the tranquilizer darts will sail right through the white wolf's body. Neither Tristan nor Cody must realize that they should be fighting Ford, not his wolf.

I thought I knew what I had to do tonight, but I can't go with Ford now. Not when his jotunn and warlock have triggered a darkness within me that is hammering inside my mind. Ford plans to crack me open, reach inside, and pull out the darkest part of me. I don't know what I'll become if he succeeds.

Before Cody can pull the trigger, Tristan shifts into his wolf form. Tristan leaps at the white wolf so fast that I can barely follow him. His claws are outstretched, his snarling jaws ready to tear the white wolf apart.

He won't be able to.

The white wolf, like my wolf's energy, is insubstantial even if he appears solid. Tristan is about to sail right through the wolf's body and Tristan will be the one who feels like he's being torn apart.

It's too late for me to scream a warning.

My muscles fire as I throw myself in the direction of Ford's human form, intending to sprint around and behind Cody.

I've only taken a few steps when a savage *thud* and a roar make me spin back to Tristan and the white wolf.

The two wolves collide, claws ripping at each other.

Tristan's wolf tears at the white wolf's shoulder, his claws cutting through flesh.

Real flesh.

I scream and nearly drop the blade.

My eyes are wide with shock. At every point of impact where Tristan attacks the white wolf, the white wolf's body ripples and becomes fully formed.

Every point of contact becomes substantial.

My wolf has walked through walls, trees—leaped through the ice jotunn himself. Ford's wolf has manifested in dark alleys. Appeared out of the night. Yet Tristan's wolf collides with him as if he's made of flesh and bone.

Flesh and bone that can be killed.

Already, the white wolf's shoulder is gashed and bleeding. Tristan isn't faring any better, the two wolves tearing at each other with their claws and teeth in a fight so fast and savage that I scream, horrified at the damage they're causing between them.

Cody's rifle glints at the edge of my vision.

Gasping, I spin toward him.

He's pivoted and now points the rifle in my direction, his breathing ragged and his hands shaking. For a horrible second, I think he's aiming at me.

Then I realize my mistake.

Ford is no longer lying on the tarmac behind Cody.

My breath catches as Ford's voice sounds directly behind me and his arms snake around my chest. "Do you see, little one?" he asks. "Tristan Masters has the power to end us when nobody else can. Our wolves are not immune to him. *He* is your enemy. Not me."

Before I can respond, Cody fires at Ford's face, but this time, Ford is ready.

Ford's hand snaps up. I groan when he opens his fist to show me the tranquilizer dart he caught.

"Wolf shifters are a worthless shadow compared to us," Ford says, curling his lip at Cody.

In the distance, Cody is pale. He pulls the trigger again, but it clicks and clicks. He's out of ammunition.

I still have the dagger, and if that doesn't work, I have my claws.

With a scream, I kick Ford's shin, spin to him, and aim the dagger at his throat.

A silver object thuds into my chest at the same time Ford leaps away from me, narrowly evading the dagger thrust.

My vision blurs as I look down at what he rammed into me.

The tranquilizer dart juts from my chest.

Oh... no...

Cody roars behind me—a sound of frustration and rage that the tranquilizer Ford caught has been used against me. At the same time, my legs wobble and my grip on the dagger fails. The blade slips from my fingers. Ford lurches forward and catches the dagger before it hits the ground.

Watching me fall to my knees, he lets out a triumphant laugh. "Thank you, little one."

He turns and throws the blade with deadly precision at the fighting wolves.

My heart stops as the dagger spins through the air, speeding toward Tristan's back.

No! Tristan!

I try to scream a warning, but my vocal chords don't work and only a garbled sound makes it past my lips.

Deep pain fills me as the dagger slices across the side of Tristan's neck, cutting through his wolf's fur to the flesh beneath.

Tristan's wolf jolts and rears back, shifting into his human form within the space of a heartbeat.

He stumbles away from the white wolf, gripping the side of his throat with his human hand, trying to stem the flow of blood, but it courses down his shoulders and chest.

As the white wolf prowls up behind him, Tristan pivots

toward me, his lips parting. His wild gaze follows the lines of my bloodied hair, the darkness of my crimson eyes, to the puddle of my tulle skirt as I kneel on the tarmac in a subservient pose.

Tristan! Don't stop fighting!

The danger is behind him. The white wolf leaps at Tristan's human back, its teeth bared for a killing blow. The pressure of a scream I can't release builds against my ribs and my heart. I can't fight, can't run to Tristan, can't help him, my arms and legs heavy and numb as Ford wrenches me backward so hard that my knees and calves scrape the ground.

Tristan roars with pain as the white wolf's jaws close around his shoulder from behind. The beast yanks him down to the ground, savaging his shoulder.

Tristan lands with a thud, his face increasingly pale as he loses more blood. He tries to twist to fight back, thumping at the wolf's side, legs, anywhere he can make contact, but his hands are bloody and his grip must be slippery and he has no hope of fighting back now…

The white wolf drags him toward the edge of the tarmac, wrenching its head in vicious pulls that yank Tristan closer and closer to a deadly fall.

A wail of pain and fear passes through my lips, defying the powerful tranquilizer pulsing through my body.

Violence rages through me, the same painful hammering inside my mind begging to be released, but I still can't move.

I can't do a thing as the white wolf drags Tristan up the safety net and over the edge.

CHAPTER FOUR

No!
My heart thuds as I scream inside my mind.
The white wolf's energy disintegrates in the air. The moment he lets go of Tristan, he is insubstantial again, disappearing into the night.
But Tristan...
His fall is so silent. He doesn't shout or make a sound.
I want to howl, roar, scream. Block out the sound of Tristan's body hitting the ground, but instead, I hear... a *splash*.
A pool? Please let there be a pool down there.
I reach out through the melding bond, trying to sense his thoughts, convincing myself that he must be alive. He has to be!
Emptiness greets me when I expand my senses and seek Tristan's presence, his feelings. The emptiness is colder than the ice jotunn's touch and it fills me with dread. Even if he landed in a pool, he was losing too much blood.
Panic builds inside me again, but I reach out once more, screaming inside my mind.
Tristan! Answer me!
I tell myself he has dragged himself out of the pool and is now unconscious. That's why I can't sense him. He isn't drowning. Not broken or bleeding out. I tell myself this isn't

the end. He promised me there wouldn't be a last time for us. It can't be the end because Tristan... *oh, Tristan*... is the most fucking fierce, the most unstoppable man I've ever met.

He can't die. He won't.

I'm confused, angry with him, even afraid of him in some ways, but I'm not done with him yet.

My vision blurs, darkness encroaches at the edges of my view, and the tranquilizer finally does its work.

I black out with only a moment's warning.

I jolt awake after what feels like only a few seconds to find myself held in an upright position.

"You're nearly there," Ford whispers against my cheek. "Your transformation is continuing."

My heart stabs, a deep emotional pain. I try to struggle against Ford's hold, but my vision begins to blur again.

I'm vaguely aware of the white wolf, returned and standing over the warlock, who is still unconscious. The wolf's big paw swipes through the warlock's shoulders, proving how insubstantial the wolf is to anyone but Tristan. The contact between the wolf and the warlock creates a jolt of electricity that crackles in the air.

The warlock's eyes fly open. He wakes with a roar on his lips.

I sense movement behind me a moment before the jotunn's icy hands close around my arms and Ford hands me off to him. I can only guess that the white wolf woke the jotunn up the same way he just woke up the warlock.

I can't see Cody now and panic billows up through me because I'm about to black out again—

After that, I catch only snatches of movement and voices, piecing together what's happening around me, struggling every time I come to, only to pass out again.

The jotunn carries me to the helicopter, where he wraps me in a blanket. He folds it around the back of my head and shoulders, catching my hair as it flies about my face in the wind. Then he slides me onto a seat in the helicopter cabin before strapping me in.

The inside of the cabin is built for luxury. It contains four seats, two on each side facing each other, made of plush leather. There are even consoles between the seats with cup holders.

Outside the chopper, the warlock scoops up his fallen wand from the tarmac and hurries to the cockpit again, settling into the pilot's seat and preparing for takeoff while Ford slips into the chair opposite me.

As soon as the warlock takes a seat, the cabin falls quiet despite the noisy whir of the rotor blades outside and the wind rushing across the open door. I can only assume he's controlling the environment so Ford doesn't have to shout.

"Nobody will be able to track you to where I'm taking you," Ford says to me with a self-satisfied nod. "Not even Tristan. Assuming he's still alive."

I black out completely again and when I come to, the ice jotunn is leaning through the door. He's so tall that he has to hunch over. He inclines his head back toward the tarmac. "What do you want to do with the shifter?"

I finally see Cody lying still on the ground. It feels like only moments ago he was upright, trying to shoot Ford. Now Cody's head is bleeding, as if he suffered a blow to the side of it. A blow I didn't witness. I'm drawn to the golden wolf's head tattoo and my blue-flamed wolf shadowing it that inks his chest.

His tattoo makes me shudder.

If sapphire blue is the color of my fear... then crimson is the color of my fate.

Ford purses his lips, narrowing his eyes at Cody. "Bring him with us. He could prove useful."

"What about his father?" the jotunn asks. "The shield has kept Baxter away from the roof, but he'll get through as soon as we leave."

Ford considers this for a moment. "Remove all evidence that his son was up here with us. All Baxter Griffin will know is that Cody has disappeared. Baxter is predictable. He will take advantage of the situation to blame Tristan, just like he blamed Tristan for what happened to his daughter."

With a nod, the ice jotunn returns to the tarmac, quickly picking up all of the fallen darts and removing Cody's weapon harnesses. He hefts Cody over his shoulder and carries his unconscious form to the helicopter cabin.

Reaching the chopper, the jotunn throws the weapon harnesses to the warlock, who catches them without a backward glance.

I black out again, this time for longer.

When I come to, Cody has been strapped into the seat diagonally from me. His head is strapped in so it doesn't loll, but his eyes are closed and his breathing remains shallow. I shudder at the internal damage that the warlock's magic might have inflicted on him, along with the bleeding gash across his forehead.

I can't help Cody.

I couldn't save Tristan. I want to scream my rage at him. At the Deceiver who kept too many truths from me.

Please let me breathe without pain.

I need to know that the heart beating inside my chest is my own, free from the threat of being torn apart...

Reaching out through the melding bond again, I try to sense Tristan again and this time... there's a spark.

It's faint, but it's there.

I convince myself it means he's alive.

The jotunn secures the cabin door, the helicopter rises into the air, and I black out again.

When I come to, we've ascended into the sky. I'm facing the window and a shadow wheels in the direction of the roof we left behind.

It's the briefest flicker, but for a heartbeat, I think it's a hawk.

My heart leaps. I imagine I can see Danika's bronze-tipped feathers, that she knows where Tristan is, that she will find him even if she can't find me...

Then the chopper changes direction, the shadow moves,

and I realize it was only the early morning sunlight reflecting off the clouds.

I'm on my own.

∽

I wake to a *click*.

Cold steel circles my ankles and my left wrist. My back is pressed to a wall while I rest in a kneeling position on a smooth stone floor. A warm pressure against my chest keeps me upright.

"She's progressed more quickly than I could have hoped, but I can't take any chances," Ford says, his voice right next to my ear. "I don't know the extent to which we've succeeded in drawing out her wolf already."

My eyes fly open.

Ford leans against me, stretched slightly to my right, his body supporting mine so I don't crumple to the floor. Because my head rests on his left shoulder, the first thing I see is the side of his neck, then the distant window on the other side of a vast stone room. The window looks directly out onto a clear, blue sky. Not a cloud in sight.

Without making any sudden movements to let Ford know I'm awake, I swivel my gaze from the distant window all the way to my left. I can just see past Ford's neck to the source of the *click*.

The warlock stands on my left. He just closed a shackle around my left wrist. My left arm is now chained to the wall in a position that forces me to stretch out at my side. The slightest shift of my feet tells me that the chains around my ankles are incredibly short, forcing the soles of my feet to remain pressed against the wall.

Someone else is gripping my right arm, but the icy pain I register shrieking through me tells me it's the ice jotunn. He's gripping my arm in two places—my forearm and my hand. I can't see that side, but my position tells me he's about to shackle my right wrist in a similar outstretched pose. If he succeeds, I won't be able to stand up. I will be forced to remain in a kneeling position with my arms at my sides.

I won't be able to defend myself.

I may not know what my next step is, what my path is, but I know it doesn't involve being chained to a wall.

Gritting my teeth, I release the claws of my right hand—right into the ice jotunn's hand, tearing through sinew and muscle.

His roar of rage breaks the quiet around me and I sense him jolt away from me, tearing his hand free of my claws.

At the same time, I bare my teeth against Ford's neck and prepare to rip out his throat.

He jumps back from me just in time, but I'm ready for that too.

The moment his weight lifts, my reflexes fire.

Focusing all of my energy into my right fist, claws retracting in the space of a beat, I lash out at Ford. My fist smacks his cheek, a perfect hit that busts up the skin across his high cheekbone, splitting it to the bone. "You will *not* chain me!"

Ford jumps back from me, avoiding my follow-up punch.

My right fist sails through the air without meeting its mark. The steel manacle around my left wrist bites into my arm, drawing blood as I attempt to pivot around it, half-leaning, half-standing, knees bent, trying to balance and to fight with only one hand.

"I will do what's best for you!" Ford shouts and bares his teeth at me, his incisors descending as he towers over me, remaining at a distance where I can't reach him. "Do as I say," he says. "Submit to the chains."

"I will not!" I scream at him.

His lips draw back from his teeth, his facial features partially shifting, his eyes glowing crimson red and his claws descending. It's the first time I've seen him shift partially from human to wolf and it's startling and violent because his human features are so nondescript, but his wolf's features are... dominant and beyond savage.

His face takes on a glow that his human features lack, his teeth sharpen, his jaw grows stronger, and his eyes become piercing.

I shudder as he narrows his gleaming, crimson eyes at me.

"You will obey me," he says, his voice carrying both a command and a warning.

I snarl right back at him. "It's not in my nature to obey."

Even Tristan learned that about me.

The shape of Ford's lips changes, lifting into a spine-tingling grin that warps the combination of his human and wolf's features. He ripples back and forth between his shifts so fast, I can't tell which is more dominant—his wolf or his human.

"Then I will make you." Daring to step within striking distance, he grabs at my fist as I swing it again at his face.

His hand moves so fast that I can't follow its arc. He catches my wrist before I can evade him. His fingers dig painfully between the delicate bones at the base of my hand, drawing a scream to my lips. The pressure of his hold and the strength in his hands threatens to break my bones, but still, I rage at him, pushing and pulling, daring him to rip through my arm.

"Stop fighting me," he roars at me. "I am not your enemy."

"You will *always* be my enemy—"

My breath cuts off when he uses the full force of his body to knock me against the wall. Still gripping my right wrist, he shoves his free hand against my face. His palm rests half across my mouth, half across my cheek, his fingertips tangling in the strands of my loose hair.

I scream against his hand, my defiant shout muffled behind his palm. Just as I bare my teeth, intending to bite him, he shoves my head into the wall.

The back of my skull hits the stone surface at close range.

Crack!

Pain explodes through me, a sickening blast, and my vision spins, blackens, ebbs… fades…

"Fuck you," I whimper.

My legs buckle. I drop so hard onto my knees on the stone floor that pain cracks through my kneecaps and shoots up through my thighs.

Now that I'm right where he wants me to be, Ford wrenches my right arm toward the final chain hanging against the wall.

The lock clicks into place, leaving me kneeling with the soles of my bare feet pressed against the wall and my arms stretched out at my sides.

My head droops toward my chest. My sense of defeat is sharp and unwelcome. I'm still wearing my tattered black dress. It's smudged and smeared with silver and black, a glittering mess that covers my skin and obscures some of the damage to my bodice and my tulle skirt. My hair is clumped, dirty, bloody and hangs across my face as I hunch.

I'm aware of the warlock and the ice jotunn standing guard on the other side of the stone room. The jotunn grips his bleeding hand but doesn't appear to have asked for help. The warlock holds his wand, ready and raised. Neither man takes his eyes off me.

Ford finally steps back from me. My only satisfaction is that his chest rises and falls rapidly, revealing the exertion it took to subdue me. He takes a deep breath, puffing it out before he touches his cheek where I hit him and split his skin.

He checks the blood that smears his fingertips before he wipes them on his white shirt. "That was more difficult than it had to be, little one—"

Fuck his pet name for me.

"Tessa!" I snarl, raising my head. "My name is Tessa Dean."

Rage flashes across Ford's face, his eyes narrowing, teeth bared. I have only a moment's warning before he drops to his knees.

The back of his hand smacks across my cheek, knocking the other side of my face into the stone wall, cutting off my scream.

Fuck... him...

The world spins and my vision blackens for a second time.

Ford's angry face blurs in front of me.

"Your name is not Tessa Dean," he says. He speaks through gritted teeth, rage dripping from every sound he makes, his lips twisting further as he continues. "That is the name given to you by a thief. A wolf shifter who was not worthy to raise you." His voice rises. The back of his hand hovers above my face, ready to strike again.

I glare at him through the strands of my hair. "Andreas Dean was—"

Crack.

The back of his hand smacks across my other cheek, forcing my head into the wall so hard that I sense the skin across my cheek split to the bone.

I try to smother my cry but fail.

"Andreas Dean was the thief who stole you from me. Hid you from me." Ford screams into my face. "Conspired to keep you from me!"

He draws back again, chest heaving, sucking air between his teeth. "And now I have no choice but to break your body, break your mind, and tear apart the human soul that cages you. I swear I will do whatever it takes to free your wolf."

I close my eyes. Ford's silhouette is blurring and it's no use trying to focus or trying to ignore the pain. I probably should have asked him where Cody is. I probably should have asked him where *I* am.

I should probably ask him what he intends to do to me.

Instead, I ask Ford the question I don't want answered.

"If I'm not Tessa Dean," I moan. "Who am I?"

Even with my eyes closed, I sense everything in this room, the way Ford's chest stills, the power growing around the ice jotunn and warlock, the strange absence of wind through a window that has no glass, the stillness in the corridor beyond the wide-open door far to my right.

Ford takes hold of my head, a firm grip across my swelling cheek. His growl whispers across the space between us.

"You are anger lingering in the back of the mind," he says. "You are revenge growing inside the heart. You are violence begging to be unleashed. You are fear that clouds judgement. You will taste the blood of gods and defy them, just as I defied them."

His grip tightens as if he senses the energy rising inside me, an energy I recognize. It's my most basic instinct, not to survive, but to *fight*.

"You are my daughter," he whispers. "And you will be my greatest instrument of war."

CHAPTER FIVE

Daughter?
Part of me knew it the moment I saw my crimson eyes. Part of me suspected ever since I met the white wolf. I should have known it months ago when Tristan crashed into the medical room at Hidden House and told me, with deep vehemence in his voice, that I didn't kill my father. My father wasn't dead.

Even with all the warnings, the foundations of my world shift.

Already tonight I found out that Tristan is the three-headed wolf, destined to become the monster that his father was. I found out that Ella is Cody Griffin's sister and that Tristan's failure to protect her led to the violent feud between Tristan's and Baxter's packs. I found out that the white wolf had a hand in Tristan's mother's death and Tristan needs revenge.

I also discovered that my quest for revenge has limits, but that I'm prepared to put myself in danger because my heart asks me to.

My *human* heart.

Now Ford Vanguard is making a claim on me that I have to deny, even if it's the truth, because it will shatter the only belief that kept me grounded my whole life—that my father,

Andreas Dean, former alpha of the Middle Highland pack, loved me, protected me, and died trying to keep me safe.

And yet... even if all of that is a lie... it is also true.

Nothing can change the fact that the wolf who raised me did his best to protect me. Nothing changes the fact that Andreas Dean taught me how to fight, he taught me to question, and he shaped me into the person I am, even if he told me to hide my strength.

I have too many questions about who I am. Far, *far* too many questions about how I came to be; about my mother's situation, how she met Ford, why she then rejected me, and why Andreas chose to protect another wolf's child... *too many questions.*

But I know one thing for certain.

I open my eyes. "Andreas Dean was right to hide me from you."

Ford's exhalation hisses through his teeth. His grip on my head tightens—crushingly tight—as if he would convince me to believe him by physically forcing the conviction into my mind. "You continue to defy me."

My cheek is swelling so much that my left eye is closing up. I can't fight back. Even my glare will carry very little force. But my tongue works just fine. "Because you want to control me."

Everyone wants to fucking control me.

I'm finished with being controlled. It ends now.

I lost my purpose when they put me in the helicopter, but now I regain it. My path is narrow and difficult, but the steps I need to take are small and simple.

My first goal will be to get the hell out of this room. No matter what it takes. My second goal will be to find Cody. Again, no matter what it takes. After that... I will do whatever I have to do to change Tristan's fate. Because changing his fate means changing mine.

"You will never control me," I say to Ford, my own teeth bared.

Ford's lips twist. "You are my daughter and you will do what I—"

I open my mouth and scream, letting out my anger in a long shriek, deliberately intended to drown out his voice. "*You. Will not. Control me!*"

His fingers dig harder into my scalp and I know he's two seconds away from hurting me again. His lips part as if he's about to shout back at me, but I continue to scream at him, tears of anger pouring down my cheeks, barely squeezing between my closing eyelids.

I wrench at the shackles around my wrists, even though they tear and cut my skin. "It doesn't matter what you do," I shout. "I won't stop fighting you. I won't stop biting and kicking and clawing at you. You will have no peace from me." I try to focus on him as blood trickles down my face and the back of my head. "No peace at all."

His free hand darts forward, grabbing the other side of my head. His fingers dig through the trail of blood that slides down my cheek, tugging at my scalp as he latches on to my hair.

His crimson eyes pierce me, but I glare right back at him.

Fuck you, Ford Vanguard. And everyone who stands with you.

"You can fight me however you wish," he says, his face shifting so far that his jaw elongates. "But it won't change who you are."

He wrenches away from me, rising to his feet and striding toward the ice jotunn and the warlock.

He grips the jotunn's shoulder. "I'm counting on you."

The jotunn gives a nod. He only takes his eyes off me to watch Ford and the warlock leave.

As soon as the sound of their footfalls recede, the jotunn crosses the distance between us. Every step he takes drops the temperature inside the room.

By the time he takes a knee in front of me, my breath is frosting.

He tips his head to scrutinize me. His blue eyes narrow as he peers between the strands of my hair.

Reaching out, very slowly, inch by careful inch, he keeps his fingers together and his palm vertical so he can angle his hand through the curtain of my hair.

His touch across my stomach and shoulders earlier felt like it was going to kill me. Now he's reaching for my head and it takes all my strength not to panic as I anticipate the pain I'm about to feel—the acidic burning.

The tips of his fingers break between the strands of my hair before he carefully tucks my tresses behind my ear and presses his palm to the side of my head.

Pain blossoms across my temple, my ear, my cheek, a sharp, cutting pain that drives rational thoughts from my mind.

My scream shrieks through my lips, but now I'm screaming with rebellion. As long as I have breath in my lungs I will resist every attempt he makes to force me to submit.

The jotunn continues to study me, searching my single open eye while his palm presses against my skin.

He must be looking for a hint that I'm about to give in.

I sense my teardrops freeze on my cheeks, tiny pearls of ice crusting the skin around my eyes and dusting my cheeks. At least the ice is cooling the swelling that's now keeping my left eye shut.

Just as darkness threatens to drive me into unconsciousness, the jotunn removes his hand.

I refuse to sag with relief, but I suck air into my chest with frenzied desperation, my breaths wheezing in and out. With every inhalation and exhalation, my moans turn into growls until I'm snarling.

"Go ahead," I say, refusing to lower my gaze. "Hurt me again."

"Hurt?" His response is sharp. "I'm giving you a gift. My power is dulling your human mind and allowing your wolf to surface. I'm giving you the chance to break free from the cage your human soul has formed around you."

"This *room* is my cage!" I shout, my voice harsh as I suck in the freezing air.

A gleam grows in the jotunn's icy-blue eyes. "If this room is your cage, then escape it."

I rattle the chains around my wrists, yanking on them. "Sure thing. Let me get right on that."

He doesn't flinch. "You think your human soul is strong," he says. "You think your spirit is worth holding on to, but it weakens you and denies you your true strength. If you were not caged by it, you would have escaped your chains already."

I grit my teeth. "Fuck. You."

He rises to his feet, staring down at me. "I will break you from your prison. It is the most important task Vánagandr has ever given me and I will not fail him."

If my face weren't so swollen, my forehead would crease. "*Vana*... what?"

"Your father." He turns his back on me, but he doesn't retreat. Kicking off his boots and removing his shirt, he's left only wearing his long pants. He strides to the side of the room and presses both of his palms flat against the stone.

Ice particles spread from his hands, rushing in every direction, covering the entire wall within seconds. At the same time, ice spreads from his feet, coating the floor in frosty patterns of snowflakes just like the myriad of ice particles that covered my skin at Baxter's home. Flurries of snow float into the air, rising from the surface of his back and arms.

I thought the room was cold before. Now the ice reaches my knees and spreads across the wall at my back, and the entire room becomes an icebox.

While his back is turned, I test my strength against the shackles, drawing on the last of my energy, but the chains are bolted into the wall. Nothing short of a sledgehammer will make them budge.

My torn and bloodied dress doesn't hold any warmth. Within seconds, I'm shaking so hard from the cold that the chains around my wrists and ankles rattle. My breathing becomes ragged, my exhalations leaving my mouth in whispered moans. My outstretched arms feel like dead weights attached to my body, causing the manacles around my wrists to cut into my skin.

As my head sags farther, my hair descends all the way to the floor, the strands swishing against the stone in time to my shivers.

I have to keep talking, have to distract myself. I test my vocal chords, my teeth chattering and my voice wheezing, a mere rasp. "My father... h-has... three... n-n-n-names."

"Yes."

"Will... you... t-tell... me?"

The ice giant glances at me. "I shouldn't have to."

A snarl rises to my lips. My face is numb now. I can't feel a thing, but that seems to be a good thing. Scorn drips from my lips. "You do my father's bidding like a good little soldier."

The ice jotunn swings back to me, his eyebrows drawn down, a betrayal of anger breaking his calm exterior. "Do not test me, young one."

"Or what?" I ask, crazy laughter leaving my lips. "You'll freeze me to death?"

He snaps. "You are freezing because your human mind tells you that you are surrounded by ice and therefore you must be cold."

He lurches toward me again, his feet thudding heavily. Ice crystals spread across the floor with every pounding step. Stopping directly in front of me, he blocks out the window of growing light in the distance. We must be approaching the middle of the day when the sun is at its highest.

"You have the power to attack and kill me," he says. "But you refuse to use it."

I blink at his fists and the snow flurries wafting around his palms. The snowflakes that fall from his hands are even brighter in the gleaming sunlight.

"You're talking about my wolf's energy." I force my stiff neck to move, raising my head to see the jotunn's face. "The second I expose my wolf, Vánagandr will seize hold of my power."

The ice jotunn suddenly focuses on my face with an intensity I wasn't expecting. "Vánagandr," he whispers, as if he just won a victory.

I glare back at him. "Do what you will. You don't have the power to break me."

Deep within the hellish storm inside my mind, deep below the pain, I have a single clear thought: *Only Tristan can break me.*

∽

After that, the hours become a mess of pain.

The chains around my shivering body provide a constant clatter that keeps me awake despite the mind-numbing cold and the sheer exhaustion that should have knocked me out hours ago.

I lose track of how long I remain on my knees on the freezing stone with the soles of my bare feet pressed against the icy wall behind me, my arms splayed out at my sides, and my breath frosting in the frigid air.

Despite the pain, I reach out through the melding bond over and over again, seeking Tristan's emotions. So distant. The smallest flickers of his essence, the faintest reminder of his scent. Maybe my mind is tricking me, but I have to believe he's alive.

At some point, the jotunn leaves the room and when he comes back, he's changed his clothing and is now dressed in jeans and a short-sleeved T-shirt that strains around his chest and biceps.

The sunlight slanting through the window has changed over the hours, brightening and now fading again. Night is falling.

I'm dehydrated. Starving.

My fingers and toes are frozen. I can't feel any of the wounds, scratches, or bruises I've sustained—certainly not the claw marks across my chest and back.

My head sags further, the weight of my tipping body pulling dangerously at the sharp manacles, cutting freshly into my wrists. New blood slips across the steel onto the floor, where it blossoms crimson on the ice before it freezes. Snow builds around my knees until it reaches my thighs. Somehow, it never melts, not even when it touches my skin.

The glistening snowflakes torment me—an unattainable source of liquid—as my thirst grows until it's unbearable.

I count the times that the ice jotunn crosses the distance to take my head in his hands until I reach twenty. Every time, he studies my eyes but doesn't seem to see what he wants, and I sense his growing frustration.

By the thirtieth time, I scream at him with a voice that becomes more and more hoarse until my vocal chords are finished and my shrieks are nothing more than whispers.

I finally lose my voice.

My own silence scares me more than the pain.

When darkness falls outside the window, the ice jotunn approaches me yet again. The whisper of every snowflake falling from the ice jotunn's shoulders grates in my hearing. He takes a knee in the darkness, overly bright moonlight gleaming around his silhouette.

He slides his palm against my cheek and, despite my wish to fill the room with screams of rage... I have nothing left.

Pain stabs silently inside my head as I press my lips together, too exhausted to wince or jolt. I swore I wouldn't stop fighting, but now my only goal is to survive.

All I have to do is stay alive.

Stay alive, Tessa...

The giant scrutinizes me, his icy-blue eyes bright and glowing in the dark. For the first time since he started grabbing my head, I choose to close my eyes. I tell myself it's not an act of weakness. I've fought back for hours. I will fight again as soon as my vocal chords heal. I just can't fight right now...

My shoulders sag and I lean into his hand, taking the pain quietly.

Without removing his hand, the ice man says, "Your wolf is breaking free. You will know your true nature soon."

I don't believe him.

I haven't sensed my wolf's energy since the ride in the helicopter even though I feel as physically strong as when I harness her energy.

Fundamentally, what the jotunn says doesn't match what I know to be true: My wolf is me. I am her. If something should break free, then it can only be *me*.

Maybe I *am* what needs to break free.

My eyes fly open. I study the jotunn carefully when he removes his hand.

"*Water,*" I mouth, unable to form sound. "*I want... water.*"

He remains on one knee in front of me, a hulking form. He watches my lips, reading my speech. It must be difficult in the darkness, but he seems to catch my meaning.

"Water will freeze before it touches your lips," he says.

"*Then give me snow.*"

"Snow?" he asks, leaning back an inch. His focus flicks to the flurries that have built around my knees before he returns to my face, his eyes narrowed and his gaze distant as if he's thinking it through.

He cups his hand. Ice particles rapidly form across his palm, building until five perfect snowflakes swirl above the surface of his hand. Every time they drop to his palm, he bounces his palm gently and they float back up.

Reaching for my face with his free hand, he presses his thumb to the corner of my mouth so that my lips part and my head tilts back.

Every touch burns, but I take it in, dragging on the sensation. I don't care what it takes to get water.

The jotunn raises his palm above my face and allows the snowflakes to float toward my lips.

"You make dangerous choices," he says, looming over me.

If he's trying to tell me that the snow will kill me or hurt me even more than I'm already hurting, then his warning is too late.

The first snowflake touches my bottom lip and melts against my skin. The second and third enter my mouth and turn to liquid that I swallow all too quickly in my desperation to quench my thirst. The fourth snowflake melts against my lips as I snap them closed.

My eyes fly wide.

I choke. Swallow. Gasp for air. Inhale the final snowflake.

The honeyed liquid slips down my throat, cool and sweet, warming my mouth like ginger, spreading across my tongue and loosening my tight vocal chords.

It doesn't hurt. Far from it.

I taste a howling wind on my tongue, the rasp of stone, the creak of ancient branches. I flail with the sensation of sinking into deep snow. Closing my eyes again, I fall into a freezing wind buffeting my body and hair, plucking at my tulle skirt and tattered bodice. Tipping my head back, my eyes still closed, I see a crisp blue sky and catch the glimmer of a wild mountain at the corner of my vision.

I open my eyes to find the jotunn watching me with an intensity that would rival Tristan's.

"This isn't snow," I say, my voice strong and clear for the first time in hours.

When Helen explained my resistance to magic to me, she told me that there are different kinds of magic, but they generally fall into four types. Light magic is warrior's magic—the magic of love and strength. Dark magic is sorcery—it drains life around it. Elemental magic is the power of nature, which is what the ice jotunn's power mimics.

But there's a fourth type: old magic.

According to Helen, old magic sits at the foundation of the world. Hidden House is formed on a foundation of old magic, which is why it is such a powerful environment. It's also why I wasn't immune to its effects while I was there. She said that no creature is immune to old magic—not even creatures of old magic themselves.

"You're not an elemental," I say. "What are you?"

The ice giant rises to his feet, takes a step to his left, and kneels beside my shackled right hand. He crouches low, leaning at an awkward angle.

"You know what I am," he says.

I gasp and close my eyes when he turns his head and presses his temple against my numb fingers. My senses flood with a rush like howling wind. It beats at my body, tears at my hair, and fills my chest with ice with every breath I take.

The environment around me doesn't change, but inside my mind, I stand at the precipice of an icy mountain, snow swirling around my legs and chest, an expanse of mountains spreading across the horizon in front of me. I sense both freedom and danger, an intoxicating mix.

On my last day at Hidden House, I went exploring and found myself ascending a set of stairs to be faced with a narrow path along a glittering mountain, rockfaces soaring up on either side of me. When I finally reached the end of the pass and stood at the cliff's edge, all I saw below me were clouds, my future hidden beneath them. I'd hoped for the courage to face it.

Now, the clouds open inside my mind, parting slowly to the crash of steel and magic. A battleground sits far below me. Creatures of all races and species are clashing, striking at each other. One side carries the flag of the white wolf and his followers scream his names—all three of them—sounds that pluck at the darkness inside me.

When I left Hidden House, Helen reminded me to guard my heart and protect myself. She urged me to be calm. Stay in control.

I am and I will.

My path is narrow. Incredibly narrow and one misstep will see me bloodied and broken on the rocks.

Opening my eyes, I consider the glittering ice particles that frost the floor around my knees. Each one is unique and glistening, reminding me of the silver flowers at Hidden House. When I sat with Helen in the afternoons, the silver vines would trail across my lap, springing to life around me. I crushed a silver flower once and watched in amazement as it sprang back to life. Now I sit on a carpet of snowflakes that float across my knees.

"You're old magic," I whisper to the ice jotunn.

Every glittering snowflake is old magic, surrounding me and piling up around me.

The jotunn continues to press his temple to my hand and I'm painfully aware that his touch doesn't hurt me now.

It doesn't hurt at all.

Now that the limitations of my human mind have lifted, I can't believe that this creature ever hurt me.

"My people rose from the rocks at the foundations of the wildest mountains," he says. "We were once giants of the earth, feared and respected."

A hum grows at the back of my throat, an echo of a wolf howling far away. "What happened to your people?"

"The new gods took away our purpose." The jotunn's voice lowers, a spark of anger in his eyes. "They tried to take away our power. When Vánagandr challenged them, they—"

"Wait." I shiver. Despite my newfound knowledge, hearing the truth spoken aloud rattles me. "You're talking about the beginning of time. He can't be that old."

"Your father is old magic." The ice man's eyes glow brightly in the darkness. "Vánagandr fought beside my people. He was hated and feared by his own family, just like you are—"

"Stop." I mean to speak with my human voice, but it's a guttural growl.

The ice jotunn suddenly grins at me, his teeth flashing white in the darkness. He draws back into a kneeling position, peering at me across the short distance. My hair has become so clumped that there's no hiding behind it now.

"You are wary of the truth," he says. "That is wise."

I drag oxygen into my chest.

With a shock, I realize that the air isn't cold.

I'm not cold.

I'm sore. Bruised. Exhausted. Starving. Thirsty. My wrists are rubbed raw, but my fingers and toes are warm despite the press of snow around my legs and what I thought was freezing air whispering across my hands.

"*I'm* old magic," I whisper.

The ice jotunn nods. "You are."

I close my eyes. *So is Tristan.* He broke through the lock that Helen placed on Hidden House. He ran through the warlock's shield. His scent has always been so strong to me: bitter orange, nutmeg, cedar, and beneath those notes, the elusive scent of a burning fire—the power of Cerberus, a creature of the gods.

The ice jotunn's teeth glow white as he takes a knee and bends his head in a deep bow. "Welcome, daughter of—"

"Fenrir," I say, speaking my father's names for the first time. "Daughter of Fenrir, Hróðvitnir, Vánagandr."

The monstrous, infamous Wolf of War.

CHAPTER SIX

"What do I call you?" I ask the jotunn.

He tips his head to the side. The corners of his mouth twitch up. "My names are difficult to pronounce."

I exhale a puff of air and pin him with my gaze, a silent compulsion to obey me.

He relents. "You can call me Brynjar." He pronounces it 'brin-yahr.'

"That's not so difficult."

"It's a shortened version."

I return his quiet gaze. I don't ask him to remove my chains because he told me I had to remove them myself. "You can get me water now, Brynjar," I say.

The jotunn arches an eyebrow at me, since he insisted before that it would freeze before it touched my lips.

"It won't turn to ice," I say. "You tricked me."

"Your human mind tricked you."

The ice jotunn's magic wreaked havoc with my human senses and my mind rationalized it by believing I was cold. Really his power has broken apart the layers of my mind that were vulnerable—all the parts of me that are not old magic. A painful, destructive process. Like removing the outer layers of an onion to get to the heart of it. Now that there is nothing left to destroy… his magic no longer hurts me.

THIS BROKEN WOLF

I shrug my shoulders, the barest acknowledging movement the chains allow me to make. "I'm thirsty. And I want to see my father."

Brynjar draws to his feet, towering over me. "He will be happy to see you."

The ice giant strides to the open doorway at the side of the room, old magic snowflakes drifting from his fingers, leaving a glittering trail behind him that sparkles in the moonlight.

As soon as he's gone, I study the chains around my hands—smooth, steel manacles. Brynjar told me that I could escape them myself.

It's time to see if he was right.

I seek my energy—the shape of a wolf inside me—tentatively calling it forward.

A savage burst of power rushes through me, stronger than I've felt before, rattling me to my core. My hands shake, my arms tremble, and my breathing increases. The chains rattle violently against the wall. The power rushing through me is intoxicating, making me moan. My head tips back and I don't try to fight it.

Brynjar's magic has done its work, but he, my father, and the warlock—they're all wrong.

There is no wolf.

There's only me and the shape of a wolf that I can fill if I wish.

I still have my heart. I still feel. I still care. Brynjar has destroyed the walls around my power, but my power is not heartless like he may believe. Even if I will make him—and everyone else in this place—believe that I am.

Exhaling slowly, I allow my energy to flow into a wolf's shape. All of me. A complete shift for the first time since this nightmare began.

My arms slip from my chains and so do my feet.

Snowflakes fall away from my knees and thighs, clinging to the shifting shape of my legs before they fall to the floor. My clothing slides off my body, the tattered skirt and bodice floating to rest on the snowflakes.

I test my ability to control every aspect of my appearance—my fur, my eyes, even my teeth and claws—sifting through my emotions, calculating my fear and my anger, the shifting colors of my power.

There are so many different shades, all the hues of my impulses and emotions, but only crimson vision—ruby-red eyes like my human hair—will allow me to walk the narrow path ahead of me.

Only perfectly crimson eyes will allow me to convince my father that I'm like him now.

While my vision burns, I choose darkness for my fur, onyx tinged with cobalt, to make myself appear slightly more vulnerable than I am.

In this form—a full shift—my body is solid, not insubstantial. Now that I'm satisfied with the shape I've taken, it's time to separate from it.

Whenever I've released my wolf in the past, I've started from my human form and sent her out from me.

This time, I'm starting from my wolf form.

I remind myself to call my wolf shape 'her.' I practice it inside my head. I have to force it to become my way of thinking. The only way I'll win this game is if I play into my father's beliefs.

Carefully, I stretch out my power, stepping from the wolf shape, pulling my human form from her. I remain substantial while she is pure energy. The instant I separate from her, my vision splits. I can see myself—all of myself, human and wolf.

My wolf is powerful, larger than before because I chose to make her so.

But *I*... am wild and hurt. Every part of my human body is beaten, bloodied, and bruised. My swollen eye is only now beginning to open—and only a little.

Once again, men have attempted to crush me with their fists.

My wolf's crimson eyes flame brightly as my anger grows.

Fuck each and every one of them.

I growl at my wolf, who growls back, both of us humming deep inside our throats until I feel calm again.

Reaching for my discarded clothing, I pull on the skirt and underpants. The bra and bodice are so badly damaged that I take the strips and tie them around my breasts like a bandeau, situating them so they cover the important parts.

My wolf's eyes and lips settle into a hard expression as she turns to keep watch over the doorway. Her point of view will allow me to see anyone who might approach while I focus on the window. I expect it won't be long before my father arrives. He once described my wolf's appearance as a burst of energy that demands he come find me.

Outside, the night sky is impossibly calm and clear. The moon seems to sit closer than I've ever seen it, a half-crescent surrounded by sparkling pinpricks. A million stars.

The window itself is wide with a broad ledge that I could sit on if I wished. We must be high up for me to be able to see the sky like this and far away from the nearest building since my view is unobstructed. My father said that nobody would find me here.

Carefully extending my arm, I dare to reach the fingertips of one hand through the opening. The hair on my bruised arm rises, standing slowly higher with every inch closer I come to pushing my fingers through the opening.

Magic tingles across the tips of my fingers as I touch a shield. It's not cloying and heavy like the warlock's magic. It's weightless, dancing across my skin as I reach farther, my entire hand submerged in it before I breach the shield and my arm extends into the chill, night air.

My eyes widen. Then my eyelids lower. The magic is calming, soothing. It feels like Hidden House, certainly not the kind of place that my father should control.

Deciding against leaning my head and shoulders through the opening, I listen carefully, making out the sound of ocean waves crashing on rocks far below. That can only mean we're somewhere on the western coast—

My father's presence in his human form is as undetectable

as mine is, but there's no mistaking the excitement in the rapid footfalls of the person I can hear hurrying along the corridor. Anticipation must be thrumming through him. The idea that he can own and control me would be thrilling him to his ancient bones.

He appears in the doorway, tall and lean, dressed in fresh black pants and a collared shirt unbuttoned at the top and rolled up at the sleeves. I imagine he has had time to eat, shower, and sleep. Although his jaw remains shadowed with growth and his cheekbones are high, his hair appears reddish brown now and slightly longer around his ears. His eyes are more blue than green. I wonder if he has changed his appearance so many times over the years that he can't quite control it anymore.

Brynjar and the warlock appear behind him—their presence strong in my heightened senses—but they remain in the shadows of the corridor.

"Daughter—" My father freezes mid-step, his gaze swiftly passing from the empty chains on the wall, across my wolf, finally landing on me. I watch him with my wolf's eyes while I remain with my back to him, my hands planted on the window ledge.

"Where is Cody?" I ask, without turning.

My father's eyes narrow at my wolf, who growls at him, baring her teeth, her lips drawn back. She snarls at him, commanding him on my behalf. "Answer her!"

My father's eyes flush as crimson as my wolf's. I read his thoughts as clearly as if he's speaking them. He's angry that I dared to command him, that I haven't bowed to him or acknowledged his strength. Maybe he even imagined I'd throw my arms around him and thank him for freeing me.

"Why do you want to know where Cody Griffin is?" he asks, a sharp demand for an answer.

I finally turn to my father, my head held high. "Because I want to kill him."

CHAPTER SEVEN

A slow smile grows on my father's face. "Of course you do," he says. "Your wolf needs blood."

I incline my head, soft and slow, but my voice is sharp. "I'm impatient."

My father's anger rises, his eyes narrowed, but he inclines his head sharply toward the corridor behind him. "Come with me."

The corridor we enter is open at both ends and appears to lead out to a platform on each side, both flooded with moonlight. The helicopter sits on the platform to my right. To my left, I make out the shape of a set of stairs right at the end of the corridor. They appear to be leading down. The flight leading up is at my back and to the side of the doorway that opens onto the platform on that side.

We must be in some sort of tower. It's eerily quiet despite the nearness of the ocean and the wind that must be blowing outside. Torches burning with flames light up as we pass, revealing more rooms on either side of the corridor. The walls of one room are partially covered in white marble, glistening tiles scattered in a haphazard pattern, many of them chipped or broken off. Maybe it was once completely white.

The room across the corridor appears the same, although what's left of the white marble flickers with tiny streams of gold. The middle of the floor bears a burn mark, as if something exploded against it.

I need to keep moving, but I also need to learn as much as I can about my surroundings. I'm aware of my father's intense scrutiny as I pause outside the room with the burn mark on the floor.

"What is this place?" I ask.

"This tower is called the Spire. It's a place of old magic, hidden from human eyes since its creation during the time of the gods. It once housed objects of the oldest magic until it was plundered for its treasures."

He points to the floor beneath our feet. "These halls were once embedded with priceless jewels." Then he gestures to the burn mark in the room I was looking into. "That room once held an eternal flame. It was stolen, like many other priceless treasures." His upper lip curls. "Until I put a stop to the plunder."

He leads me to the staircase at the end of the corridor, but again, I pause.

An archway to the left reveals a large room containing what looks like the remains of four large statues, each one discolored with age. My wolf darts into the room, quickly circling the statues so that I can see what remains of them. The most intact of the statues appears to be made out of wood —a woman, judging by her shape and dress, although her head and the top part of her shoulders are missing.

She holds her arms out, elbows bent, palms flat. From what remains of the other statues, it looks like at least one of them also holds its arms in a similar position.

My wolf stops in front of the most smashed statue. Only its white stone base remains. She nudges the pebbles that litter the floor around it. Indents on the base mark where small stone feet might once have stood—possibly a child's feet.

"These statues represent the four keepers of magic," my father says. "Some call them the pillars of magic. They once held the four books of magic: old magic, light magic, dark, and elemental. The books are said to contain the essence of each kind of magic."

"Where are the books now?" I ask.

My father folds his arms across his chest. "I've been trying to locate them, but I'm not the only one searching for them."

I turn away from the room and wait a beat for my wolf to join me. My father hasn't tried to take control of her like he did on previous encounters, but I sense that he wants to. He casts constant glances her way and his power ebbs and flows as if he's trying to decide whether or not to reach out.

The staircase we next descend is also made of stone, but its surface is uneven, bearing open indents where jewels must have once rested. I follow my father while Brynjar and the warlock walk behind me.

Before we reach the bottom of the staircase, I sense other creatures and I slow my steps, gauging the level of threat. Exiting the stairs into another corridor—this one much wider—I find the area busy with women. They smell musky like shifters, their animals appearing in my senses like colors—all honey-colored, but I'm not sure what animal they are.

One of the women waits at the base of the stairs, her fingers tapping impatiently against her thigh. She's wearing military-style cargo pants and a jacket along with a weapon belt bearing a handgun and a dagger at her waist. Her eyes are wide-set, green that fades to gold around the center, and her hair is tawny, cut short at her strong jaw. She's tall, my height.

She steps up to my father as soon as she sees us. "Can I assist you, boss?"

"Perla." My father greets her. "My daughter wishes to see the prisoner."

"Which one?" she asks, a crease appearing in her forehead. For a second, she flushes with annoyance and I catch sight of her shifting skin—a leopard's spots. She carries the same glow as the other shifters, so they must all be leopards. "I've just finished locking the women back in their shared cell. Cody Griffin is being held separately."

There's plenty of room to maneuver in this corridor. My

voice is sharp as I step up to her with my wolf at my side. "You have female prisoners too?"

Perla turns her gaze on me, her focus swiftly passing across all of my bruises, scratches, and my hardly-intimidating state of dress. She does well to hide her increasing annoyance. Or, at least, she tries. She might defer to my father, but the haughty angle of her chin tells me she's used to calling the shots.

I narrow my eyes at her. My wolf bares her teeth at my side.

"You would be wise to answer me," I say, allowing my claws to descend.

"We have three female prisoners nearly ready for transport," she says.

"Where are you taking them?"

Perla pauses, shifting on the spot and casting my father a quick questioning glance. I read her rising frustration—I imagine it's because he hasn't stepped in to stop my questioning. "Boss?"

Ford gives her a curt nod. "My business is now my daughter's business. You can tell her everything."

Perla nods, but her voice is strained, as if she disagrees with his willingness to share information. "We will take these prisoners to Mother Lavinia in a week's time. She requested new fighters. We'll see if she likes any of them."

"What happens if she doesn't?"

Perla narrows her eyes at me. "Then I haven't done my job properly."

I want to ask more questions, but there's only so much I can get away with. This is the first I'm hearing about Ford's business, but selling prisoners to a witch for fights sounds like some sort of supernatural trafficking to me. Both Cody and Tristan called Ford a butcher. I imagine this could be why.

I remain impassive. "I want to see Cody Griffin."

"Him?" Perla's gaze flickers to my father again, dismissive of me. "Doesn't your daughter wish to clean herself up first?"

My wolf prowls forward, snapping at the woman. "*His daughter* wants to see Cody Griffin."

Perla stands straighter, a backward lean the only indication that she acknowledges the threat in my wolf's growls. She abruptly spins on her heel. "He is this way."

She leads us toward another flight of stairs. This one is different to the ones before. There are two staircases side by side, both leading downward, but they are divided by a wall.

The staircase on the left carries the slightly metallic scent of stone like the rest of the tower, while the one on the right glows faintly sapphire blue and the air wafting through it smells like rain-touched grass. The sapphire blue one is guarded by two female leopard shifters.

My father pauses at my side as he gestures me toward the stone staircase. "Some of the magic in this tower is still functioning because the old magic was imbued into the very stone from which the tower was built. The weather shields around the windows are an example. The sapphire staircase is another." He points to the staircase on the right that glows faintly blue. "That staircase will lead you directly to the base of the tower in only ten steps so you don't have to climb all of the internal stairs. There's a sapphire staircase every three levels."

It sounds very similar to the old magic that governs the staircases in Hidden House, where one flight of stairs will take you wherever you want to go within the house.

Perla pauses in front of the stone staircase. "Cody Griffin is on the next level down," she snaps.

I eye the sapphire staircase—a direct route to exit the tower—before I follow her down the stairs and into the next corridor. Along the way, more female shifters stop and watch me pass. I count twenty so far. They're all wearing similar combat uniforms to Perla, all of them leopard shifters. Some frown at what I'm wearing. All of them give me a wide berth.

We finally reach a room at the end of the corridor with an arched doorway leading into it—open like mine was.

Perla stops at the side of the doorway, remaining outside.

My wolf prowls into the cell first while my father steps

aside to let me through. At the last moment, his hand snakes out to grab hold of my arm, pressing on my already aching bruises. He draws my hand into his, pushing a dagger into it.

"Take your time," he says, his eyes gleaming with crimson hues.

My wolf has already taken stock of the layout inside the room. It's much like mine with a single window magically shielded from the wind outside. The walls and floor are cold, gray stone.

Cody is chained to the wall in the same way I was, kneeling with the soles of his feet pressed to the wall and his muscular arms outstretched. His head is bowed and his eyes are closed. His sandy blond hair isn't long enough to fall across his eyes, but the strands are matted with blood from the blow to his forehead.

His face is pale, his breathing shallow. The golden tattoo on his chest is overly bright compared to the deathly shade of his skin.

Without a word, I take the dagger my father offers and carry it into the room, my feet brushing the smooth stone. If this room was once decorated or contained magical objects, then they are long gone. The walls are bare but smooth.

I kneel beside my wolf in front of Cody's unconscious form. He is completely vulnerable to me now.

He tried to hurt me once. Then he fought for me.

I am revenge growing inside the heart.

I press the flat of the blade against his tattoo, sliding the sharp edge up toward his throat, holding it the same way he once pressed my axe to my chest. To this day, I still don't know if he realized he could have killed me right then.

My father prowls across the floor behind me while Brynjar and the warlock take up position on either side of the door like guards.

"Did he hurt you badly, little one?" my father asks.

"Yes."

"Then hurt him."

My wolf considers Cody with her crimson eyes, the power

of anger that allows me to see what the person I'm looking at doesn't want me to see.

Even this close to death, Cody is at war with himself. On the night I first met him, I saw his power split into two—fear and anger—two emotions at war in him like they are in me. But what I don't see right now… is his wolf's aggression. I'm not sure why, but darkness grows where his wolf's desires once burned.

I press the blade close enough to Cody's throat to draw a tiny prick of blood. "His wolf wants me," I say, making my father pause his prowling.

I cast a sideways glance at Ford. "I can use his wolf's desire against him."

My father narrows his eyes at me. "For what purpose?"

I tip up my chin. "To inflame the war between packs."

Ford's lips part before they curl into a smile, but he hesitates. "He won't live long enough for that sort of revenge."

My lips draw back into a snarl. I rise to my feet, whisking the blade away from Cody's throat. Swiftly shifting gears, I advance on the warlock. "Whose fault is that?"

Silas stands his ground, resolute, as I stride toward him. I jab the dagger at his throat, the tip piercing his skin. His only reaction is to lean back slightly, his gaze never leaving mine.

"You will heal Cody Griffin," I say. "I want my revenge."

The warlock's gaze flicks to my father.

"Don't look to my father for orders!" I scream. "Your magic deprives me of what I want. Now, fix it."

Silas was willing to give up his only functioning eye to bring out my so-called true nature, but he doesn't seem to like being ordered around by a woman. From the corner of my eye, I see his hand twitch. He must be trying to decide whether or not to knock the dagger from my hand like he did when I fought him on the helipad.

My father also appears to be on the backfoot. "Little one, it's impossible to reverse the effects of dark magic. Power taken is gone forever. Only the purest light can return Cody's life to him." Ford paces toward me, his hands raised, taking careful steps. "Pure magic like that no longer exists."

Yes, it does. I'm sure of it.

I sat beneath tree branches made from pure magic every night at Hidden House. A garden filled with rare silver flowers in a home sustained by old magic. The challenge will be getting Cody there.

I purse my lips and meet my father's eyes, betraying nothing of my emotions because that is part of my true power —to build a wall around my inner thoughts, so opaque that it will be mistaken for a heart of darkness. "Then I'll make use of the life Cody has left."

Lifting the blade from the warlock's throat, I speak to the ice man. "Bring the wolf to my room, Brynjar." Striding to my father, I stop beside him. "I assume I have a room?"

"You do. A very special room." He gives me a smug smile. "Brynjar will show you."

I continue to stare up at Ford. "I also want painkillers. Human ones. As well as food, water, and new clothing. This body defies my will and is slow to heal."

He gives me a nod. "You'll have them. Rest tonight. Tomorrow, I'll tell you all about my empire."

"I look forward to it." I rise up onto my tiptoes and kiss his cheek, finding his skin cold. "Goodnight, Father."

"Daughter."

The cold in his eyes sears my mind before he strides from the room with the warlock close behind him.

Brynjar kneels in front of Cody to unlock the shackles around his ankles and wrists. He presses up against Cody's chest, supporting his torso before hoisting Cody's unconscious body across his shoulder. I remember what Ford told Charlotte—that the ice jotunn's skin is covered in a shield of magic so others can't feel pain if they accidentally touch him. I hope it will protect Cody now.

When I follow Brynjar out into the corridor, I'm surprised that we ascend the stairs back the way we came. We return all the way up past the level with the two platforms where I was held and then we take one more set of stairs upward.

My legs are screaming by the end. Three flights of stairs would normally be nothing to me, but my body is exhausted and my mind is beyond stretched.

The corridor on this level is much shorter than the ones below and only has two rooms—one opposite the other.

"You'll have this level all to yourself," Brynjar says.

It sounds like freedom, but it isn't. To exit the tower, I'll have to make it down three levels of stone and past about thirty supernaturals to the sapphire staircase. Not impossible, but it would be reckless to try before I know what other traps might be waiting outside the tower. Not to mention, it's impossible to leave unless Cody wakes up.

Also, I don't believe for a second that they won't spy on me somehow. Everything I do will be watched. My ability to resist magic only extends to magic that impacts my body. I can break through magical shields and survive bullets infused with dark magic, but I can't detect or affect magic that is used outside my touch, such as cloaking shields that hide someone's voice or presence. Helen had multiple private conversations with Tristan by using a spell that stopped me from overhearing their voices. The warlock and ice jotunn concealed their supernatural status from me at Baxter's party until I literally brushed up against the ice jotunn and sensed his icy skin.

I will need my wolf to remain vigilant at all times to protect me.

Brynjar points to the room on the right-hand side. "This is yours."

I peer into it and my heart sinks.

It's empty. Four bare walls, all of them scratched and marked, stare back at me. The floor is dusty and the window on the far right lets in a whistling wind where I presume the magical shield must have a crack in it.

Damn. No wonder Ford looked so smug when he told me there was a very special room for me. *Very special, indeed.*

"Go on," Brynjar says, nudging me forward by bumping his shoulder into mine. "Step inside."

I give him a dirty look. My wolf hangs back as I resign myself to sleeping on a cold, stone floor.

Stepping inside, I gasp as my bare feet settle onto smooth wood and my surroundings transform.

Light ripples from where I stand, spreading across the floor to the walls and up across the ceiling. A fireplace glowing with a warm fire forms in the opposite wall with a plush rug in front of it made of some sort of fleece. A large bed takes shape close to the window on the far right. It's covered in snuggly-looking fleece blankets. A small wooden table sits in the near right corner with two chairs and a view through the window. On the left-hand side of the room, a glistening white claw-foot bath is situated in the far corner, sitting on top of a set of gleaming white marble tiles. A showerhead extends from the wall above it. There's no privacy screen between the bath and the rest of the bedroom, but a small room leads off from the left that I presume contains a toilet.

The walls are a deep indigo blue and the ceiling opens up to a sky filled with a thousand stars that shine a soft light, mingling with the amber glow from the fireplace. Magic shimmers through the walls, silver swirls that are both warm and inviting.

This room looks like it was designed for a queen. A beautiful, starlit queen.

The scent in the room carries a faint mix of fresh night air, sweet flowers, and low notes of burnt caramel, fragrances that speak of both a man and a woman.

There is love in this room. It takes my breath away and hits me hard. This room belonged to two people who were both very powerful and incredibly in love.

My wolf whines at me, her face turned up, her instincts a mirror to mine.

I should not be here. Not with all my baggage, my anger, and my despair. Maybe the room on the other side of the corridor will be a better fit for me…

I back up—and step directly into Brynjar.

He is an immovable wall behind me. Letting go of Cody's legs, he nudges me forward again with his big hand pressed to my lower back.

"I wasn't expecting this," I say, turning my face up to his, the cold mask I've been holding over my emotions slipping.

Brynjar grins, a rare show of genuine humor. "We believe this room once belonged to some sort of priestess. Maybe a deity. Only creatures of old magic can trigger the room to come alive. It seems to have some sort of built-in protective mechanism. Unlike the rest of the tower, this room has remained intact because there are not so many creatures of old magic anymore who could plunder it."

My wolf pads across to the rug in front of the fire, lies down, and places her head on her paws, looking back at me.

I guess I should accept that I'll be sleeping in here.

Brynjar strides into the room ahead of me now. "Creatures who are not of old magic can only experience the room like this while one of us is in it."

He heads for the bed, but I stop him. "Put Cody on the rug beside my wolf," I say. "He'll be warmer there."

"Very well." Brynjar supports Cody's head as he lays Cody down on the rug. Then he straightens to give me a bow. "Goodnight, young one."

When Brynjar exits the room, I notice a ripple in the air over the doorway. I'm just about to investigate when I sense others approaching in the corridor outside.

Perla appears in the doorway with two women at her side. The doorway ripples again as they enter the room and greet me stiffly. One of the women carries a few items of clothing, which she lays down on the bed. The other carries a tray filled with food while Perla herself hands me a wooden box.

"These are the painkillers you requested," Perla says, shoving the box into my arms without a backward glance.

Without being invited, she crosses the distance to Cody and crouches to peer at him. Gripping his broad shoulder in her fist and leaning over him, she inhales deeply. Then she turns up her nose. "His wolf is pitifully weak. You will struggle to take any pleasure from him."

My wolf raises her head from her paws where she rests beside Cody, her crimson gaze alert and bright with my rising anger. She is about to snap at Perla, but I rein in my anger.

Quietly placing the medicine box on the bed before I cross to Perla's side, I *"hmm"* softly in the back of my throat, giving her no indication of my intentions as I wait for her to glance up at me.

The moment she looks up, exposing her neck, my hand whips out to grab her throat, squeezing so hard, so fast, that she makes a choking sound.

My claws graze her neck and she instantly freezes.

The two other shifters tense behind me, both of them reaching for the daggers at their waists, but my wolf is facing in their direction. She snarls a warning, baring her teeth at them, ready to attack. Helen was right when she said my wolf could watch my back.

"*My* wolf is not weak," I say. "I understand you have a place in my father's empire and are useful to him—and possibly to me—but if you lay a hand on my possession again, I will rip out your throat without a second thought."

Perla carefully unfurls her fingers from around Cody's shoulder and raises her hand into the air at her side.

"Better," I say, releasing her slowly enough for her to feel the smooth side of my claws slipping across her throat. "Now, get out."

Perla jumps to her feet, backing away from me without taking her eyes off me. The other two women also retreat, quickly exiting through the door.

Pausing in the shadows beyond the doorway, Perla exhales with the deep hiss of a big cat that tells me she has partially shifted. "You can't replace me."

So that's the source of her insecurity.

I arch an eyebrow at her. "I already have."

With a snarl, she spins on her heel and disappears into the dark.

This time, I'm certain that there's some sort of magical shield over the doorway. The ripple was even more distinct for the leopard shifters than it was for Brynjar.

I listen for Perla's retreating footfalls before my wolf rises from her position on the rug, steps lightly over Cody, and prowls to the door.

She steps through easily to the other side and turns back, showing me what I need to see. From the corridor, there is an opaque screen across the doorway. I can see out from inside the room, but someone outside can't see in.

I test the carriage of sound by sighing loudly.

My wolf's ears prick, but her perception of the sound comes from her connection with me, not because she heard it through the doorway. I'm comforted to know that somebody standing outside the room won't be able to hear me. Not that I'm anticipating conversing with Cody anytime soon.

I allow myself to sag with relief. Only I, Brynjar, or my father can trigger this room and it was empty when we arrived, so I know my father wasn't secretly hiding here. I watched Brynjar leave. That means I now have some semblance of privacy.

I've never tested whether or not my wolf's form can remain awake all through the night while I sleep, but I will need her to keep watch on the corridor. Closing my human eyes, I expand both my senses. The next level down is now empty of shifters.

I'm finally alone. I can finally stop hiding my pain.

I collapse with a groan, dropping to the floor and barely making it back toward the bed at a crawl. Managing to reach up and grab the medicine box before I slide back to the floor, I hug the box to my chest, doubling over it.

My hands shake so hard that the lid rattles when I lift it. Scanning the bottles and packets, I seek the painkillers and anti-inflammatories, forcing myself to focus and count out the dosages before I take them.

Managing to climb up onto the bed, I reach for the jug of water and the glass already poured, sipping water as slowly as I can—even though every impulse in my body urges me to gulp it at speed. I pour another glass and drink that too. Then I tear a corner off a piece of bread and chew carefully. Remaining curled up on the bed, I close my eyes, hug the piece of bread to my chest like a safety blanket, and tear strips off it until I finish it.

All I want to do now is sleep, but I can't.

Get up, Tessa.

I groan. Shout at myself inside my mind.

Tessa, get the fuck up!

Sliding down the side of the bed to the floor—my best version of *up* right now—I take stock of what else is in the medicine box. I find a variety of painkillers, ointments, and serums, along with a large syringe filled with adrenaline. I don't want to use it on Cody to wake him up, but I will if I have no other choice.

I drag myself across to him. The painkillers are finally kicking in and my head is clearing. Not much. Just a little. I have to take care of my wounds, but I know that once I do, I won't want to move again.

Cody's injuries have to come first. He was hurt in the fight with Tristan, then again on the helipad, and he has new wounds around his wrists and ankles from the shackles.

I lean over him, pressing my hand to his forehead to check his temperature, relieved that it seems to be okay. His breathing is more even now, too. So is his pulse.

"Why the hell did you use tranquilizers and not bullets?" I ask him, even though I may never get an answer. My only guess is that Cody knew bullets wouldn't kill Brynjar—or Ford, for that matter. Ford definitely seemed surprised by the substance in the tranquilizers that knocked him out.

Testing my legs, I rise to my feet, preparing to use the tap over the bath for water to clean out Cody's wounds.

I'm surprised to find the bath full of water already. It's even hot.

Thank you, old magic.

Taking a cloth from the pile of towels on the chair, I dip the soft material in the water. Wringing it out, I return to Cody and wipe it over his face and chest, paying careful attention to the wound on his forehead, cleaning it out. Turning him onto his front proves difficult even with my extra strength. When I finally succeed, I prop pillows against his chest to keep him elevated while I clean out the wounds on his back and dress them.

When I'm done with his chest and arms, I blow out a breath and consider what to do about his legs. I have no idea if he has a festering wound under the pants he's wearing. Even a small wound can be deadly.

With a sigh, I unbuckle his long pants and set about removing them, leaving his underpants in place, because, hell, there are limits.

A gash across his thigh makes me feel justified about stripping off his pants, even though it's a flesh wound and isn't deep enough to be life-threatening. I don't have a needle and surgical thread—and wouldn't know how to use them even if I did—so I cut strips of tape and use them to pull the edges of the wound together before I bandage it.

Leaning back on my heels, I bite my lip as I consider whether there's anything else I can do to keep him alive until I can get us out of here.

My care for him up to this point has been deliberately clinical, but now I consider how savagely gorgeous Cody is. His human form reminds me of his wolf. Sleek and beautiful in an aggressive way. He has perfectly muscled shoulders, biceps, and forearms, as well as a lean waist and strong thighs.

Cody is not ruthlessly fierce like Tristan, but he's dangerous in other ways. He has the ability to adapt to his surroundings—to don a suit and look completely comfortable holding a wine glass, even though his wolf would prefer to rip out someone's throat. I told Ford that Cody's wolf could be bent to my will, but I don't believe it for a second. Cody's wolf has always been in combat with mine, a battle of dominance that can only lead to destruction.

Now, his life is in my hands.

I tell myself I need to pick myself up, clean my own wounds, and check my healing progress. I need to get some sleep. The swelling around my left eye has receded enough that I can open it again, so that's positive at least.

While my wolf remains at the door, I pull off my torn clothing—all of it. Stepping fully naked over Cody's unconscious form, I throw the remnants of my ripped skirt and bodice into the fire.

What's left of the material shrivels and melts.

Finally making my way to the bath, I sink below the surface, hating the way the water quickly swirls with blood and crystalline snowflakes. Before I can think too much about what I'm about to submerge in, I take a deep breath, lower myself beneath the surface, and keep myself immersed by planting my hands on either side of the bath.

I let out my breath with a scream, allowing my vision to turn crimson, testing my control over the darkness inside me.

My rage rises, violent, clawing sensations strong enough to dominate my mind. A gift from my father, it seems. With sheer fucking determination, I pull my rage back. There's no destroying it, only containing and controlling how it manifests. What scares me is the possibility that one day... I won't be able to control it. That my true nature—my rage—will control me.

I'm now walking a dangerous, narrow path with only one destination in mind: destroying Ford Vanguard, the monstrous, ancient wolf who sired me.

CHAPTER EIGHT

I step out of the bath before the water gets cold, having cleaned and checked each of my wounds and washed my hair as best I can with the cake of soap the room provided. I'll have massive frizz issues tomorrow, but who the fuck cares?

Wrapping a towel around myself, I'm grateful that between the bath and the painkillers, most of my aches are subsiding. I can move without pain now, functioning nearly normally, even though I'm exhausted. Crossing back to the bed, I check out the clean clothing the leopard shifters left for me, hoping they brought me something to sleep in.

I was expecting standard issue uniforms like the leopards wear, but instead, they've given me multiple flimsy polyester skirts that won't reach far past my butt and two short-sleeved T-shirts. No shoes of any sort. The two bras in the pile are one cup size too small for my double-Ds.

I select one of the shirts but don't put it on since my hair is still dripping. Finding a spot in front of the fire with my back to Cody's side, I tip my hair forward to help it dry, not caring when the towel slips to my waist. The warmth of the fire is like a balm against my frayed emotions and my eyelids finally droop. The thought of curling up in front of the fire instead of sleeping on the bed is incredibly tempting.

I'm suddenly aware of Cody's forefinger brushing against my exposed thigh, the lightest touch.

"You're too beautiful for a fucker like Tristan," he says.

I startle and spin to Cody, my hair falling across my breasts, covering more than was concealed a moment ago.

"You're awake!" Tugging the towel up over my chest, I lean over Cody, my forehead creasing when it looks like he's still asleep… until I see that his eyes are open by the barest margin.

Hmm. I'm not certain now that he was unconscious for as long as I thought…

"I'm not awake." He groans, his lips pressing together and his brow furrowing. "I'm in hell, where I'm paying for my sins."

I continue to lean over him, assessing the pale shade of his cheeks, waiting for his eyes to open more so I can check his ability to focus.

When his eyelids finally open, his gaze passes across my face but doesn't stop there, descending across my shoulders, my arms, down to my thighs, pausing on every scratch and bruise, lingering on the ligature marks around my wrists, before rising to settle on the damage to my cheek, where Ford cracked my face against the wall.

"Damn," Cody whispers. "They really fucked you over."

My defenses rise. I'm not sure what to expect now that he's awake. I should take comfort in the fact that he's still barely moving, but I'm not sure how long his paralysis will last. After all, I was convinced he was unconscious and I was wrong.

I snap back a sharp answer. "I've been hurt worse than this."

He flinches. "Don't minimize your pain, Tessa. Anyone else would be curled up screaming by now."

"It's a good thing I'm not just anyone, then," I say.

"You're definitely not anyone." His faint smile fades. "But if I'd helped you escape like I intended, you wouldn't have those bruises."

I lean farther forward, tucking the towel firmly above my breasts before I drop both of my hands onto his shoulders with a snarl. "You mean if you'd taken control of me like you intended?"

I watch for the golden flecks that always build in Cody's eyes when his wolf surfaces. It's his wolf that responds to my power. It's his wolf that tried to mark me the night my father died. I need to draw out his animal while he's vulnerable so I can determine the level of threat he poses to me.

I'm unsettled when I don't see his animal or hear its growl in his voice.

"My intention was never to control you," he says quietly. "Only to offer you a safe place to—"

"Safe?" I snap. "With you?"

"Yes," he says, meeting my stern gaze. "With me."

Tristan told me to go with Cody, that he would take me somewhere safe, but I press my lips together. I'm struggling to believe that Cody's intentions were so simple. When he first appeared on the helipad, Cody said that his wolf wouldn't let me go again.

I suddenly blink, a new thought occurring to me. "What did Tristan promise you if you helped me?" My fingers tighten around Cody's shoulders, my claws threatening to release. "Tristan spoke to you before the ice man carried me away. What did Tristan offer you?"

A muscle ticks in Cody's jaw. "Not a fucking thing, Tessa. He didn't have to promise me anything."

I narrow my eyes, challenging Cody's answer. "Then what did he say to you?"

A determined light enters Cody's eyes, although he keeps his voice low and soft. In control. "He told me that the only person standing between me and what I want is myself."

I pull in a breath. *Damn you, Tristan.* He knew exactly what to say to make Cody's wolf respond.

The firm lines of Cody's lips soften as his gaze passes across my face. "You're hurt, Tessa," he says. "So am I. I don't know where the fuck I am or how I got here, but I know you didn't have those cuts or bruises the last time I saw you. I failed, and for that, I feel as much regret as a fucker like me can feel."

I withdraw a little, my eyes narrowed. "Is that meant to be an apology?"

He exhales slowly. "Call it 'accepting responsibility.'"

His eyes close again before he says, abruptly, "You should know that Tristan's alive."

My breathing is suddenly a thousand times less calm. I try to block out the memory of my father dragging Tristan's body to the edge of the roof. I'm sure I've sensed Tristan since that moment, but I can't be certain and it's tearing at my heart, adding fuel to the anger that simmers at the edges of my mind.

My vocal chords are tight in my throat. "What makes you so sure?"

Cody grimaces without opening his eyes. "The guilty always survive." His fingers twitch again, but this time, his touch is firmer against my thigh. I could almost imagine that his claws have appeared, but when I glance down, they haven't.

"Take me as an example," he says. "I'm still alive." He exhales. "Also, there's a pool below the helipad that he would have fallen into."

So there was *a pool.*

"Assuming he survived the neck wound," I say. *From the dagger I practically handed my father.*

Cody gives another heavy exhale. "Yeah, there's that."

Pushing away the deep turmoil I feel about Tristan, I study Cody carefully. I wasn't expecting him to wake up at all. Ford said that power taken by dark magic is lost forever, and I'm suddenly on edge. I haven't seen any sign of Cody's wolf, even though I've attempted to provoke him several times.

I press my palm to the side of Cody's face, running my thumb back and forth across his cheek. He closed his eyes a few moments ago and now a slight crease rests in his forehead as if he's hurting. It's probably the pain of the wounds I already know about, but I need to be sure.

"Open your eyes," I say, trying to coax him to obey me.

THIS BROKEN WOLF

He keeps his eyes closed. "Why?"

As much as I play the part for my father's benefit, dominance is not a pretense for me. It's who I am now. My inner nature doesn't like being disobeyed. My power rises and my voice becomes guttural. *"Open your eyes."*

His eyes fly open, but they quickly narrow at me.

I expect his wolf to respond to my command, but his eyes are pure hickory brown. There isn't a sign of the flecks of gold that appear when his animal takes control. The only change is a few bloodshot streaks at the edge of his irises. By now I should have heard at least a hint of a growl in his voice, should have sensed his alpha wolf's desire to dominate me.

Instead, he's lying still beneath me and taking fucking responsibility like a real man would.

Gripping his face firmly, I allow my power to surface, savage strength that surges through me and turns my vision crimson.

He jolts at the appearance of my scarlet eyes. "What the fuck, Tessa?"

I grip him harder. It's his internal struggle that alarms me. Beneath his defenses, I discern his anger, pride, the will to survive, even a surprising capacity for loyalty, along with the barest hint of honor that was long ago ripped to shreds and buried in a deep grave... but still no wolf.

"Cody," I whisper, allowing my power to drain away and my eyes to return to normal. "Where is your wolf?"

CHAPTER NINE

Cody grits his teeth. I wait for his incisors to appear, but they don't.

He's silent for a very long time and this time, I don't push him for a response.

Finally, he says, "That fucker never did me any favors." He meets my eyes. "It was him or me."

I draw a sharp breath. "You let the dark magic take your wolf's power so you could live."

He returns my gaze without flinching. "Like I said, it was him or me."

Damn. I'm shocked to my core. Not only because Cody made an unthinkable choice, but because it worked. Would I ever be willing to sacrifice my power to save myself? Or would I choose to go down fighting, even if it meant total annihilation?

My wolf whines just outside of the doorway in the corridor, expressing my worried feelings. She is me, so even though she can't see through the opaque shield with her wolf eyes, she knows everything that happens inside the room. What's more, Cody can see *her*.

He tenses, his shoulders bunching, wary now. "Who is that?"

I bite my lip. "That's me." I squeeze my eyes shut for a

moment at my slip-up. Grimacing, I say, "I mean... that's my wolf."

Cody speaks slowly. "You're in two places."

"Yes."

"Does Tristan know you can do this?"

I swallow. "No."

Cody stares up at the ceiling. I wait for him to ask me complicated questions, but instead, he makes a request. "Tell me where I am and how I got here."

I explain everything I can about where we are and what happened after he was knocked out on the helipad, although I don't know what happened to him in the time between the chopper and when I had him unchained.

I balk at talking about my father, but it's not a secret I can keep. I tell Cody who I am. Who my father is. And what my father can do. I tell him that Tristan knew who I was, but that he didn't tell me.

I *don't* tell Cody that Ford might have been involved in the events of the night that Ella disappeared, including Tristan's mother's death. I don't have concrete information about that and speculation will only worsen the confusion around the events of the past.

Talking keeps me from thinking about how complicated everything has become.

Cody doesn't have a wolf. *He doesn't. Have. A fucking wolf.*

If any part of his wolf remains, its power is so reduced that I can't sense it. Perla said Cody's wolf is weak, but I doubt she could distinguish between the remnant scent of his wolf and his wolf-less nature now.

I'm not sure how to process the destruction of Cody's wolf, so I focus on what I know.

"My father can separate from his wolf, just like I can," I say. "He can see into your mind and he will strip back your defenses. You can't fight him. You can't kill him. Only Tristan can."

Cody meets my eyes. "Then how am I still alive?"

I pause. "I convinced my father that I can manipulate you.

"You're alive because I promised him that I will use you to incite war between the packs."

Cody's jaw tenses. "You're walking a dangerous path, Tessa." The tightness around his eyes increases. "You need to tell me: What is my role in it?"

I take a deep breath and wish I hadn't. Even without his wolf, Cody smells like a field of grass warmed in the sun, a scent that speaks of safety and contentment—of the startling possibility of *friendship*—emotions I can't allow myself to feel around him.

"My father will be able to sense that your wolf is gone—assuming he hasn't already. I need you to behave as if you still want me. As if losing your wolf doesn't change that. Your motivations have to appear the same as your wolf's."

Cody's eyes narrow. A storm grows in his brown eyes. He reaches up to brush the strands of my hair from my face. Despite the growing tempest in his expression, his touch is light and careful, avoiding my bruises. "You want me to act as fucked up as my wolf made me?"

"I don't see any other way to keep you alive," I say, my voice hardening. "My father has to believe that I can manipulate you in some way." I don't release him from my gaze, allowing a hint of rage to redden my eyes. "You need to play my game until we can get the hell out of here."

He casts an angry glance at my wolf, who returns his glare without flinching.

Cody grits his teeth. "Fine."

Given the tension in his jaw and the glint of unhappiness in his eyes, I'm surprised he agreed so quickly, but I can only accept his word.

I relax against him. "Good."

I've sunk slowly toward his chest while I've been speaking and now my head rests on his shoulder, my legs curled up under me at his side. "Then we need to get some sleep."

Despite my assertion, I remain where I am, still wrapped in a towel. My limbs are heavy, the painkillers have well and truly kicked in, and I don't want to move. *Damn his field of sun-warmed grass.* I could sleep right here for days.

"I've had too much sleep," Cody grumbles, rubbing his forehead with the back of his hand. He glances at me while my eyelids droop. "You know it's fucking humbling lying here unable to do anything for myself."

"I can put your pants back on for you if you'd like?" I offer, tipping my head back to arch an eyebrow at him, wondering if he realizes that he's been moving his arms for a while now.

"I don't have pants on? *Damn.* I wondered why my legs were cold." He twists a little, his torso rising before his hand lowers to graze my arm, trailing a path between the bruises. His other arm curls around my lower back. Despite proving to himself that his arms and legs are now functioning, he doesn't try to get up.

"Daughter of the war wolf, huh?" he says, the tension around his eyes increasing again.

I yawn and rest my head back down on his chest. "Apparently."

His fingertips trace the top of the towel across my back, pushing my hair to the side, making me sigh. "Tessa?"

"Hmm?"

"Don't fucking let your guard down around me."

My forehead creases where my head rests against his chest, but I dismiss his warning. It's a simple fact that I'm stronger than he is, especially now that his wolf is gone. He can't hurt me.

I'm the one who can hurt *him.*

His fingers tighten across my back. "I'd like to blame everything on my wolf, but he wasn't responsible for breaking the rules at the Conclave. I was the one who asked Dawson to take me up the mountain."

Every muscle in my body tenses. I take a breath and hold it, allowing the rage to build inside me in case I need it.

"I had reasons for wanting to see you—reasons that feel unjustified now," he says. "But I want you to know it was more than pure curiosity. I'm telling you this because I played a dangerous game that night with no thought about the consequences, and it went very, very wrong. I won't do that again."

I tip my head back to meet his eyes. There's a hardness in his expression that wasn't there before. Only moments ago, he agreed to play my game, but it looks like he's already about to go back on his word.

"You're lying here with me like you trust me," he says, the corners of his mouth turning down. "That can't fucking happen. Ever."

Get up, Tessa. Fuck the field of warmed grass and get the hell up. Blame the painkillers. Blame my wounded body.

Cody moves faster than I do, his arm tightening around my lower back, his hand gripping the back of my neck, pulling me hard up against him.

He flips me onto my back on the rug. My legs are still bent at my knees at the side of his hips, but the towel separates all the way to my waist, clinging together at the top only by the knot above my breasts and pinned in place by the weight of his chest pressing against mine.

"I may have lost my wolf, but I can still cause you harm," he snarls, his human voice harsh. "Don't forget it, Tessa."

I try to catch my breath as he rapidly shifts his hands, one to my shoulder, the other to my hip, both pressing down hard on me. I grab his hands before he can make another move, sensing the flex of his muscles as he tests his physical strength against mine. Without his wolf, he shouldn't be strong enough to subdue me this long, but—*damn it*—I underestimated his human strength.

"Get the hell off me or my wolf will hurt you," I snap, imagining the pain I can inflict on Cody if my wolf tears through his insides. At the side of the room, my wolf lowers her head, lips drawn back and teeth bared, an imminent threat, ready to attack.

Cody glances my wolf's way. "Then do it!"

He poises above me, his hands clamped on me. He waits for me to retaliate, as if he wants me to. I glare up at him, angry at myself that I let my guard down. Angry at *him* for turning the tables on me. One minute he was stroking my back and now he's trying to make me fight with him. His wolf always provoked the violence in me and responded to my instincts to fight, but Cody was in constant battle with his wolf. Without his wolf… he shouldn't be acting like this.

For a second, I consider engaging my crimson vision, but my instincts tell me it will only inflame the situation.

A storm grows in Cody's eyes when I continue to hesitate.

"Maybe it will take a different approach," he says. His hands soften against the towel's edge, stroking across the top of my breasts. Watching me carefully, he lowers his head to mine, his lips the barest distance from my mouth.

His voice whispers across my cheek. "How far will you let me go before you end me?"

The smell of sun and fields is intoxicating as I breathe in his scent, but instead of dulling my senses, the aroma sharpens my anger. My rage intensifies that he's daring to make a move after everything that happened between us in the past. I'm not in any way afraid for my safety. I can subdue Cody easily. But a darkness rises inside me, a seductive and undeniable temptation to test my strength against his.

"Touch me that way and I will kill you," I snarl.

Ignoring my warning, he dips his head, his lips a breath away from brushing mine.

With a growl of rage, I knock my right fist into his side, hard enough to risk cracking his ribs.

He reacts quickly, rolling to avoid the hit but taking me with him, deftly pressing my left knee to the side so that I end up on top of him, straddling his hips.

His left hand strokes down my back as we finish rolling, daring to descend all the way to my backside. As I rear up over him, intending to leap back to my feet, he uses my momentum against me. Simply grabbing one side of the knot at the top of the towel with his other hand, he lets me do the rest.

My upward movement rips the towel right off me.

I freeze. Gasp.

He keeps his gaze on mine, pure challenge, before he pitches the towel to the side, where it lands at my wolf's feet.

My inner rage bursts upward, my snarl barely human. "You fucking—"

"What?" he asks. "Fucking what? What am I now?" His expression darkens. "Human? Wolf? Man?"

He arches up beneath me, openly defying the clawed hand I slap onto his chest. My claws could rip out his heart, or his throat, or any other part of his body that I wish. The way he tempts my darkness—is tempting my violence right now —shakes me.

Before I can answer, he drops back to the rug. His hands curl around my naked hips and his thumbs stroke down my stomach, past the crease at the top of my legs to rest on my outer thighs.

"Or maybe," he says, his lips parting, daring me to retaliate. "*Mate.*"

My eyes widen, outrage spurring me to attack again. I swing my left fist at his face. "You know that's impossible!"

He catches my fist, his biceps bunching as he holds my flexed hand, testing his strength against mine.

Shocking me, he says, "Just because you can't bond doesn't mean you can't fuck. I'm willing to accept the compromise."

I'm beyond angry now, barely keeping hold of the darkness inside myself, but if I let it out, I'll kill him. I don't know why he's provoking me, but he's playing a game of dominance with me that he can't win. My inner nature craves supremacy, thrives on it, wants to unleash the violence that will allow me to destroy him.

While the tension between our two fists remains, I lean over him, dragging my lower lip into my mouth, watching the bead of sweat slide down his temple, studying the way the tension around his mouth and eyes changes.

"You're exerting yourself too much, Cody," I whisper, my voice taking on the guttural tones that tell me I'm approaching dangerous territory.

The corners of Cody's mouth turn down before he releases

my hand, making the most of my forward momentum as he engages his stomach muscles and rises up beneath me into a fully seated position. Sweeping his hands down my spine, he pulls my legs around his hips and holds me tight against him.

"Is this enough like my wolf for you?" he asks.

If it weren't for his underwear, there would be nothing between us, but it's not our physical closeness that makes my heart sink.

Oh... fuck...

He asked me about his role in my dangerous game, and I told him that he had to act as if he wanted the same things his wolf wanted. I told him to act as if he hasn't lost the animal that was part of him his whole life—a crucial part of him even if he was at odds with it more often than not. Now I realize how cruel my instruction must have sounded to him.

"Cody, I—"

He cuts me off, speaking through gritted teeth. "End me, Tessa." The storm in his eyes grows wilder. "Put me out of my misery already."

My rage fades, draining away from me. "No."

"I'm dying! I won't survive without my wolf. I've only got days to live. I can sense it! I'm a liability to you." He grabs my hand and presses it to his heart again, forcing my fingers to curl so that my claws would impale him if I released them. "I failed to take you to safety. I have nothing to offer you now."

I draw back, wrenching my hand away from him. "You have *everything* to offer!"

"What can I do for you?" Narrowing his eyes, still testing my boundaries, he dares to slide his hands up my ribs and rest them beneath my breasts. "Maybe I can warm your bed? Or mark this perfect shoulder—"

"Stop." He's still trying to provoke me. I grab his hands and push them back to my hips, wrapping them around me. "Yes, you're leverage, and my father will use you against me. I have no doubt about it. But I need an ally, Cody. Someone whose face I don't hate."

His hands flex against my hips and his forehead creases deeply. "You should always hate me, Tessa."

I grit my teeth, my patience running thin. "There was a time when I would have killed you." I sigh out an exhale. "But today, I'm stuck in a beautiful cage surrounded by monsters, and I don't know if the man I love is alive..."

My voice fails. *Damn.* Admitting that I love Tristan—especially to Cody—is the most dangerous thing I've done all night.

Cody surprises me by falling quiet. His response is subdued. "You can't fucking forgive me for what I did."

"That might be so," I whisper. "But you can spend the rest of your life making it up to me."

Taking a deep breath, I ease out the tension in my body, listing objects in my mind to regain control. *Silver flowers... silver vines... silver house...*

With my diminishing anger and rising control, I become more aware of how completely naked I am. My cheeks begin to burn. Carefully placing my left arm across my breasts, I attempt to conceal them as best I can—not that he hasn't seen everything already.

Cody's hands ease away from my hips and for a beat, I catch the way his gaze follows the shape of my face, shoulders, and curves.

His lips press together in a fierce line.

"I will," he says. "Spend the rest of my life making it up to you. However short my life is."

His hands drop to the rug. I don't need my power to read the war inside his mind right now. Even without his wolf, it seems to have remained, a perpetual battle.

"We should start by getting some sleep," I say.

At the side of the room, my wolf turns away from us and focuses back on the corridor. She is a reminder that I could have put a stop to Cody's actions at any time I wished—with sheer and utter brutality.

I rise to the bed, grab the first soft T-shirt I can find, and pull it over my head, glad to find that it's long enough to cover my backside.

I'm aware of Cody rising to his feet behind me, but I continue with my resolution not to make this more awkward than it already is. After I sweep the rest of the clothing onto the floor, I remove the tray of food and water and slide myself under the bed covers. All the way to the other side.

"They will expect us to sleep together," I say, patting the space behind me.

"How do you want this to work?" Cody asks.

"However it has to," I say.

The mattress tips beneath me as he gets in. Instead of keeping to his side of the bed, he slides over and carefully pulls me up against him. The way he moves tells me he knows I can pull away from him at any time.

He settles in behind me so that he's spooning my back.

"This is how it should work," he murmurs, nudging a light kiss against the back of my neck. It doesn't feel like he's making a move, more like he's making an apology.

I don't fight him. Fighting him just brings out the beast inside me. It brings *me* out. I was born with layers of malice and destruction. Brynjar's magic has broken the barriers that my human soul constructed to constrain the darkness inside me. But still, I have my heart—a link to my humanity—and that leaves me in a bitter war with myself.

Tristan knew what I was before I did.

He knew the battle I would have to fight within myself and how hard it would be. He matched my darkness, but he knew the dangers because he fought his own darkness every day.

Struggling to contain the burn of tears at the back of my eyes, I tell myself I can't let my inner nature destroy me. I have to believe that Tristan is alive, find my way back to him, and find a way to change his fate.

It's the only way I'll change my own destiny.

CHAPTER TEN

I awake to a warning growl from my wolf.

Using my wolf's sight, I make out the ice jotunn's silhouette approaching along the sunlit corridor outside the room. Brynjar's power shimmers as he walks, luminescent in my wolf's vision. He's carrying a tray of hot food and a large satchel rests across one of his shoulders. The scent of bacon and toast wafts into the room ahead of him, making my stomach grumble.

My wolf backs up from the corridor but remains in the doorway so that Brynjar can't enter it yet.

"You will wait," she says to him.

I'm not sure if he will try to push his way past her, but the ice giant stops patiently outside the doorway, quietly holding his offerings.

I take a moment to assess my state of health. I must be healing much faster than I ever did before because my face isn't swollen anymore. I can't feel the split across my cheek. My body is stiff, but the bruises on my arms are gone. I can't see my legs yet to check them over, though. A brief pat of my hair tells me I was right about my prediction—my hair is a mess of frizz.

I turn in Cody's arms to find his eyes determinedly closed in the way of a person who doesn't want to be awake yet. The

THIS BROKEN WOLF

bedroom isn't exactly filled with light. A dark haze has dropped over the window as if the room is built to block out the rising sun.

Taking the chance to carry out a visual check of the wound across Cody's forehead, I'm pleased to see it's healing, although he sports a nasty bruise that extends back beyond his hairline. I'll also need to check the cut on his thigh once he's out of bed.

I nudge his cheek with mine, avoiding the bruise.

"It's morning," I murmur, coaxing him to give in to the day and open his eyes.

"Fuck mornings," he says, grabbing me and bundling me up so that I roll on top of him as he shifts onto his back. Wrapping his arms around me, one hand sliding into my hair, he falls still again. The unhappy crease in his forehead eases and his breathing deepens, his chest rising and falling beneath me, relaxing while my weight settles onto him.

I prop my chin on his chest, considering for a second whether or not he and Danika are cut from the same cloth. She hates mornings too. The corners of my mouth rise at the thought of my friend. Danika would tear Cody apart with her talons sooner than look at him.

My heart becomes heavy as I lower my ear to his chest, listening to his heartbeat.

It isn't Tristan's heartbeat and I can't sync with it.

I quickly bury my face against Cody's chest, allowing my hair to fall across my cheeks, trying to create a visual shield to hide my sadness in case Cody stirs again.

Yesterday, all I could think about was survival, of making it through the pain and danger that filled every second of every hour. Today, I'm stronger, but with strength comes the ability to feel sorrow and regret—to question the choices I've made that have led me here—along with a bone-deep dread for the people I care about.

I have to believe that they're all safe. That Tristan is alive—that he somehow made it to Helen, is healed, and back with Jace and the pack. I have to believe that Iyana and Danika are also safe and they've either stayed with Tristan or returned to Hidden House. But I know, in my heart, that they'll be looking for me. They are my friends, my pack, like sisters to me. They went with me to Tristan's home, gave me all the love and support they could possibly give...

My father said that nobody would find me here in the Spire. I don't think he's lying to me. It's been longer than twenty-four hours since I left Baxter's home. If Iyana and Danika could track me easily, they would have found me by now.

Closing my eyes, I take a deep breath to calm myself. I remind myself that for now, I'm alive and so is Cody. My plan for the immediate future is to keep us that way.

Tipping my head back, I find myself looking into Cody's already half-open eyes. I'm unsettled to see that his irises look more bloodshot today than they did last night. His cheeks are still pale too. Maybe he will pick up once he's eaten some food.

He gives himself a shake, the tension around his mouth easing. Cupping the back of my head, he presses his lips to my forehead and whispers, "Time to play wolf."

Turning us swiftly, he puts me beneath himself. His big hands grip my ribcage below my breasts, tugging me upward as he presses his cheek to mine. It's a rough but oddly playful gesture.

I stare up at him, wide-eyed, feeling like I was just a cub's plaything.

"Now I'm up," he says with a grin.

He draws his hands down my sides and hips as he slides from the bed. Cody is still only dressed in his underpants, but he ignores the jotunn—who can't yet see in, although we can see out—as Cody saunters straight to the small bathroom.

I'm slower to rise, carefully pulling the long T-shirt over my naked backside before I retrieve a pair of underpants from the pile on the floor and shimmy into them.

After a quick visual check of the bruises on my body, I shift my wolf out of the way so that Brynjar can enter the room.

He looks straight at the empty rug where Cody was lying last night before narrowing his eyes at the closed bathroom door.

I take the tray of food from him. "Good morning, Brynjar."

"You should eat and dress quickly," Brynjar says. "Your father is impatient."

I consider the dark screen across the window. It's difficult to tell how high the sun has risen. "What time is it?"

"Late."

"Damn." Placing the tray on the bed, I perch on the end of the bed and gobble half of the bacon and toast as quickly as I can, leaving the other half for Cody.

"I was not expecting the shifter to survive," Brynjar says, his expression revealing nothing of his inner thoughts as he removes the satchel from his shoulder and places it on the bed.

He must have assumed Cody would die in the night.

I glance dismissively in the direction that Cody went, downplaying his survival. "He's like a cockroach. Difficult to kill. But useful to me."

Brynjar inclines his head at the tangled sheets. "No doubt."

I focus on the items that Brynjar has brought us: two new sets of clothing, along with two pairs of boots.

One set of clothing is definitely for me: figure-hugging black pants and a button-up khaki shirt in what looks like my size along with a weapon harness and two daggers, both in scabbards. And a whole range of underwear that fills me with relief, since the labels confirm they're in my size this time.

The other set of clothing is also made up of black pants and a khaki T-shirt, but in a man's size. However, there's a distinct absence of weaponry for Cody.

As I swivel to check out the new clothing, my feet kick the clothes I swept off the bed onto the floor last night. "Tell me something, Brynjar," I say, pausing.

"Yes, young one?"

Swooping on a flimsy skirt in the pile of clothes Perla left me, I spear it with my claw and hold it up. "Did Perla intend to insult me?"

The corners of Brynjar's mouth turn down as he nods, a forthright response. "Perla has occupied her place in your father's empire for five years now. She finds and collects whatever he wants—people, magical objects. After you first appeared to your father, he asked her to find you. She tried but couldn't. It's the first time she's failed him. It has occurred to me that she might have deliberately failed, because she doesn't want you here, but I can't be certain." Brynjar stands back from the bed. "She will continue to test you until she feels your bite."

I consider his warning. My interaction with her last night might not have been enough to make her back off. "Then I'll need to bite sooner rather than later." My inner darkness rises, although I calm my instincts. "At a time of *my* choosing. Not hers."

Brynjar gives me a firm nod. "That would be wise."

"What about you?" I ask, popping the final piece of toast into my mouth. "Where do you stand in my father's empire?"

His attitude has been polite, almost subservient, but I haven't forgotten that he's the one who carried me screaming from the room at Baxter's home.

"I'm what you might call 'the muscle,'" he says, with a sudden cold grin.

I arch an eyebrow at him. "Does that mean you're my muscle now, too?"

"Your father has assigned me to you."

Cody's voice sounds from the far side of the room as he reappears, the best impression of a growl on his lips. "Tessa doesn't need you." His eyes narrow and his fists clench. If he had his wolf, his claws would descend. "She has me."

Brynjar returns Cody's hard stare with one of his own. "That remains to be seen." He turns to the door. "I will meet you at the top of the sapphire stairs."

I whisk my new clothing off the bed and head quickly to

the little bathroom. "I left you some breakfast," I say to Cody as I stride past him.

Cody catches my arm, lowering his voice. "I don't trust him, Tessa."

I press my lips together. "You told me not to trust you, either."

He lets go of my arm and stalks away from me, turning his back on me before he strips off his underwear and reaches for his new clothing. He doesn't have Tristan's scars, but he carries himself with the same edge of tension. As the alpha of his pack, Tristan was conscious of all of his pack members at all times. He never slept well. The dark rings around Cody's eyes this morning indicate the same.

My wolf turns back to the door to give Cody privacy while she keeps watch over the corridor. I stay conscious of what she sees while I hurry to the bathroom. It's a small room but comfortable enough with a washstand, toilet, and a mirror on the wall. Soft lamplight glows from the ceiling when I enter.

I glance in the mirror and freeze.

I expected to see bruises and a mop of ruby frizz on top of my head, but instead, I barely recognize my own face.

My irises are the brightest sapphire blue and my lashes are longer and darker than they've ever been, the outline of my eyes shadowed as if I've magically applied eyeliner. My lips are ruby red and my cheeks are flushed. What I thought was frizz is body and shape, my hair streaming around my head and shoulders. I look as if I just had the best night of my life.

Running my hand across my forehead and through my hair, I'm shocked by the way my expression alters in the soft light.

Drawing on my darkness, I shiver at the impact on my appearance as my strength flows through me. The color of my irises shifts from sapphire through magenta to a ruby hue that matches my hair and my lips.

I shudder as my incisors peek through my lips, deadly tips.

I appear mesmerizing in the way that a snake is mesmerizing, or maybe the way a lion is sleek and beautiful until it attacks.

Gripping the edge of the sink, I tell myself that I'm still me. That I'm still in control of my actions and my future, but the smallest doubt creeps in as I consider my face in the mirror.

What has my father done to me?

CHAPTER ELEVEN

We follow Brynjar down the sapphire steps to reach the outside of the Spire. I pull my wolf's shape back to my human form on the way down. With Cody at my back and Brynjar at my front, I'm covered on both sides. Not that I can completely trust either of them.

The stairs let out into an entry room in the shape of a semi-circle that contains a total of five sets of stairs. When we reach the bottom, I turn to consider each of the staircases, noticing that they have numbers listed in groups of three, from one to fifteen, etched into the top of the arches above them.

Brynjar leads us across the entry room and through an ornate wooden door. We exit onto a courtyard paved with smooth stones all fitted together to form a dais of sorts. The sound of crashing waves finally reaches me, along with a fresh breeze. It's late morning and the sun streams across a grassed area of about a hundred square feet immediately in front of the dais.

Beyond that, I'm surprised to see a larger cleared area of land containing multiple modern-looking buildings, including an enormous shed the size of an airplane hangar. The door is wide open, revealing several military-type vehicles and off-road motorcycles inside it.

If only there weren't fifty armed leopard shifter women between me and the vehicles. They stand around the large grassed area that sits at the base of the dais. Perla is shouting orders at four leopard shifters who are taking turns grappling with each other in the center of the combat area. It must be some sort of training session.

I take a moment to glance back at the tower, finally seeing it from the outside for the first time. It's like nothing I've ever seen. Constructed of some kind of black rock, its sides are jagged and it rises to a peak at the top. Two enormous landing pads extend out on either side of it about a third from the top, horizontal with the cliff's edge. Brynjar takes up position beside the door behind me while Cody stays close to me.

Ignoring the women training in the combat area, I focus on Ford, who sits at a weathered wooden table on the right-hand side of the dais.

He leans over a map.

"Daughter," he says. "Come here."

Cody's gaze burns my back as I obey Ford's command. He follows me, keeping his distance from Ford.

"Yes, Father," I say, standing at Ford's side and placing my hand on his shoulder.

The map he studies depicts the state of Oregon, but it's not an ordinary paper map. The images on the map are alive. Moving from west to east, glossy green forests give way to the city divided by the flowing river, followed by more city buildings, more forests, and then the Cascade mountains in the east. The light over the map is different in places, as if it's reflecting the actual status of the sun right now—some places shadowed by cloud cover. In other places, it's raining.

I recognize some of the artificial markings on the map as distinguishing between the Lowland and Highland territories controlled by wolf shifters, but I'm not familiar with the extra markings within the Tillamook National Forest at the west of Tristan's territory.

"What are those?" I ask.

"The current territories controlled by the witches," Ford

says. "They've been waging war against each other for over three years now."

Tristan told me the same thing. He said I should never go into the forest because it's a war we don't want to get involved in.

"Mother Lavinia has slowly conquered more ground through a series of challenges and battles," Ford continues. "This larger southern portion belongs to her coven now. These four northern sections are governed by other covens. Mother Zala is perhaps the most ruthless of them. She lost territory to Mother Lavinia last year because Zala is more inclined to take risks."

He talks me through the map of what he calls his western empire, which encompasses the area all the way up the coastline and inland as far as the Cascades. He mentions the witches and their covens—all five of them—and he speaks briefly about the witch who once controlled the entire forest: the woman called Mother Serena. She apparently lived for hundreds of years by stealing powers from other witches. At the height of her power, her coven had mastered control over the trees and earth. They were said to be unbeatable—until they were all wiped out. Nobody knows by whom. Ever since then, the forest has been in chaos.

"Why don't the five witches battle it out once and for all?" I ask.

Ford's eyes twinkle. "Because I've convinced them not to."

I stare back at him. "You're playing them off against each other."

He gives me a sly grin. "I am."

"To what end? How does this benefit you?"

"War gives me control," he says. "As long as the witches are at each other's throats, they need my help. I am not needed in a time of peace."

He returns to the map. "Do you see these areas?" he asks, sweeping his finger from the west across to the east. "These are the only places I don't control in one way or another."

Ford circles two locations on the map with his finger. One

is the reduced territory within which Tristan's pack now lives—the clock tower and surrounding blocks up to the edge of the river.

The second place surprises me.

Ford jabs his finger at a small section of blocks within Baxter's territory. Given the way Baxter seems to be in Ford's pocket, I'm surprised that anywhere in Baxter's territory is off-limits to my father.

"Where is that?" I ask.

"It's where your mother lived."

My forehead creases. It's nowhere near the Middle Highland territory where my mother grew up. That is, assuming I believe everything about the woman I was *told* was my mother. A shiver runs down my spine as I allow myself to contemplate all the doubts I have about my birth. So much of it was a lie. I want to rip answers from my father, but if he intends to toy with me, then I'll have to play along for now.

Ford rises from his seat. "Walk with me."

I incline my head, aware that Brynjar doesn't try to follow us, but Cody steps away from the wall.

Ford stiffens, his nostrils flaring and incisors descending as he growls. "Without your lapdog."

I cast Cody a warning glance combined with an upraised palm, telling him to stay behind. His eyebrows lower and his lips press in an unhappy line, but he doesn't disobey me.

Following Ford down the steps at the side of the dais, I step onto a pebbled path that leads toward the far edge of the clearing and around the perimeter.

"Your shifter has lost his wolf," Ford says, inclining his head back at Cody. "He won't last long without his animal. Can you still control him?"

I stifle my shudder at my father's comment about Cody's life expectancy. I was prepared for this conversation, so I focus on what Ford wants to hear.

"He's angry with his father for handing me over to you. Even without his wolf, he wanted me for himself." I compose my features into a haughty expression, playing a dangerous card that could either work for me or backfire. "Cody thinks he can convince me to escape this place."

Ford's eyebrows rise, but his hand suddenly darts out to grip my arm. "Do you want to?"

I meet his eyes. "What is there to escape? You've given me more freedom in the last night than I've had my whole life. I've been captive at Tristan's will for months. Before that, I was forced to remain on the top of a Middle Highland mountain." I tentatively reach out to curl my fingers around Ford's shoulder. At the same time, I take a deep, audible breath, closing my eyes, and then exhaling. "*This* is freedom."

Opening my eyes, I find him smiling at me, as cold as he always is, but there's a glimmer of crimson in his irises.

"I will give you all the freedom your wolf wants, Tessa," he says. "You may fight, kill, and control others to your heart's content. All I ask in return is your loyalty."

I'm relieved that he's moved on from the subject of Cody. For now, it seems my father is prepared to accept my word.

I arch an eyebrow, playfully challenging him. "Are you calling me *Tessa* to toy with my feelings or because you concede it's my name?"

Ford shrugs, urging me into a walk again. "I'm assuming it's the name your mother chose for you. Despite her deception, I've decided to accept your name."

"My mother is a bitch," I say, but with a laugh on my lips as if I don't care. "So if that's your reasoning, then I'm afraid you're insulting me."

Ford draws back a little, his eyes narrowing. "I'm talking about the woman who gave birth to you. I'm assuming you never knew her. If you did, you would have known about *me*."

I stop walking again, my fake laughter gone. "You're trying to tell me that the woman I think is my mother... *isn't* my mother."

He shakes his head. "That's correct."

Despite telling myself I'm prepared for anything now, my mind spins to hear it confirmed. It means that *neither* of the people I thought were my parents actually *were* my parents.

Denial rises to my lips. "But my eyes are the exact same color and shape as my half-brother's eyes," I say.

Ford reaches out to slide his fingers through my hair—his constant obsession. "Only because you adapted to your surroundings."

My response is flat, disbelieving. "What?"

I want to pull away from him, but he closes his fist around my hair.

"You have already learned how to make changes to your wolf's appearance," he says. "We can also make subtle changes to our human features if we need to. Your eyes are naturally blue, but you adjusted the shade to match the people you thought were your family."

He gives a short laugh. "I had a little trouble at the moment that our human forms came face to face for the first time the other night. I wasn't sure what appearance would make you trust me more."

I can't stop my gasp. When Ford emerged from the shadows beside the stairs at Baxter's home, his voice was rough, but also smooth. His hair appeared light brown, but the longer I looked at him, I thought maybe it was dark blond. His eyes had cycled from hazel green to pale brown. Only some of his features remained static—his strong jaw, perfectly curved lips, and high cheekbones.

If I can change some parts of my appearance… does that mean the face I saw in the mirror this morning is my chosen form? Or have I been pretending all my life and the person I see in the mirror now… is the *real* me?

I suppress my shudder as Ford considers my hair. He purses his lips before he says, carefully, "Perhaps you hoped that if you looked more like that woman, she might love you."

I inhale sharply, worried that he can see more deeply into my emotions than I want him to.

My mother—the woman who was supposed to raise me but didn't—publicly rejected me. She hated me. I thought it was because of my freakish nature. That she was embarrassed to have brought me into the world. But what if I was never hers?

And how would such a trick even be practically possible?

My power rises, the deepest anger triggered by confusion and the pain of rejection and abandonment that has followed me my whole life. I tell myself that there are a hundred other explanations, but my deepest pain rears its ugly head at the possibility that my birth mother hated me too. That neither of my mothers wanted me.

Ford releases my hair to brush my cheek, coaxing my crimson rage to calm. "Don't be angry with me, Tessa. I understand your pain. My mother rejected me, too."

I jolt away from his touch. If he believes I'm angry at him, then so be it.

Nothing I believed about my life is true. *Nothing.*

Everything that grounded me has been torn to shreds, piece by fucking piece over the last few days.

I want to run. I could turn right now and sprint into the forest. Escape this nightmare. I need Helen right now. And Iyana and Danika. I need their ability to cut through all of the bullshit and restore my foundations. I need their friendship, their love.

But I can't run because I've left Cody behind on the dais.

I see now how clever Ford was to separate us while he spoke to me. He may not be able to see into my innermost thoughts, but he doesn't trust me. He dangles this wide open space in front of me, telling me I'm free to do whatever I want, but I'm not.

The only way I'll escape this place—and not get Cody killed—is by convincing Ford to let us go as part of his plan for me.

I know I should calm down. Regain control. Continue to play the game I need to play, but the rage inside me is unquenchable.

So are the questions I need answered.

"Why don't you control the place where my mother lived?" I ask. "What could possibly stop you?"

He sucks at his teeth before he snarls. For a second, I glimpse the violence in his eyes that he has been keeping in check during our conversation. He may feign calm, but the monstrous wolf lurks close to the surface.

"That place is controlled by powerful assassins," he says. "Your mother was one of their best."

CHAPTER TWELVE

My mother was an assassin, a woman who killed people for a living. My father is a monstrous wolf who cages and kills people for a living. It's no wonder I'm so messed up.

But something else sticks out about what he said.

"*Was?*" I ask.

"She's dead," he says, his incisors descending even farther, warning me that my questions are making him angry.

Sudden pain strikes through my heart.

My mother is dead.

I found out about her and lost her all at once. But maybe... just maybe... she wanted me after all. Maybe she died and then... Andreas took me in... because despite all the lies and all the questions, one thing remains certain: Andreas Dean was determined to keep me alive no matter what it cost him.

My questions might make my father angry, but pain makes me reckless. "Who was she?" I ask, determined to have answers even if I provoke him into taking a swipe at me. "Was she a wolf shifter or something else?"

"Her name was Natalia. She was human," he says. "A beautiful, deadly human."

I freeze. "That's... impossible..."

His fist darts out, clamping around my shoulder, his claws

pricking my skin through the khaki T-shirt. "Natalia gave you the human soul that I despise."

I remember when he assailed me in the park on the night Brynjar and Silas attacked. I told Ford that my human soul makes me who I am. He told me I was too much like my mother.

"Did she try to kill you?" I ask. "Were you a target?"

"No. I met her in my human form. She didn't know who or what I am." His voice is so guttural now, his eyes flashing crimson, warning me to stop asking questions. The last time he looked at me with this much hatred was when I defied him while I was chained in the Spire. That was when I was stopping him from getting something he wanted.

His intense anger now is the same. It's emotional.

He lost something he wanted.

My eyes widen. *Damn...*

"You loved her," I whisper. And... if she didn't know what he was, then maybe... "She loved you."

The corners of his mouth shoot down. He jolts away from me, his claws catching in the shoulder of my shirt and tearing a rip in it. "I'm not capable of love. You would do well to remember that."

I stare at him. The shock now streaming through me eases some of my anger. "How did she die?"

He inhales deeply, but his breathing remains ragged. His responses are short. Sharp. "Natalia disappeared. I tried to find her. A year later, I found her gravestone. That is the end of it."

He falls silent and I discover that now... I'm numb.

I wobble, reaching out for the nearest tree, pressing up against its trunk. I don't know how Andreas pulled it off. How he made it look like I was his. And the woman I thought was my mother...

"How could they do it?" I ask, rubbing my forehead with the back of my hand. "What happened when I was born? You can't just suddenly produce a baby without a pregnancy..."

Ford steps beneath the shade of the tree, the shadows

under his eyes accentuated without the sun. "I know who your mother is because you have her hair. It is a part of your features you can't change. But I don't know what happened when you were born."

"I guess that means only my *fake* mother can tell me and she's the last person I want to go near," I say.

Ford becomes more alert, his eyes brightening again. "You want to kill her."

"Both her and my half-brother—" I stop myself, shaking off the thoughts of killing that came so quickly and naturally to my mind. Talking about killing without a second thought. "My *not* half-brother."

Damn. My eyes widen again. If Ford's telling the truth, then Dawson isn't my brother. All those years he tormented me. I was trapped, not only by my situation, but also by the belief that Dawson was family and I could never really escape him. Now I have no familial connection with him at all.

Ford begins to pace in the shadows. "What is her name—this woman who mistreated you?"

I clamp my shaking hands together. I tell myself I conquered this fear, all the years of pain at Dawson's hands, but somehow it always returns to me. Irrational and panicky.

"Her name is Cora," I say, forcing myself to breathe. "She was Andreas Dean's mate. But she abandoned both him and me the day after I was... *supposedly*... born. She's with Peter Nash now—Dawson's father."

Ford purses his lips. Then shakes his head. "I've heard of her, but I haven't met her."

"But you *have* met Dawson," I say. "You sent him after Tristan's pack. And after *me*."

Ford's eyes narrow to glittering crimson strips. "I didn't send him after you, Tessa. Dawson was a convenient diversion so that Brynjar and Silas could break into Tristan's territory. I convinced Baxter Griffin that my men could go with Dawson that night to assist him."

My thoughts churn for the thousandth time. "The attacks on Tristan's pack were a diversionary tactic?"

"For me, they were," Ford says. "For Baxter, they were an act of revenge."

Again, I stare. My voice becomes a cautious whisper. "You're playing the wolf shifters off against each other. Maintaining the war between them. Just like you're playing the witches. Aren't you?"

"A war wolf without a war is not a wolf," Ford says.

Looking at him now is like watching a ghost emerge from the shadows. He must have lurked behind every act of aggression Baxter's pack committed on Tristan's pack, encouraging and enflaming the violence.

"Why did you need a diversion?" I ask. "What was your real target?"

Ford clears his throat as he reaches for my arm and urges me to continue walking, leaving the shadow of the tree. "A year ago, I found out that an object of great value may be hidden in the library near Tristan's home. It's an object that is impossible to retrieve in my wolf form. I finally persuaded Baxter to attack the heart of Tristan's territory so that I could reach the library in my human form. Unfortunately, Tristan got in the way that day. You prevented the second attempt."

Unfortunately? Baxter and Dawson had nearly killed Becca and Carly, two shifter girls, that day—both of them young and innocent. And Ford had incited them to do it.

I clamp down on my returning rage as memories flash back to me of how frightened and hurt the girls were, how desperate Tristan was to save them—desperate enough to break the lock Helen had placed on Hidden House. I remember looking down on the city from Tristan's penthouse window when he told me not to be fooled by how peaceful it looked—that Baxter and Dawson had attacked two blocks down, right outside the library. And then... on the night Dawson attacked again near the bridge, I demanded to know what he was doing there, and he said...

I'm here to borrow a book from the library.

"You want a book."

THIS BROKEN WOLF

Ford inhales sharply. "Dawson must be smarter than he appears. I take it he talked."

There's a question in Ford's statement—he wants to know what Dawson said to me that night—but I don't answer it. "Why do you need this particular book?"

"It's the book of old magic stolen from the Spire," my father says. "I've been searching for centuries, chasing breadcrumbs around the world. That book contains the secrets of old magic. *Our secrets.* In the wrong hands, it could end us."

I shiver as a cloud stretches across the sun, casting us into sudden shadow. The air smells like rain again. "Then we need it," I say.

"It will also tell me everything I need to know about Cerberus and how to end him once and for all," Ford says.

I suppress another shiver, but this time, it's sudden and undeniable anticipation, not fear.

If the book of old magic can tell us everything there is to know about Cerberus, then it could also tell me how to save him. This book that Ford has been desperately trying to retrieve could hold the answers I need. Answers to change Tristan's fate. To defeat the Deceiver, Coward, and Killer. To stop the three-headed wolf once and for all. But not in the way Ford wants.

All this time, the book was a mere two blocks from Tristan's home. All the answers I need so close to where I was.

If I can convince Ford that I'm on his side—help him get the book—then I'll have what I need to save Tristan.

I continue walking, continue taking deep breaths, focusing on the movement of my feet.

"You formed a bond with Tristan Masters," Ford says, but I'm prepared for where he will take our conversation next. He has shocked and surprised me at every turn this morning, but now I can read his intentions clearly.

"When your human heart ruled your mind, you were willing to sacrifice your freedom for Tristan," he continues. "I understand the power of attachment. But…"

His lips stretch into his most fatherly smile, his head tilted, eyes soft and sad, as if he understands what it means to give up something you want. And maybe he does. He says he can't feel love, but he must have come close or he wouldn't hate my biological mother so vehemently for keeping me from him.

"You know about your power and your heritage now," he says. "Every descendant of Cerberus is a threat to us—one of the few creatures of old magic who can kill our wolves."

He takes my hands. "I've told you everything I know about your mother. I've opened your mind to your power. You *must* believe me now: Tristan Masters is our enemy."

I raise my chin and continue to hide my emotions. I need my father to believe that I'm willing to kill Tristan get the book.

"I saw into Tristan's heart," I say. "He wants to kill me. But I will kill him first. For both of us." I curl my fingers around my father's. "The book will tell me how."

Ford closes his eyes, exhales a relieved sound, and nods his head. "Remember what you are, Tessa. You are violence begging to be unleashed. All you have to do is whisper inducements into the ears of the willing and they will follow their instincts to an end of your making. You must destroy Tristan before he destroys us."

Turning my face up to my father's, I ask, "How can I meet your expectations? I have so much to learn."

He scratches his chin. "Help me with this next batch of fighters I'm sending to Mother Lavinia. Prove yourself to me, Tessa. When the time is right, I'll send you back to Tristan. You will make sure he trusts you. Then you will retrieve the book from the library and we'll have the answers we need to end him."

Back to Tristan... where all the answers I need are waiting.

My heart feels lighter, a dangerous hope rising inside me. As long as I play his game, my father will send me right back to Tristan, where I want to go.

"I won't fail," I say.

CHAPTER THIRTEEN

We continue along the path around the perimeter near the trees until we reach a second path that cuts back to the combat area where the leopard shifters were training.

As I draw nearer to the combat area, it's apparent that the fighters have changed. The leopard shifters remain standing in a loose arc around the edge of the grassed area while Perla paces inside the circle they form.

She grips her dagger, spinning it around and around in her fist. The texture of her skin changes, glistening in the shadows of the growing clouds above us as she ripples in and out of her shifts, her leopard's spots manifesting and fading in turns.

Inside the combat area, three women spar with each other.

The glow of power around each of them is different, which means they're from different species, but I'm still learning how to identify them.

The women wear tank tops and tight sports shorts, showing off their muscled arms and legs, but it's the muzzles around their mouths that really draw my attention. The muzzles are made of shaped leather that sits beneath their noses, obscuring their mouths in a way that will prevent them from biting. The contraptions have holes along the surface so the women can breathe, with straps that tie around the backs of their heads. My focus flashes to the metal cuffs hugging the women's wrists and ankles—along with the gloves they're wearing. The tops of the gloves are tucked tightly beneath the cuffs around their wrists so it would be difficult to remove them.

They must be the three female prisoners Perla mentioned yesterday.

While the muzzles will prevent biting, the gloves will stop them from using their claws—assuming they have claws.

Aware of Ford's gaze on me, I slow my pace to consider the prisoners carefully. I know nothing about them, who they are, what they've done in their lives, or how they came to be here.

"These are the prisoners you want me to help with?" I ask my father, keeping my voice low.

He leans toward me as we come to a stop just outside the line of guards. His speech is equally quiet. "If you can convince Perla to let you help."

There's a challenge in his gleaming eyes and I'm not sure how to read it.

Watching the prisoners fight, I assess their strength and balance. They are all clearly trained already, fighters in some way or another. They're also already bloodied, bearing split skin across their arms and legs, including what appear to be recently healed wounds, perhaps from a previous fight.

Any two of them could easily gang up on the third, but they don't, which I find interesting.

They are nearly equally matched, but the smallest woman is the fiercest. She has golden flaxen hair streaked with pink highlights, which is tied back in braids. Her skin is bronzed and she wears a tattoo of a snarling lion across her upper arm, the image of the beast's mane swirling across her skin. It's impossible to see the shape of her face beneath her muzzle, but the tattoo is a giveaway. She has to be a lion shifter.

The tallest woman has silver hair, hanging loose beneath the back of her muzzle. Her eyes are the palest blue, her skin alabaster, the glow around her an icy white, but she doesn't wear a tattoo that allows me to quickly identify her power.

The third woman has olive skin, the darkest brown hair and dark-brown eyes that match. While the lioness is fierce, and the silver-haired woman is athletic, the woman with the dark brown eyes is lithe, her movements fluid as she evades more often than she strikes.

My attention is drawn back to Perla when she screams at them from the side. "You will fight until you bleed!"

I blink as she darts between them, spinning from one to the other, deftly avoiding their fight while nicking their bodies with her knife.

A cut to an arm. A shallow slash to a thigh.

The women flinch but don't scream, and I sense the force of will it takes for them to stay focused on each other.

My blood boils.

I mistook the bleeding wounds on their arms and legs as injuries they'd inflicted on each other. Now I see that Perla is trying to enrage them, the same way you would provoke an otherwise peaceful animal to fight.

This is not training. It's fucking barbaric.

Just when the silver-haired woman is about to defend herself against a punch from the lioness, Perla swipes the prisoner's feet out from under her, knocking her to the ground. The woman quickly rolls out of the way as Perla stomps her foot right where the woman's head was.

"You will keep on fighting until I say it's enough!" Perla screams as she resumes pacing around them again, twisting her dagger in her hands.

The lioness makes a swift move on the woman with silver hair, spinning behind her and kicking the back of her knee to force her to the ground. At the same time, the lioness defends against a hit to her temple from the brown-eyed woman, deflecting the blow with her forearm and landing two quick jabs with her right hand to the brown-eyed woman's ribs that knock her backward. The lioness does it all while gripping the silver-haired woman's neck, keeping her pinned on her knees.

Perla darts forward just as the lion shifter swings her fist back for a knock-out blow to the silver-haired woman's head.

Attacking from behind, Perla's knife slices once again across the lion shifter's upper arm—the one without the tattoo—leaving another shallow cut behind.

The lion shifter screams with rage. I'm surprised, since she's been cut several times already but has swallowed her cries until now.

I lean forward, watching closely as Perla steps back.

The silver-haired woman suddenly drops her weight and pulls the lion shifter into a roll that takes them both to the feet of one of the watching guards.

The guard hustles out of the way, growling at the two women. "Get the fuck back!"

The two prisoners jump to their feet, but instead of attacking each other, they leap at the guard.

My eyes widen at their coordinated move.

The silver-haired woman's fist collides with the guard's neck in a quick jab while the lion shifter steals the dagger resting at the guard's waist. The silver-haired woman attacks the nearest guards, dropping two of them with her fists in quick succession, but the lioness twists, dagger in her fist, and runs at Perla.

The dark-eyed prisoner is a couple of steps ahead of the lioness, timing her run at Perla.

The brown-eyed woman screams with rage.

My lips part in anticipation. She's the distraction, creating a visual barrier between herself and the lioness who charges up behind her.

I hold my breath at the sheer courage of the move.

The dark-eyed woman leaps at Perla, grabs Perla's dagger arm, succeeding in wrenching it behind her just as the lion shifter darts forward, legs pumping. The lioness leaps, her dagger perfectly aimed to slam it through Perla's throat and kill her—

The lioness screams, yanked to a stop midair as if she hit an invisible wall. Light flashes around the cuffs on her wrists and ankles, wrenching them together behind her back before she drops to the ground. Her wrists end up bound together along with her ankles, her limbs pulled together so that she lands heavily in a hog-tied position. The dagger she was holding jolts from her clenched fist and floats up into the air above her as she screams through her muzzle.

At the same time, the dark-eyed woman reaches desperately for the dagger Perla grips before the woman is also flung backward. Her wrists and ankles snap together as she flies into the ground. Her head hits first and she sags against the grass, unconscious.

Silas steps through the doorway at the base of the tower, his hand casually raised as he strides from the dais and down the stairs. Both Brynjar and Cody have remained on the dais, but they've both moved toward the fight, stopping when Silas passes them.

I feel the burn of Cody's focus, as if he reads my mind and he's silently telling me not to follow my instincts.

Perla swings on Silas with a snarl when he reaches her. "I had it under control!" she says.

"You didn't," he replies, a blunt rebuke. "These ones are high-spirited—"

"That's what Mother Lavinia wants!"

"She won't want them if she can't control them," Silas says, light glowing around the edges of his eyepatch. I picture the orb beneath it, swirling with magic that continues to bind the women's hands and ankles behind their backs, leaving them completely unable to defend themselves. Only the silver-haired woman remains unbound, but she crouches in the center of the combat area on her own now, chest heaving, her anxious gaze passing across the other two prisoners.

As Perla and Silas continue to trade words, I consider my father's challenge, meeting his eyes where he stands beside me. He returns my gaze, impassive, uncaring of the women.

He wants me to train them, but he told me I would first have to go through Perla. I also hear Brynjar's warning inside my mind that I need to show Perla her place sooner rather than later.

These three woman were incredibly brave to try to overpower her. They must have known they wouldn't get far and wouldn't get away, but they were willing to work together to end her.

Perla's training method consists of inflicting pain, not creating skill. I don't know if she chose her life or was forced into it, but I can't let any uncertainty stop me now.

It's time for me to bite.

Slipping between the guards, I release my wolf, her fur rippling through blue-black to the darkest charcoal. Together, we prowl toward the woman with the silver hair.

I bend to her, catching her muzzled chin in my hand, holding tightly. She could be an ice witch, but her musky-sweet scent makes me think she's also a shifter.

She gasps, her eyes widening, her focus flickering from me to my wolf and back again. The tension around her eyes increases, fear tightening her features as she sucks air into her chest, heaving against the muzzle.

It hits me hard—twists my heart—that she's afraid of me. More fearful than she is of Perla. I guess she recognizes that I am like Ford, and he is to be feared.

I won't look like a friend.

"I suggest you stay here," I murmur to her before I glide to my feet.

My boots are whisper quiet in the grass as I rapidly cross the distance to the lion shifter's position on the ground. The dagger that she stole taunts her, floating tip down beside her face. The muscles in her arms and legs strain as she struggles to break free from the magic holding the cuffs together.

She fell only a few paces away from where Perla and Silas continue to argue, now trading insults, their voices rising, but I sense they will be done with their conversation soon.

I need to act fast.

I approach from behind the lioness and crouch at her side without touching her, keeping Perla in my sights. She glances my way but dismisses my presence at the lion shifter's side.

She *still* doesn't recognize the threat I pose to her.

With a firm hand, I take hold of the back of the cuffs keeping the lioness tied.

Silas's magic dissolves at my touch.

The lioness startles as her hands and feet are freed, glancing back at me, her eyes partially shifted, irises golden and lashes dark.

I incline my head from the dagger to Perla with an arched eyebrow, as if to say: *Now's your chance. Will you take it?*

The lioness's eyebrows draw down, determined. She doesn't hesitate. Snatching the dagger from the air at her side, she propels herself forward with an animal roar. She can't get enough height from her current position, but she rams the dagger into Perla's thigh.

Perla screams. Her eyes fly wide with shock.

She reacts reflexively with a fist to the lioness's head, followed by a knee to her chin that knocks the lioness out and flips her onto her back.

Perla's shout turns into a furious howl of pain as she wrenches the dagger out of her thigh. She partially shifts, her leopard's skin glowing. She aims a savage kick with her good leg at the unconscious lioness's head—so close to where I crouch that she nearly kicks me instead.

She really should have thought it through.

I grab Perla's foot before it can meet its mark and sweep her off her feet with my upward momentum. My fist darts down at the same time, smacking into her stomach and winding her as she falls onto her back.

She stares up at me for a beat as my second fist descends. With a gasp for breath, she rolls to the side before I can crack her cheekbone.

My hand hits the grass instead, but I rise slowly as she backs away from me.

"Tessa." Perla spits, gripping her side where I struck her. Her fingernails sharpen into short, leopard claws. "You don't want to challenge me."

"This is not a challenge," I say, prowling after her so that she is forced to move farther away from the lioness. "A challenge would mean I thought you were worth fighting. This is a lesson."

She backs into clear ground while I advance on her.

The leopard shifters around the edges shuffle where they stand, uncertainty flashing across their faces. They would be used to taking orders from Perla and attacking any prisoner who causes trouble.

But I am a different creature with a different place in my father's world. My wolf darts toward any who look like they're about to make a move, ensuring none of them try to get in my way. Their gazes flick back and forth between Perla and me—and then across to Ford, who remains at the edge of the group.

I'm aware of the lioness groaning as she wakes up. With a glance back at me, she crawls as fast as she can to the brown-eyed woman, who is still bound and cuffed but is also regaining consciousness. The silver-haired woman hesitates only another beat before she races across the clearing to her friends.

Behind them, Silas takes a careful step back, also looking to Ford.

Closer to the tower, Brynjar has stepped to the front of the dais and Cody has descended to the bottom of the steps, but he stops when I give him a quick shake of my head.

I turn to Ford. I need him to know that I will obey him. He has the final say here.

He folds his arms across his chest and gives me a nod.

I have his consent.

What I choose to do next will take me one step closer to Tristan.

"Perla," I say, removing my boots and beginning to unbutton my shirt. "You will fight until you bleed."

CHAPTER FOURTEEN

"You first," Perla snarls.

She yanks off her boots and weapon belt, dropping them to the ground before removing her pants and shirt. She nearly rips through her clothing by shifting before she's even fully removed the garments. I recognize the strategy behind the quickness of her movements. She's trying to hide the wound in her thigh. It's bleeding—and quite a bit—which makes it a significant liability to her right now.

If I were the one injured, I'm sure she'd take advantage of it, but I want to beat her without availing myself of her existing weakness.

Like most shifters, she isn't afraid to strip naked in front of everyone before she shifts completely into her leopard form. Her leopard form is bulky, bigger than I was expecting with tawny fur, like her hair, and spots that are rimmed in dark brown.

My feet sink into the soft grass. It's perfectly moist from what must have been a rain shower in the night or early morning. It will help with traction. I take another beat to remove my shirt and pants, remaining in my underwear as I circle around Perla while her cat hisses at me.

I've never pulled my wolf back to me and at the same time

shifted completely into her shape before. We need to merge completely, and it doesn't look like Perla is going to give me time to complete the task.

She leaps at me, her back legs bunched and claws outstretched, aiming for my human heart and going straight for the kill.

My wolf's energy rushes back to me, streaming into my body in a massive hit. At the same time, my power explodes inside me like a bomb I didn't know I'd set alight. In less than a beat, I fill the shape of my wolf, shifting completely and leaving my clothing behind. Crimson fire fills my vision and Perla's attack is reduced to shades of energy. Her beating heart seems so fragile, pounding rapidly within her ribcage. Her muscles, claws, teeth, torso—every part of her body—appears weak to me as I rise up in a rush of power.

I bat at her attack, my paw slashing at her front leg as it reaches me first. My back legs bunch, my reflexes hammering at a speed that makes her oncoming wrath seem slow.

Leaping at her, I spread my claws and swipe them across her exposed stomach, only making shallow cuts before I retract my claws and use the full force of my shoulder to knock her to the side.

Her scream splits my hearing.

She contorts midair and hits the ground with a *thud*. She paws at the ground, trying to get up, her legs churning before she finally makes it to her feet.

She hisses at me and I wait for her to make a decision.

She could yield, but... she doesn't.

Racing at me, she veers off to the side, headed for her discarded daggers, shifting rapidly into her human form to snatch them up. She spins, crouches, and throws them at me.

I dodge each one as I prowl toward her, snapping my jaws at her. She shifts again into her leopard form, but the flow of her energy is sluggish in my vision.

Before she can complete the shift, I leap at her, my claws extended.

This time, I separate my human form from my wolf, timing my own shift perfectly.

My solid human weight knocks into her chest, shoving her onto the ground where she lands on her back. At the same time that I pin her with my human body, my wolf's form lands half across her chest, resting on the ground perpendicular to her body where its claws can hook into her beating heart.

Her eyes are beyond wide, her face draining of all color.

She screams with pure agony. It's the same sound I made when the jotunn took hold of me and it chills me, but I close my ears to it, listening only to the violent rage storming inside me.

Perla thrashes against me, mindless thrashing, but I punch her shoulders, keeping her down. I'm vaguely aware of my father running at the side of the combat area, following our fight. He stops only a few paces away from us and leans forward in anticipation as I strike her cheek, keeping her down and extending her pain.

I am violence begging to be unleashed.

"You will fight until I say it's enough," I snarl at her.

"Tessa!" Cody's shout cuts through my rage.

My head snaps up to find him standing at an equal distance from me as my father is.

Cody's face is as bloodless as Perla's. His eyes are wide, his lips pressed together. In my crimson rage, I can feel his pain, the memory of *my* screams. "Tessa. Stop."

Silas hovers close behind him. The warlock's hands are raised in Cody's direction and the power growing around him makes my heart sink. If Cody tries to get in my way—if he tries to counteract my father's commands—then Silas will kill him.

On my left, my father's lips part. He is about to speak and I anticipate what he's going to say. He's going to command me to kill Perla. He will tell me he wants me to take her place.

At the same time, I sense his power curling around my wolf—a tentative touch. He's preparing in case I relent and release her. If I choose to give her mercy—if I show any sign of listening to Cody—Ford will seize my wolf.

If my father forces my actions, I will lose the power that I need to gain. I need to show him that I am not merciful, make him believe I prefer torture to death.

The temptation to give in to the darkness once and for all is nearly overpowering, but I won't become a killer at his command. I will only act according to my own will.

Perla's last dagger lies on the grass within reaching distance. Snatching it up with a scream that drowns out my father's voice, I drive the dagger at Perla's face, stopping its downward trajectory just before it reaches her rapidly blinking eye.

Her sobs break the thick silence that descends around us.

My father's hold on my wolf loosens but doesn't break completely.

"What do you think, Silas?" I call to the warlock. "Can she manage without an eye?"

I raise my head to stare at Silas. He's wearing all black today, his hair slicked back, a tall and somehow gaunt figure. I beat him badly on the helipad, forced him to use much of the magic stored in the orb he carries with him. I wonder if he's still recovering his energy.

He glares at me but steps away from Cody.

Ignoring Perla as she writhes beneath me, I turn my attention to my father, making sure he feels he has control of this situation, that my scream to drown him out before was inadvertent. "Are you pleased with my strength, Father?"

He waits a beat, looking down at Perla, extending her agony. Finally, I sense his power retreat completely from my wolf.

"I am," he says.

Returning my attention to Perla, I keep the dagger above her face while I ease my wolf from her body, withdrawing my claw from her heart. She cries with relief as my energy releases her, her eyes streaming with tears. Some enemies, if left alive, will strike back, but Perla's spirit is open to me in my crimson vision. Her most basic instinct is survival at all costs.

She won't try to come after me. She understands that will only get her killed.

While my wolf takes up position beside us, I seize Perla's chin in my hand and lower my voice. "Listen to me carefully. I will train the fighters from now on. You will continue to do whatever my father asks you to do, but you won't get in my way. Understood?"

She makes a strangled sound that I assume means 'yes.'

Releasing her and rising to my feet, still butt-naked, I keep hold of the dagger and wait for her to get up.

Perla wobbles, pressing her hand to her heart as she turns onto her side and pushes up onto her hands and knees. Her eyes are bloodshot and her skin remains pale. When I take a step toward her, she flinches, her hand flying up in a defensive gesture. She reaches for her clothing as she hurries to make it back to her feet on her own.

One of the female guards standing behind Ford snickers as she watches Perla struggle to make it the rest of the way up.

With a snarl, I spin to the woman and storm toward her, forcing her to back up so fast that she trips and lands on her backside.

She lets out a scream as I loom over her. Quickly hunching her shoulders, she bows her head in a submissive gesture as best she can while she sits on the ground.

I shout at the guards. "Perla lasted longer than any of you would have. She is your superior, but now she answers to me. Do you understand?"

They are quiet.

"Do you fucking understand?" I roar.

They break into snarls, their eyes lighting up, screaming back at me. "*Yes, mistress.*"

"Good," I say. "Now get back to work."

Once they disperse, I take a deep breath, clench my fist around the dagger, and stride to my clothing. Quickly scooping it up, I return the dagger to my weapon belt, and pull everything back on.

My damn hands are shaking.

Ford thinks he broke my humanity in the tower, but echoes remain, deep echoes that remind me I have a mind and a heart.

I am not only made of the impulses that storm my body.

Tristan's voice returns to me and I miss a step. *My impulses are nothing without actions.*

Regaining my composure, I stride directly toward the prisoners. The lioness and silver-haired woman stand protectively on either side of the dark-eyed woman, who remains bound by magic on the ground. They tense as I approach. Nothing I can do or say to them will make them trust me—and they shouldn't. All I need is for them to follow my orders. I'm determined that they'll live. I don't care who they are or what they've done. Every woman has the right to determine her own fate.

I swiftly bend to the dark-eyed woman, releasing the magic that binds her. She rolls swiftly away from me before leaping to her feet, immediately on her guard.

I'm conscious of my father's scrutiny as he continues to watch me interact with them. My expression is hard as I address the women. "You will be sold to the witch named Mother Lavinia. Your future is set and can't be changed. Don't try to fight it. But if you want to survive, you will do exactly as I tell you. Brynjar will fetch you at sunrise tomorrow morning and bring you here for training. Until then, you will rest and eat."

Raising my hand, I call Brynjar over to me. "These women belong to me now. Make sure they get safely back to their cells. Give them the same food you bring me. I want them to have clean clothing and bandages for their wounds. They must be strong and fit. I'm determined that Mother Lavinia will pay more for them than she's ever paid."

Hopefully in her own blood.

"I'm determined to make my father happy," I say.

Brynjar gives me a nod, but I catch his arm before he turns away. "I'm returning to my room now and I don't want to be disturbed until it's time for dinner. I'm still adjusting to my new power."

"Of course," he says.

Turning away from him, I seek my father where he stands nearby. I raise my chin and wait for him to respond.

He considers me for a moment, lips pursed before he gives me a cold smile.

With a quick nod of acknowledgement, I call my wolf back to me, reuniting her with my human form. Her body glides into mine, a seamless action before I stride back to the dais, ignoring Silas on the way.

I meet Cody at the bottom of the steps. I can't tell if the tension around his mouth and eyes is concern... or anger. *Deep anger.*

"Not a word," I snap. "Unless you want me to hurt you."

He presses his lips together and follows me into the Spire's entry room. I take the sapphire staircase situated to the far right. Even though it bypasses many of the floors, it still lets out two floors below the fifteenth, which leaves us in tense silence for longer as we ascend.

My hands won't stop shaking and my heart is beating too fast. With every step I take, my heart pumps harder inside my chest, a quickening hammer until I'm audibly hauling in my breaths by the time we reach my room.

I race into it, causing the room to transform from a dusty, bare space into a bedroom I don't belong in. Even though it's daytime, the ceiling is darker than it was last night, the window obscured by a black screen, not a spot of sunlight gleaming through. Even the fireplace is dark, only a soft lamp sitting on the mantelpiece providing light around us.

I have barely enough rational thought left to release my wolf to guard the corridor before I swivel to the wall directly beside the door and press my back against it, trying to center myself in space and time. Sweat drips down my face, my body overheating by a thousand degrees. My shirt and pants cling to me as I gasp for breath. Bracing against the wall, I rip off my boots, hoping that will cool me down.

Cody keeps his distance, but it seems he's done being silent. "Tessa?" His voice is sharp. Angry. "What the hell was that?"

I don't answer him. Can't answer.

"You could have killed that woman."

"Which one?" I cry. "I could have killed all of them. Or gotten them killed. You could have been killed too."

Panic attack. I'm having a panic attack.

"Fuck!" I slide down the wall. "I can't do this. I thought I could, but I can't."

I press my hands to my stomach and bring my knees to my chest, trying to squeeze myself into the smallest space possible.

My hands are shaking so hard that they rattle against my legs and I can't fucking make them stop. I try to compress myself, try to hold my edges together and not fall apart. I hear Tristan's voice over and over. *Fight it, Tessa. You're strong enough to fight it.*

But I'm not.

"I am anger lingering in the mind," I whisper, rocking back and forth. "I am revenge growing inside the heart... I will taste the blood of gods... and defy them..."

"Tessa?" Cody lowers himself carefully, reaching out for me, his hand sliding between my back and the wall, curling around me.

"I'm not strong enough." I gasp. *"I'm not, I'm not, I'm not..."*

Very carefully, he hooks his other arm beneath my knees, pulling me into his arms and away from the wall. I'm sweating so much that my hair is slick against my face, my palm leaving a print against his shirt as I lean into him.

Quietly, he carries me to the bath, pausing beside it only to ditch his boots before he steps right into it and lowers us both in. It's full of cool, fresh water—the shocking beauty of old magic that reads my emotions and provides for me like Hidden House did.

Tears spill from my eyes and suddenly I'm sobbing, gasping in every breath and crying every exhale. Ford tried to break me when I was in chains, but I stayed whole. I thought only Tristan could break me—and maybe one day he will. But it turns out that I might break myself first by willingly walking down a path to malice and pain.

Without speaking, Cody has settled in behind me, extending his legs on either side of mine so that my back presses to his chest. I sense him move carefully behind me as I continue to cry. One of his arms leaves me to reach back before he returns and immerses two small cloths in the water in front of me. He sweeps my hair to the side without forcing me to move in any way, working with my hunched posture to press one of the cold cloths to the back of my neck.

Gently and slowly, he uses the second cloth to wipe the edges of my face as far as he can reach, cooling my cheeks and chin before pressing the cloth to my hair and wiping down the strands to cool my head.

He doesn't try to wipe my tears, doesn't try to stop my crying. Doesn't say anything or ask me anything.

He rinses the cloth that he placed on my neck when it gets warm, cooling it and putting it back again. He continues doing this until my sobs finally stop, my body is cool again, and the silence between us is broken only by the soft lap of water at the sides of the bath.

I never dreamed that I would ever be so vulnerable in front of Cody Griffin. Or that he would respond in the way that he has.

I exhale quietly. Tristan kept so much from me. He didn't ask for help, and it only led to pain and damage. I can't make the same mistake. I can't do this alone.

I have to take a chance…

"Are we enemies?" I ask.

Cody remains quiet behind me.

I give him time. I need truth, not a kneejerk response.

"No," he says.

I close my eyes, quietly releasing my held breath. "Do you want me in your bed?"

His response is faster this time. "My wolf did."

I consider the distinction between himself and his wolf. "What about you?"

He leans forward a little, pressing his cheek to mine from behind. "I can't answer that question."

"Can't or won't?"

"Won't." He hesitates another beat and then he sighs quietly. "We don't need that sort of complication right now."

"But last night—"

"Last night was me fucking things up again," he says. His forehead creases at the corner of my vision.

"You said I shouldn't trust you." I squeeze my eyes closed, feeling like I'm stepping onto the thin branch of a Spire-height tree that extends out above ocean rocks. "But I need someone to trust. Can I trust you, Cody?"

He is quiet again. For a really long time.

Just when I think he's not going to respond—that I've made a terrible mistake—he says, "I've lost my wolf. I shouldn't be alive. I don't know if any minute will be my last."

He leans back, running his hand through his wet hair. This time, I swivel to face Cody, my movement causing liquid to slosh around us. Droplets of water run down the side of his face past his hickory-brown eyes and catch in the growth across his jaw.

"Fuck, Tessa," he says, drawing his hand down the strands of my hair, his thumb grazing my cheek. "Even if I don't die, there's a significant chance that I'll lose my shit in a bad way. I nearly did last night."

His lips form an intense line. "Tristan doesn't have a monopoly on savage behavior. You saw what my wolf was capable of. I nearly killed you with a fucking axe. That's a mere glimpse of the darkness I could descend into if my mind breaks because I've lost my wolf."

"Then we'll stop each other," I say, pressing my palm to his chest over his heart as I turn to face him completely. "The same way I'll stop Tristan."

Cody's dark gaze passes from my eyes to my hand pressed against his chest. "How?"

"By finding an answer."

"And if the answer can't be found?"

It can. Somewhere in Hidden House, there's an answer to Cody's lost wolf. I'm sure of it. If I can trust him enough to take him there.

"I promise I'll end you before you hurt anyone you love," I say.

He nods once before pressing his palm to the side of my face. "You can trust me."

Wrapping his arms around me, he pulls us both upright, balancing us carefully so we can climb out of the bath safely.

We separate then, turning our backs to peel off our wet clothing and dry ourselves off. I reach for the T-shirt I wore last night, pulling it on to find Cody standing with the towel slung around his hips, giving his clothing choices a disgruntled look. He only has the second set of clothing that Brynjar brought him this morning.

I bite my lip. "I won't think you're being impolite if you need to sleep only in your underwear."

His lips rise into a grin that lights up his eyes. "I usually sleep naked. Last night was an exception."

I clear my throat. "Consider underwear compulsory."

"As you command."

It's only early afternoon, but I head straight for the bed and crawl onto it.

Cody slips in behind me—wearing underwear—and reaches across me to pull the blanket over from the other side, wrapping us both in a cocoon.

He settles in behind me, pressing a kiss to the back of my neck like he did last night.

"What do I need to know?" he asks.

Starting slowly, I tell him everything from the start of my life up to now; everything I know and all the things I can guess. I tell him that as long as I prove myself, Ford will send me back to Tristan so I can steal the book of old magic.

The only thing I leave out is Hidden House and all of the women there. I want to tell him about Ella, but that would reveal the whereabouts of many other women whose lives need to be protected. I don't have the right to make that decision. Only Helen does.

At the end of the story, I yawn but fight my exhaustion, desperately trying to keep my eyes open. He must have questions. I certainly do.

"How the hell did my fake mother fake a pregnant belly?" I ask.

"Maybe she didn't." Cody exhales softly against the back of my neck, his arms tightening around me. His voice is low, a depth of pain in it that I haven't heard him express before. "Female wolf shifters often miscarry. My mother lost two cubs between me and Cameron. Obviously, I wasn't old enough to understand her pain at the time, but she mourns the anniversaries every year."

My eyes burn with sudden tears as he falls silent for a moment.

"She lost two daughters. I lost two sisters," he says. "Losing Ella after that nearly killed Mom."

I pull his arms closer around me. "I'm sorry for your loss, Cody. I didn't have a chance to say that before, but I mean it."

He clears his throat, but he still sounds strained when he speaks. "I'm not saying it happened in Cora Dean's case, but if the timing matched, it's an answer to your question."

An awful, painful answer. If Cora lost her cub and was asked to raise me instead... she wouldn't have been able to mourn or recover emotionally. And then, I was *me*. Different and unexplainable. It doesn't excuse the way she treated me, though.

"I still don't know how Andreas crossed paths with my birth mother," I say. "She was an assassin located in the Eastern Lowland. I only have pieces of the puzzle and I can't see it clearly..." My voice trails off as a powerful yawn overtakes me.

Cody is quiet for another beat, but I don't think much about it because he's been taking his time speaking and I'm okay with that. "Keeping your wolf awake all night is exhausting you," he says.

"She needs to keep watch. Keep us safe..."

"I don't know much about your power, Tessa, but every alpha needs to recharge. You can't keep her awake all day, as well as all night. You need to let her sleep at some point. While we're awake."

My protest is smothered by another yawn. I can barely keep my eyes open now. "I need her to watch my back."

"You have me," he says, quietly.

I force my eyes open as I consider his offer.

He told me we aren't enemies. He told me I can trust him.

"Okay, then," I say.

CHAPTER FIFTEEN

My human form sleeps, but my wolf form is awake. Cody wants me to rest my mind during the day, but that doesn't count when my human form needs protection so she can sleep.

I must remain awake and alert to protect myself.

Quietly rising from the floor outside the opaque doorway, I prowl across the corridor to the room opposite my bedroom, treading lightly in the dust that has gathered over untold years.

I didn't dare stray from my bedroom doorway last night, but today, I edge closer to the room that sits across the corridor.

The writing carved into the floor within its doorway tempts me to enter it.

The Near-Apart Room.

Expanding my senses, I remain alert for any sound or movement along the corridor, using my crimson vision to see through the stone floor and distinguish the power of the supernaturals on the level below me. I've been worried about someone spying on me by being cloaked in one of Silas's spells, but I can sense his presence two levels down, where he's working on a spell right now. I can distinguish the sparks of his power, and I'm confident I will recognize his power if someone attempts to approach under a spell of invisibility.

Sniffing at the writing on the floor, I inhale the scent of ice and snow. I recoil a little, reminded of Brynjar's power, but this scent doesn't seem magical. More like real ice.

Edging closer, I peer inside the room.

It's as bare as my bedroom appeared at first, a large window on the left-hand side allowing the early afternoon sunlight to stream inside. It's lined with wood instead of bare stone. Cobwebs float across the ceiling, the floor is covered in dust, but writing is scratched across the wall opposite me.

The writing is jagged, gouged into the wall as if by a dagger, a sequence of sentences forming a rough spiral from the center of the wall down to the floor. Every sentence appears to be written in a different hand, but each is a question.

Where are you? Why did you leave? Who took you? Why didn't you come back? How did you die?

It's painful to read. Like I'm listening to the cries of different voices calling to lost loved ones, asking for answers that won't come.

Stepping into the room, I expect it to transform like my bedroom did.

Nothing happens. Unless I count the dust bunnies that float into my nose. I sneeze into the quiet, a weird sound to my wolf ears.

Warily crossing to the other side of the room, I follow the gouged questions from the center all the way to the floor. Maybe I have to write my own question before the room will answer me?

I shudder away from the wall. I have too many questions, but if this room is a place to seek answers about loved ones—or maybe to mourn them—then there's only one question I could write.

Only one scream into the dark that might give me enough peace about Tristan so that I can keep going.

Even if I wasn't afraid to ask it, I can't make a mark on the wall or the floor in my wolf form. My paws barely disturb the layers of dust, let alone scratch anything.

Backing away from the room and through the doorway, I consider the layers of grit across the floor. Nobody has set foot in this room for a long time—except perhaps my father in his wolf form, but he would have had the same experience as me. Nothing would have happened for him.

He hasn't released his wolf since the fight on the helipad. Come to think of it... Tristan injured him. I wonder if Ford is nursing wounds he doesn't want anyone to know about. I've been in fights where my human form has been hurt, but this was a fight between Ford's wolf and Tristan's wolf. The wounds might not show up on his human body.

Returning to the doorway into my bedroom, I keep watch over the corridor until the light fades outside and I sense Brynjar approaching from the level down, bringing food to us again.

I duck my head inside the bedroom and growl a sharp warning to my human form, satisfied when she stirs beneath the covers.

Cody surprises me by waking up faster this time. Definitely not a morning person but certainly an evening person. He pounces on my human form like a cub, pulling her up into his arms and tangling them both in the sheets before he nudges her cheek and neck. It doesn't feel like he's making a move on me, more like he's pouncing on and playing with a close member of his pack, re-establishing a connection that's becoming closer with every hour we spend together.

This time, my human form laughs and swats at him before she leaps from the bed, but her laughter fades rapidly as she meets my eyes. Everything I've seen while she was asleep passes into her mind, immediately becoming her knowledge too.

Her gaze shifts beyond me to the doorway that leads into the Near-Apart Room. Her hand twitches in the direction of the dagger in the weapon harness she dropped to the floor—a dagger she's now determined to use to carve a question into the wall.

The question that burns in our mind and won't let go.

Is Tristan alive?

CHAPTER SIXTEEN

*D*ressing quickly, I pull my wolf back to my human body. I'm ready when Brynjar arrives with the food. Cody is a glowering sentinel at my side, his wolfish playfulness gone the moment that Brynjar appears in the doorway.

Devouring the meal while Brynjar waits, I ask him to tell me where the kitchen is—and how the hell we can get toothbrushes, deodorant, and more clothing. He takes us down the nearest sapphire staircase to the bottom of the Spire and then up another sapphire staircase to the third floor, where there are both supplies and food stores—along with a group of very cranky cooks, the kind who don't care who you are; they'll swat you with a wooden spoon if you get in their way.

We leave with more clothing, including pajamas, and the necessities for basic hygiene.

When dusk sets in, I decide to test the boundaries of my freedom by roaming each of the levels of the tower—under Brynjar's watchful eye—including inspecting the prisoners' shared cell. It's larger than the room that Cody was kept in and flanked on either side by two more cells that are currently empty. I'm satisfied that the space is generally clean and has light and fresh air.

Cody stands at my side, a step away, in exactly the right

position to watch my back like he promised. We're both dressed in black pants and khaki shirts—his a short-sleeved T-shirt that pulls across his biceps and chest, mine button-up with the sleeves rolled up.

I'm pleased to see the women now dressed in clean clothing similar to what I'm wearing, bandages visible where their sleeves are rolled up, and no chains around their wrists or ankles.

After Brynjar orders them to line up for me, he tells me, "They've been fed."

"Good." I step up to the women, looking them over. They return my gaze with varying expressions of defiance and uncertainty.

"My name is Tessa," I say. "Ford Vanguard is my father. I want your names and species."

The lioness narrows her eyes at me. Her golden flaxen hair is braided today in a way that allows the pink highlights to crisscross each other. Her snarling lion tattoo is hidden beneath her shirt. "We were told we no longer have names," she says.

I arch an eyebrow at her. "I'm only going to say this once. If I ask you a question, you will answer it. Fully and truthfully. If you lie to me, I will know, and I will react without mercy." I stop and level my gaze with each of theirs. *"Names and species."*

"I'm Reya," the lioness says, her amber eyes flashing wide with caution. "Lion."

The silver-haired woman speaks without betraying any emotion. "Neve. Snow leopard."

Hmm. That explains the icy white glow around her.

"I'm Nalani," the dark-eyed woman says, considering me warily. She was the one I interacted with least yesterday. I didn't free her during the fight like I freed Reya or speak to her like I spoke to Neve. "I'm a panther."

They're all big cats, fierce shifters. I'm used to training with a vampire and a hawk shifter. In fact, I was the one being trained. But I'll have to adjust fast when we start tomorrow. I plan to take them through the same training routine Iyana and

I started with. That way, I'll get a sense of their strengths and weaknesses first, their balance and agility. It will be trickier with three trainees because I'll have to continually swap them out, but I'll manage.

"Follow my instructions during training and you'll walk away stronger," I say to them. "Disobey me and you'll end up weaker. Understood?"

They each nod, their real feelings hidden behind masks now. I'm okay with that. Keeping them alive doesn't require friendship.

"Good. Then we'll begin tomorrow."

I'm leaving the cell with Brynjar and Cody when my father appears at the side of the corridor.

Ford prowls up to us, narrowing his eyes at Cody, who returns the stare without budging.

Fuck, Cody has balls.

"You will need to hurt them if you expect them to obey you, daughter." Ford growls at me, a challenge in his voice, his eyes glowing crimson. He's back to calling me 'daughter,' and I'm not sure whether or not I should read anything into it.

"If that's what it takes," I say, uncaring. "You can observe my methods tomorrow if you wish."

"Oh, I will," he says. "I'm always watching you, Tessa."

And now it's *Tessa*. I narrow my eyes at the veiled threat in his statement. It should probably unsettle me, but my inner darkness sparks, wanting to push back. Today, in front of all the leopard shifters, I had to be careful to make him feel in control, but now I sense an opening to push a boundary.

"How is your wolf, father?" I ask, allowing my own vision to blush crimson. I slide up to him, placing my hand on his shoulder and allowing my expression to soften, as if I'm concerned. "I haven't seen him since I arrived. I was hoping our wolves might run together."

"Indeed." He draws back. "Perhaps tomorrow."

I need to test my ability to take hold of his wolf like he can take hold of mine. Until I know whether I can do that, I will always be at a disadvantage. He will always be able to overpower me.

When Cody and I return to my bedroom, I pause in the corridor opposite the Near-Apart Room. If my father is concealing his wolf's wounds, then I need to access the Near-Apart Room sooner rather than later. He said he was watching me, but his ability to overpower me will be limited until his wolf is healed.

Cody has remained with me the whole time, watching my back like he promised. As he stops beside me, I roll my shoulders, trying to ease out my tension as I weigh up the risks of leaving Cody alone with my wolf.

"I need you to do something for me," I say. "But it comes with a risk."

"What do you need?"

"Watch the corridor with my wolf?" I ask.

Cody's forehead creases, but he follows my line of sight to the writing etched in the floor of the doorway to the Near-Apart Room. Cautiously, he peers inside the room, taking in the dust and cobwebs. His gaze lingers on the questions carved into the opposite wall, his expression becoming blank, but not before I catch the flash of pain in his eyes.

"I need to know if Tristan's alive," I say.

"Only painful questions are written on that wall, Tessa," Cody says, taking a step back. "I think whoever wrote them already knew the answers. Are you sure you want to do this?"

I grip his shoulder while I remove the dagger at my waist. "I have to know. I need you to keep watch while I'm in there. Can you do that for me?"

The crease in his forehead deepens. He blows out an exhale, his lips pressed in an unhappy line, but he gives me a brief nod. "I can."

At his agreement, I release my wolf, who immediately sets about prowling up and down the corridor, her senses alert to any risk. I've already ascertained that Brynjar isn't nearby and both Silas and Perla have avoided me since this morning.

I pause at the door, my tension rising since I can't determine where my father is. "Cody, if my father approaches while I'm in there—"

"I'm not helpless, Tessa," he says, cutting me off. "Your father's too smart to kill me while your back is turned. If he wants to end me, he'll do it at a time that has the greatest impact on you. I'm more worried about what you'll find in that room."

I shudder at Cody's prediction about my father's intentions, determined that it won't come true.

"I'll give you privacy." Cody strides away down the corridor to take up position near the top of the staircase.

My hand is sweaty around the dagger as I cross the threshold into the room. I'm not sure where to carve my question since the spiral already reaches the floor, but I kneel in the dust next to the last mark and begin there. I take note that every letter of every word carved into the wall already touches the letter before it so that they're all connected.

Dragging the dagger through the floor, I pull it over and over to make each line. It's not easy work. The floor is hardwood and every letter needs to be clear. I'm sweaty and my arms ache only halfway through, every movement of the dagger getting harder.

I remind myself that I've worked harder than this, chopping wood and lugging buckets of water up the mountain before I left.

My senses buzz with an increasing pressure around me, as if I'm now pulling the dagger against another force that is trying to stop me from finishing my question.

My exhales become heavier and my muscles scream as I pull the dagger in the curve that will complete the question mark.

I take another look at the questions before mine. The dot at the bottom of the question mark is separated from the others.

Just as I finish carving the curve of the question mark, the letters I already carved begin to fill with a glistening black substance that slowly oozes along each connected line.

A sense of dread fills me. I don't know what will happen if I don't finish the question before the liquid reaches the last mark.

Leaning back for momentum, I grip the dagger poised above the floor. I have to make this count.

With a grunt of effort, I ram the dagger into the wood. The moment it hits, the room explodes into a whirlwind around me, dust and grit rising and spinning, the wind trying to rip the dagger from my grasp.

I hold tight. With all my might, I twist the dagger from side to side to form the final circle.

Cody suddenly appears at the door, but I raise my hand to stop him from coming inside, hoping he can see my gesture through the whirling debris. *Stay back.*

He retreats just before the dust thickens and the inky substance filling my question bubbles up around the final circle. Darkness descends like shutters across the window and door, shields that increase the pressure inside my ears, telling me I'm now locked into this room. I have no idea if someone outside the room can see or hear what's going on, but my instincts tell me they can't. I can't sense any life beyond this room now.

I'm alone.

Leaving my dagger in the floor, I tip my head back, nearly choking on dust as I scream. "Tristan! Are you alive?"

The dust continues to swirl, gritty pieces that beat and scrape across my face and forearms. I throw my arm across my mouth, trying to breathe. The whirlwind becomes even angrier, like a living force that wants to answer my question, but... somehow... I haven't got it right...

My heart stills and my eyes close. I'm not asking the wrong question. I'm asking it about the wrong person.

I groan against the sudden squeezing of my heart and tip my head back again, protecting my eyes with my arm.

"Are you alive... *Deceiver, Coward, Killer?*"

The whirlwind drops. The air clears and the pressure

inside my head eases. Slowly lifting my arm away from my face, my eyes widen at where I am.

I'm standing in Tristan's penthouse, but I'm facing the wide windows where he always stood in the mornings while he connected with his pack and made sure they were safe. It's where he wanted me to stand if everything had gone according to his plan for me to take over his pack. The risk he took with his plan defies belief. He knew what I was, but he still thought his pack would be safer with me than with him. Maybe... he truly believed I could fight my fate. He told me that he doesn't have a choice about his future, but I have a choice about mine. I guess he really believed it.

I'm wearing the same clothing as I was in the Spire: boots, black pants, and my button-up khaki shirt. The elevator into his apartment is to my left, the ceiling-to-floor paintings of a forest covering the wall on either side of the elevator exactly as I remember them. Plush lounge chairs are at my back, a large rug situated on the floor between them, and the tiled kitchen sits farther to my right.

As I turn to face the room, a shiver runs down my spine, my focus drawn to the doorway into Tristan's bedroom, where a figure rises from his lean against the doorframe.

"Tessa Dean."

Tristan's deep growl makes me shiver. His muscled silhouette is clouded in the shadow of the dark bedroom before he emerges.

CHAPTER SEVENTEEN

The strands of Tristan's raven-black hair fall across his eyes, but his hair is wilder and slicked with sweat.

He's wearing the same black suit pants from the night we parted, but they're torn at the knee and unbuttoned and unzipped at the top, barely hanging on to his hips.

His chin is shadowed with longer growth than the last time I saw him and his shoulders are hunched, his biceps bulging, arms corded with muscle as if he stepped from a fight and every muscle in his body is already pumped.

He pulls his shoulders back, rising to an intimidating height as he steps into the center of the lounge room, returning my fierce stare. His gaze passes across my ruby-red hair, my cobalt eyes, and crimson lips, running slowly all the way to my toes before rising again.

I inhale all the layers of his scent, drowning in bitter orange, nutmeg, and cedar… but beneath them is the scent of blood.

My focus flashes to his neck. The wound has closed and a scar is already forming. "You're alive."

"Am I?" he asks, his head lowering, eyes narrowing. "Why don't you come over here and see for yourself?"

Somehow, I've been transported to his penthouse, but if Tristan himself is an illusion, then I need to know.

I round the lounge chair at the elevator end of the room and stride toward him. I tell myself I'm not afraid of him. Even without my wolf, my power is as strong as his.

He turns to face me, his shoulders hunching, biceps tensing in a way that makes my instincts tell me to stop, uncertain if he's bracing to defend himself or attack. I hesitate two paces away from him, suddenly wary.

"Why stop there, Tessa Dean?" he asks with a challenging growl in his voice. "Why not come closer?"

I reevaluate him and our surroundings. The room is exactly as I remember it, right down to the scuff marks outside the elevator, but when I glance upward, the ceiling appears more gray than white—more like the rock ceiling of the Near-Apart Room at the Spire.

I gasp when it suddenly begins to rain inside his penthouse. Real raindrops dampen my head and shoulders within seconds. First the Near-Apart Room produced a dust storm; now it must be producing rain. I don't understand why or how. I tell myself it doesn't matter right now. Whatever strange marvels the room has to produce to bring us together, I'll accept them. What matters is that Tristan is here.

His gaze washes across me before it lifts to the ceiling above us. His upper lip curls, a fierce growl releasing from his mouth, his expression becoming even more aggressive as the rain falls onto his face. "What magic brought you to me?"

I'm suddenly aware of a splatter of blood washing down Tristan's arm as the water gathers across his shoulders, but I can't see where it came from. I don't know whether or not it's from a wound or if it could be someone else's blood.

I shudder. "Magic that is strong enough for me to see that you aren't Tristan."

I might have been brought here by the magic within the Spire, but the scent of blood from his body is very real and it sets my instincts on edge.

"Which are you?" I demand to know, standing my ground

without taking another step toward him. "The Deceiver, the Coward, or the Killer?"

A dark gleam enters Tristan's eyes. "Which do you think?"

"The one I haven't met before," I say.

The Killer.

I've met both the Deceiver and the Coward before now. Tristan lied to me multiple times, not least by keeping his true nature from me. He also shied away from telling me the truth about my past. But while I've seen Tristan at his most ruthless, the cold efficiency with which he killed was always in defense of his pack, never mindless or bloodthirsty. It was only when he fought Ford's wolf that I saw him strike in a way that was—

My heart skips a beat.

Did fighting Ford's wolf allow the Killer to take over Tristan's mind?

"How long has Tristan been keeping you at bay?" I ask.

"His whole life," the Killer says. "But that was destined to change. Your father gave me the chance I needed to finally emerge." The Killer takes an aggressive step toward me. "What do you want, *Tessa Dean*? Or should I call you 'Daughter of War'?"

My jaw clenches. "I need to know if Tristan is alive."

"So you can move on without guilt?" the Killer asks, giving a snarl, his shoulders hunching over again. His eyes shift into the shade of his wolf so that they glow with amber flecks that clash with the crisp green of his irises.

"No!" I take a step forward. "So that I can make it back to him."

The Killer's eyes darken. It's the only warning I have before he darts forward, closing the gap and pulling me close. His arms wrap around my waist and back, a seductive pull that tugs at the beast inside me.

My crimson rage rises to meet the heat in his hold, my head tipping back as he tangles his hand in my hair, cupping the back of my neck.

Even though his touch triggers a conflicting mix of anger and desire inside me, I groan with deep relief.

He's solid, not an illusion like our surroundings.

His power washes around me, streaming through my senses like an explosion. My lips part as his head tilts to mine, water sliding down his face and chest.

He nudges the corner of my mouth on his way to my neck, inhaling my scent, his lips drawing through the moisture on my flesh to brush the skin beneath my ear, making me shiver.

"Why did you push me away on the rooftop?" he whispers against my neck. His voice has become suddenly softer and when he draws back, his eyes are crisp and green again. They appear nearly human, possibly the most human he's ever looked.

"Tristan?" I search his eyes, slipping my right hand between us, my palm to his heart, sensing his breathing.

It's already aligned to mine.

Oh... thank everything holy.

I let out my breath and a sob comes with it. I try to smother it, but it's impossible. I start to cry and break into a smile at the same time. "It's you."

"Tessa." He murmurs my name.

I bite my lip hard, trying not to completely lose my composure as he bends to press his cheek to mine, a soft touch, staying there, his arms wrapped around me.

Tears of regret fill my eyes. "I was afraid of what I saw in your heart," I whisper, answering him honestly. "I wasn't in control and I acted out of fear and confusion. I know what it means now to fight the darkness inside. I know you won't hurt me."

"But I could," he whispers, drawing back. "You saw it for yourself. Your wolf isn't protected from me."

His quiet gaze follows the line of tears down my cheeks. The last time I cried in front of him, he followed the shiny rivers of my tears and he hid his true response behind an emotional shield.

But now, he's surprisingly open to me, his eyes softer than I've ever seen them. Maybe even... too soft.

"Why couldn't you let me do the right thing?" he asks.

I draw in a shocked breath. "You mean… why didn't I let you die at Baxter's hand?"

He gives me a single nod, waiting for my response.

Pressing my hand firmly to his chest, I lift my chin. "Because I will do the impossible," I say. "I will stop your fate."

"No." He shakes his head, untangles his hand from my hair, and starts to pull away, but I hold on to him.

Until this point, I haven't accessed my power, but now I let some of my strength flow through me, allowing me to hold on to him for the moment it takes for me to say, "I need to stop your fate, Tristan, because then I know I can stop mine, too."

He pauses, his hands flexing against my back. "That's not a good enough reason, Tessa. You could have changed your fate by letting me die."

He is more quiet, more subdued than I've ever seen him, and it's starting to scare me. By now, he should be raging at me. He should have flipped the kitchen table, maybe clawed a cushion. I haven't seen his incisors or his claws since the Killer disappeared.

While he remains standing in front of me, not trying to pull away, I slide my hand cautiously up his chest, along his shoulder, to press my palm against the side of his neck where he was cut. "How did you survive?"

His eyes meet mine and I sense a shift in him. I don't want to use my crimson vision to see inside his heart because doing that will only show me his impulses, not his decisions, but a sense of unease is growing inside me.

His eyes narrow at me and the corner of his mouth curls up, shockingly sly. "What makes you think Tristan survived?"

I jolt in his arms, finally realizing what's wrong.

"Coward!" I shout. "You're the fucking Coward!" I plant my hands on his chest and shove him away from me. "You're the one who wanted to die."

The Coward's far-too-green eyes twinkle at me as he rights himself. "When you forced Tristan's hand at Baxter Griffin's party, you opened a door wide open for me, Tessa. For that, I should thank you."

When I growl at him, his eyes merely narrow.

"Is this when I should run away?" he asks, exaggerating wide-eyed terror.

Within a blink, his expression shifts into a threatening snarl that matches mine in ferocity.

Rapidly switching gears, his claws descend, his shoulders hunch, and his muscles cord. The Killer appears within a blink. "Or should I make you cry again?"

"You can fucking try," I say, the rain running down my face as my own claws descend. "Let me speak with Tristan."

"Or what?" The Killer's incisors are sharp as he challenges me. "What will you do, Daughter of War? Slit my throat? Throw me off a roof? Leave me there to die?"

Before I can gasp, he drives his own claw toward his heart.

I lurch forward to stop him. *What the hell is he doing...?*

"You can't save Tristan." The Killer snarls, a look of concentration falling over his face, as if he's fighting a force inside himself.

I let out a scream, but it's not only of anger. A hundred knives suddenly raked through my heart like the Killer is clawing me instead of himself. I double over before I can reach him, my knees buckling.

The Killer digs his claw deeper, succeeding in breaking the skin so that a trickle of blood slides down his chest, mingling with the rain.

"What are you doing?" It feels like my heart is breaking apart inside my chest and I don't understand it. I gasp for breath, suddenly realizing that the melding bond I have with Tristan must be allowing me to feel his pain as if it's mine. The only way that could happen is if Tristan himself is allowing me to feel it.

"I'm breaking the true mate bond Tristan formed with you," the Killer says. "Until the bond is broken, we can't kill you."

CHAPTER EIGHTEEN

"Tristan will never hurt me," I cry.

"Tristan is already dead," the Killer says. "We're all that's left."

"I don't believe that."

I can feel him. Tristan is in there somewhere. He's alive. I just have to find him. *Somehow...*

Closing my eyes, ignoring what I see and hear, I breathe deeply, inhaling Tristan's pure scent. All the layers of power, all the nuances of his heart, all the internal conflict and the violent darkness that I didn't see until he let me see it.

Keeping my eyes closed, I allow my crimson rage to rise, enabling me to see the power around me without opening my eyes. Flames burn at the edges of my vision, the immense power of the Spire sustaining my presence here, keeping us together.

Confusingly, I glimpse streams of other ancient powers in the walls behind Tristan. They snake from the ceiling toward the floor, thick and rope-like. I can't make out what they are, but right now, it doesn't matter.

Tristan is my focus.

Streams of immense energy cascade through his body. They cut across each other, looping like the snake that glides through the eye sockets of the wolf inked into his chest. A million small nooses, closing tighter with every passing moment, form a web around his heart and strangle it.

Darting forward, I grab the Killer's free hand before he can impale me when he fights back. I push his left arm wide. Allowing my power to rush through me, giving me strength to hold off his left arm, I grab the claw he's using to attack his own heart. Stopping him.

Sweat drips down my face as I plant my feet and brace, testing my strength against the Killer's.

"Let him go," I snarl.

We're equally matched and my muscles scream, but I maintain my hold on him as I rise up on my tiptoes. My arms shake with effort, but I hold on as I seek Tristan's mouth.

My lips brush against his incisors, daring him to hurt me.

"Let him go." My voice hardens. "Or I swear I will fuck with you so badly, there won't be anything left."

The Killer's arms suddenly drop to his sides, taking my hands with him.

Tristan's mouth presses against mine, his incisors disappearing in a heartbeat.

"Fuck." He inhales against my mouth. "Tessa."

My eyes fly open to find Tristan's blistering gaze raking from my mouth to my eyes. His hands rapidly glide up my arms to my shoulders and behind to my shoulder blades, flexing near my spine. "How are you here? You shouldn't be here." A muscle tenses in his jaw. "Are you an illusion?"

"I'm here." My heart hammers inside my chest, my power kicking like a drum inside me. "I found a way to see you, but I don't know how long it will last."

Leaning forward, I press my lips to his, a light touch, testing his response. My incisors are a heartbeat away, ready in case the Coward or the Killer surfaces again. I know what they look like now—the Killer with his corded muscles and hunched shoulders, the Coward with his soft green eyes. It's the Deceiver I'll need to worry about. I don't know what he looks like, but his appearance is bound to be subtle.

Tristan releases his hold on my torso, reaching for my face

instead, his thumbs brushing across my cheeks, a firm touch. Somehow, despite the rain that continues to fall, his gaze follows the path of my tears down my cheeks.

He growls beneath his breath. "The fucking Coward did this." Holding my gaze, refusing to let go, he says, "Don't you ever cry for me, Tessa."

I release my breath. Tristan once commanded me never to beg.

Only the real Tristan would tell me not to cry.

It's really him.

Biting my lip, I remain so close to Tristan that I could close the gap in the space of a breath and kiss him again. In the days I've been apart from him, I've experienced soul-tearing pain and walked a fine line between light and dark.

Quietly, I press my lips to his.

"The Killer said you were dead," I whisper, pulling back and nearly breaking his command not to cry.

"Fuck the Killer." Despite the vehemence in Tristan's speech, his gaze runs carefully across my face before he dips his mouth to mine, but only for a moment.

"You feel real," he says. "You need to tell me how you're here."

My heart breaks a little that he can't seem to believe we're together right now.

"I'm being held in a place called the Spire," I say. "It's a place of old magic. I found a room that allowed me to connect with you."

"Are you safe?" His gaze passes urgently across my face. "Is your appearance a trick? You don't look hurt."

"I'm not hurt." *Not anymore. Not now.*

"How long do we have?" he asks.

"I don't know," I say, nudging my mouth against his again, all of the tantalizing kisses drawing out my body's need for him. "A minute. An hour. Not long enough."

Not long enough to ask him all of the things I need to know.

Even if I had time, I have to treat every piece of information he gives me with suspicion until I know what the

Deceiver looks like. It won't stop me asking questions—I just need to be careful what I do with his answers.

"Is your pack safe?" I ask. "Is Baxter Griffin honoring the deal?"

"My pack is safer than they've ever been," Tristan says, but a hint of darkness enters his eyes, the amber flecks of his wolf's eyes growing. "You made a deal that was too good for Baxter to pass up. Ford owes him a favor now. Baxter won't fuck that up by making a move that dishonors your sacrifice."

"Not even to find out what happened to his son?" I ask, thinking of Cody.

"Not even if his son's life is in danger," Tristan says. "It's the only thing Cody Griffin and I have in common. Both of our fathers are fucking monsters."

"And me," I whisper. "You have me in common now too. Since you sent Cody after me."

Tristan takes his time responding. His warm hands stroke down either side of my neck, running through the water that has collected against my skin as the rain eases to a drizzle around us.

"You're free to make the choices you want to make, Tessa," he says.

I take a beat to respond, understanding that he's trying to tell me he won't stop me from following my heart, but I need to be open and clear about my feelings. "Cody is complicated. He's facing a lot right now. But he's a friend. An ally. Someone I can trust." Just saying it lifts some of the weight off my heart.

"Then he's alive," Tristan says. "Even without his wolf."

"You knew his wolf was gone?"

"I sensed it as soon as I saw him on the helipad."

Faster than me, then.

My hands tighten around Tristan's shoulders. "I'm trying to play my father's game, but Cody's running out of time and I'm scared I'm going to lose. I'm scared other people will get hurt."

"Sometimes you have to lose to win," Tristan says. He's quiet. His fingers swoop lightly across my cheeks and lips, up across my temple and forehead, before stroking through my hair, all the way down my back.

Before I can respond, he says, "Your power isn't constrained anymore, Tessa, but you're controlling it. That's the most important thing."

I let out my breath. "I know what I am. I know who my father is. I understand why you didn't tell me about the three-headed wolf or about who I am. We should be enemies, but we aren't."

Tristan's hands knead my back, easing out all the tension in me. "You met the Coward and the Killer," he says.

I grimace. "Nice guys."

He drops a kiss on the corner of my mouth, lingering, but not long enough to quench my growing need. "It's the Deceiver you need to worry about."

I meet his eyes. "You hate liars because you're forced to become one."

"I need to know that the people around me are telling the truth," he says. "So I can keep things straight in my head. I've been the Deceiver for a long time. Ever since I was born, I've pretended to be like other shifters when—fundamentally—I'm not. I've been an imposter since birth, just like my father and his father. Sometimes, the three personalities skip a generation, but they always resurface."

I draw my hands through Tristan's wild, wet hair, grazing my fingers across the growth on his jaw. "What do you know about the book of old magic?"

His forehead creases. "I don't know what that is."

As he speaks, an edge of tension grows around his mouth. He quickly continues. "Or I could be lying to you right now. I might know exactly what book you're talking about, but I won't tell you what I know."

I consider that possibility. "Do you know when you're lying?"

"The Killer and the Coward take over my mind completely —they control my actions and I don't know what's happening until I surface again—but the Deceiver is subtle. I find myself saying something I know isn't true." Tristan's hands tighten around me. "I don't always want to do it."

"Oh, so you only want to lie *sometimes*," I say, biting my lip as I arch an eyebrow at him, trying to make light of something too heavy to face.

"I don't want to lie to you right now," he says, focusing on my mouth, his chest rising and falling faster beneath my hands. "Don't ask me any more questions."

Slowly, he closes the gap between us. Nudging my lips apart, he tastes my tongue, coaxing me to allow him to explore my mouth. I respond with a low growl that hums in my throat, my body heating at his touch, the needy ache in my center growing more intense.

Swiftly breaking contact with my mouth, he searches my eyes for a heartbreaking second. "Tell me truthfully: Are you really here or am I dreaming?"

"I'm here," I say, as certain as I can be. Running my hands across his chest, I explore the shape of his wolf tattoo, circling the spot where the Killer's claw drew blood.

Leaning forward, I press my lips to the damaged skin. Carefully, feeling like it's the right thing to do, I dab the tip of my tongue against the wound, my wolf's rage urging me to clean it, to show my care for him.

When I raise my eyes to Tristan's, I find his lips parted, his inhalations rapid. "You are more wolf than you know, Tessa," he says, his voice low.

I allow a smile to ghost around my mouth, my palms resting lightly on either side of his chest, bracing against his muscles.

I don't know how long we have—or if I'll have the chance to be with him again.

"Show me," I challenge him.

CHAPTER NINETEEN

With a deep growl, Tristan pulls me up against him.

This time, his mouth is scorching on mine, drawing my simmering need bursting to the surface. Deftly dealing with the buttons at the front of my shirt, he grips my torso and lifts me so that my lips fit completely together with his. Taking his time, he explores my mouth with heady strokes of his tongue that ignite the need inside me.

Still kissing me, he removes his long pants before he draws my shirt off my shoulders and down my arms. I reach for the button at the top of my own pants, but he grips my hands before I can begin to remove them, running his fingers up the insides of my arms with an intensity that makes my heart hammer inside my chest.

His touch brands me as he turns me in his arms so that my back presses to his chest. With one arm firmly fitted across my hips, the other across my chest, he remains behind me as he maneuvers us to the floor.

My body fits to his, responding to all of the pressure points he applies until I'm lying on my stomach on the rug on the floor.

His weight presses against my back with the perfect pressure to tantalize me but not cage me. He sweeps my hair to the side, his hands stroking down my back to my hips and all the way back up again. His lips follow the trail of his hands, his tongue swirling across my back in warm strokes that make my thighs clench.

He explores my back and neck until I'm gasping, wanting more.

Responding to my moans, he draws my pelvis up off the floor, finally unzipping my pants and sweeping them down my legs and past my feet, pulling off my boots at the same time. Starting at my ankles, he glides his hands up the inside of both of my legs all the way to my inner thighs, stroking toward my center. I moan as he slips his finger inside me, stroking me, but not easing the ache, teasing me with the promise of climax.

"Tristan," I say, arching to catch his ruthless smile. "I want more."

This time, he moves fast, reaching around me and placing me onto my back so that he can kneel between my legs.

I arch against him as he thrusts inside me, driving deep, drawing a moan to my mouth as intense pleasure ripples through me. He draws out slowly, waiting another beat before he thrusts again. I fist the rug, bracing and meeting his movement. But this time, he leans close, his chest rising and falling rapidly as he pauses while he's deep inside me.

The desire in his eyes is so intense, I nearly climax at the sound of his voice. "Come get me, Tessa."

My eyes widen as he withdraws completely, leaving me empty and moaning with need. *What?*

He remains poised above me, dipping his head to nudge my mouth with his. Then my neck. He dips his mouth toward my breast as if he's going to stroke it, but he pauses, his lips slightly parted.

My chest heaves. I scream with need as he rises off me without easing the ache inside me. I challenged him to show me how much like a wolf I really am. It seems he's determined to prove to me any way he can that there's a wolf inside me.

Following him up, I pounce on him, driving him onto his back on the floor. He gives me a searing smile as his arms close around me, waiting for me to make my move.

Reaching down, I'm just about to draw him inside me, moaning with anticipation, when he grabs my torso and tips us to the side, rolling with me so that I end up on my back again.

He swoops down and closes his mouth around my breast. Mindless pleasure rides me as his hands stroke my neck, my side, and my pelvis while his mouth works its magic. The pleasure is so intense, I nearly climax when his hand brushes across my center, but he stops again, his expression filled with increasing challenge as he hovers above me.

"You are a wolf," he says, his gaze burning mine.

I growl deep in my throat.

Come and get him? Fuck, yes.

My wolf's energy rises to the surface. Planting both of my hands on his shoulders while I remain beneath him, I arch my hips up against his stomach and wrap my legs around him. Sliding downward, I move in a way that will make him believe that I'm determined to take him from beneath if I have to.

At the last possible moment, I push with my hands and tip my hips, rocking us to the side, pushing him onto his back.

His eyes narrow at me, the intense challenge in them growing. The muscles in his biceps and thighs bunch as if he's going to roll us again, but this time, I'm ready to let my darker nature speak.

Planting my hands on his chest, I push him back onto the floor, pinning him. I allow my incisors to peek through my lips as I growl at him, a deep, needy snarl.

"I want you, Tristan," I say. "All the fucking ferocity and imperfection of you. *Now.*"

One of his incisors appears, his expression both deadly and beautiful.

Burning heat fills me as his gaze passes from my eyes to my lips all the way down to my hips. He takes me all in, his hands resting lightly on my hips, and the need in his eyes is everything I want.

With a sudden dangerous glint of amber in his eyes as his wolf appears, he grasps my hips, lifts me off his pelvis and positions me where I can draw him inside me.

"Yes," he says, giving me permission.

My body is beyond ready, all the aching need building as I fit my body to his, controlling the first thrust.

I sense his darkness rise with mine as I drive him as deep as I can inside me, riding the powerful wave of pleasure. My need for him is reckless and wild, destruction only a heartbeat away with every plunge of my body onto his, every thrust of his body into mine. Gripping his shoulders to keep myself anchored, I demand as much from him as he wants from me.

His eyes shift, the glowing amber flecks of his animal growing and receding as danger and release draw closer.

Hurtling toward climax, I seek his mouth, my incisors receding as I press my lips to his. I inhale every nuance of his scent—all the power, danger, menace, and the promise of the ultimate pleasure—before I arch back, holding his scent on my tongue as I crash against him.

I tip my head back and scream out every moment of pain and heartache since we were torn apart. My body matches the ferocity of Tristan's need, crashing against him, not satisfied until he orgasms with me.

My chest heaves as I drop toward his chest, planting my hands on either side of his head before I run my hands into his wild hair. I study him as intensely as his gaze follows every curve of my face in a slow movement.

It's like he's determined to memorize this moment.

He suddenly rears up beneath me, our bodies still joined. I don't know when the rain stopped, but we're still damp, glittering droplets clinging to our skin.

His animal snarls at me before he darts forward, his mouth closing over my shoulder, his teeth bared, the move he would make if he were about to mark me.

I don't flinch, don't pull back.

His eyes meet mine as his lips draw away from his teeth, his incisors pressing against my skin without breaking it.

"One day, Tessa," he whispers, his lips easing across my shoulder. "You will want this as much as I do."

His tongue swirls across the soft edge of my shoulder and along my collarbone. I close my eyes, soaking up his touch as he plants kisses up my neck, his mouth pressing against mine in a lingering touch.

"Tessa, promise me—"

His speech cuts short and his arms flex around me. At the same time, a cold breeze swirls at my back.

My head snaps up.

The air in the room is hazy, the rug suddenly disintegrating around my kneeling legs, rising upward into a growing dust storm.

No! It's too soon!

At the same time, the rain starts to fall again, harder this time, washing down our bodies.

My heart hammers inside my chest. "I'm about to be torn away from you."

He takes hold of my face. "Don't come after me, Tessa. Promise me!"

I search his eyes, suddenly confused. Then stubborn. "I will find my way back to you. No matter what it takes."

Tristan glances up again, turning his face to the ceiling like the Killer did when the rain first began falling. His expression hardens. The wind howls around us, the dust turning to mud and clinging to my face and arms, my torso.

The raindrops slow, the breeze carrying the dust chills my skin, and the room shimmers in a blur around me. The walls, the floor, the furniture—it's all disintegrating.

Only Tristan remains crystal clear in the whirling darkness.

"Don't you fucking come for me," he snarls. "It's not safe—"

The darkness rises in his eyes a second before his body disintegrates from beneath me, turning to dust in my arms.

"No!" I reach for him, my arms swilling through the air

before the debris becomes so thick that I'm forced to throw my arms across my face, doubling over my knees. My stomach churns, my head hurts, and my heart is stretched as thin as paper.

The wind dies down as quickly as it began, dropping me into sharp silence, leaving me reeling.

I open my eyes to find myself kneeling on the floor in the Near-Apart Room exactly where I carved my question. The dagger rests on the floor beside me. I'm dressed in my clothes again, every garment in place.

A shudder runs through my body and a scream builds inside my chest.

I feel... *untouched*. As if my time with Tristan never happened. All I want is to have him back.

"Tristan?" I whisper into the silence.

My carved question is the only answer I receive. *Are you alive?*

I stare and stare at the question while it echoes around in my mind.

Tristan is alive, but his final command was a warning. He told me not to come for him because it's not safe. But... why wouldn't it be safe at the Tower?

He warned me not to trust what he told me. He cautioned me that the Deceiver is subtle. He told me Baxter won't mess up his chance of a favor from Ford. He also told me his pack is safe. He told me that sometimes we have to lose to win. He commanded me not to come after him. And... he told me not to cry for him.

But a lie is not always spoken. A lie can happen by omission.

I jolt because suddenly, what's more important is what Tristan *didn't* say.

He didn't ask me why it was raining in his penthouse. In fact, he turned his face up into the rain as if he expected it. I thought the rain must be a strange effect of the Near-Apart Room, but what if it wasn't? What if he wasn't in his penthouse after all and the rain was a weather effect he brought with him? When he told me that his pack was safer than they've ever been, he didn't tell me where he was or how his pack is now safe from *him*—from the Killer and the Coward.

I asked him how he survived and he didn't tell me that, either.

Scooping up the dagger, I jump to my feet, considering the brightness of the moonlight streaming through the window.

The only way Tristan's pack would be safer than they've ever been is if... Tristan isn't with them. If he's not with his pack—not with his beta, Jace—then he's in trouble, and I need to get to him before the beast inside him takes over completely.

A slight breeze kicks up the dust on the floor, sending it whirling around my feet like a mini tornado. It's as rapid as my thoughts.

My father brought me to the Spire to break my human soul. He told me that if I train the women and prove my loyalty to him, he will send me back to Tristan. His purpose is to steal the book of old magic from the library. It's a perfect opportunity for me to return to Tristan.

But my father is continuously playing his enemies off against each other: Baxter and Tristan, the witches. For all I know, he played a game with the assassins and my mother too.

He gave me a simple path back to Tristan—train the fighters and my father will willingly send me back.

It's *too* simple.

My father doesn't do simple.

I tip my head back, a growl building in my throat as realization burns hot and relentless within me.

I fucking fell for it.

He said it to me himself: All he has to do is whisper inducements into the ears of the willing and they will follow their instincts to an end of his making.

My father will dangle Tristan in front of me like candy for as long as he can, but he'll never send me back to Tristan. He will use me for as long as it takes to get the book from the library and I'll never be free.

I don't know where Tristan is. I don't know how to find him. He tried to make me promise not to come for him.

But... when have I ever obeyed him?

CHAPTER TWENTY

My heart is hammering inside my chest as I stride from the room, meeting my wolf at the door and instantly acquiring all of her knowledge.

From my wolf's memories, I ascertain that I was gone for the equivalent time that I spent in the room—no more than two hours. The dust storm had risen around me and after that, she and Cody couldn't see or hear anything from outside the room.

I also discover that Cody has dropped to a crouch beside the bedroom doorway, his head resting in his hands. He's rubbing his temples and doesn't seem to have heard my approach, even though I stormed out of the Near-Apart Room.

I consider him with sudden concern. He's even paler than he was a few hours ago. He said he doesn't know how long he has and now I'm trying to push away my panic that maybe he doesn't have very long at all.

He suddenly looks up, sees me, and lurches to his feet. Striding right over to me, he looms over me in the way of an alpha, ignoring my personal space. "Did you get the answer to your question?"

"I did. And so much more." I reach out to press my hand to

his shoulder and incline my head toward my bedroom, where we can talk privately.

Once we're inside the room, I remove my boots, carefully deciding how to ask him if he's okay, keeping my question casual. "How are you feeling?"

"My head's pounding, but I'm fine." He brushes it off. "What did you find out?"

Forced to accept his answer, I begin to pace, crossing from one side of the room to the other, my bare feet whisper-quiet. I need to think, to understand my options for our escape.

Eyeing me warily, Cody waits for me to speak. When I continue to pace and think, he rolls his shoulders and stretches his neck, actions that indicate he's trying to relax, despite the building tension between us. Finally, he lowers himself into a sitting position on the rug in front of the fireplace, which lit up when I entered the room.

For another five minutes, I pace while he patiently waits.

I thought that I'd already worked through all of my father's moves and countermoves this morning, but I was so wrong.

Pulling to a stop in front of Cody where he sits on the rug, I finally drag in a deep breath.

"I can't see the game my father's playing," I say. "It's as though I'm blindfolded and parts of the board are in shadow. On top of that, I don't have the same pieces as my father. Without knowing what he knows, I can't fight back."

Cody's focus shifts from my eyes to my hair for a second. It's a prolonged glance and I'm not sure why, but then he focuses back on my face. "My instinct is to tell you to play your own game, but you'd still only be playing with what you can see," he says.

I grimace. "I thought I could beat him at his own game, but it's been barely two days and I've spent them playing into his hands."

"You have to force him to make a mistake," Cody says, "A last-minute change that weakens his position."

"To do that, I need to play with what I know," I say,

rubbing my forehead in thought. "But only in a way that won't get you killed... or the prisoners hurt..."

Cody gives me a stern look. "Trying to protect me and those women weakens you. The only reason you're here to begin with is because you were trying to protect Tristan's pack. They aren't even your own pack and you tried to help them." He rises to his feet and takes a step forward, angry for the first time today. "If you cut everyone loose, you could fight your way out of here. Right now."

I grit my teeth and return his stare. "If I cut everyone loose, then I'll become my father. That's when he wins."

"Then use what you have," Cody says.

In all the unknowns, one thing is clear to me: my father will use Cody and the women as leverage against me. But what if I can use that against *him*?

"If I keep my plan to myself, will you trust me?" I ask, biting my lip so hard that I break the skin.

Cody slowly exhales, the tension in his shoulders easing as he reaches for my hands.

Slowly, he turns our hands over so that my palms are resting on top of his. He uncurls his fingers. He isn't holding on to me. I'm completely free to take my hands away whenever I wish.

I don't move. I meet his eyes.

His expression softens and he inclines his head toward the rug.

"Sit with me?" he asks.

When I lower myself to the rug, Cody sits close by, one leg stretched out. He leans on the bended knee of his other leg and contemplates the fire.

"You asked me if I want you in my bed," he says. "I want to give you an answer, but it involves telling you a story."

I tilt my head. "I'm listening."

He stares at the fire for another moment before he starts to speak. "There's a room in my father's house that we call 'the den,'" he says. "It's big and has a fireplace in it that's a lot like this one, but it's far off in the eastern wing, so nobody ever really went there. When we were kids, Cameron was afraid of the dark and I had nightmares—"

He stops. Catches my raised eyebrows. I try to lower them quickly, but he gives me a half-smile.

"Yeah," he says. "I'm admitting a weakness, Tessa. I had a lot of nightmares as a kid."

My reply is soft. "Go on."

"One night, when I couldn't sleep, I was roaming the house and I found Cameron in the den trying to build up a fire so he could sleep somewhere that wasn't dark. I helped him. We made a fire and we dragged our blankets down there and fell asleep. When we woke up in the morning, we discovered Ella fast asleep on the rug with us. She must have come looking for us.

"Two nights later, three of our cousins whose parents lived with us turned up in the night. Then four of the guards' kids. We never turned anyone away and we never slept in our own beds after that. We were our own pack."

I'm quiet as he continues. "Eventually, we established our only rule: It didn't matter what happened between us, even if we were angry with each other, we always turned up at the den at night and that's where we slept on rugs and pillows."

He rubs his jaw. "I didn't realize until Ella died just how much she was the glue that bound us together. After her death, the cracks appeared and we all fell apart. She was our den alpha."

He falls silent and it feels like the silence will break into dangerous shards if I speak.

"I want you in my den, Tessa," Cody says, finally looking at me. "I want to fall asleep on pillows and rugs knowing that you're part of my pack."

He hunches over his knee, his posture vulnerable as he takes a deep breath, clears his throat, and says, "But that's not all. There's something you should know. I assumed you already knew, but I don't think you do."

I frown but say, "Go on."

THIS BROKEN WOLF

"Andreas Dean—the man who raised you—was from my pack. He was Eastern Lowland. He grew up with my father."

A quiet laugh escapes my lips. "That's not possible. Andreas Dean was the alpha of the Middle Highlands—the mountain pack where I grew up."

"Not always." Cody is subdued. "I found out about it a week before the Conclave. Your name came up and my father let it slip. He said it was only by good luck that you weren't part of our pack. I asked him what he meant and that's when he told me."

I feel like stone, devoid of emotions. "Explain."

"I only have patches of information, not the full picture."

I sigh. That's pretty much the story of my life. "I'll take whatever you've got," I say.

"Andreas Dean grew up in the Eastern Lowland pack, but he was strong enough to challenge my father and become alpha," Cody says. "As you can imagine, that made my family extremely nervous. Andreas's strength threatened generations of Griffin family dominance. They needed him gone.

"As soon as Andreas was old enough, my grandfather made an agreement with the old alpha of the Middle Highland pack. Andreas was mated to the alpha's daughter and everyone was happy. Our pack got rid of a potential challenger and the Middle Highland got a strong alpha-in-training—which, apparently, they needed."

My jaw clenches. "You're seriously telling me that Andreas Dean grew up in the city."

"It's why I asked Dawson to take me to you at the Conclave." Cody rolls his shoulders as if he's trying to ease the tension in them. "If it weren't for Andreas Dean's move to the Middle Highland, you could have been part of my pack. Hypothetically, at least. We could have grown up together. With a sire as strong as Andreas, I knew you had to be powerful."

His gaze burns mine. "I had to meet you. As soon as I saw you, I knew you were strong. My instincts went haywire. My fucked-up wolf's instincts told me that I should force you to

185

come with me—to make a new den with me. But I fucked it up."

I consider the hunch of Cody's shoulders. His alpha wolf's instincts must really be fading because that's the second time in days he's admitted responsibility for what happened at the Conclave.

"You're an alpha," Cody says. "You've always been an alpha. Tristan knows it. *I* know it." He speaks carefully. "Every alpha needs a beta. Someone who will challenge their decisions without breaking trust or loyalty."

He pauses long enough that my forehead creases. "What are you saying? You want me to be your beta?"

"No," he whispers. "Fuck, no. I'm asking if you'll take me on. If you won't join my den, then I sure as fuck want to join yours."

My lips part in surprise. When I looked into Cody's most basic impulses, I saw a surprising capacity for loyalty, a necessary trait for a beta. I also remember the way he responded to my unspoken plea to stop Tristan getting himself killed.

I try to catch my breath. "I'm confused. You're an alpha-in-training. You're far stronger than your father. You're as much an alpha as I am."

"Because I had to be," he says. "Ella should have been my pack's alpha-in-training. My father has outdated ideas about women in positions of power. He chose me instead of her. But it was always Ella who kept us together."

My jaw has well and truly dropped. "Would you really choose to leave your pack for me?"

He winces. "If I'd succeeded in getting you away from Ford, I would have asserted my rights as alpha-in-training of the Eastern Lowland pack to keep your deal. But Ford has you. My father got what he wanted. Now I need to choose what I do with the days I have left. I can't be part of my father's pack anymore."

He clears his throat. "If you're worried about challenge, don't be. Aside from my numbered days, remember that Jace is strong enough to challenge Tristan. A strong beta only raises their alpha's reputation."

I remember the first night I met Tristan and Jace—my surprise that Tristan would choose a beta as strong as Jace but also the way the other alphas had become even more wary of Tristan the moment that Jace had appeared. Jace's presence at Tristan's side had tipped the balance of power.

I'm speechless. "I… um… This is…"

"Think about it," Cody says. "Until you decide, I'll keep doing what I'm doing." He shrugs his shoulders with a twinkle in his eyes. "Which is acting like your beta."

I reassess everything he's done for me today. Watched my back. Questioned my thoughts. Kept me from falling apart… a lot of the things I saw Jace do for Tristan.

Damn.

I exhale quietly. I'd asked Cody if he would trust me, even if I don't tell him my plan and now he's offering to be my beta. "Is this your way of saying that you'll trust me?" I ask.

"It is. I will." He reaches across suddenly to run his hand gently through my hair, carefully disentangling a small object from the strands.

He holds it up for me to see.

A bright, green leaf.

I wondered what he was looking at before.

Cody's lips purse before he draws the leaf up to his nose, inhaling. "I don't know this scent. It's from somewhere I've never been. Where did the room take you?"

I pat my hair, feeling uneasy before I take the leaf from Cody and raise it to my nose. It smells like moss and rain. "To Tristan's home in the city," I say.

Cody hums at the back of his throat as he shakes his head. "That leaf didn't grow in the city."

My unease increases, but I reach for Cody's hand, open his palm, and press the leaf into it. The tension around his eyes returns, the crease in his forehead nearly permanent. He squishes the leaf in his palm as he rubs his temples with his knuckles.

"Damn," he says. "This headache…"

"You need to rest," I say. "Let's get some sleep. Follow my lead tomorrow. Stay where you can see me at all times. Don't lose sight of me, even if that means you have to run."

He tips his head, a curious gleam entering his eyes, but he proves his trust by not asking me what I mean.

CHAPTER TWENTY-ONE

*A*s soon as my human body falls asleep, I prowl the corridor in my wolf form, my senses alert to all of the supernatural creatures sleeping in the Spire or, in Cody's case, *not* sleeping.

I poke my nose into the bedroom, settling down on my paws where I can see him while I guard the corridor.

He tosses and turns for an hour before he finally rises and heads to the bathroom, where I hear him splashing water. He emerges again with water dripping down his face and across his broad shoulders. He's dressed only in black underpants, his concession to my mandate against nakedness in my bed.

Proceeding to the fireplace, he grips the edge at the top of the mantelpiece, leaning forward, the muscles across his back flexing. He stares into the flame before he steps back, running his hand through his hair, pressing his forearm against his forehead.

After reaching for his long pants and pulling them on, Cody retrieves my weapon harness and the dagger I used to carve my question into the floor of the Near-Apart Room.

I cast my human form a worried glance, but she's fast asleep under the covers, her breathing deep and even. She's exhausted. *I'm* exhausted.

Cody crosses to me where I wait in the doorway. He

surprises me by taking a knee in front of me, as if he's paying homage to me. He holds the dagger at his side, its tip pointed down and away from me.

His eyes are increasingly bloodshot, the strain showing in his face. He's in pain, but he conceals it from my human form better than he's hiding it from my wolf.

"I asked Tessa to make me her beta, but she hasn't accepted yet. There's one thing I have to do for myself and I don't have the luxury of choosing my timing," he says.

"What are you doing with that dagger?" I ask.

"I have to know," he replies, fearless despite my growl.

"Know what?"

"How my sister died," he says. "I heard Tristan on the helipad. He said that Tessa's father had something to do with Ella's death. I have to know who killed her."

I startle. "You intend to scratch your question into the floor of the Near-Apart Room?"

He bows his head. "I can't die without knowing the truth. I promised Tessa I'll be there for her and I will, but I need to take this last step for me."

"But—"

His head snaps up. "I'm not afraid of pain or death, but I am afraid of dying without knowing who killed Ella."

But she isn't dead.

I don't know what the room will do if Cody asks a question that it can't answer. Before I got my question right—before I spoke a question that the room could answer—a dust storm had swirled around me, threatening to suffocate me. I'd feared that the old magic in the room might end me.

"You can't ask the wrong question, Cody," I say.

"Then I'll have to get it right," he replies.

He rises to his feet, shoulders back, and strides past me. His quietly moving feet kick up dust into the midnight moonbeams as he determinedly crosses the corridor behind me.

I can't use my wolf to stop him. There was a time when I used my energy as a healing force—to calm a wounded girl—

but now I'm afraid that my energy can only cause pain. In his weakened physical state, I could kill him.

I need my human self to get through to him.

Racing toward my human form, I leap onto the bed. My energy maintains enough traction that I can cross it and pass my paw through my human's shoulder. She barely reacts and for a moment, I'm forced to consider her quiet features in the flickering firelight.

My human face is commanding and sultry. Dark lashes rest against my cheeks. I have ruby lips that can twist with scorn or harden with malice. But my external features hide what I'm really feeling. All the fear and turmoil. A transformation that I'm still fighting with every breath I take.

"Wake up," I growl, snapping my teeth at her. "Cody needs you!"

I sense the moment she wakes, a deep tug pulling at my heart that connects us, our energy melding into one.

Her eyes fly open and everything I've seen in the last hour transfers to her. She jolts upright and the energy and power inside me rushes back to her, our forms uniting again.

Returned fully to my human form, I jump out of bed, tangling in the sheets and falling to the floor with a *thud* that jars my knees. I tear through the material and jump back to my feet, running across the corridor in my T-shirt and underpants.

On the far side of the Near-Apart Room, Cody has already started carving his question. Sweat drips down his face and chest as he scrapes the dagger back and forth across the floor. His muscles bunch as he digs deep and forms the connected letters of his question.

Who killed you?

The Near-Apart Room is driven by old magic. He's asking it a question that can't be answered because Ella isn't dead. She wasn't killed and... *fuck...* I don't know what the room will do.

I'm about to step into the room when a force shoots up in

front of me. An opaque wall forms, obscuring the room and stopping me from entering.

Damn. If it's the same barrier that went up while I was in the room, then Cody won't be able to see or hear me now. Just as I can no longer hear or see him.

I fight my panic—the need to scream through the barrier is nearly too much. Shouting will only bring my father and Brynjar running and that's the last thing we need.

I have to get in there.

Pushing my palms against the barrier that has formed across the doorway, I harness as much of my energy as I can. I remind myself that I'm old magic, the Spire is old magic, and old magic is not immune to itself.

The barrier shrieks as I break through it and push my way into the room. The moment I step inside, the power inside the room bites at my skin, prickling me like a thousand needles. At the same time, it feels like my feet sank into mud. I am an intruder now and the room seems determined to stop me from continuing on my path.

Across the way, Cody's hands shake visibly, the dagger trembling. The effort he puts into every movement of his arms and shoulders tells me that the energy inside the room is building around him too, just like the pressure increased around me when I carved my question.

I expect him to look up, but he doesn't.

"Cody! Stop!" I cry, but the sound of my voice is swallowed, as if the moment I open my mouth, my speech is stolen from me. As if the room is cocooning my presence.

Damn room.

Damn broken man needing answers.

Even now that I'm inside the room, Cody doesn't seem to be able to see or hear me. I need to get to him. I have to believe that the room will let me speak as soon as I reach him.

With a grunt of effort, I grit my teeth and push through the force surrounding me, heaving every step. A wind grows, tugging at my long, gray T-shirt and whipping it up around my waist.

I had my reasons for keeping the truth about Ella from him. Good reasons. Right reasons. But I have to speak the truth now. He has to know that she's alive.

I continue shouting—trying to shout—with every step. I scream for him to stop. I scream that Ella is alive, but my voice is swallowed at every attempt. Each step takes too long and with the passing seconds, Cody continues to carve his question.

The letters begin to fill with golden liquid that shines brightly in the moonlight. It's not black like the liquid that filled my question, and it's streaming through the connected strokes toward his position much faster than I experienced.

As he continues to drag the dagger back and forth, a surge of power suddenly flashes up from the golden liquid like a lightning strike. It courses across his chest, making him jolt.

Despite the impact, he drives the dagger onward, preparing to carve the start of the question mark. The golden lightning strikes again, hitting his shoulder, this time hard enough to knock him onto his back. It's as if the room is trying to stop him asking a question it can't answer, the old magic trying to repel him before he goes too far.

He lands heavily before he rights himself, clutching his chest but apparently determined to continue. His need for answers must be too strong for him to care about the pain.

Hell, I understand it. Not knowing whether Tristan was alive ate at me. Cody has lived with the unknown for years.

But I can't let him finish that question. He's already physically vulnerable. Another lightning strike could kill him.

I hold my breath as he rams the dagger back into the floor. I'm still five paces away, a scream of fear rising in my throat as another electrical pulse flashes from the question and wraps around his neck like a rope before it disappears. He jolts, writhes, but refuses to let go of the dagger.

Groaning against the heavy weight I'm pushing through, I harness my energy, brace, and burst through the final steps, breaking through the last barrier of old magic to reach Cody's side.

His question is almost complete.

"You can't ask that question!" I make a grab for the dagger, my hands closing around his.

He freezes before he jolts. "Tessa! No! You shouldn't be here." Blood drips from his chest and neck where he was struck. I sense the force building again, ready to strike the moment he twists the dagger to complete the dot at the bottom of the question mark.

I cast a panicked glance at the golden liquid filling the letters. The fiery lightning crackles around its edges, appearing to be created directly from the question he's asking. The last strike wrapped around his neck. I'm terrified of what the next one will do.

I need to explain everything to him, but there's no time. Lightning builds across the surface of the golden liquid that now rushes around the upper curve of the question mark, speeding toward the dagger's tip.

Keeping my left hand firmly on the dagger's handle so I'll take the brunt of the room's power, I pivot so that I'm facing Cody. Swiftly, I slide my leg over his into a straddling position. I wrap my right arm around his chest, ready to wrench the dagger from the floor.

Cody's fierce eyes meet mine, straining to maintain control of the dagger. "Don't deny me this, Tessa! I need to know what happened."

I lean close, quieting my voice, prepared to take the lightning strike. "Cody, the room can't answer that question."

The crease in his forehead deepens as he searches my eyes. "Why not?"

"Because Ella isn't dead."

He stills. A storm of emotions passes across his face. Disbelief, surprise, rage, distrust, hope, despair, all jumbled together. I sense the war inside him rising again, but his grip on the dagger eases, giving me the opportunity to retract it.

Bracing for impact, I wrench the dagger from the floor. The lightning crackles behind me, its light reflecting in Cody's eyes, golden flecks appearing in his irises.

For a second, it looks like his wolf has returned.

I grit my teeth as the bite of magic washes across my back, prickling my neck where my hair has parted and burning across the backs of my arms.

Inhaling, I hold my breath and count another heartbeat.

The glow fades, sparks dissolving and falling to the floor, where they disappear.

The sudden silence in the room tells me I stopped the question just in time. With a quick glance to the side, I see that the golden liquid is rapidly seeping away into the floorboards and the wood is healing itself, joining together the cuts of Cody's question as if he never asked it.

We're left kneeling on the floor, tangled up around each other and now, the silence is heavy.

"Ella's alive," I say, deciding against trying to pull away from him. "I've met her."

His forehead creases, then smooths. Then creases. "If she were alive, she would have come home."

"She can't," I say softly, carefully. "She was hurt and she needs to heal."

He tenses up and I know that if he still had his wolf, it would be raging now, the protective instincts for his sister going wild. I hurry to continue. "She's protected and loved, Cody."

"Where?"

"It's not safe for me to tell you. That's why I haven't told you anything before now."

He falls quiet. His head is bowed so low that his forehead nearly touches my shoulder. "What happened to her?"

"I'm sorry, but I don't know," I murmur quietly. "When I met her, I was only told her name. It was important that I didn't ask questions."

Helen will know. Tristan will know. But neither of them has ever told me.

Cody's arms are warm around my back, but his breathing is more rapid than it should be. "My father told me that Ella died in the forest. He said Tristan's father took her and killed her. But she was alive. All this time." Cody raises his head, his teeth gritted, his arms clamping around my back. "We should have fucking gone after her."

His voice rises. "The witches weren't a threat at that time. Mother Serena was dead. The covens were in chaos. We should have burned the fucking forest to the ground looking for her!"

"Cody—"

"She was hurt and we fucking abandoned her!"

He tries to pull out of my arms, agitated, but I take hold of his shoulders, then his face, wrapping my legs around him, forcing him to look at me.

"Cody!" I make myself meet his gaze even though his sudden focus on me tears at my heart. "You didn't know."

"But did my father?" he asks. "Did he know?"

Cody's question makes my eyes widen.

He continues, his voice harsh and uncontrolled. "My father used Ella as an excuse to rage against Tristan's pack. He called it justice." Cody snarls. "But he and Ford Vanguard have been in each other's pockets for years and Ford was there that night, right? Ford and his wolf were fucking there when Tristan's mother died and Ella was taken.

"Did Ford know where Ella was? Did he tell my father?" Cody's grip on my sides is painful. "Did my father fucking know where she was? Did he use his own daughter to justify a power grab over Tristan's territory?"

Cody is asking me questions I can't answer, but they make my heart sink. My father has demonstrated the power of manipulation. My father could have taken Ella without telling Baxter Griffin anything. Or he could have told Baxter everything and played to Baxter's baser emotions: greed, the thirst for power, the glory that would come with taking Tristan down.

I try to calm my hammering heart. I'm surprised to realize that in the last few minutes, the dark rage inside me has quieted. My heart feels more human than it has in days.

"I don't know the answers to your questions," I say. "But I want to help you find out."

"I won't live that long," Cody says, putting voice to the fear that I haven't wanted to acknowledge. "These headaches are getting worse." He exhales a heavy sigh. "I'm a fucking idiot for asking to be part of your den. What use is a dying, wolfless shifter to you?"

My eyes burn. I bite my lip. Dare to lean forward and press my cheek to his.

"Anyone can be pack," I whisper. I pull back and give him a crooked smile. "Besides, I like you better without your wolf."

He arches his eyebrows before he returns my lopsided grin. A moment of peace between us.

My sense of calm fades too soon. "If I thought for a second that we could run right now—escape from this place and take the other prisoners with us—I'd do it. But between my father, Brynjar, and Silas, I'd be leading you to your death. I'm the only one who would get out alive."

Cody is agitated again, his hands clamping on my arms. "Then do it! Get the fuck out of here, Tessa." His grip is so tight that it hurts. "*Run. Right now.* Forget me. Forget the prisoners. Go to the place where your mother lived. There's a boxing gym there where Andreas Dean used to train. I was going to take you there. They can help you."

I startle. "You were going to take me... where?"

"To the boxing gym where your father trained. The assassins own it." He plows on. "Nobody can touch you there—not your father, my father, not even Tristan. The assassins can protect you."

"Wait. Back up." There's too much information in what he said and it's making my head spin. "Boxing. Gym. Assassins."

I'm reduced to single words. My thoughts are churning, but I try to vocalize them, try to focus on one thing at a time. "Andreas learned to box at a gym run by assassins."

"My father said Andreas was a rule-breaker," Cody says. "My family knew he was training there and it made them even more uneasy."

Fuck. I press my hands to my temples. "That's the connection between Andreas and my mother. He must have met her at the boxing gym." I sway a little. "The boxing... that he taught me since I was little..."

Cody is quiet again. "I didn't know your mother was an assassin. I wasn't keeping that from you, I swear to you. I wanted to take you there because it's the only place nobody would come after you."

I stare at Cody, my thoughts in pieces. "If you didn't know about my mother, what made you think a group of assassins would protect me? It's all well and good that nobody would come after me there, but what made you think they wouldn't kill us both as soon as we stepped into their territory?"

Cody takes a deep breath and speaks even more carefully this time. "Because I spent the last two months forming an alliance with them."

At my shocked jolt, he grimaces. "It didn't start out that way. After Andreas died, I sought them out because I wanted to hand myself in. I asked them to end me."

My lips part, but my voice fails me.

"It turns out they don't operate that way," Cody says. "They aren't what I expected. They were willing to train me in the gym. Just like they trained Andreas. They offered me an alliance."

Cody has surprised me at every turn. Once again, I reevaluate what I know of him—or what I thought I knew. When I went to his father's home, I discovered Cody changed. He was far more sure of himself, his body honed, as if he'd spent the time since the Conclave working out. His silhouette had a finely chiseled edge that it didn't have before. He was quieter, more controlled in his actions, more considered in expressing his thoughts. He told me that he regretted the past and that the person he'd been was dead. That he had killed that part of himself. I never imagined how literally he had tried to achieve that.

And then... on the helipad, he chose to give up his wolf.

"The assassins are feared for very real reasons," Cody says.

"They're human, but they derive their power from old magic —the magic of the gods bestowed on them. They gave me the tranquilizers that knocked out the ice jotunn and your father on the helipad. I don't know how much the assassins know about your father, but I'm sure they can help you, Tessa."

I remember the shock on Ford's face when Cody shot him with the silver liquid that knocked him unconscious. He asked Cody how the hell Cody had gotten the darts. I guess he never imagined that Cody would have sought an alliance with assassins, of all people.

Cody presses his forehead to mine. "I walked down the path my father set me on and I'm not proud of the things I did. I don't want that to happen to you. I want you to go to the assassins. I want you to be safe."

Quietly, I consider Cody's request. He wants me to give up his safety for my own, but I can't do it. Exhaling heavily, I lean in to press my cheek to his, the same nudge he gives me in the morning.

Somehow, the touch seems to calm him. Maybe it's a wolf thing that I don't understand, an expression of connection. Maybe it's simply soothing. Somehow, it makes me feel calmer too.

"I'm not leaving you here," I say, closing my eyes and hugging him, making myself more vulnerable than I ever thought I would. "I'm not going to let you die. Escape won't be easy or quick. It will be difficult. But I promise you, I'm taking you with me and I'm getting you to a place where…" I squeeze my eyes closed, knowing the danger of promising something, of giving hope, that could be impossible. Taking him to Hidden House could be impossible. "I'm going to do everything I can to help you heal."

His arms close around me, warm, firm, but not tight. He allows me to rest there with him, both of us taking as much as we can before I pull back to brush my hand across his forehead. He's overly warm, but I have to expect that his symptoms will worsen until I can get help.

"You need to sleep now," I say. "I still have some human

medicine. You'll start taking it right away for the headaches. From now on, you tell me when you're in pain. You don't hide it. Tomorrow... the new game begins."

He seeks my hand, curling his fingers around mine. "Fuck," he says. "I'm in your den now, aren't I?"

"Be careful what you wish for," I whisper.

CHAPTER TWENTY-TWO

I wake the moment that the first hint of dawn lightens the horizon. It's still dark outside and the screen across the window will soon cast the room into shadow, but my anxiety levels are rising like a tidal wave. I have to stay calm. Have to remember to breathe.

I remind myself that I'm not alone. Just like Iyana and Danika backed me up, Cody will do everything he can to help me today.

His arm is heavy across my torso, his forearm curled up against my chest. I measured out the right dose of human painkillers last night and he finally fell asleep. I'll need to give him more this morning and tuck some extra pills into my pocket to have them on hand.

Carefully maneuvering around in his heavy arms, I expect him to grumble at me, but he's quiet. Really quiet.

Too quiet.

I don't hear him breathing.

Fuck!

I leap upward, gripping his upper shoulder. "Cody?"

He's perfectly still. Unresponsive. His sandy blond hair is slicked to his forehead as if he had a raging fever while he slept.

My heart rises into my throat, my jaw clenched with fear. I

shake him as savagely as I can. When he doesn't respond, I'm ready to scream. "Cody!"

He pulls in a deep breath but doesn't open his eyes. "I'm awake. I'm okay."

I exhale a fuck-load of fear, dropping my head to his chest, pressing my shaking hands to his broad shoulders, trying to calm myself down. "You weren't breathing."

He still doesn't move. "Of course I was breathing. I'm just a deep sleeper." He inhales quietly as if to demonstrate. "Deep breathing. See?"

I tip my head back. "Then open your eyes." When he doesn't obey me, I run my hands across his face.

It scares me when he barely responds.

I nudge his cheek with mine, a firm stroke, trying to elicit a response. "Open your eyes, Cody."

His eyelids rise at an excruciatingly slow speed.

Damn. I press the back of my hand to my forehead, biting my lip hard.

His pupils are dilated, but it's not because I've lost control of my power during my panic. He's unfocused. The whites of his eyes are badly bloodshot, jagged crimson threads spearing all the way to the edges.

I'm not sure how I'll get him to Hidden House, let alone convince Helen to help him, but I need to move up my plan. I was hoping I would have another day to get beneath my father's skin and pave the way to rebellion, but I'll have to make a move this morning.

"Hey," Cody says, his forehead creasing. He reaches up to press his palm to my cheek. "Alphas don't cry."

"I'm starting a new trend." *Damn him for being more lucid than I thought.* I swipe at my cheeks, clearing my throat. "All alphas are required to cry at least once. It's the new alpha way."

He closes his eyes with a heavy exhale. "That sounds suspiciously like you'll miss me."

"Fuck no." I swallow. "I'll be happy when you're gone."

"I'll stick around longer to piss you off, then." A smile plays around his mouth. With a deep inhale, he finally lifts both of his arms, grips me around my ribcage like he has done the last two times we've woken up in this bed, and rolls me onto my back. He dips his cheek to mine, nudging me, his usual wolfish good morning but much less boisterous.

Rolling over and away from me, he takes a moment to sit on the edge of the bed. Without looking back, he picks his clothing up off the floor, walks slowly to the bathroom, and closes the door.

Now that the sun is rising, the shade over the room becomes darker, the shield across the window blocking out the light. It's a mystery to me why this room reacts to the day by trying to turn the room into night. I wish I could have stayed here under different circumstances, maybe discovered its secrets or learned about the people who once lived in this room. They were happy. I'm sure of it.

I dress in my black pants and khaki shirt for what I'm determined will be the last time. I can't wait to wear a flannel shirt again. It's naïve to think that merely putting on a flannel shirt will make me feel like myself again, but I have to hang on to the simple things.

Quickly picking out the medicine from the box, I memorize the different colors and doses. Then I tear a strip off one of the skirts Perla brought me and wrap the medicine in it, tucking it into my pocket.

When Cody emerges from the bathroom, water droplets still clinging to the side of his face, I take a swift look at him across the room. He moves a lot faster now and his eyes have cleared a little, not as bloodshot. His breathing appears more even, too.

"I'm okay," he says, pausing at my scrutiny before he crosses the distance between us and reaches for the painkillers I hold out for him. "I've got a few days left in me yet."

I quell the worry inside me and give him a nod before I finish up my preparation for heading outside.

When we exit the Spire into the cool morning air, the first full rays of sunlight break the horizon, gleaming over the combat area. I pull my wolf's energy back to my body to conserve my energy as much as I can. Even in his weakened state, I trust Cody to watch my back and I can call my wolf out rapidly if I need her.

Our boots beat softly as we cross the dais before we stop and wait for Brynjar to bring the three shifter women out for training.

The women look a lot fresher than they did yesterday—well-rested and fed. I give Brynjar a firm nod, since he took my orders seriously.

I greet each of the women without niceties, checking over their wounds first. The bruise on Reya's—the lioness's—jaw is nearly healed; the ligature marks around Nalani's—the panther's—wrists and ankles from her extended period in the cuffs have faded; and the cuts on Neve's—the snow leopard's —arms have closed up.

I remind them: "Obey my orders and you'll live another day. Disobey me and you'll meet a swift end."

I work them hard—much harder than Iyana ever worked me—but I need my shouts to be heard above the increasing bustle around me. I need the fighters to make a visual impact on every leopard shifter passing by. Every maneuver, every sequence of moves, has to be powerful.

The women respond with the skill of those who are already trained but see the benefit of expanding their skills. Especially when I teach them a sequence that means they can defend each other against a common enemy. I place myself in the move, making myself a player in it, practicing it with them.

That's when a gleam enters Reya's eyes and she gives me a quick onceover, as if she's reassessing what I'm doing.

I don't give her any indication of my intentions, simply continuing with the training.

I'm gratified when my father comes out to watch. I catch his presence from the corner of my eye, but I don't stop the training session right away, pushing the women for another half an hour to really get his attention before we break to hydrate.

The women are exhausted, but they don't complain, gathering at the corner of the dais to drink from the water flasks that Brynjar has brought out. He's a constant presence this morning—my guard in the guise of a helper.

I take note of his location close to the women, as well as the locations of each of the leopard shifter women coming and going in and out of the Spire and the buildings at the other end of the clearing. The only potential assailant who isn't within sight is Silas. Expanding my senses, I detect a hint of his dark magic on the third level of the tower. It will take him a few minutes to reach us when hell breaks loose.

Cody has remained on my right and slightly behind me the whole time, shadowing my movements as I trained the women. He stays close now that I've stopped. I've kept a constant eye on him, watching for any indication that he's not doing okay, but his eyes remain clear and as the morning has gone on, his energy levels have picked up.

After we drink as much water as we need, Cody follows me up onto the dais, where my father stands.

Ford's wearing black pants and a khaki shirt this morning, just like we are. His hair is slicked back and today, he has settled on blue eyes and dark brown hair. The breeze is cool as we approach, a promise of winter to come, but as it swirls around my father, it carries the scent of malice back to me, stronger than the salty ocean air. It's the same scent as when his wolf appeared on the helipad.

I shiver with anticipation. I need to use his wolf so I can force my father's hand. The animal is near. I can sense it. I just can't see it yet...

I brush my hand against Cody's arm when I slow my pace, a touch I hope he will interpret as a warning, before I greet my father.

"Did you sleep well, Tessa?" Ford asks.

"You know I did," I say.

My response makes his forehead crease sharply.

I clarify. "Since you were watching me like you promised. All night long. Right, Father?"

His eyes narrow at me, but I gesture at the women. "Do you like the soldiers I'm producing for Mother Lavinia?"

"You're teaching them to fight as a team. Not against each other," he says with a disapproving scowl.

"You find that unsettling." I ignore the way his eyes narrow even more. I cast my gaze across the women. "I have my reasons."

He snatches my shoulder into his clawed grip, his eyes flooding with crimson power. I sense him searching the streams of my power for what I could be hiding, but our power doesn't work on each other. Our impulses are like a black void to each other.

"I don't like secrets," he says beneath his breath.

I react slowly, turning my face up to his. "Neither do I, but some secrets must be kept, don't you agree?" In the next breath, I ask, "Where is your wolf, Father? Is he still weak from his fight with Tristan?"

"Weak?" Ford growls, his voice low and dangerous.

Just as I hoped, the provocation works. The white wolf is a bright swirl of light as he streams and ripples into shape at Ford's side, within touching distance. The wolf bursts with energy so strong that the hairs on the back of my neck stand on end. Electrified.

The white wolf snarls at me, his lips drawing back over glowing, sharp teeth while his crimson eyes gleam in the sunlight.

"I am never weak," the white wolf says to me.

Holding my head high, I look down at him. "Of course you aren't."

Side-stepping Ford as if his human form were insignificant, I kneel in front of the white wolf, taking a knee in a subservient pose. "You will always prevail. You're the Wolf of War. My true father. And I... have inherited all of your power."

Holding the white wolf's gaze, I allow my crimson rage to

rise, controlling the rush of fury that threatens to dictate my thoughts and actions. Last night I felt my human heart's pure emotions, untainted by my fury for the first time in days. Now, I have to put those feelings aside and become the wolf my father thinks I am.

I slide my hand under the white wolf's chin, daring him to pull away from me. It's a test of his resolve in front of the prisoners, Cody, Brynjar, and all of the leopard shifters whose attention I have been grabbing all morning.

My posture will appear submissive. My head is bowed slightly while I extend my hand, as if I'm requesting the honor of connecting with him, paying homage, maybe declaring my loyalty.

His fur is harsh against my palm, taking solid form where I press my hand. He is real beneath my touch, not insubstantial.

A memory flashes through me of the night the white wolf held my wolf captive in the park. I'd lunged at him with a dagger and caught the flash of fear in his eyes as he disappeared before I could make contact. I wasn't sure why he was afraid of me at the time, but the way his insubstantial wolf takes solid form at my touch confirms it.

I can't stop my elation.

Tristan is not the only one with the power to end my father. I can too.

Stroking the white wolf's chin, I lean toward him. Pressing my face against his, feeling the breath of his snarls near my neck where his teeth could sink into me and end my life, I whisper into his ears. "You gave me all the power I need to overthrow you."

CHAPTER TWENTY-THREE

The white wolf leaps away from me with a snarl, his crimson eyes blazing. He will think I've made an empty threat, but I'm about to make good on it.

I release my dark wolf from my body. She flies from my chest, her claws extended and teeth bared, sailing through the air toward him.

She thuds into the white wolf's side, raking her claws down his neck and drawing his blood before he can leap out of the way. The impact knocks both of our wolves across the dais. Recovering quickly, they leap away from each other, circling, their teeth bared.

I'm not about to lose the advantage of surprise. I draw both of my daggers and spin to Ford, driving one blade at his throat, the other at his stomach. He blocks my upper arm, protecting his neck, but doesn't deflect my lower arm fast enough. The blade scrapes across his side, slicing through his shirt and grazing the flesh across his ribs.

His scream of rage and pain draws the attention of every leopard shifter in the clearing. At the corner of the dais, Reya, Nalani, and Neve burst into action, all three leaping away from Brynjar before he can grab them. They dart toward clear ground and take up defensive positions back to back like I taught them this morning.

The leopard shifters don't wait for Ford to command them. They head straight for the prisoners. The first leopard to strike at Reya with her dagger meets a kick to the face that throws her backward. Nalani deflects the second leopard with a crunching blow to her ribs. Neve deftly evades a third leopard, her snow leopard's agility evident in her lithe attack as she sweeps her assailant's feet out from under her. Nalani's panther's strength reveals itself when she follows up Neve's move with a cracking blow to the fallen leopard's temple. So far, none of the leopard women have shifted, but a few in the back are preparing to remove their combat uniforms so it won't be long before the clearing is filled with at least twenty leopards.

Perla is among them, but she stands back from the fight, watching the interaction between me and my father carefully. She has felt my strength. She knows I could have killed her and didn't. Her lips press together in indecision, but it's hard to read her true intentions when she backs away from the fight and retreats to the other side of the clearing.

My greater worry is Brynjar. He has frozen at the side of the dais, the same indecision written on his face as Perla's. What I know of his nature is that he is dedicated to the old magic that streams through both Ford and me. His loyalty is to Ford, but he won't want to see me die. Even so, the minute he takes a step toward Cody, I will need to send my wolf after him.

Cody has taken up position right beside the door of the Spire, his attention wide, taking in the leopard shifters, the prisoners, me, my father, and Brynjar. Cody is tense, poised, and I know he'll be ready for either Brynjar to attack or for Silas to storm through the Spire's door.

I scan the fight around me within a split second and now my attention returns to my father.

Ford snarls at me. "This is not the time to challenge me, daughter."

"I drew your blood already, Father. I'd say this is the perfect time."

"You can't take my empire." Ford pivots to avoid a second thrust of the blade I aim at his throat. "I made you. You will never be as strong as me."

"I'm *stronger*," I say, playing on his fears. Still in control of both daggers, I flip them one after the other in my hands, a threatening gesture before I grip them in a fighter's hold, ready to slash the blades across his chest. "You broke my human soul too well."

Only a few paces away from us, our wolves snarl and leap at each other again, their teeth closing around each other's shoulders. His white wolf suddenly yelps and I suspect my wolf has caught one of his freshly healed wounds. She gnashes at the same spot again, but his wolf darts to the side.

"Surrender, Father," I say to Ford, continuing with a lie. "You can have a place in my new empire. I won't abandon you."

I tense as Brynjar makes a move, but only to step into the shadows at the side of the Spire. I guess he's decided to stay out of this fight after all.

My heart sinks when Silas appears inside the door, his power blazing so brightly that he lights up the shadowed entryway. Cold, blue lightning flickers around his hands, arms, and torso, casting electric color across his black clothing.

Cody is ready. The moment that Silas steps foot outside the door, Cody moves at rapid speed. He throat-punches Silas with one hand, aiming for the spot where Silas's magic hasn't extended. At the same time, he rips off Silas's eyepatch with his other hand, exposing the magical orb that holds Silas's power. Cody makes a grab for the orb—the smartest move he could make—but the warlock's magic blazes too quickly.

With a shout, Silas sends a stream of lightning at Cody, who is forced to leap to the side. The lightning crashes against the Spire's wall. I expect a few stones to fall, maybe some hairline cracks to appear, but a force bursts outward at the impact and I sense the old magic in the Spire react. The lightning is deflected and splintered, a shower of deadly light shards falling around Silas and Cody.

I was preparing to take another stab at Ford's heart, but I'm suddenly caught by the indecision that I need to protect Cody first. I freeze and prepare to throw my weapon at Silas, readying my wolf to leap at him if I have to.

My father's shout rages across the dais. "Stop, Silas! I need that shifter alive! Contain him but don't kill him. *Yet.*"

Silas is poised, ready to strike again, his magic becoming softer but no less deadly, while Cody is tense and takes up a defensive stance, both of them located on the dais where it meets the Spire's outer wall.

Ford hunches his shoulders as we circle each other. "What do you want, daughter? Let's make a deal."

"A deal." I scoff. "You have nothing to offer me that I can't take for myself."

I'm prepared for this game to go one of two ways. Either I defeat my father now and take control of my fate, or I force him to make a mistake that gets me, Cody, and the prisoners out of here, and *then* I'll take control of my fate.

"I think I can offer you something you want," he says.

Shaking my head, I say, "No."

He's stalling for time—I can read it in the way his gaze flicks from me to my wolf. His fingers twitch at his sides and I sense his powerful energy reaching out toward my wolf, preparing to take hold of her. Once he captures her, it will be game over.

His wolf's energy is bright and burning in my senses.

It's time to test whether I can take control of his wolf the same way he takes control of mine. Allowing my crimson rage to rise across my vision, giving in to the malice inside me, I sense the streams of energy making up the shape of his wolf, the flow of his power, as well as the flow of my own power. The streams are like ropes and if I can just use them like a noose…

I'm shocked when my power responds to the mere thought

of catching hold of his power. A thread of energy, imperceptible except in my crimson vision, extends from my wolf's body like a rope as she prepares to lunge at the white wolf again.

The thread twines around his neck, around and around, drawing tighter and tighter...

"Taking my empire and controlling it are two very different challenges," Ford snaps. He's either unaware of the attack I'm about to perpetrate on him or he thinks I won't be strong enough to be a threat to him. "You don't have any alliances yet."

I give him a slow shake of my head. I intend to plant a seed of doubt in his mind, one that I hope will rattle him. After all, he told me I can create fear that clouds a person's judgement. "I will take the prisoners to Mother Lavinia and make a new alliance with her. Once she's on my side, everyone else will fall into line."

He scoffs. "How do you propose to ally yourself with the most ruthless witch alive?"

"I will annihilate her enemies for her. I will do what you've failed to do: give her the forest," I say. "She will come to understand that following me brings her glory."

Ford twitches. For the first time since he called a halt to Silas's magic, he seems unsettled.

"You won't succeed," he snarls.

I look him directly in the eye. "I disagree." I raise my voice. "What do you think, Brynjar? Can I bend a power-hungry witch to my will by whispering promises into her ears?"

The ice jotunn is an unreadable mountain of muscle where he remains on the far side of the dais, separated from Silas and Cody. I sense his growing inner conflict in the way his gaze passes from my father to me. He has served Ford since Ford gave him purpose. Now, he must wonder... who will give him the greater purpose in the future: my father or me?

I lower my voice as I return my focus to Ford. "I will leave today. Right after I destroy you."

My wolf's energy suddenly tightens around the white wolf's throat, drawing closed. The white wolf jumps, his crimson eyes widening. He whines, shakes his head, and draws his lips back before he drops his head to his paws, desperately trying to scratch at the power that chokes him.

The power that I sensed Ford extending toward me, slowly reaching to take control of my wolf's energy, dissipates.

Ford clutches his own throat and drops to his knees. His eyes are as wide as his wolf's. I guess he really didn't think I'd have the strength to place a chokehold around his wolf's neck.

"Silas!" He gasps. "Kill the wolf-less shifter. And the prisoners."

Cody is already moving, his fist crashing into Silas's face, another into the warlock's stomach. The warlock doubles over, but only for a moment. Silas recovers in time for Cody to get in another hit to his chin before Silas's magic explodes from his hands, knocking Cody against the wall and wrenching Cody's arms out to the sides, pinning him against the Spire.

"Silas will rip your lapdog apart at my command." Ford gasps at me, clutching his throat. "Do you want another person to die because of your actions?"

He's referring to Tristan, trying to weaken my resolve with guilt about what happened on the helipad. It won't work, but even so, I have a choice to make.

Unless I kill Ford right now, Silas will rip Cody apart. The energy I'm using to hold Ford is coming directly from my wolf, so I can't move her to defend Cody. Even if I kill Ford in a single strike, I will need my wolf to move as fast as possible to prevent Silas from striking and killing Cody at the same time. I know Ford was afraid of me striking him in my human form, but I don't know what it will take to end him. The fight between him and Tristan lasted minutes and both of them ended up injured but not dead.

With a growl, I test my ability to choke Ford by tightening the thread of energy around his wolf's neck, but it meets resistance. It seems that I can hurt him this way, hold him captive, but it doesn't look like I can kill him.

Fuck. My chances of taking control of my fate right now are fading. I'm now headed down the second path of forcing Ford to make a mistake.

It's time to play-act my part.

I snarl at my father but twitch in Cody's direction, a fearful gesture, as if I'm worried about him, but I'm trying not to show it. It doesn't take a lot of acting because I'm genuinely fucking afraid for him right now. At the same time, I loosen my hold on the noose around the white wolf's neck. Then my eyes widen, as if I realized the danger of losing hold of the white wolf and now I'm afraid of retaliation.

I jolt and fumble, my hands shaking, the noose loosening even farther as I let it slip. At the same time, I pull my wolf's energy back to my body, a fierce enough tug that it forces me to release my father from my power completely.

It means that my wolf's energy is safe and he can't take hold of me.

It also means surrender.

With a roar, my father rises to his feet.

The white wolf leaps forward and snarls at my back, jubilant in his victory. With my father on one side of me, and the white wolf on the other, I must look helpless.

Closer to the tower, Silas throws his head back, triumphant, while Cody remains pinned against the wall. In the clearing beyond the dais, the prisoners have gathered back to back again while the leopard shifters circle around them. Their fight is paused as the leopard shifters take glances at Ford and me, waiting for the final outcome.

I catch the sweat and wounds on the prisoner's faces. The moves I taught them this morning kept them alive, but their disappointment is palpable. My heart sinks because I can't explain to them that I'm not giving up, that this is only Plan B.

"Brynjar," my father shouts.

The ice jotunn's boots thud in the silence. He stops beside

my father, a massive sentinel. Brynjar gives a heavy sigh. "I apologize if I failed you, boss."

"On the contrary, old friend," Ford says. "You broke her so well that she is everything I could hope for. She longs for blood. As she should." Ford's eyebrows draw down, a spark of anger in his eyes. "But I must teach her that my blood is not to be craved. Biting me will only bring pain."

He sneers. "We will take her to Mother Lavinia today, just as she wishes. All of the prisoners will come with us. Then we will see whether or not my daughter is willing to bend to my will."

Inside, I'm relieved. The seed of doubt I planted in his mind has grown. He needs to reassert his alliance with Mother Lavinia and teach me a lesson at the same time.

I'm getting the hell out of here and Cody and the prisoners are coming with me.

It's a small step to freedom, and I'm not sure yet what price I'll pay for it, but any step away from the Spire creates the opportunity for escape.

Brynjar doesn't seem to need instructions from my father. He strides right up to me. I force myself not to react violently, not to slash at him with the daggers when my breath suddenly frosts in the air. I adjusted to his power when he broke me. It doesn't feel cold to me anymore, more like a fist.

Snowflakes drift from his hands when he catches my wrists, twisting the daggers from my hands and yanking me off my feet, nearly dislocating my arms. He dangles me so high that my booted toes barely touch the ground.

I face off with him. "One day, Brynjar, you will need to make a choice," I say, planting another seed of doubt, one I hope will come to fruition.

He tips his head to the side and considers me with his icy-blue eyes. "Today is not that day, young one."

"Maybe not, but soon."

In response, Brynjar's lips press in a straight line.

He zeros in on my face.

I read his intentions and brace for the pain.

The ice jotunn knocks his head into mine, a mountain of rock impacting my forehead, his icy magic streaming through my mind at the same time.

My head snaps back and the effect is instant.

Agony tears through my mind, followed swiftly by darkness.

CHAPTER TWENTY-FOUR

I regain consciousness in increments.

I'm aware that the ice jotunn is carrying me into a building and I make out the shape of the vehicle hangar. He carries me in his arms this time. I can now see that there's another door at the other end of the building so that vehicles will be able to exit from either side.

Two military-style vans stand closest to the front with their back doors open. Inside the large, windowless back compartment of each vehicle, a cage has been built into the left-hand side while a bench seat is situated on the right.

I catch sight of Reya, Nalani, and Neve being loaded into the vehicle on the left and I give in to a moment of relief that Ford is really carrying through. Brynjar steps aside, revealing Cody with his hands bound behind his back, his mouth gagged. Silas shoves him into the cage of the nearest vehicle ahead of me.

Blinking slowly, taking mental stock of my limbs, I look up to find Brynjar staring down at me.

He's already aware that I'm awake.

"It's only a cage if you think it is," he murmurs, adjusting his arms so he can curl his hand across my forehead. A single tap of his finger is like a rock against my head.

Damn. The ice jotunn's hand is like a mountain dropping

on me.

I black out again.

~

The hum of an engine fills my hearing.

I jolt awake to find myself lying on my side in darkness.

I can't move my arms or legs and a blindfold rests around my eyes, but I can sense others in the back of the van with me. Cody's scent calms me—the field of warmed grass that I cursed a number of times is now as effective at calming me as making lists inside my head. He's nearby. Somewhere near my head.

I also smell Silas—a dark, oily scent like his magic. But I can't scent the final person and that tells me everything—it must be my father.

I assume I'm now in the cage in the back of the van. I could harness my crimson rage to see beyond the blindfold, but my eyes would glow behind the material and I want to take a moment before Silas and my father realize I'm awake.

Cold metal circles my ankles and wrists, all four of my limbs pulled tightly behind me and attached so close to each other that I can actually touch the soles of my feet with my hands. Steel bars press against my face like fingers. Anger settles in my stomach at the realization that the metal extends around my mouth, chin, and the sides of my face. Some sort of strap is clamped across the back of my head—every part of it pressing against my scalp.

It's a muzzle. Not leather, like the women's, but steel.

Well, that's just glorious.

I hold my anger at bay. I can slip these chains like I slipped the shackles in the tower, but I need to determine my best move first.

The intense pain of Brynjar's headbutt has receded, but my skull aches, a dull throb that worsens as I test my physical strength against the chains around my wrists and ankles just in case I can break them in my human form.

The sound of a match lighting makes me pause.

The flare of light builds around the edges of the blindfold. I'm about to draw on my crimson vision, but thick fingers brush against my face and the blindfold is pulled up, but only from one of my eyes.

Silas leans back on his heels outside the cage, smiling at me.

His eyepatch rests once again over his magic orb. I guess he likes the symmetry between us now—each of us watching the other with only one eye. Keeping his balance as the vehicle turns a corner, he lowers the burning match so that I can see what rests across his lap.

A semi-automatic rifle. No magic bullets for me this time.

It's ironic to me that magic flows off my human form, but bullets designed by humans can kill me. *Maybe...*

I consider it more carefully. My father has survived through the ages. Killing him—and me—can't be as easy as killing our human form. My father is most afraid that his wolf's power will come to an end. He told me that only Tristan has the power to end us. I know I can end my father too. It has to mean that my human form can survive a mortal wound. I might be hurt badly—I *have* been hurt badly—but I won't die as long as my power remains intact.

I reconsider my fear of the human weapon, convincing myself that while it can hurt me, it won't kill me.

The light within the van confirms that my father sits on the bench seat behind Silas. Tipping my head back slightly, I finally make out Cody, sitting with his back pressed to the side of the vehicle, his hands behind him. The clank of metal indicates he's cuffed to a bar. He's still gagged, but he doesn't try to speak as he focuses on me.

"Why do you fight your path?" Silas asks, allowing the match to burn all the way down to his thumb and forefinger. His gaze from his uncovered eye drills into me for a second before he puffs on the match to blow it out and leave us in darkness. "You are war and you can't escape it."

My response is a growl. "When I'm free, I'll rip out your eyes. Both of them."

As the vehicle bumps along what I assume is forest terrain, I'm unable to balance myself, even though I try to dig my knees in. Rocking on the spot, I end up crammed against the bars between Silas and me. For all my bravado, my head is pounding.

Silas gives a heavy sigh. He lights another match, lifting it recklessly close to his lips. "You can fight your future, but you will fail. Then you will realize that the only path is your father's."

The flickering amber fire casts a glow across the warlock's cheeks and lights up his uncovered eye, now brighter than it was before.

He inhales the flame, pulling it right off the match.

His cheeks glow amber, but the fire blazes through the veins in his neck, glowing beneath his shirt as it travels down his arm. He turns his palm up as the flame bursts into life in his hand, hovering above the surface of his skin, growing and spinning.

"Your father would order me to light you on fire if he thought it would make you understand your path," the warlock says.

This flame is magical and my fear of it is minor, even though it's stronger and brighter than a real flame.

Keeping his fiery palm outside the cage, Silas reaches through the bars with his free hand to grip the back of my head, twisting his fingertips through my strapped hair.

His touch is suddenly overwhelming. Beneath the sickening depth of his dark magic, I sense a mind that is older than it should be. The source of his life has to be his second eye—the magical orb. He releases me with a shove before he leans back, still holding the fire in his palm.

It's Ford's turn to slide forward—right to the edge of his seat. Silas's firelight glitters in his eyes when he speaks. "I've told you about the five witches who control parts of the forest, but have you heard the stories about Mother Kadris?" he asks.

THIS BROKEN WOLF

It's an odd change of subject. I sift through the names of the witches Ford told me about—the ones he deals with—but Mother Kadris isn't one of them.

"No," I say, but not before Cody tenses at the corner of my vision. He remains half in the shadows where I can't quite see his face.

Ford casts Cody a sharp glance. "Your lapdog obviously has." He touches Silas's shoulder with an order. "Silas, allow the shifter to speak."

Silas swills his hand across the air and Cody's gag disintegrates from his mouth. Cody inhales sharply in a way that indicates the gag wasn't only physical, but also magical. Silas must have been preventing Cody from making a sound. I kick myself because I should have realized. I need to be more alert to Silas's tricks from now on.

"Tell my daughter about Mother Kadris, lapdog," my father says.

I tip my head back again, trying to keep Ford in my sights at the same time as I see Cody, remaining impassive about the insulting name Ford keeps calling him.

Cody opens and closes his mouth, working his jaw for a moment. He pauses a beat as if he's not going to obey Ford but finally says, "Mother Kadris is a myth. A story told to scare children into behaving themselves."

Ford gives a gusty laugh. "Mother Kadris was real. Trust me, I met her. Tell my daughter what she did that was so terrifying to children."

"She would offer a favor in exchange for your soul," Cody says. "At first, the favor would grant you what you wanted, but her victims were left soulless and eventually they all became monsters. Finally, she granted a favor that cost her the life of someone she loved. After that, she disappeared."

Casting my father a hard stare with my single visible eye, I ask, "This is supposed to mean something to me because…?"

Ford returns my steady gaze. "She was once a member of Mother Serena's coven," he says. "You remember the witch who once controlled all of the forest? I met Mother Serena and Mother Kadris centuries ago when they were at the height of their power. The dark magic they wielded and the chaos they caused was truly magnificent."

He rubs his chin. "But Mother Kadris became too confident, too sure of herself. She lost someone she loved, just like the story goes." Ford gives a shrug. "Someone else paid the price for her pride. After that, her heart was broken, her powers diminished, and she vanished. Now she is nothing more than a bedtime story."

He slips off the bench seat and reaches through the bars, stroking my arm, making me shudder. "It's a warning to us all about the dangers of playing a game we can't win, Tessa."

My father's gaze passes pointedly to Cody before returning to me. "Someone we care about will die."

When Ford begins to lean back, apparently satisfied that he's delivered his threat, I draw on my wolf's energy and allow my eyes to flicker crimson.

"That story assumes we all have someone we love more than ourselves," I say, studying Ford as hard as he's now studying me. My speech implies that I don't care about Cody's life, after all—which I already proved isn't true—but even so, I can't resist the urge to draw a little blood.

"Isn't the real message that love makes us weak?" My lip curls as I snarl at my father. "Whether it is love for a friend… or a mother… or perhaps a lover who disappeared without a trace and hid a child—"

Ford's hand darts between the bars, grabbing my muzzle and yanking me toward him. His nostrils flare and his breathing rasps at the verbal claw I just drove into him about his feelings for my mother.

"I warned you," he says. "I am incapable of love."

"But not resistant to bonding. You and I are very alike—but not in all respects," I say. "Perhaps you bonded with her because you are the original war wolf, but I can't bond. I'm incapable of feeling that connection. The absence of a bond makes me stronger than you. You will see."

"No," he snarls. "*You* will see. Very soon."

CHAPTER TWENTY-FIVE

*A*fter traveling through the forest for another two hours, the van finally draws to a stop.

Brynjar's large body blocks out the dappled mid-afternoon sunlight as he opens the van's doors wide for my father and Silas to climb out. The fresh air brings the scent of the forest, triggering a memory.

Damn. This place smells like the leaf that Cody plucked from my hair. I was afraid that Tristan might have retreated to the forest. It's the only place his pack wouldn't come after him.

The ice giant unlocks the cage, reaches in to slide me toward him, and releases the chain keeping my feet bound to my hands. He leaves the cuffs around my wrists and ankles, and I discover that they are tied with their own chains so that my hands remain behind my back and a chain extends between my ankles.

Brynjar gathers me into his arms to lift me out and place me on my feet, where I discover that the chain between my legs is only long enough for me to shuffle along the mossy ground. I groan as the blood rushes to my hands and feet now that I can stretch my limbs.

Cody shuffles up beside me as soon as Brynjar releases him

from the cuffs that chained him to the inside of the van and lets him out.

The vehicle is parked beside an enormous tree. All of the trees soar far above me, the canopy overhead allowing only soft mid-afternoon sunlight to reach the ground. A drop of water lands on my cheek when I tip my head back to follow the height of the nearest tree all the way to its top. It must rain constantly but lightly here because the ground is moist beneath my boots but not soggy.

The other vehicle pulls up beside ours a moment later and two leopard shifters jump out of it. One of them is Perla. I watch carefully as she pulls Reya, Nalani, and Neve from the back. The women appear mostly unharmed, but I'm conscious of their focus on me. I'm now bound up like they are—muzzle and all.

Cody's the only one who isn't muzzled and I guess that's because his teeth are basically human-shaped now.

I take note when Silas leaves his weapon inside the vehicle and the two leopard shifters also remove their weapon harnesses and leave them behind. For a moment, my mind whirls as I consider whether or not now is the time to escape, but the chains around our ankles make that difficult. I can slip my bindings, but Cody and the prisoners won't be able to.

Damn. I swallow my moment of hope.

"We walk from here," Brynjar says as my father strides away ahead of us. Silas waits for us to advance, taking up the rear with Perla at his side. She steers well clear of me, although Silas breathes down my neck along the way.

A winding pathway through the trees awaits us.

Stone pillars are placed at intervals along each side with runes carved into their flat surfaces.

My senses buzz with all of the magic in the air around me. The thick layers of protective spells that surround this place make the exposed skin on my arms, neck, and face tingle. I sense eyes in the trees. Witches must be watching us from cloaked positions. I also have no doubt that we wouldn't be able to pass along this path at all unless they had already lowered their defenses to allow it.

Well, for the others, that is. I could walk right in like my father could. I guess that makes for a significant power imbalance when the witches know that Ford can stride right through all of their defenses and attack them if he wishes.

Brynjar slowly falls back until he walks beside me while Cody shuffles along on my left. At Brynjar's appearance, Silas backs off behind me.

Brynjar and Silas were working together as a team when I saw them during the fight in Tristan's territory. They also worked in tandem to break my human soul, but since then, I haven't sensed the same unity of purpose between them.

"My father intends to teach me a lesson in humility," I say to Brynjar, not bothering to whisper. He will be able to hear me if he wishes. "I understand what you meant about the cage, though. I can slip these chains at any time. But for now, I will endure the shame."

He nods, and I wish I could hate him more for choosing to stand at my father's side.

"You have decided to bite at a time of your choosing," he says with an icy gleam in his pale blue eyes.

I nod. "I believe my father would expect nothing less."

Two enormous stone pillars sit on either side of the end of the path. Passing between them feels like walking through a snowstorm—another magical barrier.

Once I pass through, what appeared to be an empty forest ahead of us transforms into a series of wood cabins built into the sides of even more enormous trees than the ones where the vehicles are parked. A large, circular clearing is located directly ahead with a diameter that stretches as far as two hundred feet, while the cabins sit around its edges in a solid horseshoe pattern. The entrance where we stand appears to be the only opening in and out of the clearing.

I'm unsettled that the trees remind me of the trees in my bedroom at Hidden House—like the enormous trunk that hid an entire bathroom. These ones are even bigger, the cabins seeming to have been formed from the wood and bark at their bases while gleaming crystal windows refract the light onto the clearing.

A single woman stands in the middle of the open space wearing pure white clothing consisting of white ankle-height boots, pants, and a cowl neck top that dips low enough to show off her cleavage. A long, silk jacket flows to her calves. Her copper hair is loosely curled, her lips are the color of tangerines, and her eyes are like hazel wood. The wand she holds casually at her side is also pure ivory and could possibly be made out of bone. She looks no older than forty, but it doesn't take my crimson eyes for me to sense that she's much older.

Ford slows his pace as he approaches her, giving her a formal bow when he stops a few paces from her. "Blessings on your power, Mother Lavinia."

She inclines her head. "You've brought your offerings early."

"I thought you would be pleased."

Her eyes gleam as she licks her lips. "I can't wait to see what goodies you've brought for me to play with this time."

Ford sweeps his arm wide while Brynjar and Silas line us up nearby—Reya, Nalani, and Neve closest to Lavinia while Cody and I are farther to her right. Perla and the other leopard shifter take up position off to the side and out of Mother Lavinia's way.

The witch starts on the left, making appreciative noises as she squeezes Reya's bound arms, pats down Nalani's torso, and stares hard into Neve's eyes.

"Very nice," Lavinia says with a visible shiver of delight. "Very strong. They look spirited, like I asked."

"They should be good for early fights," Ford says. "They will maintain your reputation."

"Only early fights?" Mother Lavinia asks. She grabs Reya's shoulder. "I like the look of this lion shifter for a final fight. I'm keen to take more of Mother Zala's territory. That witch is like a claw in my side. I need to teach her a lesson."

"I have something better for you," Ford says, pointing at Cody and me.

Mother Lavinia stops in front of Cody and her eyebrows draw down with displeasure. "This one is dying." She turns her fierce glare on Ford. "Why have you brought him to me?"

Ford gives her a soothing smile. "Because he will allow you to keep the next one under control."

Mother Lavinia blinks at Ford, her lips pressed together as if she suspects he's deceiving her before she moves on to me.

I allow my crimson rage to rise a second before she meets my gaze.

She takes one look into my angry eyes and jolts back a step, her hand flying over her heart, after which she lets out an embarrassed laugh.

"Oh, dear!" she exclaims. "But, Ford, darling, you mean to trick me. This must be your daughter, is she not? She has your eyes." Lavinia turns to Ford, her fingers tapping against each other greedily. "Your daughter can't really be on offer... can she?"

Ford's expression is hard. "Tessa is offered on loan. She needs to learn her place. I'm hoping you will teach her."

"Gladly." Mother Lavinia licks her lips as she looks me up and down. Moving back to Ford, she places a perfectly manicured hand on his arm, squinting a little apologetically as she says, "You do realize, darling, that I might not return her to you in *exactly* the same untouched condition in which you've brought her to me today?"

Ford's glare at me deepens. "I'm counting on it." He lowers his voice. "She comes with a warning, however. Like me, she is highly resistant to magic. I suggest you keep weapons handy and make the most of the dying shifter to keep her in line."

"I will. How delicious." Mother Lavinia licks her lips again. "We should celebrate." She raises her hands, her white sleeves falling away from her forearms as she claps her hands twice.

So far, I haven't seen any other witches, but I can sense their magic glimmering at intervals around us.

The corners of the cabins around the clearing shimmer

and suddenly become fluid. Women take shape, pulling their bodies from the wooden edges of the buildings, the varying colors of their skin gleaming through all of the wooden hues, their diaphanous dresses floating around them as they step from the wood and gather behind Mother Lavinia. Ford told me that Mother Lavinia has the largest coven and I count twenty witches, all dressed in white like she is, their clothing varying between pants and low-cut tops to dresses with and without shawls around their shoulders.

"Sisters," Mother Lavinia calls. "We have a new fighter who is sure to win us more territory and bring us glory!"

One of the witches steps forward eagerly. She looks younger than the others with straight, brown hair cut short at her shoulders and big, green eyes. "As strong as Daisy?" she asks.

"Sister Tia!" Mother Lavinia flushes and her eyes narrow at the young witch. Her voice loses its pleasant tone, a sharp edge to it. "We do not speak of Daisy. She is dead to us and that is the end of it."

My forehead creases. Daisy must have been a fighter for Mother Lavinia, but it's hardly an intimidating name. Maybe that was the point—to make her opponents underestimate her.

Mother Lavinia lifts her chin, takes a deep calming breath, and pastes a serene expression on her face. "Sisters, prepare a feast. We will eat tonight and plan our next challenge tomorrow."

She turns to Sister Tia. "You will take the fighters down below and make them pretty for the feast. They need to keep their strength up."

Sister Tia folds her hands in front of herself. "I'm sure I don't have to tell you to behave yourselves," she says. "We can make your lives very unpleasant if you don't."

She waits another beat for her message to sink in, then continues, overly bright. "You can follow me now."

I glimpse Reya eyeing the stone pillars at the entrance to the clearing—how close they are to us—but I give her a quick shake of my head. She won't get far in her shackles and she isn't resistant to magic, like I am.

She presses her lips together and I sense her frustration as she focuses back on Tia, who waves us forward. "This way."

We follow Tia to the cabin at the back of the clearing, shuffling up its wide front steps to the door. Cody stays close to me on my right-hand side while the shifters remain on my heels. The door opens into a homely-looking lounge room with a fireplace burning in the hearth. It's not exactly a cage.

Tia waves her wand, whispers beneath her breath, and the rug in front of the fire lifts into the air. A large trapdoor opens up in the floor and the top of a set of wooden stairs is revealed.

"It's a good thing you're here," Tia says as she leads us down the overly warm stairwell. "Our last fighter was killed two weeks ago in a silly bet. She wasn't very strong."

It's difficult to maintain balance walking down the stairs with our hands chained behind our backs and our feet shackled together. I find myself leaning against the side of the stairwell, finding the warmth in the wooden walls disconcerting. It should be getting cooler the farther we descend, not warmer.

"If you love fights so much," I ask Tia, "why don't *you* fight?"

Tia halts on the stairs and whirls to me. "Are you trying to provoke me?"

"Maybe," I say, arching an eyebrow at her.

"You might be on loan, but that doesn't mean we can't hurt you," she threatens, raising her wand. I guess she didn't hear Ford tell Mother Lavinia that I'm resistant to magic.

I brush off her threat. "It seems strange to me that you don't use your own magic to fight against each other."

Tia draws herself upright. "We did in the beginning. We lost too many sisters that way. After what happened to Mother Serena..." She shudders. "She destroyed her whole coven in a fight she thought she could win. Those fucking assassins..."

Tia stops on the middle step and covers her mouth with a little laugh. "Oh! Forgive my language." She takes a beat to compose herself, smiling sweetly again, but her eyes are cold. "We won't risk total annihilation."

Tia turns away from me, but I'm not done asking questions. I sense Cody and the three women also listening intently as they navigate the stairs behind me. Tia seems overly talkative and I don't want to let the opportunity for answers pass.

"Who was Daisy?" I ask, since whatever happened to the former fighter might give me a clue about what awaits us.

"A wolf shifter. Like you, I guess. One of the best fighters we had."

"What happened to her?"

Sister Tia stops on the bottom step. "Daisy never wanted to fight. Ever. Mother Lavinia had to force her to do it. But once provoked—*damn*—Daisy was glorious in a battle to the death." She sighs. "Then, one day…"

She stops speaking, a deep scowl forming on her face. "We don't talk about that." She proceeds into the room with a shrug of her shoulders. "Never mind. Now we have you."

I step into a large room with a floor and walls made of wooden boards. Cody and the three women join me, all five of us pausing to consider our new cage.

I was expecting cold stone. Wood is a surprise. Rugs and pillows have been piled up in the far right-hand corner of the room. Two clothes racks with both men's and women's clothing hanging on them sit against the far wall, along with a ceiling-to-floor mirror. There appears to be a small bathroom to the left, but that's it.

The temperature has increased with every step we took downward and now it's overly warm and stuffy. When I look down, I make out a glow beneath the floorboards, as if there's another level below us, but it's difficult to sense what's down there. Nothing living, that's for sure.

Tia catches me looking. "This room is set within a bed of flames," she says, licking her lips, a dangerous glint appearing in her eyes. "The fire burns all night and day, but don't worry. Protective spells sit between you and the flames. Do what you're told and we won't incinerate you."

I shudder, worried that I could disrupt the protective shields by setting foot in this room. "Where are the spells?" I ask.

She waves her hand. "On the other side of the walls and floor."

I exhale my relief. That means I'm not in direct contact with them. I remind myself that my ability to resist and break magic is directly connected with touch.

I force myself to breathe again.

"You're really lucky to be here, you know," Tia continues, glancing from me to Cody and the women. "Mother Zala keeps her fighters in a deep pit in the ground. It's open to the rain."

With a bright smile, Tia strides to the rack of clothing and pulls out both a flowing dress and a leather bodice. "Hmm. What to go for tonight? Elegant or battle ready?" She casts an eye over us. "Let's go with elegant."

Pulling multiple dresses and a man's suit from the racks, she throws them onto the floor and glides toward the staircase. "Knock yourselves out. Don't fight over the dresses. I'll be back when it's time for the feast."

She hasn't gone far when she pops her head back around the corner. With a wave of her wand and a whispered spell, the shackles fall away from our feet and ankles, clanking onto the floor.

"You can remove your own muzzles," she says before she disappears again, as blasé as if she'd told us to help ourselves to coffee.

Reya, Nalani, and Neve back away from Cody and me, turning to each other to remove their muzzles. Cody reaches for the back of my head and finally succeeds in untangling the buckles from my hair. Silas must have tied the muzzle on. I'm sure Brynjar would have taken more care.

Cody pauses behind me, his hands resting on my shoulders. "What now, Tessa?"

Turning, I take a careful look at his eyes. They're increasingly bloodshot. Luckily, Brynjar didn't empty my pockets because I still have the packet of medicine. "First, you need painkillers. Then we go to this feast, scope out our surroundings, and figure out an escape route. My father doesn't control this environment and he won't stay long. As soon as he's gone, I'll kill the witches and we're getting out of here. I'm not spending another night in captivity."

While Cody heads to the bathroom to change, I scoop up one of the dresses that rests on the floor between me and the shifter women. It's cobalt blue with thin straps, a plunging neckline, and a miniskirt that sits beneath a sweeping diaphanous overlay. The overskirt joins at the center of the waist at the front. It splits to either side and will allow for good leg movement.

Reya's voice sounds beside me as she reaches for a pale pink dress that will work with the pink highlights in her golden flaxen hair. "You make escape sound simple."

"I can fight witches," I say. "I can even fight the ice jotunn and the warlock. My father is impossible to beat."

Reya grips the dress so hard that she threatens to tear it with her extending claws. She's afraid. Even if I couldn't smell her fear, I read it in the tension around her eyes and the way she scrunches her hands into the delicate material. "Where do we fit in this plan?"

"I need you to stay out of danger and protect each other. Whatever you do, don't try to help me. My father will use you as leverage against me."

"So we live or die by your decisions," Reya says, her lioness surfacing in her amber eyes.

"You will *live* by my decisions," I say.

"How do we trust you?" Nalani asks, her dark eyes wide. She and Neve stand a little to the side. "You're his daughter. This could all be a trick to get us to fight. Like that Daisy woman they spoke about."

THIS BROKEN WOLF

I take a breath. "I won't ask you to trust me. You need to judge my decisions for yourselves. If you feel like I'm making the wrong choice, then do what you think is best for you."

I pull off my black pants and khaki shirt, but I'm careful with the fold of material containing the painkillers, placing my clothing in a pile against the wall for now. I'll need to find somewhere to hide the medicine since there are no pockets in the dress I shimmy into. The bodice is a size too small, gripping my torso and giving me significant cleavage, but when I riffle through the other dresses on the rack, I don't find anything closer to my size. Apparently, it's one-size-fits-all in this firepit.

Reya, Nalani, and Neve have similar struggles with dresses that either pinch their waists or their hips. Reya is the broadest in her shoulders and has to leave the back zip of her pink dress undone at the top to fit into it.

When Cody emerges from the bathroom, he's pulled on a pair of long, navy-blue pants and a white collared shirt that he left open at the top, but he leaves off the jacket. He looks like a Griffin through and through, his family more powerful than any other shifter family, and yet privately broken. His external appearance, every perfect muscle, his broad shoulders, sculpted chest, and lean waist, every part of him, hides the cracks.

I find makeup in an open box sitting on the floor of the bathroom. There's also a toilet and a sink, but no cupboards where I could stash the medicine packet. I shun the makeup. The face I wear is already alluring and seductive. It makes me wonder how Cody can look past my shape, my shell, to the sheer fucking terror and determination beneath. Maybe he wonders the same thing about the way I see him now. How I can look away from the past, put it to the side, and ask for his help?

Taking a deep breath before I exit the bathroom, I consider tucking the medicine packet into my bra, but the bodice is so tight that the lump will be visible no matter where I put it. I scan the room for a place to hide the painkillers, eyeing the

233

pile of rugs and pillows in the far corner. Climbing over them, I reach down into the very corner and push the medicine packet into it. It will have to do.

My hand brushes a sharp object when I withdraw it and I'm surprised when blood blossoms. I peer into the corner, carefully pulling away the corner of the heavy rug that sits up against it, hoping I might find a concealed weapon.

The wooden paneling is chipped, a sharp piece jutting from a slightly warped board. Something glints right beneath it. A chain maybe…

"Tessa?" Cody reaches across the pile of rugs. The way I'm lying, my backside is up in the air, my head in the corner.

"There's something down here," I mumble, carefully fishing beneath the rug and prying up the warped section of board. I carefully tug on what turns out to be a fine, gold bracelet with four flat charms attached to it. They're shaped like tiny canaries, each enameled in a different color with extraordinarily detailed wings, bodies, and beaks.

Carefully depositing the medicine into the corner, I replace the board and the rug before I pop my head back up.

The blood drains from Cody's face.

"What is it?" I ask, scrambling across the uneven pile to reach him. "Are you okay? Do you need more painkillers?"

"Can I see that?" he asks, holding his hand out for the piece of jewelry.

I pass it over, pressing the bracelet into his palm.

He is like stone, staring at the birds without moving, not even to close his fist. "This is Ella's."

"What?" My forehead creases. "Are you sure?"

"Mom gave it to her. She loved canaries. She never took it off."

I'm suddenly taken back to Hidden House and all the mornings that Ella recited the colors of canaries that coasted around her upraised hand. "But—"

Bouncy footfalls on the steps interrupt us and Tia appears, swathed in a new gown, white again but with a shimmering skirt and a fitted, sleeveless bodice.

"Oh, goody!" She claps her hands, immediately zeroing in on Cody's open palm. "You found Daisy's bracelet. I've been looking for that."

She swoops at Cody and snatches the bracelet before he can close his fist.

Cody's eyes narrow, his lips pressing together until they're bloodless. He returns my gaze silently as we both process what this means.

Tristan's father supposedly brought Ella into the forest, but we know Ford had a hand in it. This must be where he brought her—straight to Mother Lavinia, who needed to establish dominance without risking her own life or the lives of her witches.

I want to scream. *Cowards. Cold, fucking bitches.*

Ella should have been the alpha of the Eastern Lowland pack. She would have been as powerful as Cody. She never would have wanted to fight, but Lavinia made her…

I squeeze my eyes closed. I shared a room with Ella for two months, walked quietly with her, listened to her make lists and whisper the color of canaries. This place broke her.

Fuck. Fuck. Fuck.

Seeming oblivious to the rising tension in the room, Tia slips the bracelet onto her wrist and admires it.

Reya, Nalani, and Neve take a step away from me, casting cautious glances between us.

I give Tia a cold stare. "Her name was Ella," I say. "Why did you call her 'Daisy'?"

Tia's gaze flicks to me. She rolls her eyes as if I'm stupid. "Because of her hair."

"Right." I nod. "White-blonde hair the color of daisy petals." I fight to pull back my incisors, battle the urge to drag them through Tia's throat. "How long was she here?"

"I don't remember." Tia frowns, barely glancing up. "Maybe a year. I loved dressing her up before a fight. She was like a pretty doll."

My rage rises beyond my control, but as I take a step toward Tia, my claws descending and my wolf's energy surging inside me, Cody's hand clamps around my arm and stops me.

"We're looking forward to the meal," he says to Tia through gritted teeth. "You're here to escort us, aren't you?"

Tia spins on her heel. "This way."

I follow closely behind her, matching the speed of her bouncy stride. When we exit the firelit cage into the living room above, I catch Cody's eye before I say to Tia, "Are you sure you should be wearing that bracelet, Tia? Mother Lavinia told you not to speak of Daisy. She might be angry to see you wearing an object that reminds her of Daisy."

Tia scowls at me, her cold eyes boring into me. Glaring at me, she wriggles the bracelet off her wrist and leaves it on the mantelpiece. "Fine."

As we follow her out into the lamplit clearing, I make a promise to myself.

I will burn these fucking witches to the ground.

CHAPTER TWENTY-SIX

We exit into the cool night air. The clearing has been laid out with tables that glitter with crystal goblets and are filled with bowls brimming with food. Bright lamps float in the air above the tables, keeping the encroaching dark at bay.

It's been a hot minute since I ate and my stomach grumbles fiercely. I need to keep up my energy, stay alert, but I'm wary of the food and drink. It could be laced with all sorts of substances that could dull my reflexes and instincts.

I need to stay sharp.

I count all twenty witches, elegantly dressed, some seated at the tables while others mill around the clearing. Each woman carries her wand attached to a holster at her waist.

Mother Lavinia glides toward me, dressed in a sweeping, pure white gown with a fitted bodice that barely contains her cleavage. A crystal goblet hangs between her fingertips while she stretches her arms toward me as though we're old friends. "There you are! My contender! Come, sit with me, Tessa."

Within seconds, Cody, Reya, Nalani, and Neve are pulled away from me and whisked off to separate tables. Once seated, each of the shifter women is flanked by two witches who set plates in front of them and set about plying them with food and drink. Cody has no less than four witches surrounding him, one of whom sits on his lap and immediately tries to feed him berries. Even from a distance, I can see how hard he's fighting to restrain his dislike of her. If he still had his wolf's teeth, that witch would have lost her fingers by now.

"We don't have to be enemies, Tessa," Mother Lavinia coos at me. "We can have a symbiotic relationship."

I refocus on her as she draws me past the table where Ford, Silas, Brynjar, Perla, and the other leopard shifter are eating. They're all dressed in evening wear that seems to fit them perfectly. Either they keep a stash of clothing here for these occasions—which is possible, since my father regularly procures fighters for the witches—or Mother Lavinia bestowed some magic upon them.

"I asked your father for a little alone time with you at my table," Lavinia whispers to me. "I don't want us to get off on the wrong foot."

My father watches me pass with a cold stare. It looks like he's content to let Mother Lavinia try to manipulate me for now.

She urges me into a seat at the head table that sits closest to the stone pillars at the entrance to the clearing. Nobody else is sitting at this table, and I'm now separated from Cody and the others, who are all located farthest from the way out.

Walking past the cabins has confirmed for me that they are connected at the sides, living tree trunks and branches forming barriers between them. There are no alleyways or paths from the clearing at ground level. The only way out is through the entrance pillars. It's possible to veer off the path once we're out of the clearing, but getting out will be the challenge.

I cast a casual glance at the cabin roofs. There are spaces between the tree trunks higher up. If we can't make it to the entrance pillars, we will have to find a way up and over the cabins and through the gaps.

Mother Lavinia wastes no time leaning across me to fill

my plate with sliced meat, roasted vegetables, and gravy that looks the color of blood.

"There," she says, sliding into the seat beside me. "We can feed you and tend to your needs. In fact, we can give you every pleasure you could desire."

She strokes my arm, an overly familiar gesture, as she continues. "All we ask in return is that you fight for us. The more fights you win, the more rewards we will lavish on you. I understand your father brought you here to teach you a lesson, but maybe you'll find you like it here."

I stare back at her. *Is she fucking delusional?*

She pops a berry into her mouth, sucking on it a little before swallowing. I narrow my eyes at the smear of what appears to be blood on the forefinger of her right hand.

I point. "You have a little something on your..."

She laughs, raising her forefinger to her lips. "So I do."

Opening her mouth, she places her finger on her tongue and licks the blood off it, giving a little moan of satisfaction at the same time. "Delicious. You should try it."

She reaches across to run her finger along the back of my hand. "I think you'll like it."

Assuming she means the berries, I rise slightly in my seat, reach for the nearest bowl, and place a single berry on my plate. I don't touch it.

"You know, Tessa..." Mother Lavinia slides closer to me, nudging my overlaid skirt to the side to rest her hand on my bare knee. "I'm really surprised that Fenrir made such a beautiful daughter. He's an ugly beast, don't you think?" She brushes her free hand through my hair, her voice breathy. "But you are mesmerizing."

I blink at her. I can't tell if she's trying to butter me up or hit on me. Thinking of Ella, I push at the berry with my finger. "What if I'm not in the mood to fight? How will you make me?"

"You don't want to find out," Lavinia says, a suddenly cold light entering her eyes. Her hand closes around my thigh in an uncomfortable squeeze. "I expect you to kill for me, Tessa. If you don't have the stomach for it, then I'll find a very unpleasant way to force you."

"Don't worry." I smile. "I'm my father's daughter. I have the stomach for killing."

"Good." She leans back in her seat. "Eat, dear. I promise it's not poisoned."

My stomach growls again. I have to eat something or I'm not going to make it through the rest of the evening. I poke my fork at what appears to be a simple baked potato. I lift it to my nose to smell it before I chew carefully.

"Good girl." Mother Lavinia darts forward again, planting a kiss on my neck. She's still stroking my knee and I fight my rising anger. If she doesn't stop touching me soon, she won't only lose her fingers, I'll break her arm.

A shout from the end of the clearing makes us both turn in our seats.

A bare-footed witch in a flowing, white dress races toward us between the stone pillars. Her face is pale and her black hair flies out behind her.

"Mother!" she shouts.

A hush falls over the other witches as the black-haired woman drops to her knees on the other side of Mother Lavinia, speaking in a muted voice. "Mother Zala is here. She demands an audience."

Lavinia's upper lip curls. "How dare she enter my territory!" she hisses. "What makes her think I won't kill her for this trespass?"

The black-haired witch is ashen. "She wishes to make a challenge."

Mother Lavinia laughs, a bubbling sound that eases the growing tension around us. "With what? Her last contender was a sorry mess. We did her a favor when we put the poor creature out of her misery."

The dark-haired witch's gaze flicks nervously to me. "Her new contender is far from a sorry mess, Mother."

Mother Lavinia narrows her eyes, but she doesn't ask about the contender. "What exactly does Mother Zala want?"

THIS BROKEN WOLF

"She demands an audience under the rules of challenge," the messenger replies.

"Very well," Mother Lavinia says. "I suppose she may come in peace."

Lavinia grips the edge of the table before she turns to me. "You will soon learn, Tessa, that the only rules we recognize between covens are the rules of challenge. They prevent total desolation. However, they will only stretch so far. Mother Zala may approach, but she must not set foot beyond the entrance. If I don't like the wager she proposes, I'm entitled to refuse and send her on her way." Lavinia gives an abrupt exhale. "We will see what she has to say."

Rising to her feet, Mother Lavinia calls, "Sisters, clear the tables."

To me, she says, "You will wait beside me, Tessa."

All of the witches rise from their seats. My father and his entourage have already left their seats. I'm unsettled by the smug smirk on my father's face as he moves to a position in front of one of the cabins on my left.

The witches surrounding Cody, Reya, Nalani, and Neve take hold of my allies' arms, pulling them to the other side of the clearing on my right. Cody and the shifter women return my wary look as the witches continue to hold them.

Beside me, Mother Lavinia lifts her wand, focusing on the tables and chairs. She murmurs in a sing-song voice, "Clear to create clarity."

The furniture lifts into the air, each piece folding in on itself—food and all—rapidly becoming smaller. Seven witches stride forward, catching the tiny, flat squares of wood that are left floating in the air. They slip the squares into their bodices. While five witches, including Tia, remain with my allies at the side, the remaining witches gather in loose rows facing the entrance pillars.

Mother Lavinia takes my arm, only releasing me once I turn to face the pillars with her.

High above us, it suddenly begins to rain, a soft drizzle.

Mother Lavinia grumbles beneath her breath. "Mother Zala and her fucking rain…"

She waves her wand with a quick whisper: "Simple shield."

The rain instantly meets a transparent dome that forms across the clearing above us, causing the water to run off it onto the peaks at the top of the cabin roofs. A single drop slides down my cheek.

The dark-haired witch who left to tell Mother Zala she could approach races toward us again along the path. She hurries between the pillars and joins the ranks behind us.

Rain continues to fall over the pathway we're now facing as two figures take shape in the darkness beyond. The first is a woman with a stocky figure whose stride is no-nonsense, her boots thudding against the mossy ground. She's wearing dark-colored pants, low-slung with a studded belt, together with a black button-up long-sleeved shirt and a dark vest, both open at the front to reveal the top of her lacy bra. Her hair is long and brown but with blond tips at the end. She wears black gloves and carries an ebony black wand. She appears to be in her thirties, slightly younger than Mother Lavinia, and her eyes are a cold gray. The rain continues to fall on her as she walks, but she doesn't seem to get wet. The water runs off her head and shoulders and splashes at her feet.

She must be Mother Zala.

The person behind her is shrouded in shadows that are too thick to be natural. I can only just make out the raindrops hitting the top of the person's head through the haze, but I can't tell if they're male or female.

I can scent Mother Zala—an unpleasant smell of stagnant water—but not her fighter, so the shadows must be some sort of cloaking spell that moves with the fighter like a cocoon. I'm not sure if the intention is to conceal the fighter from us—or us from the fighter.

When Mother Zala stops between the entry pillars, the shadows gather behind her, thickening the cocoon around her fighter.

THIS BROKEN WOLF

Zala's speech is as cold as her eyes. "Mother Lavinia, I'm here to make a challenge."

Lavinia's tangerine-colored lips twist. "Clearly. What do you wish to wager?"

"My entire territory."

The clearing falls deathly quiet and Mother Lavinia stiffens beside me. "What do you expect me to wager in return?"

Mother Zala's expression remains cold and calculating. "Your entire territory, of course."

Mother Lavinia snorts. "My dear, let me understand you. If I win, I receive your meager quarter of the northern forest. But if you win, you want all of the southern forest?" She rolls her eyes. "I don't think so."

Mother Zala's lips rise, revealing a gold tooth. "You obviously haven't heard. I'm not surprised that you haven't—anyone who could have told you is dead." She takes a step forward but remains poised exactly between the entrance pillars, not breaking the rules. "I now control all of the northern forest."

Mother Lavinia is suddenly like stone beside me, no longer derisive. "Since when?"

"Since I carried out three challenges over the last three days and won all of them."

Mother Lavinia's hazel eyes grow wide. "What did you do with those covens?"

Mother Zala smiles again. Sweetly this time. "I syphoned all of their power. Then I killed them." She turns her wand around within her gloved palm as she licks her lips. "Are you afraid of losing, Mother Lavinia?"

Mother Lavinia tips her chin up, glaring past Zala at the fighter shrouded in shadow. "You've made your challenge, but you haven't revealed your contender. I wish to see her before I consider the wager."

"Very well." Zala steps to the side of the wide path, her wand carving a slow swirl in the air.

243

The shadows disperse, revealing broad shoulders and a lean waist—the muscular silhouette of a man, not a woman.

A metal collar glints around his neck. It's reddish-brown and studded with what looks like copper.

Still shrouded in dispersing shadows, he tips his head back and snarls at the rain before he actively shivers, shaking the water off his shoulders as if he's shaking out his fur.

My heart thuds as Tristan steps into the lamplight.

CHAPTER TWENTY-SEVEN

I can't breathe.

The clearing breaks into shouts of outrage around me.

"How dare you bring him here!"

"That's Tristan Masters. We should kill him!"

The witch standing closest in the row behind me shouts, "How dare you challenge with a fucking man!"

Their outrage washes over me as Tristan focuses on me, his animal gaze raking down me from my head to my bare toes. His muscles are corded, his shoulders hunched, chest slicked with sweat and rain, and his eyes are shrouded by his wild hair. He's wearing different long pants now—black jeans that don't have the same rips as the black suit pants I saw him in last.

Except that the man I'm looking at now isn't Tristan.

He's the Killer.

I knew from his omission during my time in the Near-Apart Room that he wasn't with his pack. I suspected that he was here in the forest. But... with Mother Zala?

Zala said she won three challenges over three days. That's one for each day that Tristan and I have been apart. What I don't know—what fills me with dread—is whether or not he's here by choice.

Or rather—by the Killer's choice.

Mother Lavinia snarls beside me. "That's Tristan Masters." She leaves my side to pace in a wide semi-circle around Mother Zala. "He is a known enemy of this coven. A thief who once stole my best fighter from me—as well you know, Mother Zala! How dare you bring him here!"

"What a shame for you that he's now my captive," Zala says, unaffected by Lavinia's outburst. "I'm sure you've craved his blood for some time. However, the rules state that I may challenge with any captive I choose."

"You stole him from his pack?" Mother Lavinia asks, her eyes narrowed with disbelief. "How did you accomplish such a feat?"

Mother Zala tips up her chin. "I found him dying in unfriendly territory. He was suffering from a near-fatal wound and couldn't fight back." She runs her fingertip across her exposed throat to demonstrate the neck wound. "Now, he's mine."

Lavinia tips her chin up. "Fenrir's daughter will make light work of Tristan Masters... *if* I accept your challenge."

My heart is hurting. My father dragged Tristan to the edge of the helipad. Tristan fell into the pool and then... I try to picture the moments after that. Anything could have happened. Baxter could have found him and sent a message to Zala. Or Zala could have already been at Baxter's home. It's a large enough house that I might not have seen her. Or...

While Lavinia and Zala continue to trade insults, and the tension among Lavinia's coven rises, I half-turn to where my father stands with his entourage in the shadows at the side of the clearing.

He gives me a smile colder than the ice jotunn's touch.

My heart sinks.

He told Zala where to find Tristan. He's been playing the witches off against each other for years. He's an expert at it. He handed Mother Zala a fighter she couldn't refuse. He's now created a situation that tempts Mother Lavinia to risk her territory so she can control the entire forest.

But... two things don't make sense. First, if a single witch controls the forest, they won't need my father's help anymore; he'll become redundant. Second, with Tristan in captivity, my father has had three whole days to breach the library in Tristan's territory and retrieve the book of old magic—but he hasn't.

Now, my father leaves Brynjar, Silas, and the two leopard shifters in the shadows so he can prowl toward me. I tense as he slinks to my side and leans in to stroke my hair. "I warned you, Tessa. You will lose everyone you love if you choose to challenge me."

He threatened in the van that I won't win a game against him and that someone I care about will die. I thought he meant Cody, but now I know he means Tristan, too. Everyone I care about in this clearing will die.

The witches are holding tightly to Reya, Nalani, and Neve behind us, but they're having more trouble with Cody. He strains against the two witches attempting to restrain him until Tia brandishes her wand in his face.

I don't hear what she says to him over the increasing murmurs of the crowd, but he snaps something back at her and struggles even harder to free himself. He seeks me across the top of Tia's head, his focus rapidly switching between Tristan, my father, and me.

Cody gives me an urgent shake of his head, his brow furrowed, fierce. I could interpret his gesture any number of ways, but the alarm on his face when he looks at Tristan and the way Tristan's killing me with his eyes...

I can practically hear Cody's warning: *That isn't Tristan. Don't fight that fucking beast.*

Tia snaps at Cody again, slapping his face with her wand at the same time and sending a wash of golden light across his cheeks.

My blood pressure rises when Cody jolts and stops struggling, his shoulders slumping, even though he remains upright. In his weakened physical state, he won't be able to take many more magical assaults.

Ford forces my attention back to himself by grabbing my face. "Do you see, Tessa? Your wolf-less friend will die and Tristan will continue to live at the mercy of his inner demons. I won't stop there. I will hunt down anyone who ever cared about you and I will kill them."

His claws extend across my cheek, his grip so hard that it feels like he would knock my head against a wall if he had one handy. Suddenly releasing my face, he scratches his claws down my back, making me gasp and arch away from him.

Damn him.

"You did all of this to put me in my place," I say, swallowing my whimper of pain. "But why were you willing to risk peace between the witches?"

Ford lowers his voice to a mere murmur, barely audible, his claws still pressing into my shoulder blades. "They won't respect the outcome of this fight. They have too much to lose. Even now, Zala's coven will be fortifying her territory in case Lavinia wins. If Zala wins, Lavinia will strike back. She won't concede. The forest will descend into even greater chaos."

"So you win," I say. "No matter what happens… What about the book of old magic?"

He blinks at my sudden change of topic. "What about it?"

I grab his hand, returning his violence, my claws extending so fast that if he pulls away, I will gouge valleys into his flesh. "Tristan has been captive in the forest for days. The library has been unguarded all this time. Why haven't you raced to steal the book you want so badly?"

A muscle in my father's jaw clenches. "We don't need to talk about that right now."

I seem to have hit a nerve. *Finally.* I purse my lips, recklessness growing inside me as a perilous possibility occurs to me. "You can't retrieve it, can you? You need me to do it."

My father flinches and his eyes flash crimson, a sign that I've struck truth.

"Maybe there are protective spells around it that are so deadly you won't risk your own life, but you're willing to risk mine," I continue. "Maybe you've tried before and nearly died in the process." A deep growl grows inside me. "Stop me when I'm getting warm, Father."

His lips twist as he grinds his teeth. "Do what I command, and your friends won't die tonight. I will make sure Tristan goes free. You won't have to fight him. I will make sure your friends survive. I'll even find a way to save your wolf-less friend."

All of his lies wash over me, empty promises as my father leans in so close that his lips touch my ear, his claws dragging upward to prick my neck and my earlobe. "Give in to my power and you will bask in my glory and my protection. Defy me and I will make you writhe."

He pulls back far enough to see my face and read my response.

I sense a trickle of blood sliding down my neck. I'm deadpan now. Blank. I don't protest. My claws retract and I let go of his hand without drawing his blood, even though he drew mine.

He tips his head to the side, his fingers softening against my neck, stroking down my hair as he takes my silence as agreement. "Good girl."

He turns away from me and strides toward Lavinia and Zala. He spreads his arms wide as he approaches them. "Mothers," he says with a placating tone. "I think we can work this out."

The Killer has remained at Zala's side, but he shakes off the new raindrops that have gathered on his shoulders, his focus remaining unnervingly on me as he seems to ignore everything else around him, including my father.

I'm beyond my tipping point, my anger boiling to the surface.

I need to scream.

I need to cut down my father and every single witch in this clearing, including Zala and Lavinia. I need to turn back time and make a different choice on the helipad—to trust Tristan the moment he told me to fight the darkness inside me.

More than anything, my heart hurts.

I've kicked and clawed and tried to maneuver my way to freedom, only to end up deeper inside this pit of rage and darkness. Only to end up standing across from Tristan while the Killer undresses me and cuts me into tiny pieces with his eyes.

I can't sense Tristan's thoughts or intentions while the Killer controls him. The Killer's nature seems to strangle the melding bond I formed with Tristan. But I don't need the bond to know the Killer's intentions. He revealed them to me when I met him in the Near-Apart Room.

The Killer has only one purpose: *Death.*

Specifically: *Mine.*

Tristan and I are both creatures of darkness, fighting against our own inner natures that thirst for pain and blood. Fighting our fathers, who bestowed the gift of darkness on us.

Since the moment I met Tristan, I've known that a fight between us must never happen, but that is the hope of a person who no longer exists.

I can't be that person anymore.

As the two Mothers turn to Ford, I take a deep breath and meet the Killer's eyes across the distance.

Holding my head high, I roar, "I will fight Tristan Masters!"

CHAPTER TWENTY-EIGHT

The clearing falls silent.

Mother Lavinia spins, her white gown floating around her hips and thighs with the suddenness of her step toward me. Her cheeks flush. "I will make that decision," she snaps. "Not you!"

I ignore her.

So does the Killer.

The Killer gives me a savage smile. "I accept this fight."

He steps forward as if he's going to break the barrier within the entrance pillars, but Mother Zala screams at him. "Stop!"

Swiftly raising her wand, she taps the collar around his neck. A jolt of electricity sizzles through the collar, flickering across the Killer's neck. He grabs at the collar as the power crackles around his shoulders and face, driving him to his knees.

My senses don't buzz in the same way that they would if the current running through the collar were magical. It was certainly triggered by Zala's wand, but the collar must be converting it into real electricity.

"Do *not* pass across the threshold until Mother Lavinia accepts the challenge," Zala snarls at him, threatening to tap her wand against the collar again. "Or the shields will kill us both!"

The Killer turns his face up to Zala's, considering her for a beat. "You forget. I'm not susceptible to magic."

He launches to his feet and his arms dart out. Wrapping them around Zala's torso, he wrenches her off her feet.

Her eyes fly wide.

She screams, kicks her legs, and rams her wand against his collar.

At her touch, electricity jolts through the Killer's neck and back again, sizzling and steaming from his wet shoulders. He roars with pain but doesn't stop. Swinging to face the threshold, he grips Zala in front of himself and steps right through.

The breath stops in my lungs. I sense the witches behind me gasp. Ford and Lavinia are closest to the Killer and they both leap backward.

Zala's scream of terror cuts short as the Killer takes two steps into the clearing and then halts. There's a moment of tense silence as Zala remains, quiet and still, no longer struggling in the Killer's arms.

The Killer casts me a deadly grin as he closes his arms more tightly around the witch's body.

She disintegrates quietly.

Her body, even her clothing, disperses into a fine crimson mist that floats up and out of his arms, silently dispersing.

Mother Lavinia rushes back to her coven, her hand over her mouth, her white dress covered in fine spots of blood. Ford remains for a beat longer, snarling at the Killer. For a second, his body glows as if he's going to release his wolf, but instead, he storms past me, quickly returning to Brynjar and Silas, who draw him as far back as they can.

I'm left standing opposite the Killer as the mist settles at my feet.

The Killer is impassive. He swills his forefinger through the fine vapor floating in the air in front of him, carving the winding shape of a snake that slithers toward the ground before it rises up, perfectly noose-shaped like the snake tattoo killing the wolf on his chest.

He reaches up to the collar around his neck and extends his claw into the back of it. The collar gives a *click* as it opens. He promptly drops it to the ground.

The Killer speaks into the heavy silence. "Mother Zala was no longer useful to me." He points at me. "Tessa Dean is mine to kill."

Mother Lavinia gasps behind me, her face flushed. Now that Zala is dead, she has the opportunity to claim the rest of the forest, but only if I win. If I lose… well, I guess that's up to the Killer.

She throws back her head, her copper hair flying around her shoulders. "Sisters! Take hold of the prisoners and move to the back of the clearing. If Tessa wants her friends to live, she will win this fight for me."

Cody, Reya, Nalani, and Neve struggle against the witches who force them to the very back of the clearing. The witches form two rows between me and my friends, their wands raised and ready, their white clothing bright in the shadows. Mother Lavinia stands at their head and a glittering protective shield forms over their position.

Maybe it makes her feel better. The Killer and I could easily barrel our way through any shield they put up.

The Killer's gaze rakes up and down my body over and over like claws, trying to strip away my defenses.

The corner of his mouth hitches up as I return his gaze without flinching. Now that Mother Zala is dead, the rain has stopped, and he gives a final shake of his shoulders, water droplets following every dangerous curve of his sculpted chest and muscular arms.

"Tessa Dean," he says, his hair falling back over his eyes after he shakes it out. "You look too beautiful to kill."

I draw on my wolf's energy, taking comfort in its flow through my chest and my mind, welcoming the heat inside the darkness. My back stings from the claw marks my father inflicted on me, but drawing on my power dulls the pain.

"You won't kill me," I say, taking a confident step toward the Killer. "The true mate bond won't let you."

The Killer tips his chin up. "Only if the bond still exists. I've had time to destroy it. Is that a risk you're willing to take?"

"It is," I say, keeping my declaration calm and quiet.

I've chosen not to draw on my incisors or claws, taking careful steps, my bare feet whisper-quiet on the mossy ground. I got through to Tristan before by maintaining my calm, drawing him out through touch. I'll only succeed by making myself vulnerable.

It's an even riskier gamble now than it was in the Near-Apart Room.

The Killer remains where he is, watching my approach, his chest rising and falling evenly, but the muscles in his arms and chest are corded, pumped, ready to retaliate.

"I want to speak with Tristan," I say, keeping my hands slightly raised, soft without my claws.

The Killer lowers his voice. "Maybe I'll let him out if you're willing to do what I want."

"What is that?" I ask.

The Killer moves so fast, his power shockingly strong in his Killer form, but even at this speed, I can follow his movements, read his intentions.

I allow him to wrench me off my feet, his arms wrapping around me, plastering me against his chest. I throw my arms up reflexively in a defensive gesture and now they're trapped between us.

I'm aware of my father's snarl, the scent of malice that tells me he's on the verge of releasing his wolf. I'm also aware of Cody's shout of alarm behind me. He will only be able to see that the Killer grabbed me and not that I'm okay.

The Killer ignores them both.

"Kiss me like you kiss Tristan," the Killer says. "Convince me not to kill you."

"You're taunting me," I murmur, slowly inching my arms upward to free them from the crush between us. Making no sudden movements, I slip my hands up to his shoulders, then one hand farther up his neck, my thumb grazing the edge of his jaw. "Let Tristan out and I'll kiss him all you want."

The Killer's crisp, green eyes are flecked sharply with amber, his hands forming claws across my back. "Now you're taunting *me*."

"Maybe." I drag my lower lip between my teeth. "Maybe I just need to know how badly you want to win."

"Testing me, then," he growls.

My heart hammers. I curl my fingers around the back of his neck, stroking up into his hair while my other palm presses against his chest, flexing against his muscles.

"Always," I murmur. "I will always test you. We're cut from the same cloth. We both want the same thing."

He follows the tip of my tongue as I wet my lips. "What is that?" he asks.

I slide upward, pressing my body against his, creating friction between us as I angle for his ear and whisper, "To dominate."

He growls against my throat, swooping to graze his lips across my neck.

I close my eyes. I can't deny the answering darkness building inside my heart. I thought that I would need to grow strong enough to be with Tristan, but now I'm not the one who needs strength.

Staying on tiptoes as the Killer gives a throaty growl against my neck, I take my chance to whisper into his ear again. "Tristan… You're strong enough."

The Killer jolts. His claws scratch my back, digging through the wounds my father already gave me, but I clamp my hands around his face, tangling my fingers in his damp hair. The water on his chest has already seeped through my dress, smearing the red mist between us.

I pull the Killer down to me, parting my lips and arching up to kiss him, demanding that he accept my embrace.

He pauses for a beat, his lips a whisper away from mine. "I will win, Tessa Dean."

"Hmm." My tongue darts out to taste the rain beneath his bottom lip. "You've already lost."

He doesn't seem to care, his mouth crashing against mine with a violence that triggers every impulse of my inner nature that I fight, the deepest need to control, dominate, and destroy.

I struggle to stay afloat, to remember what I'm fighting for, my hand gripping the back of his neck, repeating Tristan's name over and over in my mind to keep myself from giving in.

I gasp for breath as the Killer suddenly breaks contact and his hold on me changes, his claws retracting.

My eyes fly open to meet Tristan's gaze.

"Tessa?" His focus darts around the clearing in the way of someone who is waking up and doesn't know where they are. "Where the hell—"

"Stay with me," I say, clamping my hands around his face, desperately willing him to listen. "I need you."

His focus flies to Ford, Brynjar, and Silas. Tristan's claws reappear as suddenly as they disappeared.

"Look at me," I order him, my hands tightening, trying to draw his attention back to me. "You told me to command, order, even rage, but never beg. I'm commanding you now, Tristan." I grit my teeth. "Stay with me. Don't go…" My eyes fill with hot tears and I fight my wavering voice. "Don't go away again."

His hand brushes my cheek, running through my tears. "Fuck, Tessa. What the hell have I done?"

"It doesn't matter. I need you to fight with me now. I can't beat my father on my own."

Tristan grips the back of my hands as I continue to hold his face. "You're not safe with me, Tessa. I don't feel the true mate bond with you anymore."

I inhale sharply and try to exhale. "The Killer broke it?"

"He must have."

I press my forehead to his. "It doesn't matter. You're here now."

He dips his head to kiss my lips and I taste the saltiness of my tears along with the earthy scent of rain on his cheeks before he pulls back. His eyes shift a little, but it's his wolf, a determined gleam growing. He places me back on my feet, releasing me as he rolls his shoulders and stretches his neck, his focus intense. "It's time to end your father."

At the side, Ford draws himself upright. His growls of unhappiness have increased ever since Tristan reappeared. He won't wait for us to attack. His claws descend as he strides toward us, releasing his wolf at the same time. The white beast materializes faster than ever before, glowing and electrifying.

I check the realization on Tristan's face as he says, "They're the same creature."

If Tristan is shocked, he recovers quickly. With a flick of his fingers, he releases his claws and his incisors appear. I do the same, both of us taking up offensive stances.

Behind Ford, Perla and the other leopard shifter retreat completely, pressing up against the nearest cabin. Brynjar takes a step forward, his icy-blue eyes gleaming while Silas prepares for a fight, lightning crackling around his hands. Even without weapons or a wand, Silas is dangerous because of the power-filled orb he carries with him.

Brynjar calls, "Boss! We should leave this fight."

"No," Ford replies, his wolf's voice in his growl. "An alliance between Cerberus and the Daughter of War will never hold. They're enemies by birthright."

Without pause, the massive white wolf leaps at Tristan, its teeth bared. At the same time, Ford himself launches at me, his fist aimed at my face.

Tristan takes a knee, driving his claws directly at the white wolf's eyes. When the wolf twists in the air to evade the strike, Tristan's foot connects with its side, making it yelp.

I block Ford's hit with my forearm and revert to a boxing combination that Andreas taught me—a quick jab to Ford's stomach, followed by retracting my defensive arm and aiming a knock against his ribs, then an uppercut to his chin. Anyone else would be flat on their back, but my father merely grins through his now-bloody teeth.

"Tristan will kill you, Tessa." He strikes out at my face again and I block the blow, but he's still speaking. "Why don't I show you the truth of the fire you've been playing with..."

He grabs hold of my arm and twists it so that I'm forced to turn. With a rapid movement, he pulls me up against him.

A scream of agony burst from me as he drives the claw on the forefinger of his free hand right into my arm, impaling me all the way to the bone. He doesn't stop there, grunting as he drives the claw deeper, as if he's drilling into the bone itself.

I writhe as Ford's claw is more than a weapon cutting through my flesh. Power pulses through me at the connection, a deep, primal power that cuts through my foundations, threatening to shatter my thoughts, tearing at my insides.

Kicking my foot back into his shin, I attempt to wrench myself away from him, twisting to angle my arm at the last moment so that his claw slides out. I'm lucky it doesn't slice my arm apart.

I back up, ready to release my wolf, ready to scream for Tristan to help me kill Ford, when a deep inky substance oozes from the wound in my arm.

It doesn't look like blood. It's ebony black shimmering with streams of mahogany red.

Ford's lips draw back from his teeth. "The blood of gods runs within you, Tessa."

I sway as the scent of my deep blood filters through my senses.

I smell like a wolf, but not like a wolf. I smell like death and power and deceit, like the haze that shrouds a bloody battlefield when the blood sprays and the bodies hit the mud and I'm the only one left alive while everyone dies around me.

Dropping to my knees, I press my palm over the wound, trying to stop the flow, the scent. It must be the same scent of my power that I worked so hard to control—the scent that once drove Cody to violence and that Tristan has fought to resist ever since he met me.

Ford stands over me, my blood dripping from his elongated claw, my scent hanging dangerously in the air.

"Tessa!" Tristan's shout reaches me as he grapples with the white wolf, holding its jaws open in his hands as if he could rip them apart. He retracts his hands and punches it in the face before it can bite back. Tristan leaps away from it at the same time.

"No!" I cry, throwing my hand out to stop him as he runs toward me. "Don't come near me."

It's too late.

His nostrils flare and he digs in his heels, every visible muscle in his body tensing and cording. In an instant, his shoulders hunch and his green eyes become hard as they rake across me.

No. Please, no.

I sag, still pressing my palm against my arm, trying to stem the blood that has already brought the Killer back. Tristan's gone, and he won't return as long as my deep blood seeps down my arm. This scent belongs only to monsters—and a true killer is what I've brought out in him.

Ford towers above me as I slump over my knees.

He draws his wolf back to his body in a rush of light that splashes power across his chest before the white wolf disappears again.

My father gloats as he backs away from Tristan and me. "Now we'll see who kills whom, Tessa."

My breathing is erratic. My own scent is wild and heady in my senses. Just like it triggered the Killer, it also draws out my worst impulses, a hot rage that wants to hurt, that craves the quiet scream.

I have only one line back to myself now.

If I can draw Tristan back to me, then I'll know I'm not lost.

Wiping my bloody palm across my dress, I stride straight at the Killer as he waits for me to attack.

"Let Tristan go," I command him.

"Never!"

My fist cracks across his jaw, but he barely flinches. I allow the surge of my animal's energy and instincts to flow through me without restraint. My other fist crashes against his shoulder and this time, I knock him backward. He twists at the waist to absorb the blow before he spins back to me, his head lowered, his teeth bared.

"I will fight you," I shout. "I will tear you apart to get to Tristan. I will rip you to so many pieces that you will never stand between us again."

I duck the Killer's fist and swing my own so hard at his ribs that I split my knuckles on impact. The air whooshes from his lungs as he bends reflexively. He's winded and he'll have an almighty bruise, but I didn't crack his ribs. The Killer's body may as well be made of steel.

He fights back, dodging my kick to his jaw while he's doubled over. Grabbing my foot, he twists my ankle so that I have to flip midair to avoid a broken bone. His fist on the back of my calf is like a rock, as heavy as the ice jotunn's fist, but I drop to avoid the impact—and another broken bone.

I'm aware of a struggle and shouting in the background— Cody's voice—but I can't take my eyes off the Killer. Any distraction could get me killed.

The Killer still has hold of my foot and now I'm facing the ground. Punching both of my fists against the mossy earth, I bend the knee of my held foot and kick back with my other leg, smacking his nose hard enough to force him to release me.

Just as I attempt to leap to my feet, he throws himself forward, his weight dropping onto my back, his fists on either side of my head. He drops his lips to my ear as I struggle to breathe, trying to plan a way out from beneath him.

"My instincts tell me to end you," he says, his incisors brushing against my neck. "But imagine the carnage we could cause together. You and me, Tessa Dean."

As I buck beneath him, his arms snake around my waist, dragging me up against him. My skirt is caught around his arm, his other hand pressing higher around my ribs beneath my breasts. I prepare to drive my elbow back into his stomach when he nudges the side of my neck, dropping a kiss beneath my earlobe that startles me.

"Why tear each other apart when we could destroy your father, conquer the forest, and make a new pack filled with the supernaturals others don't want? The strong supernaturals who need strong alphas."

His palm presses against my stomach, stroking through the material as I'm suddenly frozen in his arms.

"Together," he says. "Side by side. Two alphas leading a single pack for the first time."

The anger I felt before disappears and in its place is a dark void that fills with a whisper I don't want to hear.

I am anger, revenge, and violence begging to be unleashed.

The Killer's claws form across my stomach, scraping through my dress, shredding the material and yet... a wild euphoria rises inside me. The angrier the Killer grows—the more he unleashes his violence—the more I'm drawn to him, as if there's a part of me, a very dark, empty space inside me, that his anger and violence fill.

I want it.

A shout makes me jolt, the sounds around me suddenly rushing back in. At the back of the clearing, Cody is struggling to break through the barrier of witches, trying to get to me, while the women attempt to hold him back.

To my left, Silas has harnessed his lightning, his magic flickering around his palms, but now he's pointing in the direction of the entrance pillars.

"Boss!" Silas shouts to Ford. "Incoming!"

Ford spins in that direction. At the same time, the Killer wrenches me to my feet and pivots so that we're both facing the entrance, where Silas pointed. I don't fight the Killer's hold yet, my back still pressed against his chest.

My lips part with shock. A power so immense I've never sensed anything like it washes across the very air I'm breathing.

At first, I think it must be Mother Zala's coven rushing

toward us, because no single supernatural could control that much power...

A female silhouette appears in the darkness of the path. She runs toward us, shrouded in shadow so I can't make out her features, only her outline and that her hands are outstretched.

She doesn't carry a wand, but a magical force blasts from her hands, rippling through the air from her fingertips in a bright explosion that gusts through the entrance ahead of her. The pillars shatter and pieces of rock fly outward.

I flinch as the Killer pulls us both downward, his arms flying across my head as he turns his back to take the impact.

Now that I've turned, I can see the witches raising their wands in unison a second before a shield forms around them that blurs their figures behind it. Cody had just made it to the edge of their number and he bashes against the shield with his fists and feet. His mouth moves—he must be shouting—but I can't hear what he's saying.

Just as I brace for impact, another bright wave sweeps from the newcomer's outstretched hands, rushing around the hurtling debris and sucking it back to the mossy ground like an explosion in reverse.

She bursts through the entrance, her dark hair flying, gray eyes alight with power that makes her glow. She's wearing black pants and a comfortable-looking sweater rolled up at the sleeves. There's a smudge of dirt across her cheek. Her chest heaves as she skids to a stop just past the broken entrance, both hands upraised, light swirling around her fingertips, pulsing power demanding to be released.

I stumble to my feet, prying myself free from the Killer's arms. He rises with me, letting me go, but remaining like a shadow behind me.

I can't tear my eyes away from the witch in front of me. "Helen?"

CHAPTER TWENTY-NINE

*H*elen focusses on me but keeps her hands up. "Tessa! Are you okay?"

"I'm..." My wild gaze passes across her outstretched hands. How could I not know she controlled this much power? *Dear fuck.* I suddenly remember what she said to me when I first arrived at Hidden House. She told me that my senses would be dampened. I wouldn't be able to sense anyone's movements, catch their scents, or detect their supernatural status. She told me it was important because many of the women who live there are extremely powerful.

I didn't stop to think she might mean herself.

Another three figures race up behind her. One of them is Iyana, the mercury-drinking vampire, her long, black hair caught up on her head in a tight knot, her large, blue-gray eyes quickly taking in the scene while her rose-bud lips press together, a cautious expression. She's wearing tight black pants, a long-sleeved jacket, and her knee-high boots, along with a weapons belt sporting multiple handguns and daggers at her waist. She deftly races through the debris on the ground to take up position on Helen's far right.

The other two figures are nearly identical, both with tawny brown hair streaked with golden highlights and sage-green eyes. They're wearing skirts and sweaters, their tops also pushed up to their elbows, but they both carry a pack of cards fanned out in their hands, gripped securely as they take up position on either side of Helen. I never expected to see Luna and Lydia, the card mage twins, outside of Hidden House. Luna's cheeks blush peach as she accesses her power, silently communicating with Lydia, who immediately zeroes in on the Killer and me.

I look for Danika, the hawk shifter, but she doesn't appear behind them. If she's here, she'll be hiding in the trees with a sniper rifle, providing cover.

"Tessa?" Iyana calls to me. Her eyes pass desperately across my face, as if she's looking for the person she knew and doesn't find me. She refocuses on the Killer, becoming even more cautious. "Tristan?"

With a jolt, I remember how much my appearance has changed, how much I don't look like myself anymore. For all I know, right now, I could appear even more fierce than I did in the mirror this morning. A fine mist of blood has settled over my neck and bodice, the material torn across my stomach. My eyes are a brighter blue now and darkly rimmed. I adapt to my surroundings and the last hour has demanded that my ferocity rise to the surface.

"Careful, Iyana," Helen says, her voice as soft as I remember, as soothing, but there's a warning tone in it. "We don't know who Tessa and Tristan are right now."

My heart cracks inside my chest, making space for a little more anger. I tell myself they need to protect themselves, that I would be guarded in their shoes if confronted by me and Tristan right now. Neither of us looks like ourselves anymore, but I desperately need them to have faith in me, to trust that I won't hurt them…

I gasp against the rising pain inside my chest. "How are you here?" I ask.

"We've been searching for you and Tristan ever since you were taken," Iyana says. "Both of your trails went cold at the edge of the forest. We couldn't locate either of you until this afternoon. Your energy was hidden from us until now."

Ford had taken me to the Spire, which is cloaked in old magic. It wasn't until today that I emerged from it. I'm not sure what magic Mother Zala was using to mask Tristan's location, but it must have been effective.

While Iyana speaks, Helen's gaze passes over me. Her expression becomes distant and I sense the immense power around her reaching out and curling around me, seeking answers. It only lasts a moment, and I don't fight against it before she refocuses.

"I see now," she says quietly, the tension around her eyes increasing.

All at once, it's as if she knows everything about who and what I am.

When I first arrived at Hidden House she asked Tristan what he knew about me. She told him that my power was nothing she had sensed before, but that my human soul was masking an essence she couldn't identify. I guess now that my father has broken through my human soul, she can see everything she needs to see.

I want to tell her that I'm still me, but I don't know if it's the truth.

"They came to save you, but they fear you now." The Killer growls, a rumbling whisper at my ear. "Just like they fear me."

His arm clamps around my waist, sudden and vise-like, and he pulls me back against him.

My father, Silas, and Brynjar remain ready to attack at the side, but my father moves to the front, calling across to Helen.

"Mother Kadris," he says. "How nice to see you alive after all these years. Where have you been hiding?"

I stare blankly from my father to Helen, confusion rising inside me.

Mother Kadris...? Where have I heard that name before?

It comes to me in a rush. She was the center of the cautionary tale Ford told me in the van: a witch, centuries old, who gave favors in exchange for souls but lost someone she loved. She once ruled the forest with Mother Serena.

If Helen is Mother Kadris, then she is one of the most

powerful witches in our history. She always used a wand in Hidden House, but now she isn't carrying one with her. Either the house dulled her power or she was carrying out a ruse so that we didn't ask questions about why she didn't need a wand.

"Fenrir," Helen says, acknowledging my father.

Behind me, Mother Lavinia gives a shriek of rage and breaks through the shield her witches formed. "Mother Kadris!" Brandishing her wand, she storms toward Helen, muttering spells beneath her breath.

A cascade of crackling magic spews from Lavinia's wand toward Helen, Iyana, and the card mage twins, but Helen merely shifts her hands and the onslaught of magic hits a transparent shield, exploding and rippling across it without causing any harm.

"Trespasser!" Lavinia shrieks.

Helen arches an eyebrow. "Actually, it's the other way around. This forest belongs to me."

"You gave up your territory decades ago," Lavinia screeches. "Leave! Now! Or I will make your blood boil and your veins burst. I will tear out the eyes of your companions and rip off their skin."

The sultry persona Lavinia was projecting earlier tonight is long gone. Her copper hair glows a harsh color, her eyes dark and shadowed, her threats vicious.

The shield the witches were maintaining breaks fully and all of them rush forward, wands raised.

Freed from the shield, Cody sprints away from the witches with Reya, Neve, and Nalani close behind him. They form a tight semi-circle on my right between me and my father, and now there are four groups formed in the clearing.

My father, Brynjar, and Silas stand on my far right. When I peer into the shadows behind them, I make out Perla and the other leopard shifter clambering up over the nearest cabin roof, headed for the forest outside. Perla crouches and glances back for a moment, her eyes wide before she climbs onward. I never liked her, but even so, she's choosing to leave rather than fight against me. Now that Helen has broken the protective spells around the clearing, it's most likely safe to get through.

Perla jumps out of sight and I hope I never see her again.

Mother Lavinia stands on my far left while her witches crowd behind her in an arrow shape like flying birds, angling through the gap between me and the cabins on the far left.

Cody, Reya, Nalani, and Neve have formed a neat arc on my direct right, flanking the Killer and me. I catch Cody's eye as the Killer continues to hold me close. The tension in Cody's body, the darkening rings beneath his eyes, and his rapid breathing make my heart hammer. He has to be in serious pain by now, but he must be fighting it.

The friction rises around me with every breath I take.

"Calm yourself and your coven, Lavinia," Helen says, soothing again. "I'm here for Tessa and Tristan. Nothing more."

"You can't have them!" Lavinia screams, her face flushed as she angles around in front of me. "You will take nothing from this place. Everything you see is mine!"

Her voice echoes inside my mind.

Mine. Mine. Mine. How many times have I been claimed?

The Killer's voice sounds at my ear, a deep rumble. "Make your choices, Tessa Dean," he says.

Before Helen arrived, he said we could stand side by side, two alphas leading a single pack. I tell myself I can't take his offer at face value. I remind myself that the Deceiver lurks inside him, the hardest nature to identify. But I want what he's offering. A place in the forest for all the supernaturals like the women who live at Hidden House, the ones who don't fit the mold. A powerful pack that doesn't have to hide.

To punctuate his offer, the Killer releases me, his arms sliding away from me. I tip my head to see the challenge in his menacing eyes before I turn to Helen, Iyana, and the mage twins.

"Helen," I call. "I know you're afraid of what you see in me, but I need you to know that I'm more than my impulses. I need you to believe in me." I pause. Take a breath. "I'm coming with you. It's up to the Killer whether or not he comes with us."

Stepping away from the Killer, I reach for Cody, my hand curling around his arm, urging him to come with me.

At my touch, he closes the gap between us. "They won't let us go easily, Tessa," he says, scanning the witches as well as my father's group.

I cast an urgent glance at Reya, Nalani, and Neve, who also step back toward me. They quickly take up position facing outward so we're guarding each other's backs. Now that I'm turned slightly, I meet the Killer's eyes, arching a questioning eyebrow at him. "Are you with me?"

His biceps flex as he hunches his shoulders. "Will I get to kill along the way?"

"Only my enemies."

He shrugs. "That will do." His eyebrows draw together as he gives a threatening snarl before he turns to complete the defensive circle that we've formed. "For now."

We're now flanked by Mother Lavinia and her witches on my left with my father, Silas, and Brynjar on my right.

"We're all coming with you," I call to Helen, but my glare is for Lavinia and my father, who stand closest to us on either side, turning from one to the other. "You will let us go or I will burn both of you."

Ahead of us, Helen braces, her protective shield extending in front of Iyana and the card mage twins, but it won't help us until we reach her. Iyana draws a dagger and a gun while Luna and Lydia both flick several cards into the air. The cards circle around their heads, glowing at the edges.

"Your threats are futile, Tessa," my father says. "I will never let you go."

On the other side of me, Mother Lavinia narrows her eyes at me a moment before she screams at her witches and they all raise their wands in unison.

The ground erupts beneath our feet, tree roots shooting upward and twining around our legs. Lavinia and her witches may have brought the roots to the surface by magic, but the wood is real and doesn't break at my touch. Our group nearly separates from our protective formation as we try to evade the twining ropes, but then an immense force settles around my legs and the roots are pushed back to the ground, writhing and trying to rise again. In the distance, Helen's hand is outstretched in our direction, maintaining the protective shield around their position as well as counteracting the witch's spell.

Luna and Lydia let their cards loose. The glittering cards speed across the distance, hitting the witches at intervals and exploding into nets that stun half the witches and pin them down on the ground.

At the same time, Iyana takes aim at my father and Silas. She fires in quick succession, but they're both ready. My father evades the first bullet and snatches the second two from the air, holding them up for her to see how futile her action is. Silas waves his hand across the air and the bullets aimed at him fly into the external wall of the nearest cabin.

"Hurry!" Helen shouts to me as the card mage twins elevate another set of cards into the air above their heads and prepare to let them loose on the witches who remain standing and are still trying to resurrect the tree roots around us.

The Killer reaches for the nearest two witches, crashing their heads together, dropping them to the ground before he sets his sights firmly on Lavinia. She screams a spell at him that turns the tree roots at his feet into fire. The flames leap around his legs, but he runs toward her, punching through the rising furnace. I see him leap and then—

My father roars. "Silas! Brynjar! Bring Tessa to me."

CHAPTER THIRTY

𝓐 cold pit opens inside my stomach when Silas drops to a knee, extending both of his hands.

Dark light blasts across the clearing, a direct stream hitting my chest and knocking me onto the ground before a second wave floods the air above me. The dark light is so thick, covering the air so fast, that I can't see more than a few inches around me. Within the space of a single breath, the dark magic coats my tongue and sears my chest.

Dazed from the blow, I scream at myself to get up.

I know the cost of dark magic and I won't let my friends pay the price.

My vision bursts into crimson so that I can see through the haze. At the same time, I release my wolf's energy. I have to use her against Silas before he harms another person—even if I risk my father taking hold of her.

The moment I harness my crimson vision, an immense brightness fills my field of view—not Silas's magic, but Helen's power at the front of the clearing. It's so bright that I'm momentarily blinded. I can't even make out the shape of the Killer or Mother Lavinia where they were last standing.

Throwing myself in the other direction, away from the light, I freeze at what I can now see. Reya lies only a few paces away from me. She's curled up on the ground, clutching her stomach, the light rapidly fading from her body. Nalani and Neve are also curled up on the ground nearby, their power being syphoned from their bodies.

No.

Panic fills me when I can't see Cody.

"Cody!" I scream, suddenly desperately frightened for him.

I need to stop Silas right away.

Dashing to my feet, I'm confronted by Brynjar's bright figure, light pouring from his silhouette as he powers toward me through the darkness.

Silas knocked me down. I guess it's Brynjar's job to retrieve me.

Not this time.

As I swing farther to the right, I locate a group of witches huddled together, casting spells at Helen. Their magic flares, obscuring my view, but not before I locate Silas standing beside them.

I launch into a sprint toward him, sending my wolf's energy ahead of me, suddenly aware that I'm not the only one running for him.

Cody darts toward Silas from my left, much closer to Silas than I am. I recognize the golden aura of Cody's silhouette, which is brighter than I expected, the impulses of his heart a burning fire that stuns me as he runs straight for Silas's position.

Cody swoops to snatch up a slender object from the ground as he runs—maybe a dropped wand. He takes another three steps and leaps at the warlock, the wand clutched like a dagger aimed high at Silas's face.

Silas's energy sparks with lightning, his left hand flooding with deadly electricity, pointed directly at Cody's leaping body.

My heart stops. "No! Cody!"

My wolf's energy streams ahead of me, speeding across the distance faster than my legs can carry me, but she's still seconds away from reaching Silas to stop him.

Silas's lightning shoots through the air as fast as Cody's makeshift weapon flies toward Silas's eye.

Both hit at the same time.

Cody drives the wand into Silas's face at the same moment that Silas's lightning bursts across Cody's chest.

I scream, my heart thudding as Cody is flung backward. He gains air before he hits the ground, rolls to a stop, and doesn't move.

Silas roars with pain. He grabs at the wand jutting from his eye, but my wolf flies into him before he can remove it. I sense my wolf's energy tearing at his insides on her way through his body, her claws and teeth gnashing, ripping at every nerve inside him, shredding his pain receptors, interrupting his reflexes.

Silas screams and the dark magic fades from his hands, the oily blackness finally receding.

Dropping to his knees as the air clears, Silas grabs at the wand again, still trying to remove it, but my wolf isn't done with him. She turns and leaps through his body a second time, ripping and shredding all over again as he flails and screams and slumps to the ground.

My heart is in my throat as I skid to a stop beside Cody, finally reaching him. I drop to my knees, my crimson vision fading to normal.

His eyes are closed.

He's lying on his side, his shoulder hunched over his chest, his lower leg bent at the knee.

"Cody?" I bend over him, frantically reaching for his face. He doesn't respond, his shoulder shifting under the pressure of my hands, his arm sliding farther down toward the ground.

"Cody?" I ask again. Taking a breath, telling myself he's okay, I bend to gently nudge his cheek with mine, the same way he nudges my cheek in the mornings. "Wake up."

My voice rises when he doesn't respond. "Cody!"

I nudge his cheek again, harder this time, my palm pressed against his heart, waiting for a beat, waiting for him to respond. Patiently waiting. Because he will respond. He has to.

My father rises up from behind the witches, standing from a crouch. He won't have been affected by Silas's dark magic, but he must have used the witches' bodies to shelter from the haze.

"I warned you, Tessa," he says. "No matter what you do, you will lose everyone you care about."

My father's clothing is coated in a fine charcoal dust, a mist of dark magic. He has made his eyes brown now—a hickory brown too much like Cody's—and his incisors peek between his lips, his high cheekbones glowing with triumph.

Gleaming with power over me.

My breathing increases as my hands harden around Cody's shoulder, gripping him tightly.

"Cody!" I scream, shaking him. "Wake up!"

He's quiet. Still. He isn't breathing.

Oh, fuck, he isn't breathing.

I rock on the spot, clutching his shoulder, refusing to acknowledge what I see and know. I can't accept it because despite my belief that subverting Tristan's fate will subvert my own, it was Cody whose loyalty kept my heart warm. It was Cody who made me feel human and not like a monster. Cody wanted me in his den and held me when I panicked. He reminded me that I had a friend.

"Find your hate, Tessa," my father whispers. "Take out your pain on the weak. Reject your human soul and all its failings. Once and for all."

My wolf prowls in a circle around me and the Killer's footfalls crunch in the dry dust at my side. His looming presence is a darkness that casts a shadow across me, but somehow, impossibly, it's like finding shelter from the burning sun.

I'm aware of all the silent patches around me as the pain and anger inside me grow. Silence peppered with sound.

Silas moans in the dirt he lies on, the moss stripped away from the earth as a result of his magic. The shifter women groan as they push up onto their hands and knees at the far corner of my vision, wobbling and struggling to rise. The nearby group of witches are bent double, coughing out bursts of charcoal air from their chests, their faces pale.

Brynjar hangs back on my left, glittering snowflakes falling from his hands as he silently bows his head. He is old magic, like me. He wasn't affected by Silas's dark magic.

Helen's magic burns brightly behind me. I'm not surprised that she was able to protect herself, Iyana, and the card mage twins. If she really is Mother Kadris, then she may have absorbed the souls of old magic creatures in the past. Even now that I know her savage history, the warmth of her magic is too kind. Too generous.

It is not for me.

I stare up at my father as a quiet rage settles inside my chest. It is the moment after a hammer hits the surface of an icy lake, but the surface has yet to crack.

I could tell my father, the Wolf of War, that I will kill him.

I could promise to tear him apart. Just like I promised to avenge Andreas Dean's death, but I failed. I promised myself I would find a way to stop Tristan's fate, and I failed.

I promised to keep Cody alive, and *I... fucking... failed.*

Tipping my head back, I take a deep, strong breath, the deepest breath I can manage, filling my chest with dirty, dark, oily air, dragging all the darkness into me that I can possibly inhale.

My hair falls down my back, my cobalt-blue dress pools around my knees, my eyes turn up to the canopy of glittering branches overhead, and my fingernails become claws around Cody's shoulder and head as I hold my breath in, letting the weight of pain drown me, and then...

I let it out.

My scream rises up and out, washing across the clearing, a shrieking force that explodes into everyone around me.

Ford crouches. The witches flinch. Helen's shield flickers, her power eroded against the force of my scream. Only the Killer remains standing upright, a violence like my own reflected in his fierce green eyes.

My wolf's form ripples and changes. Her fur bleaches from

ebony-blue to gold, and her legs turn russet. I always thought that Cody's wolf looked like it had waded through blood, his golden fur savagely bloody around his legs. Now my wolf mimics his, a ferociously gorgeous golden beast with bloodstained paws.

Cody's wolf is gone.

He is gone, but I will take the pain that his death has caused me and I will use it to destroy this place. I vowed to burn this fucking coven to the ground and in that, at least, I won't fail.

Leaping over Cody to reach Silas where he is still slumped on the ground, I wrench the wand from the warlock's face. It's ivory with a rounded tip and feels like it's made of bone. An instrument crafted from death to cause death.

Rising to meet my father's eyes, I say, "You finally did it, father. You broke my human soul."

Behind me, Tia has recovered fast enough to scream mindless and furious orders at the other witches. "Mother Kadris dies tonight! We will tear her apart! We will tear them all apart! They will die screaming. They will all fucking die—"

Turning, I stride toward Tia. I grip the ivory wand in my hand like a dagger. Jace once told me that knives are visceral—up close and bloody—and that's how shifters fight. Cody used this ivory wand as a makeshift knife. I will use it too. Along with my wolf.

Tia spins to me, still spewing threats, her shrill voice washing across me, unintelligible in her rage.

My wolf snaps her jaws as she leaps for Tia, flying through her torso and dropping her to her knees before my wolf plows through the witch standing beside her, ripping at both their bodies from the inside.

Even on her knees, Tia points her wand at me, attempting to hurt and kill me. The air buzzes around my body, sharp and crackling as she throws curses that roll off me, leaving nothing more than smears across my dress.

I don't bother knocking her wand to the side, letting its tip rest against my chest as I quietly grab her shoulder with my free hand and drive the ivory wand through her throat. I don't wait for her life to fade from her eyes before I drop her body to the dust and stride to the next witch.

I follow my wolf through the witches, using my strength to end them swiftly, more painlessly than they deserve, dropping them all within moments. Until I finally reach Mother Lavinia.

She already lies in the dirt, her neck broken.

My breathing is deep and even as I pull my wolf's energy back to me, merging with her again. My cobalt dress is splattered with blood. Crimson liquid drips from the tip of the ivory wand onto the dirt where I stand. My deep blood also continues to ooze down my arm from the claw wound my father gave me.

I'm calmer than I've ever been.

I finally turn to face Helen, Iyana, Luna, and Lydia. They are silent and ashen pale, but Helen lowers her hands and the magical barrier between us disappears.

Before I can speak, a shadow passes overhead and my senses buzz as a giant hawk with bronze-tipped wings swoops across the air above my head. Danika lifts up toward the canopy of branches before she soars back to the ground, dropping a duffel bag that was clutched in her talons.

The barrel of a rifle extends through the bag's opening.

Danika lands nimbly beside Helen and shifts back to her human form. Her honey-colored wings and powerful legs change into equally strong human arms and legs, and her feathers morph into tousled light brown hair with golden highlights that cascades across her shoulders. She's completely naked unless I count the intricate tattoo of a bird's wing decorating her entire left shoulder and bicep.

"If you weren't aiming your rifle at me, you should have been," I say to her.

She is quiet, pale, more tense than I've ever seen her.

"You should aim every weapon you can at me now," I say.

Danika presses her lips together and her eyes fill with tears. "Tessa, what happened to you?"

"What happened?" I tip my head, cautiously narrowing my eyes. Helen taught us at Hidden House that a little knowledge can get us killed. "That's the forbidden question."

"Fuck, Tessa," Iyana says, her fangs descending and her blue-gray eyes widening as she strides toward me, gesturing at the bodies. "It doesn't matter. *This* doesn't matter—"

I take a step back when she reaches for me, evading her arms. "You arrived too late," I say. "It was too late the moment my father chained me to a fucking wall and beat the shit out of me."

"It's never too late." Lydia speaks up and I know she's voicing both her own and her sister's thoughts. They are connected, Lydia always speaking for Luna. When I was at the house, they struggled with space and time. Now, she seems to understand exactly what she's saying.

Maybe in a perfect world, it wouldn't be too late. But I'm painfully aware of what happens to people who care about me.

My father is true to his word. He will kill everyone I love.

If I go with them now, my father will follow me to Hidden House. Just like Tristan, my father will be able to break in. My actions would jeopardize the safety of every woman living there.

The only way to keep them safe is to push them away.

"I am what you fear I am," I say. I wish it were a lie, but I honestly don't know. Either way, they will be safer if they view me as their enemy.

"No." Helen's voice is urgent, her eyes filling with tears as she holds out her hand to me. "I've done terrible things, Tessa. Things I regret deeply and will never stop atoning for. I know what you're going through. Come back with us. Come away right now. We can help you."

I shake my head. "Those three shifter women need your help. Their animals may be dying." I point to Reya, Nalani, and Neve. "They won't survive unless you help them. Just like Cody… didn't…"

I grit my teeth. Raise my chin. I resolve that my heart must now be hard and misshapen like a piece of iron that is melted in a furnace and is thrust into water before it is shaped properly.

"Tessa, please—" Helen begins.

"There's a bracelet on the mantelpiece inside the back cabin." I gesture to the end of the clearing. "It's Ella's. She should have it back."

Helen takes another step toward me, reaching for me, but I back away from her. A drop of blood splashes onto my foot. "You should leave now. I don't want you here."

Turning on my heel before they see my breaking heart, I stride back to my father.

I raise my eyes to meet the Killer's gaze along the way. He has relocated himself to stand beside Reya, who kneels in the dirt. She looks up at me and recoils at all the blood.

The Killer watches me, his shoulders hunched, his claws never far away, but now a gleam enters his fierce eyes. His expression reminds me of Tristan, the way Tristan's gaze always felt sharp, as if he were trying to peel back my defenses to get to the heart of me. The Killer told me that I opened the door for him when I pushed Tristan away, but the Killer must have been hovering right beneath the surface all along. He was waiting, the same way that my rage was waiting.

Switching the wand to my left hand, I continue toward my father, every step I take across the lifeless ground crunching in my hearing.

Cody is facing me from where he lies in the dust, his chest smeared with the mist of dark magic, his tattoo of a golden wolf still glistening with the shadow of my cobalt wolf. I never found out if he had my wolf inked into his skin because he wanted a reminder of the danger I posed to him. A danger that turned out to be very real.

As I draw nearer to him, step by step, I tell myself he's only resting.

He's simply... deep breathing.

Because that's what I need to believe now.

Several paces beyond Cody's position, my father leans over Silas, whose magic flares visibly as Silas begins to heal himself where he lies. A new eye begins to form in Silas's face, layer by layer, and the color returns to his cheeks. He will always survive, as long as he carries the orb concealed behind his eyepatch.

Brynjar stands to my father's right, an emotionless sentinel, the first hand to break through my human soul to the depth of my power.

I step carefully around Cody before I lower myself into a kneeling position in front of Silas's chest, opposite my father and Brynjar, my head slightly bowed.

I compose my features, my lips soft, my claws gone, the wand held loosely in my left hand.

"I hope you're pleased, Father," I say, extending my right hand to gesture gently at the perished witches.

"Very, Tessa," he says. His eyes glow crimson, a blazing color that lights up his cheekbones as he rises to his full height. "You're ready to stand at my side. Together, we will defeat gods and defy the stars themselves."

I breathe in. Breathe out. Smile.

My hands move fast. I ram the wand into Silas's throat with my left hand and rip off his eyepatch with my right, my claws spearing around the magical orb at the same time.

Silas jolts, a shout on his lips, but the sound stops abruptly.

He once said that he would die for me.

My father leaps back, his claws and incisors extending, eyes flushing crimson, his wolf only seconds away from appearing.

I crouch over Silas, gripping the wand where it juts from his throat before I open my right hand to show my father the magical orb I ripped from Silas's face, his eyepatch scrunched beside it. The magic inside the orb continues to swirl, the connection with Silas's body broken, but the power remaining.

"You should run, Father," I say, baring my teeth at him.

My father snarls at me, his eyes wide and lips pinched. It's the first real shock I've ever seen him reveal. His muscles bunch as he prepares to leap at me, but Brynjar's big hand clamps around his shoulder, wrenching him back.

"No, boss," the ice jotunn says. "Your daughter is no longer yours to command."

"Let me go," Ford snarls, but Brynjar shakes his head.

"No." Brynjar wraps his big arms around my father's chest and drags him backward toward the tree branches blocking the space between cabins. Halfway there, Ford stops struggling and Brynjar places my father back on his feet. My father visibly thrums with anger, staring back at me, but I return his glare without flinching.

Behind him, Brynjar punches the branches that block the gap between the two cabins. His frosty power streams through the greenery, turning the wood black and brittle before he knocks his fists into it again. He quickly clears a way through.

The open forest waits through the gap.

Brynjar strides along the path he created but pauses to wait for Ford to follow.

My father raises himself up, his fists clenched before he turns on his heel, strides through the clearing, and breaks into a run at Brynjar's side.

Within seconds, they disappear into the forest.

I still can't breathe.

I lift myself away from the dead warlock, finally leaving the wand behind, but I grip the magical orb in my fist. It's mine now.

When I stand, I turn into the Killer's shadow. His big body blocks out my friends—the women with strong hearts who wait for me to change my mind. Even now.

His presence also stops me from looking down at Cody one last time.

The Killer says, "Neither one of us can go back to the life we had. They will fear us. As they should." His jaw clenches and the more he speaks, the more he sounds like Tristan. Or maybe Tristan always sounded a little bit like the Killer. I'm not sure anymore.

"We're walking the same path," I say. "There's no escape for either of us until we reach the inevitable end."

I'm set on this path and there's no way to step off it now.

Looking up into the Killer's eyes, I say a final, silent goodbye to the person I was.

I can't fight the darkness inside me now.

I need to set it free.

It's the only way I'll survive.

CHAPTER THIRTY-ONE

The Killer's gaze rakes across my face before he inclines his head toward the gap between the cabins.

My father and Brynjar are long gone already.

I don't hesitate, strength flooding my legs and arms as I sprint across the clearing, leaping over the debris that litters the path before I burst into the forest beyond. The enormous trees rise up in every direction, an ancient forest that holds magic—and freedom.

The Killer remains close behind me, his powerful strides urging me to go faster, to leave my past behind.

I run on, my legs pumping, the diaphanous cobalt overskirt I'm still wearing flying behind me, my hair a crimson wave around my face as I dart between the trees.

The Killer is a constant presence at my back as we race farther north, heading into the very heart of the forest. He keeps pace with me easily, veering off a couple of times to run parallel with me. His body gleams with sweat, every muscle in harmony as he remains visible to me between the trees before he rejoins me on the same path.

With every step I take, I peel away my emotions one by one, discarding every moment of pain that I don't want but holding on to the moments I need.

I can't forget what has brought me to this.

As we continue to run, my senses expand and I anticipate each obstruction in our path, sense every living creature—every owl, every snake in the forest floor, every mouse—all of the creatures flying or scurrying away at our approach.

Other than the creatures of the forest, we're completely alone.

The ground beneath our feet becomes increasingly soft and mossy and the sound of bubbling water grows louder. I veer toward it until we're running alongside a creek. The trees thin a little near its edge, their roots sometimes visible on the opposite bank while the moonlight sparkles across the surface of the water. Dashing along the mossy edge, I navigate the uneven ground. The quiet is only broken by our breathing, our footfalls, and the softly running water.

The Killer stays on my heels until he suddenly darts to the side.

My hair flies around my face as I whirl to follow his path.

I gasp as he runs right to the edge of the embankment and dives off it into the water below.

He disappears beneath the surface with a quiet splash. I press my palm against the nearest tree, my chest rising and falling rapidly from running, my toes digging into the earth. Silas's orb of dark magic is still clutched in my right hand. I don't have anywhere to carry it other than my hands—no pockets or a bag—and I'm not about to give it to the Killer.

I hold my breath, waiting for him to reappear.

Moments pass and the silence thickens. I could be completely alone with the trees and the small creatures scampering across the mossy earth.

I tip my head back to scrutinize the branches spreading above me, multiple large boughs extending across the creek. Two trees sit side by side, their enormous roots spreading at an outward angle down the side of the embankment and to either side of the creek's edge. The branches above and the thick roots below create a sheltered cavern of sorts at the side of the bank.

The Killer breaks the surface below, shakes out his hair, and tips his chin at me as if he's challenging me to join him. The water is dark around him, although its surface sparkles, a cold beauty.

I'm suddenly aware of the blood on my clothing and my need to wash off the violence of the last few hours.

I crouch, take hold of the nearest tree root, and swing myself down into the cavern formed between the enormous tree roots. I land lightly on the remarkably dry ground.

Safely depositing the orb into a small crevice at the top of the nearest tree root, where it won't roll away, I step up to the edge of the creek where the moonlight falls.

Diving into the icy water, I brace as it encloses me. I plummet beneath the surface, welcoming the cold against my skin as I swim deeper, circling around the spot where the Killer treads water.

I'm surprised by how clear the water runs, how deep the creek is, and the way I can see the mossy rocks far below me… until the water swills brown with the blood that washes off me.

Then I thrash backward, trying not to swim through it, the darkness inside me becoming as icy as the liquid around me.

The water suddenly churns as the Killer dives toward me, his arms closing around me, pulling me upward. My dress drags in the water before I break the surface.

Gripping the Killer's arms, I inhale air and scream it back out, uncaring of the echoes of my furious voice. There's nobody else to hear me cry.

I scream long and loud until my head tips back and I'm howling. Howling like the dangerous creature that I am, ready to destroy every person who ever hurt me.

The Killer's arms are warm—my only source of heat—as he pulls me to the creek's edge. By the time he hoists me from the water into a sitting position, my teeth are chattering but my exhalations are angry, my incisors fully descended and my claws threatening to cut across his back where I grip him.

He doesn't seem to care that I could rip his skin to shreds.

I can't seem to hurt him.

His darkness is perfectly matched to mine.

He takes hold of my dripping hair, scooping the strands to one side, his head swooping toward my exposed neck to plant a kiss beneath my ear. I inhale Tristan's bitter orange scent, but this time, the aroma of ash and fire is stronger. The blistering notes of his darkest power, the three minds of a creature whose purpose was to guard the gates of hell itself, are becoming stronger.

"Let Tristan out," I whisper, turning my lips to the Killer's, punctuating my demand by pressing the tips of my claws into his back.

He pauses, his palms flattening against my shoulders. "I'm already here, Tessa."

I sweep his hair away from his face, the black strands dripping between my fingers as I search his eyes. Crisp, green eyes flecked with amber. Just like Tristan's. But his arms are still corded with muscle and his scent is even more fiery.

I exhale slowly, knowing that, logically, I should probably be afraid of the most dangerous combination of his minds: the Killer and the Deceiver.

My heartbeat is calm as I lean forward, soaking up his body heat, defying the cold air pressing in around us. I study the way his eyes change as I move closer, the way his minds shift far more rapidly than I expect, all of his impulses converging on a single, unrelenting instinct.

"Deceiver, Coward, Killer... *and* Tristan," I whisper, addressing all of his minds that have merged in this moment.

The most dangerous combination.

"All of me," he says, his hands stroking lightly down my arms as he continues to hold my gaze. "We all want the same thing. Whatever it takes."

A droplet of water rests on his upper lip. I fight the urge to kiss it. "What is that?"

His response whispers against my lips as he closes the gap between us. "You."

My breath hitches, my power rising to meet the undeniable conviction in his eyes. I glide my fingers carefully through his hair, stroking down the back of his neck as I allow my crimson vision to rise, sifting through the brilliant threads of his power and impulses. All of his minds are open to me.

The Coward wants my strength.

The Deceiver wants my intellect.

The Killer wants my violence.

And Tristan...

"All of you," he says, quietly stroking my lower back. "Every part of you, strong and vulnerable, trusting and reserved, protective and dangerous, vengeful and forgiving. Heart and mind, Tessa."

His hands come to rest on my hips. "Even when you can't sense me, part of me will always be with you. It might not be the part you want or need. It might not be the part of me that I want for you. But I'm here."

With a quick inhale, I press my lips to his, tasting his thrumming growls, wanting to draw out this moment while I can still feel and hear him. *Tristan's* hands. *Tristan's* voice.

I won't ask him to stay with me, because I know he can't. Not yet. Not while his darkness plays havoc with his soul.

He is broken and so am I, but one day... *one day...*

Soon.

I will free us both.

I steal every strength I can from his lips, his taste, his scent, the firmness of his hands where he grips my hips, the flex of his muscles as he pulls me closer. I don't care about the cold when my skirt slips up my thighs. I don't care about the rough ground beneath my knees when I straddle him, or how close I am to losing myself to need. I can even ignore the prickling sensation at the back of my neck that warns me this moment is about to break—

Tristan's touch hardens and the Killer's voice returns.

"Tessa Dean," he says, lifting his head from mine to cast a furious glance at the opposite bank of the creek. "We are no longer alone."

I scan both sides of the water, trying to pinpoint the source of his unease—and the reason for my prickling skin.

The forest is silent and still. Even the small creatures have disappeared.

The Killer pulls me to my feet, his hand wrapped firmly around my wrist. His shoulders are hunched again—this time protectively in my direction.

I nod at his unspoken command. "We need to move," I say.

The Killer releases me so that I can stretch for the warlock's orb, scooping it out of its nest in the tree root. Then I take a step back for momentum and run up the root to the top of the embankment.

The Killer moves fast despite his bulk, leaping up behind me so that we arrive at the top at the same time. I don't waste a second, racing away from the creek and into the thicker part of the forest, my feet flying.

While the Killer stays on my heels, I expand my senses again, detecting only the natural wildlife. No matter how hard I try, I can't identify a presence that would explain my heightened awareness of danger.

A sudden metallic *click* sounds in the shadows to my right.

I spent enough time in the gun range with Iyana and Danika to know when a weapon is being primed.

The sound comes out of nowhere and my senses go wild trying to pinpoint its source. I duck and roll, skidding to a stop at a crouch, my teeth bared, my chest heaving. I've stopped in the middle of a small clearing, the trees here slightly more sparse before they thicken again farther along.

The Killer sprints up behind me, hunching over as he skids to a stop at my side.

The forest around us is silent.

I don't sense… anything. Nothing living in this spot, but I'm sure I didn't imagine the sound.

Without a word, the Killer rises up sooner than I do, his animal eyes flecked amber in the moonlight. He tips his head as he inhales the air.

I smell it too now. Peony flowers, a feminine scent.

A woman's silhouette takes shape in the shadows at the edge of the clearing. I make out long, wavy hair, a slim figure, along with the curve of guns and daggers strapped to her waist.

As she steps partly into the moonlight, a loaded crossbow precedes her.

The bolt is pointed directly at me.

A ring on her left hand glints as she grips the weapon with both hands. The ring is an intricate silver band shaped like a sequence of leaves with a single diamond set like a flower in the top of it.

Other than her perfume, I can't sense an aura or any kind of supernatural scent. She must be human, but I'm immediately on my guard. The last time I assumed someone was human, they turned out to be my psychotic father.

"Tristan Masters," the woman says, her face remaining concealed in the shadows. "You will step aside, please. I'm not here for you."

Her voice is clear, light, the kind of voice that should sing lullabies and shouldn't make threats.

The Killer remains exactly where he is, his claws slowly descending as I rise up beside him to meet this new threat.

The woman's crossbow is unwavering, held steady as she finally steps completely into the beam of moonlight streaming into the clearing. She's dressed in a full body black suit that covers her from beneath the top of her black boots all the way up to her neck.

Her hair is ruby-red, her eyes sapphire blue, her gaze piercing. She's my height, her cheekbones high like mine, her lips curved... *like mine*. I could be looking into a mirror of myself, except that she's older.

My breath catches.

Ford told me she was dead.

"Get out of my way, Tristan Masters," my mother says, her gorgeous voice becoming harsh. "I'm here to kill my daughter and nothing will stop me."

Read the conclusion to Tessa and Tristan's story in This Caged Wolf (Soul Bitten Shifter 3).

Then get ready for a new urban fantasy romance: Hunt the Night (Supernatural Legacy 1).

THIS CAGED WOLF: SOUL BITTEN SHIFTER #3

Read the conclusion to Tessa and Tristan's story in This Caged Wolf.

I am a wolf shifter torn apart.
Hunted. Broken. Destined to spark a war.

My freedom has come at a cost. Anyone who cares about me will be hurt by the true nature of my power. To protect the ones I love, I must push them away.

Only Tristan Masters may stand beside me, but his fate is closing in as fast as my options are running out.

Surrounded by enemies, our hope lies in a secret that has been guarded for millennia—the truth about Tristan's past.

He is my future, but he could just as easily be my end.

My heart is already broken. Now I must risk my mind and soul to save us both.

This dark wolf will break free.

This is a dark urban fantasy romance, the final book in the Soul Bitten Shifter series. Recommended reading age is 17+ for sex scenes, mature themes, and language. This book fully concludes the series. No cliffhanger.

ALSO BY EVERLY FROST

SOUL BITTEN SHIFTER

(Dark Urban Fantasy Romance)

1. This Dark Wolf
2. This Broken Wolf
3. This Caged Wolf

SUPERNATURAL LEGACY - Angels and Dragon Shifters coming soon!

1. Hunt the Night
2. Chase the Shadows
3. Slay the Dawn

BRIGHT WICKED - COMPLETE

(A Fantasy Romance)

1. Bright Wicked
2. Radiant Fierce
3. Infernal Dark

ASSASSIN'S MAGIC - COMPLETE

(Urban Fantasy Romance)

1. Assassin's Magic
2. Assassin's Mask
3. Assassin's Menace
4. Assassin's Maze

ASSASSIN'S ACADEMY - COMPLETE

(Dark Urban Fantasy Romance)

1. Rebels

2. Revenge

STORM PRINCESS - COMPLETE

(Fantasy Romance - Coauthored with Jaymin Eve)

Storm Princess Complete Set: Books 1 to 3 (with bonus scenes and a life after story)

1. The Princess Must Die
2. The Princess Must Strike
3. The Princess Must Reign

MORTALITY - COMPLETE

(Science-Fantasy Romance)

Mortality Complete Set: Books 1 to 4

1. Beyond the Ever Reach
2. Beneath the Guarding Stars
3. By the Icy Wild
4. Before the Raging Lion

Stand-alone fiction

The Crystal Prince (short story)

ABOUT THE AUTHOR

Everly Frost is the USA Today Bestselling and award-winning author of YA and New Adult urban fantasy and science-fiction romance novels. She spent her childhood dreaming of other worlds and scribbling stories on the leftover blank pages at the back of school notebooks. She lives in Brisbane, Australia with her husband and two children.

- amazon.com/author/everlyfrost
- facebook.com/everlyfrost
- twitter.com/everlyfrost
- instagram.com/everlyfrost
- bookbub.com/authors/everly-frost